Gravity's Angels

Gravity's Angels

Michael Swanwick

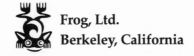
Frog, Ltd.
Berkeley, California

Published by Frog, Ltd. Frog, Ltd. books are distributed by:
North Atlantic Books
P.O. Box 12327
Berkeley, California 94712

Cover design and illustration by Michael Dashow
Book design by Jan Camp
Printed in the United States of America

North Atlantic Books are available through most bookstores. To contact North Atlantic directly, call 800-337-2665 or visit our website at www.northatlanticbooks.com.

Substantial discounts on bulk quantities of North Atlantic books are available to corporations, professional associations, and other organizations. For details and discount information, contact the special sales department at North Atlantic Books.

Library of Congress Cataloging-in-Publication Data

Swanwick, Michael
    Gravity's angels / by Michael Swanwick.
        p. cm.
    ISBN 1-58394-029-4 (alk. paper)
    1. Science Fiction, American. I. Title.

PS3569.W28 G69 2001
813'.54–dc21

                                 CIP
                               00-048375

1 2 3 4 5 6 7 8 9 / 05 04 03 02 01

BECAUSE ON FIRST LEARNING TO WALK
YOU DEMANDED TO BE PUT DOWN AND
IMMEDIATELY RAN AWAY, DWINDLING
UP THE SIDEWALK AND LEAVING ME
STUNNED IN PERFECT ALLEGORY,
I DEDICATE THE MAJOR CHUNK
OF MY LIFE CONTAINED
WITHIN THIS VOLUME
TO MY
BOLD
A N D
FEAR-
LESS
S 0 N
SEAN WILLIAM SWANWICK

CONTENTS

ACKNOWLEDGEMENTS ix

A MIDWINTER'S TALE 1

THE FEAST OF SAINT JANIS 19

THE BLIND MINOTAUR 53

THE TRANSMIGRATION OF PHILIP K 73

COVENANT OF SOULS 93

THE DRAGON LINE 135

MUMMER KISS 155

TROJAN HORSE 197

SNOW ANGELS 241

THE MAN WHO MET PICASSO 267

FORESIGHT 283

GINUNGAGAP 295

THE EDGE OF THE WORLD 333

ACKNOWLEDGEMENTS

THE AUTHOR WOULD like to acknowledge indebtedness to Jack Dann for select portions of his personal history used in "A Midwinter's Tale"; to John Muller, whose Chanty wine was transported to the Moon in "Trojan Horse," a story that also benefited greatly from Marta Randall's labors on behalf of the legendary New Dimensions 13; to the necessarily unnamed protagonist of "The Man Who Met Picasso" for its wizard quest; to Patrick McGrath for long nights discussing Tolkien; to Sandy Meschkow for technical research; to Bill Franz for the black-hole mechanics of "Ginungagap"; to John DeChancie for the mail-stealing robot in "The Transmigration of Philip K"; to Jim Turner for correcting or providing a great many technical details; to Sheila Williams, George Scithers, Ellen Datlow, the late Terry Carr, Robert Silverberg, and "Team Spectra" for doing their jobs; and to Virginia Kidd for keeping them from doing their jobs too well. Many words and ideas herein were stolen from Susan Casper, Meg and Thierry Phillips, Tim Sullivan, Greg Frost, the Philford workshoppers, and Tom and Sara Purdom, among others, none of which shall ever be acknowledged. The character of Mordred in "The Dragon Line" was originally developed in an unpublished Arthurian fantasy by the late Anna Quindsland. The greatest debt, as usual, is to Gardner Dozois, story doctor par excellence, whose delicate touch is present in all but the most recent stories here.

Health coverage was provided by a grant from the M. C. Porter Endowment for the Arts.

A Midwinter's Tale

MAYBE I SHOULDN'T tell you about that childhood Christmas Eve in the Stone House, so long ago. My memory is no longer reliable, not since I contracted the brain fever. Soon I'll be strong enough to be reposted offplanet, to some obscure star light-years beyond that plangent moon rising over your father's barn, but how much has been burned from my mind! Perhaps none of this actually happened.

Sit on my lap and I'll tell you all. Well then, my knee. No woman was ever ruined by a knee. You laugh, but it's true. Would that it were so easy!

The hell of war as it's now practiced is that its purpose is not so much to gain territory as to deplete the enemy, and thus it's always better to maim than to kill. A corpse can be bagged, burned, and forgotten, but the wounded need special care. Regrowth tanks, false skin, medical personnel, a long convalescent stay on your parents' farm. That's why they will vary their weapons, hit you with obsolete stone axes or toxins or radiation, to force your Command to stock the proper prophylaxes, specialized medicines, obscure skills. Mustard gas is excellent for that purpose, and so was the brain fever.

All those months I lay in the hospital, awash in pain, sometimes hallucinating. Dreaming of ice. When I awoke, weak and

1

not really believing I was alive, parts of my life were gone, randomly burned from my memory. I recall standing at the very
top of the iron bridge over the Izveltaya, laughing and throwing
my books one by one into the river, while my best friend Fen-
nwolf tried to coax me down. "I'll join the militia! I'll be a sol-
dier!" I shouted hysterically. And so I did. I remember that
clearly, but just what led up to that preposterous instant is
utterly beyond me. Nor can I remember the name of my second-eldest sister, though her face is as plain to me as yours is
now. There are odd holes in my memory.

That Christmas Eve is an island of stability in my seachanging
memories, as solid in my mind as the Stone House itself, that
neolithic cavern in which we led such basic lives that I was
never quite sure in which era of history we dwelt. Sometimes
the men came in from the hunt, a larl or two pacing ahead content and sleepy-eyed, to lean bloody spears against the walls,
and it might be that we lived on Old Earth itself then. Other
times, as when they brought in projectors to fill the common
room with colored lights, scintillae nesting in the branches of
the season's tree, and cool, harmless flames dancing atop the
presents, we seemed to belong to a much later age, in some
mythologized province of the future.

The house was abustle, the five families all together for this
one time of the year, and outlying kin and even a few strangers
staying over, so that we had to put bedding in places normally
kept closed during the winter, moving furniture into attic lumber rooms, and even at that there were cots and thick bolsters
set up in the blind ends of hallways. The women scurried
through the passages, scattering uncles here and there, now
settling one in an armchair and plumping him up like a cushion, now draping one over a table, cocking up a mustachio for
effect. A pleasant time.

Coming back from a visit to the kitchens, where a huge
woman I did not know, with flour powdering her big-freckled
arms up to the elbows, had shooed me away, I surprised Suki

and Georg kissing in the nook behind the great hearth. They had their arms about each other, and I stood watching them. Suki was smiling, cheeks red and round. She brushed her hair back with one hand so Georg could nuzzle her ear, turning slightly as she did so, and saw me. She gasped and they broke apart, flushed and startled.

Suki gave me a cookie, dark with molasses and a single stingy crystallized raisin on top, while Georg sulked. Then she pushed me away, and I heard her laugh as she took Georg's hand to lead him to some darker forest recess of the house.

Father came in, boots all muddy, to sling a brace of game birds down on the hunt cabinet. He set his unstrung bow and quiver of arrows on their pegs, then hooked an elbow atop the cabinet to accept admiration and a hot drink from Mother. The larl padded by, quiet and heavy and content. I followed it around a corner, ancient ambitions of riding the beast rising up within. I could see myself, triumphant before my cousins, high atop the black carnivore. "Flip!" my father called sternly. "Leave Samson alone! He is a bold and noble creature, and I will not have you pestering him."

He had eyes in the back of his head, had my father.

Before I could grow angry, my cousins hurried by, on their way to hoist the straw men into the trees out front, and swept me up along with them. Uncle Chittagong, who looked like a lizard and had to stay in a glass tank for reasons of health, winked at me as I skirled past. From the corner of my eye I saw my second-eldest sister beside him, limned in blue fire.

Forgive me. So little of my childhood remains; vast stretches were lost in the blue icefields I wandered in my illness. My past is like a sunken continent with only mountaintops remaining unsubmerged, a scattered archipelago of events from which to guess the shape of what was lost. Those remaining fragments I treasure all the more, and must pass my hands over them periodically to reassure myself that something remains.

So where was I? Ah, yes: I was in the north bell tower, my

hidey-place in those days, huddled behind Old Blind Pew, the bass of our triad of bells, crying because I had been deemed too young to light one of the yule torches. "Hallo!" cried a voice, and then, "Out here stupid!" I ran to the window, tears forgotten in my astonishment at the sight of my brother Karl silhouetted against the yellowing sky, arms out, treading the roof gables like a tightrope walker.

"You're going to get in trouble for that!" I cried.

"Not if you don't tell!" Knowing full well how I worshiped him. "Come on down! I've emptied out one of the upper kitchen cupboards. We can crawl in from the pantry. There's space under the door—we'll see everything!"

Karl turned and his legs tangled under him. He fell. Feet first, he slid down the roof.

I screamed. Karl caught the guttering and swung himself into an open window underneath. His sharp face rematerialized in the gloom, grinning. "Race you to the jade ibis!"

He disappeared, and then I was spinning wildly down the spiral stairs, mad to reach the goal first.

It was not my fault we were caught, for I would never have giggled if Karl hadn't been tickling me to see just how long I could keep silent. I was frightened, but not Karl. He threw his head back and laughed until he cried, even as he was being hauled off by three very angry grandmothers, pleased more by his own roguery than by anything he might have seen.

I myself was led away by an indulgent Katrina, who graphically described the caning I was to receive and then contrived to lose me in the crush of bodies in the common room. I hid behind the goat tapestry until I got bored—not long!—and then Chubkin, Kosmonaut, and Pew rang, and the room emptied.

I tagged along, ignored, among the moving legs, like a marsh bird scuttling through waving grasses. Voices clangoring in the east stairway, we climbed to the highest balcony, to watch the solstice dance. I hooked hands over the crumbling balustrade and pulled myself up on tiptoe so I could look down on the procession as it left the house. For a long time nothing happened, and I remember being annoyed at how casually the adults were taking all this, standing about with drinks, not one in ten glancing away from themselves. Pheidre and Valerian (the younger children had been put to bed, complaining, an hour ago) began a game of tag, running through the adults, until they were chastened and ordered with angry shakes of their arms to be still.

Then the door below opened. The women who were witches walked solemnly out, clad in hooded terrycloth robes as if they'd just stepped from the bath. But they were so silent I was struck with fear. It seemed as if something cold had reached into the pink giggling women I had seen preparing themselves in the kitchen and taken away some warmth or laughter from them. "Katrina!" I cried in panic, and she lifted a moon-cold face toward me. Several of the men exploded in laughter, white steam puffing from bearded mouths, and one rubbed his knuckles in my hair. My second-eldest sister drew me away from the balustrade and hissed at me that I was not to cry out to the witches, that this was important, that when I was older I would understand, and in the meantime if I did not behave myself I would be beaten. To soften her words, she offered me a sugar crystal, but I turned away stern and unappeased.

Single-file the women walked out on the rocks to the east of the house, where all was barren slate swept free of snow by the wind from the sea, and at a great distance—you could not make out their faces—doffed their robes. For a moment they stood motionless in a circle, looking at one another. Then they began the dance, each wearing nothing but a red ribbon tied about one upper thigh, the long end blowing free in the breeze.

As they danced their circular dance, the families watched, largely in silence. Sometimes there was a muffled burst of laughter as one of the younger men muttered a racy comment, but mostly they watched with great respect, even a kind of fear. The gusty sky was dark, and flocked with small clouds like purple-headed rams. It was chilly on the roof, and I could not imagine how the women withstood it. They danced faster and faster, and the families grew quieter, packing the edges more tightly, until I was forced away from the railing. Cold and bored, I went downstairs, nobody turning to watch me leave, back to the main room, where a fire still smoldered in the hearth.

The room was stuffy when I'd left, and cooler now. I lay down on my stomach before the fireplace. The flagstones smelled of ashes and were gritty to the touch, staining my fingertips as I trailed them in idle little circles. The stones were cold at the edges, slowly growing warmer, and then suddenly too hot and I had to snatch my hand away. The back of the fireplace was black with soot, and I watched the fire-worms crawl over the stone heart-and-hands carved there, as the carbon caught fire and burned out. The log was all embers and would burn for hours.

Something coughed.

I turned and saw something moving in the shadows, an animal. The larl was blacker than black, a hole in the darkness, and my eyes swam to look at him. Slowly, lazily, he strode out onto the stones, stretched his back, yawned a tongue-curling yawn, and then stared at me with those great green eyes.

He spoke.

I was astonished, of course, but not in the way my father would have been. So much is inexplicable to a child! "Merry Christmas, Flip," the creature said, in a quiet, breathy voice. I could not describe its accent; I have heard nothing quite like it before or since. There was a vast alien amusement in his glance.

"And to you," I said politely.

The larl sat down, curling his body heavily about me. If I had wanted to run, I could not have gotten past him, though that thought did not occur to me then. "There is an ancient legend, Flip, I wonder if you have heard of it, that on Christmas Eve the beasts can speak in human tongue. Have your elders told you that?"

I shook my head.

"They are neglecting you." Such strange humor dwelt in that voice. "There is truth to some of those old legends, if only you knew how to get at it. Though perhaps not all. Some are just stories. Perhaps this is not happening now; perhaps I am not speaking to you at all?"

I shook my head. I did not understand. I said so.

"That is the difference between your kind and mine. My kind understands everything about yours, and yours knows next to nothing about mine. I would like to tell you a story, little one. Would you like that?"

"Yes," I said, for I was young and I liked stories very much.

He began:

When the great ships landed—

Oh, God. When—no, no, no, wait. Excuse me. I'm shaken. I just this instant had a vision. It seemed to me that it was night and I was standing at the gates of a cemetery. And suddenly the air was full of light, planes and cones of light that burst from the ground and nested twittering in the trees. Fracturing the sky. I wanted to dance for joy. But the ground crumbled underfoot and when I looked down the shadow of the gates touched my toes, a cold rectangle of profoundest black, deep as all eternity, and I was dizzy and about to fall and I, and I . . .

Enough! I have had this vision before, many times. It must have been something that impressed me strongly in my youth, the moist smell of newly opened earth, the chalky whitewash on the picket fence. It must be. I do not believe in hobgoblins, ghosts, or premonitions. No, it does not bear thinking about. Foolishness! Let me get on with my story.

—When the great ships landed, I was feasting on my grandfather's brains. All his descendants gathered respectfully about him, and I, as youngest, had first bite. His wisdom flowed through me, and the wisdom of his ancestors and the intimate knowledge of those animals he had eaten for food, and the spirit of valiant enemies who had been killed and then honored by being eaten, even as if they were family. I don't suppose you understand this, little one.

I shook my head.

People never die, you see. Only humans die. Sometimes a minor part of a Person is lost, the doings of a few decades, but the bulk of his life is preserved, if not in this body, then in another. Or sometimes a Person will dishonor himself, and his descendants will refuse to eat him. This is a great shame, and the Person will go off to die somewhere alone.

The ships descended bright as newborn suns. The People had never seen such a thing. We watched in inarticulate wonder, for we had no language then. You have seen the pictures, the baroque swirls of colored metal, the proud humans stepping down onto the land. But I was there, and I can tell you, your people were ill. They stumbled down the gangplanks with the stench of radiation sickness about them. We could have destroyed them all then and there.

Your people built a village at Landfall and planted crops over the bodies of their dead. We left them alone. They did not look like good game. They were too strange and too slow, and we had not yet come to savor your smell. So we went away, in baffled ignorance.

That was in early spring.

Half the survivors were dead by midwinter, some of disease but most because they did not have enough food. It was of no concern to us. But then the woman in the wilderness came to change our universe forever.

When you're older you'll be taught the woman's tale, and what desperation drove her into the wilderness. It's part of your history. But to myself, out in the mountains and winter-lean, the sight of her striding through the snows in her furs was like a vision of winter's queen herself. A gift of meat for the hungering season, life's blood for the solstice.

I first saw the woman while I was eating her mate. He had emerged from his cabin that evening as he did every sunset, gun in hand, without looking up. I had observed him over the course

of five days, and his behavior never varied. On that sixth night-
fall I was crouched on his roof when he came out. I let him go a
few steps from the door, then leapt. I felt his neck break on
impact, tore open his throat to be sure, and ripped through his
parka to taste his innards. There was no sport in it, but in winter we will take game whose brains we would never eat.

My mouth was full and my muzzle pleasantly, warmly moist
with blood when the woman appeared. I looked up, and she
was topping the rise, riding one of your incomprehensible
machines, what I know now to be a snowstrider. The setting
sun broke through the clouds behind her, and for an instant
she was embedded in glory. Her shadow stretched narrow
before her and touched me, a bridge of darkness between us.
We looked in one another's eyes . . .

Magda topped the rise with a kind of grim, joyless satisfaction.
I am now a hunter's woman, she thought to herself. We will
always be welcome at Landfall for the meat we bring, but they
will never speak civilly to me again. Good. I would choke on
their sweet talk anyway. The baby stirred, and without looking
down she stroked him through the furs, murmuring, "Just a
little longer, my brave little boo, and we'll be at our new home.
Will you like that, eh?"

The sun broke through the clouds to her back, making the
snow a red dazzle. Then her eyes adjusted, and she saw the
black shape crouched over her lover's body. A very great distance away, her hands throttled down the snowstrider and
brought it to a halt. The shallow bowl of land before her was
barren, the snow about the corpse black with blood. A last curl
of smoke lazily separated from the hut's chimney. The brute
lifted its bloody muzzle and looked at her.

Time froze and knotted in black agony.

The larl screamed. It ran straight at her, faster than
thought. Clumsily, hampered by the infant strapped to her
stomach, Magda clawed the rifle from its boot behind the sad-
dle. She shucked her mittens, fitted hands to metal that stung

like hornets, flicked off the safety, and brought the stock to her shoulder. The larl was halfway to her. She aimed and fired.

The larl went down. One shoulder shattered, slamming it to the side. It tumbled and rolled in the snow. "You sonofabitch!" Magda cried in triumph. But almost immediately the beast struggled to its feet, turned and fled.

The baby began to cry, outraged by the rifle's roar. Magda powered up the engine. "Hush, small warrior." A kind of madness filled her, a blind anesthetizing rage. "This won't take long." She flung her machine downhill, after the larl.

Even wounded, the creature was fast. She could barely keep up. As it entered the spare stand of trees to the far end of the meadow, Magda paused to fire again, burning a bullet by its head. The larl leaped away. From then on it varied its flight with sudden changes of direction and unexpected jogs to the side. It was a fast learner. But it could not escape Magda. She had always been a hothead, and now her blood was up. She was not about to return to her lover's gutted body with his killer still alive.

The sun set, and in the darkening light she lost sight of the larl. But she was able to follow its trail by two-shadowed moonlight, the deep, purple footprints, the darker spatter of blood it left, drop by drop, in the snow.

It was the solstice, and the moons were full—a holy time. I felt it even as I fled the woman through the wilderness. The moons were bright on the snow. I felt the dread of being hunted descend on me, and in my inarticulate way I felt blessed.

But I also felt a great fear for my kind. We had dismissed the humans as incomprehensible, not very interesting creatures, slow-moving, bad-smelling, and dull-witted. Now, pursued by this madwoman on her fast machine, brandishing a weapon that killed from afar, I felt all natural order betrayed. She was a goddess of the hunt, and I was her prey.

The People had to be told.

I gained distance from her, but I knew the woman would catch up. She was a hunter, and a hunter never abandons wounded prey. One way or another, she would have me.

In the winter, all who are injured or too old must offer themselves to the community. The sacrifice rock was not far, by a hill riddled from time beyond memory with our burrows. My knowledge must be shared: the humans were dangerous. They would make good prey.

I reached my goal when the moons were highest. The flat rock was bare of snow when I ran limping in. Awakened by the scent of my blood, several People emerged from their dens. I laid myself down on the sacrifice rock. A grandmother of the People came forward, licked my wound, tasting, considering. Then she nudged me away with her forehead. The wound would heal, she thought, and winter was young; my flesh was not yet needed.

But I stayed. Again she nudged me away. I refused to go. She whined in puzzlement. I licked the rock.

That was understood. Two of the People came forward and placed their weight on me. A third lifted a paw. He shattered my skull, and they ate.

Magda watched through power binoculars from atop a nearby ridge. She saw everything. The rock swarmed with lean black horrors. It would be dangerous to go down among them, so she waited and watched the puzzling tableau below. The larl had wanted to die, she'd swear it, and now the beasts came forward daintily, almost ritualistically, to taste the brains, the young first and then the old. She raised her rifle, thinking to exterminate a few of the brutes from afar.

A curious thing happened then. All the larls that had eaten of her prey's brain leaped away, scattering. Those that had not eaten waited, easy targets, not understanding. Then another dipped to lap up a fragment of brain, and looked up with sudden comprehension. Fear touched her.

The hunter had spoken often of the larls, had said that they were so elusive he sometimes thought them intelligent. "Come spring, when I can afford to waste ammunition on carnivores, I look forward to harvesting a few of these beauties," he'd said. He was the colony's xenobiologist, and he loved the animals he killed, treasured them even as he smoked their flesh, tanned their hides, and drew detailed pictures of their internal organs. Magda had always scoffed at his theory that larls gained insight into the habits of their prey by eating their brains, even though he'd spent much time observing the animals minutely from afar, gathering evidence. Now she wondered if he were right.

Her baby whimpered, and she slid a hand inside her furs to give him a breast. Suddenly the night seemed cold and dangerous, and she thought: What am I doing here? Sanity returned to her all at once, her anger collapsing to nothing, like an ice tower shattering in the wind. Below, sleek black shapes sped toward her, across the snow. They changed direction every few leaps, running evasive patterns to avoid her fire.

"Hang on kid," she muttered, and turned her strider around. She opened up the throttle.

Magda kept to the open as much as she could, the creatures following her from a distance. Twice she stopped abruptly and turned her rifle on her pursuers. Instantly they disappeared in puffs of snow, crouching belly-down but not stopping, burrowing toward her under the surface. In the eerie night silence, she could hear the whispering sound of the brutes tunneling. She fled.

Some frantic timeless period later—the sky had still not lightened in the east—Magda was leaping a frozen stream when the strider's left ski struck a rock. The machine was knocked glancingly upward, cybernetics screaming as they fought to regain balance. With a sickening crunch, the strider slammed to earth, one ski twisted and bent. It would take extensive work before the strider could move again.

Magda dismounted. She opened her robe and looked down

on her child. He smiled up at her and made a gurgling noise.

Something went dead in her.

A fool. I've been a criminal fool, she thought. Magda was a proud woman who had always refused to regret, even privately, anything she had done. Now she regretted everything: her anger, the hunter, her entire life, all that had brought her to this point, the cumulative madness that threatened to kill her child.

The larl topped the ridge.

Magda raised her rifle, and it ducked down. She began walking downslope, parallel to the stream. The snow was knee deep, and she had to walk carefully not to slip and fall. Small pellets of snow rolled down ahead of her, were overtaken by other pellets. She strode ahead, pushing up a wake.

The hunter's cabin was not many miles distant; if she could reach it, they would live. But a mile was a long way in winter. She could hear the larls calling to each other, soft coughlike noises, to either side of the ravine. They were following the sound of her passage through the snow. Well, let them. She still had the rifle, and if it had few bullets left, *they* didn't know that. They were only animals.

This high in the mountains, the trees were sparse. Magda descended a good quarter-mile before the ravine choked with scrub and she had to climb up and out or risk being ambushed. Which way? she wondered. She heard three coughs to her right, and climbed the left slope, alert and wary.

We herded her. Through the long night we gave her fleeting glimpses of our bodies whenever she started to turn to the side she must not go, and let her pass unmolested the other way. We let her see us dig into the distant snow and wait motionless, undetectable. We filled the woods with our shadows. Slowly, slowly, we turned her around. She struggled to return to the cabin, but she could not. In what haze of fear and despair she walked! We could smell it. Sometimes her baby cried, and she hushed the milky-scented creature in a voice gone flat with futility. The night deepened as the moons sank in the sky. We forced the woman back up into the mountains. Toward the end, her legs failed her several times; she lacked our strength and stamina. But her patience and guile were every bit our match. Once we approached her still form, and she killed two of us before the rest could retreat. How we loved her! We paced her, confident that sooner or later she'd drop.

It was at night's darkest hour that the woman was forced back to the burrowed hillside, the sacred place of the People where stood the sacrifice rock. She topped the same rise for the second time that night, and saw it. For a moment she stood helpless, and then she burst into tears.

We waited, for this was the holiest moment of the hunt, the point when the prey recognizes and accepts her destiny. After a time, the woman's sobs ceased. She raised her head and straightened her back.

Slowly, steadily, she walked downhill.

She knew what to do.

Larls retreated into their burrows at the sight of her, gleaming eyes dissolving into darkness. Magda ignored them. Numb and aching, weary to death, she walked to the sacrifice rock. It had to be this way.

Magda opened her coat, unstrapped her baby. She wrapped him deep in the furs and laid the bundle down to one side of the rock. Dizzily, she opened the bundle to kiss the top of his sweet head, and he made an angry sound. "Good for you, kid," she said hoarsely. "Keep that attitude." She was so tired.

She took off her sweaters, her vest, her blouse. The raw cold nipped at her flesh with teeth of ice. She stretched slightly, body aching with motion. God, it felt good. She laid down the rifle. She knelt.

The rock was black with dried blood. She lay down flat, as she had earlier seen her larl do. The stone was cold, so cold it almost blanked out the pain. Her pursuers waited nearby, curious to see what she was doing; she could hear the soft panting noise of their breathing. One padded noiselessly to her side. She could smell the brute. It whined questioningly.

She licked the rock.

Once it was understood what the woman wanted, her sacrifice went quickly. I raised a paw, smashed her skull. Again I was youngest. Innocent, I bent to taste.

The neighbors were gathering, hammering at the door, climbing over one another to peer through the windows, making the walls bulge and breathe with their eagerness. I grunted and bellowed, and the clash of silver and clink of plates next door grew louder. Like peasant animals, my husband's people tried to drown out the sound of my pain with toasts and drunken jokes.

Through the window I saw Tevin-the-Fool's bonewhite skin gaunt on his skull, and behind him a slice of face—sharp nose, white cheeks—like a mask. The doors and walls pulsed with the weight of those outside. In the next room, children fought and wrestled, and elders pulled at their long white beards, staring anxiously at the closed door.

The midwife shook her head, red lines running from the corners of her mouth down either side of her stern chin. Her eye sockets were shadowy pools of dust. "Now push!" she cried. "Don't be a lazy sow!"

I groaned and arched my back. I shoved my head back and it grew smaller, eaten up by the pillows. The bedframe skewed as one leg slowly buckled under it. My husband glanced over his shoulder at me, an angry look, his fingers knotted behind his back.

All of Landfall shouted and hovered on the walls.

"Here it comes!" shrieked the midwife. She reached down to my bloody crotch, and eased out a tiny head, purple and angry, like a goblin.

And then all the walls glowed red and green and sprouted

large flowers. The door turned orange and burst open, and the neighbors and crew flooded in. The ceiling billowed up, and aerialists tumbled through the rafters. A boy who had been hiding beneath the bed flew up laughing to where the ancient sky and stars shone through the roof.

They held up the child, bloody on a platter.

Here the larl touched me for the first time, that heavy black paw like velvet on my knee, talons sheathed. "Are you following this?" he asked. "Can you separate truth from fantasy, tell what is fact and what the mad imagery of emotions we did not share? No more could I. All that, the first birth of human young on this planet, I experienced in an instant. Blind with awe, I understood the personal tragedy and the communal triumph of that event, and the meaning of the lives and culture behind it. A second before, I lived as an animal, with an animal's simple thoughts and hopes. Then I ate of your ancestor and was lifted all in an instant halfway to godhood.

"As the woman had intended. She has died thinking of the child's birth, in order that we might share in it. She gave us that. She gave us more. She gave us *language.* We were wise animals before we ate her brain, and we were People afterward. We owed her so much. And we knew what she wanted from us." The larl stroked my cheek with his great smooth paw, the ivory claws hooded but quivering slightly, as if about to awake.

I hardly dared breathe.

"That morning I entered Landfall, carrying the baby's sling in my mouth. It slept through most of the journey. At dawn I passed through the empty street as silently as I knew how. I came to the First Captain's house. I heard the murmur of voices within, the entire village assembled for worship. I tapped the door with one paw. There was sudden, astonished silence. Then slowly, fearfully, the door opened."

The larl was silent for a moment. "That was the beginning of the association of People with humans. We were welcomed into your homes, and we helped with the hunting. It was a fair trade. Our food saved many lives that first winter. No one needed to know how the woman had perished, or how well we understood your kind.

"That child, Flip, was your ancestor. Every few generations we take one of your family out hunting, and taste his brains, to maintain our closeness with your line. If you are a good boy and grow up to be as bold and honest, as intelligent and noble, a man as your father, then perhaps it will be you we eat."

The larl presented his blunt muzzle to me in what might have been meant as a friendly smile. Perhaps not; the expression hangs unreadable, ambiguous in my mind even now. Then he stood and padded away into the friendly dark shadows of the Stone House.

I was sitting staring into the coals a few minutes later when my second-eldest sister—her face a featureless blaze of light, like an angel's—came into the room and saw me. She held out a hand, saying, "Come on, Flip, you're missing everything." And I went with her.

Did any of this actually happen? Sometimes I wonder. But it's growing late, and your parents are away. My room is small but snug, my bed warm but empty. We can burrow deep in the blankets and scare away the cave-bears by playing the oldest winter games there are.

You're blushing! Don't tug away your hand. I'll be gone soon to some distant world to fight in a war for people who are as unknown to you as they are to me. Soldiers grow old slowly, you know. We're shipped frozen between the stars. When you are old and plump and happily surrounded by your grandchildren, I'll still be young, and thinking of you. You'll remember me then, and our thoughts will touch in the void. Will you have nothing to regret? Is that really what you want?

I thought once that I could outrun the darkness. I thought— I must have thought—that by joining the militia I could escape my fate. But for all that I gave up my home and family, in the end the beast came anyway to eat my brain. Now I am alone. A month from now, in all this world, only you will remember my name. Let me live in your memory.

Come, don't be shy. Let's put the past aside and get on with our lives. That's better. Blow the candle out, love, and there's an end to my tale.

All this happened long ago, on a planet whose name has been burned from my memory.

The Feast of
Saint Janis

Take a load off, Janis,
And
You put the load right on me . . .
　　　　—THE WAIT (TRAD.)

WOLF STOOD IN THE early morning fog watching the *Yankee Clipper* leave Baltimore harbor. His elbows rested against a cool, clammy wall, its surface eroded smooth by the passage of countless hands, almost certainly dating back to before the Collapse. A metallic grey sparkle atop the foremast drew his eye to the dish antenna that linked the ship with the geosynchronous *Trickster* seasats it relied on to plot winds and currents.

To many the wooden *Clipper,* with its computer-designed hydrofoils and hand-sewn sails, was a symbol of the New Africa. Wolf, however, watching it merge into sea and sky, knew only that it was going home without him.

He turned and walked back into the rick-a-rack of commercial buildings crowded against the waterfront. The clatter of hand-drawn carts mingled with a mélange of exotic cries and shouts, the alien music of a dozen American dialects. Workers, clad in coveralls most of them, swarmed about, grunting and cursing in exasperation when an iron wheel lurched in a muddy pothole. Yet there was something furtive and covert about them, as if they were hiding an ancient secret.

Craning to stare into the dark recesses of a warehouse, Wolf collided with a woman clad head to foot in chador. She flinched at his touch, her eyes glaring above the black veil, then whipped away. Not a word was exchanged.

A citizen of Baltimore in its glory days would not have recognized the city. Where the old buildings had not been torn down and buried, shanties crowded the streets, taking advantage of the space automobiles had needed. Sometimes they were built *over* the streets, so that alleys became tunnelways, and sometimes these collapsed, to the cries and consternation of the natives.

It was another day with nothing to do. He could don a filter mask and tour the Washington ruins, but he had already done that, and besides the day looked like it was going to be hot. It was unlikely he'd hear anything about his mission, not after months of waiting on American officials who didn't want to talk with him. Wolf decided to check back at his hostel for messages, then spend the day in the bazaars.

Children were playing in the street outside the hostel. They scattered at his approach. One, he noted, lagged behind the others, hampered by a malformed leg. He mounted the unpainted wooden steps, edging past an old man who sat at the bottom. The old man was laying down tarot cards with a slow and fatalistic disregard for what they said; he did not look up.

The bell over the door jangled notice of Wolf's entry. He stepped into the dark foyer.

Two men in the black uniforms of the political police appeared, one to either side of him. "Wolfgang Hans Mbikana?" one asked. His voice had the dust of ritual on it; he knew the answer. "You will come with us," the other said.

"There is some mistake," Wolf objected.

"No, sir, there is no mistake," one said mildly. The other

opened the door. "After you, Mr. Mbikana."

The old man on the stoop squinted up at them, looked away, and slid off the step.

The police walked Wolf to an ancient administrative building. They went up marble steps sagging from centuries of foot-scuffing, and through an empty lobby. Deep within the building they halted before an undistinguished-looking door. "You are expected," the first of the police said.

"I beg your pardon?"

The police walked away, leaving him there. Apprehensive, he knocked on the door. There was no answer, so he opened it and stepped within.

A woman sat at a desk just inside the room. Though she was modernly dressed, she wore a veil. She might have been young; it was impossible to tell. A flick of her eyes, a motion of one hand, directed him to the open door of an inner room. It was like following an onion to its conclusion, a layer of mystery at a time.

A heavyset man sat at the final desk. He was dressed in the traditional suit and tie of American businessmen. But there was nothing quaint or old-fashioned about his mobile, expressive face or the piercing eyes he turned on Wolf.

"Sit down," he grunted, gesturing toward an old overstuffed chair. Then: "Charles DiStephano. Controller for Northeast Regional. You're Mbikana, right?"

"Yes, sir." Wolf gingerly took the proffered chair, which did not seem all that clean. It was clear to him now; DiStephano was one of the men on whom he had waited these several months, the biggest of the lot, in fact. "I represent—"

"The Southwest Africa Trade Company." DiStephano lifted some documents from his desk. "Now this says you're prepared to offer—among other things—resource data from your North American *Coyote* landsat in exchange for the right to place students in Johns Hopkins. I find that an odd offer for your organization to make."

"Those are my papers," Wolf objected. "As a citizen of Southwest Africa, I'm not used to this sort of cavalier treatment."

"Look, kid, I'm a busy man, I have no time to discuss your rights. The papers are in my hands, I've read them, the people that sent you knew I would. Okay? So I know what you want and what you're offering. What I want to know is *why* you're making this offer."

Wolf was disconcerted. He was used to a more civilized, a more leisurely manner of doing business. The oldtimers at SWATC had warned him that the pace would be different here, but he hadn't had the experience to decipher their veiled references and hints. He was painfully aware that he had gotten the mission, with its high salary and the promise of a bonus, only because it was not one that appealed to the older hands.

"America was hit hardest," he said, "but the Collapse was worldwide." He wondered whether he should explain the system of corporate social responsibility that African business was based on. Then decided that if DiStephano didn't know, he didn't want to. "There are still problems. Africa has a high incidence of birth defects." *Because America exported its poisons; its chemicals and pesticides and foods containing a witch's brew of preservatives.* "We hope to do away with the problem; if a major thrust is made, we can clean up the gene pool in less than a century. But to do this requires professionals—eugenicists, embryonic surgeons—and while we have these, they are second-rate. The very best still come from your nation's medical schools."

"We can't spare any."

"We don't propose to steal your doctors. We'd provide our own students—fully trained doctors who need only the specialized training."

"There are only so many openings at Hopkins," DiStephano said. "or at U of P or the UVM Medical College, for that matter."

"We're prepared to—" Wolf pulled himself up short. "It's in the papers. We'll pay enough that you can expand to meet the needs of twice the number of students we require." The room was dim and oppressive. Sweat built up under Wolf's clothing.

"Maybe so. You can't buy teachers with money, though."

Wolf said nothing. "I'm also extremely reluctant to let your people *near* our medics. You can offer them money, estates—things our country cannot afford. And we *need* our doctors. As it is, only the very rich can get the corrective surgery they require."

"If you're worried about our pirating your professionals, there are ways around that. For example, a clause could be written—" Wolf went on, feeling more and more in control. He was getting somewhere. If there wasn't a deal to be made, the discussion would never have gotten this far.

The day wore on. DiStephano called in aides and dismissed them. Twice, he had drinks sent in. Once, they broke for lunch. Slowly the heat built, until it was sweltering. Finally, the light began to fail, and the heat grew less oppressive.

DiStephano swept the documents into two piles, returned one to Wolf, and put the other inside a desk drawer. "I'll look these over, have our legal boys run a study. There shouldn't be any difficulties. I'll get back to you with the final word in—say a month. September twenty-first, I'll be in Boston then, but you can find me easily enough, if you ask around."

"A month? But I thought . . . "

"A month. You can't hurry City Hall," DiStephano said firmly. "Ms. Corey!"

The veiled woman was at the door, remote, elusive. "Sir."

"Drag Kaplan out of his office. Tell him we got a kid in here he should give the VIP treatment to. Maybe a show. It's a Hopkins thing, he should earn his keep."

"Yes, sir." She was gone.

"Thank you," Wolf said, "but I don't really need . . . "

"Take my advice, kid, take all the perks you can get. God knows there aren't many left. I'll have Kaplan pick you up at your hostel in an hour."

Kaplan turned out to be a slight, balding man with nervous gestures, some sort of administrative functionary for Hopkins. Wolf never did get the connection. But Kaplan was equally puzzled by Wolf's status, and Wolf took petty pleasure in not explaining it. It took some of the sting off of having his papers stolen.

Kaplan led Wolf through the evening streets. A bright sunset circled the world, and the crowds were much thinner. "We won't be leaving the area that's zoned for electricity," Kaplan said. "Otherwise I'd advise against going out at night at all. Lot of jennie-deafs out then."

"Jennie-deafs?"

"Mutes. Culls. The really terminal cases. Some of them can't pass themselves off in daylight even wearing coveralls. Or chador—a lot are women." A faintly perverse expression crossed the man's face, leaving not so much as a greasy residue.

"Where are we going?" Wolf asked. He wanted to change the subject. A vague presentiment assured him he did not want to know the source of Kaplan's expression.

"A place called Peabody's. You've heard of Janis Joplin, our famous national singer?"

Wolf nodded, meaning no.

"The show is a re-creation of her act. Woman name of Maggie Horowitz does the best impersonation of Janis I've ever seen. Tickets are almost impossible to get, but Hopkins has special influence in this case because—ah, here we are."

Kaplan led him down a set of concrete steps and into the basement of a dull brick building. Wolf experienced a moment of dislocation. It was a bookstore. Shelves and boxes of books and magazines brooded over him, a packrat's clutter of paper.

Wolf wanted to linger, to scan the ancient tomes, remnants of a time and culture fast sinking into obscurity and myth. But Kaplan brushed past them without a second glance and he had to hurry to keep up.

They passed through a second roomful of books, then into a hallway where a grey man held out a gnarled hand and said, "Tickets, please."

Kaplan gave the man two crisp pasteboard cards, and they entered a third room.

It was a cabaret. Wooden chairs clustered about small tables with flickering candles at their centers. The room was lofted with wood beams, and a large unused fireplace dominated one wall. Another wall had obviously been torn out at one time to make room for a small stage. Over a century's accumulation of memorabilia covered the walls or hung from the rafters, like barbarian trinkets from toppled empires.

"Peabody's is a local institution," Kaplan said. "In the twentieth century it was a speakeasy. H.L. Mencken himself used to drink here." Wolf nodded, though the name meant nothing to him. "The bookstore was a front, and the drinking went on here in back."

The place was charged with a feeling of the past. It invoked America's bygone days as a world power. Wolf half-expected to see Theodore Roosevelt or Henry Kissinger come striding in. He said something to this effect, and Kaplan smiled complacently.

"You'll like the show, then," he said.

A waiter took their orders. There was barely time to begin on the drinks when a pair of spotlights came on, and the stage curtain parted.

A woman stood alone in the center of the stage. Bracelets and bangles hung from her wrists, gaudy necklaces from her throat. She wore large tinted glasses and a flowered granny gown. Her nipples pushed against the thin dress. Wolf stared at them in horrified fascination. She had an extra set, immediately below the first pair.

The woman stood perfectly motionless. Wolf couldn't stop staring at her nipples; it wasn't just the number, it was the fact of their being visible at all. So quickly had he taken on this land's taboos.

The woman threw her head back and laughed. She put one hand on her hip, thrust the hip out at an angle, and lifted the microphone to her lips. She spoke, and her voice was harsh and raspy.

"About a year ago I lived in a row house in Newark, right? Lived on the third floor, and I thought I had my act together. But nothing was going right, I wasn't getting any . . . action.

Know what I mean? No talent comin' around. And there was
this chick down the street, didn't have much and she was doing
okay, so I say to myself: *What's wrong, Janis?* How come she's
doing so good and you ain't gettin' any? So I decided to check it
out, see what she had and I didn't. And one day I get up early,
look out the window, and I see this chick out there *hustling!* I
mean, she was doing the streets at *noon!* So I said to myself,
Janis, honey, you ain't even trying. And when ya want action,
ya gotta try. Yeah. Try just a little bit harder."

The music swept up out of nowhere, and she was singing:
"Try-iii, Try-iii, Just a little bit harder . . . "

And unexpectedly, it was good. It was like nothing he had
ever heard, but he understood it, almost on an instinctual
level. It was world-culture music. It was universal.

Kaplan dug fingers into Wolf's arm, brought his mouth up
to Wolf's ear. "You see? You see?" he demanded. Wolf shook
him off impatiently. He wanted to hear the music.

The concert lasted forever, and it was done in no time at all.
It left Wolf sweaty and emotionally spent. Onstage, the woman
was energy personified. She danced, she strutted, she wailed
more power into her songs than seemed humanly possible. Not
knowing the original, Wolf was sure it was a perfect re-creation. It had that feel.

The audience loved her. They called her back for three
encores, and then a fourth. Finally, she came out, gasped into
the mike, "I love ya, honeys, I truly do. But please—no more. I
just couldn't do it." She blew a kiss, and was gone from the
stage.

The entire audience was standing, Wolf among them,
applauding furiously. A hand fell on Wolf's shoulder, and he
glanced to his side, annoyed. It was Kaplan. His face was
flushed and he said, "Come on." He pulled Wolf free of the
crowd and backstage to a small dressing room. Its door was
ajar and people were crowded into it.

One of them was the singer, hair stringy and out-of-place,
laughing and gesturing widely with a Southern Comfort bottle.

It was an antique, its label lacquered to the glass, and three-quarters filled with something amber-colored.

"Janis, this is—" Kaplan began.

"The name is Maggie," she sang gleefully. "Maggie Horowitz. I ain't no *dead* blues singer. And don't you forget it."

"This is a fan of yours, Maggie. From Africa." He gave Wolf a small shove. Wolf hesitantly stumbled forward, grimacing apologetically at the people he displaced.

"Whee—howdy!" Maggie whooped. She downed a slug from her bottle. "Pleased ta meecha, Ace. Kinda light for an African, aintcha?"

"My mother's people were descended from German settlers." And it was felt that a light-skinned representative could handle the touchy Americans better, but he didn't say that.

"Whatcher name, Ace?

"Wolf."

"Wolf!" Maggie crowed. "Yeah, you look like a real heartbreaker, honey. Guess I'd better be careful around you, huh? Likely to sweep me off my feet and deflower me." She nudged him with an elbow. "That's a joke, Ace."

Wolf was fascinated. Maggie was *alive,* a dozen times more so than her countrymen. She made them look like zombies. Wolf was also a little afraid of her.

"*Hey.* Whatcha think of my singing, hah?"

"It was excellent," Wolf said. "It was"—he groped for words—"in my land the music is quieter, there is not so much emotion."

"Yeah, well I think it was fucking good, Ace. Voice's never been in better shape. Go tell 'em that at Hopkins, Kaplan. Tell 'em I'm giving them their money's worth."

"Of course you are," Kaplan said.

"Well, I *am,* goddammit. Hey, this place is like a morgue! Let's ditch this matchbox dressing room and hit the bars. Hey? Let's party."

She swept them all out of the dressing room, out of the building, and onto the street. They formed a small boisterous group, noisily wandering the city, looking for bars.

"There's one a block thataway," Maggie said. "Let's hit it. Hey, Ace, I'd likeya ta meet Cynthia. Sin, this is Wolf. Sin and I are like one person inside two skins. Many's the time we've shared a piece of talent in the same bed. Hey?" She cackled, and grabbed at Cynthia's ass.

"Cut it out, Maggie." Cynthia smiled when she said it. She was a tall, slim, striking woman.

"Hey, this town is *dead!*" Maggie screamed the last word, then gestured them all to silence so they could listen for the echo. "There it is." She pointed, and they swooped down on the first bar.

After the third, Wolf lost track. At some point he gave up on the party and somehow made his way back to his hostel. The last he remembered of Maggie she was calling after him, "Hey, Ace, don't be a party poop." Then: "At least be sure to come back tomorrow, goddammit."

Wolf spent most of the day in his room, drinking water and napping. His hangover was all but gone by the time evening took the edge off the day's heat. He thought of Maggie's half-serious invitation, dismissed it and decided to go to the Club.

The Uhuru Club was ablaze with light by the time he wandered in, a beacon in a dark city. Its frequenters, after all, were all African foreign service, with a few commercial reps such as himself forced in by the insular nature of American society and the need for polite conversation. It was *de facto* exempt from the power-use laws that governed the natives.

"Mbikana! Over here, lad, let me set you up with a drink." Nnamdi of the consulate waved him over to the bar. Wolf complied, feeling conspicuous as he always did in the Club. His skin stood out here. Even the American servants were dark, though whether this was a gesture of deference or arrogance on the part of the local authorities, he could not guess.

"Word is that you spent the day closeted with the comptroller." Nnamdi had a gin-and-tonic set up. Wolf loathed the drink, but it was universal among the service people. "Share the dirt with us." Other faces gathered around; the service ran on gossip.

Wolf gave an abridged version of the encounter, and Nnamdi applauded. "A full day with the Spider King, and you escaped with your balls intact. An auspicious beginning for you, lad."

"Spider King?"

"Surely you were briefed on regional autonomy—how the country was broken up when it could no longer be managed by a central directorate? There *is* no higher authority than DiStephano in this part of the world, boy."

"Boston," Ajuji sniffed. Like most of the expatriates, she was a failure; unlike many, she couldn't hide the fact from herself. "That's exactly the sort of treatment one comes to expect from these savages."

"Now, Ajuji," Nnamdi said mildly. "These people are hardly savages. Why, before the Collapse they put men on the moon."

"Technology! Hard-core technology, that's all it was, of a piece with the kind that almost destroyed us all. If you want a measure of a people, you look at how they live. These—*yanks,*" she hissed the word to emphasize its filthiness, "live in squalor. Their streets are filthy, their cities are filthy, and even the ones who aren't rotten with genetic disease are filthy. A child can be taught to clean up after itself. What does that make them?"

"Human beings, Ajuji."

"Hogwash, Nnamdi."

Wolf followed the argument with acute embarrassment. He had been brought up to expect well from people with social standing. To hear gutter language and low prejudice from them was almost beyond bearing. Suddenly it *was* beyond bearing. He turned his back on them all, and left.

"Mbikana! You mustn't—" Nnamdi called after him.

"Oh, let him go," Ajuji cut in, with a satisfied tone, "you mustn't expect better. After all, he's practically one of *them.*"

Well maybe he was.

Wolf wasn't fully aware of where he was going until he found himself at Peabody's. He circled the building, and found a rear door. He tried the knob; it turned loosely in his hand. Then the door swung open and a heavy, bearded man in coveralls leaned out. "Yes?" he said in an unfriendly tone.

"Uh," Wolf said. "Maggie Horowitz told me I could drop by."

"Look, pilgrim, there are a lot of people trying to get backstage. My job is to keep them out unless I know them. I don't know you."

Wolf tried to think of some response to this, and failed. He was about to turn away when somebody unseen said, "Oh, let him in, Deke."

It was Cynthia. "Come on," she said in a bored voice. "Don't clog up the doorway." The guard moved aside, and he entered.

"Thank you," he said.

"*Nada*," she replied. "As Maggie would say. The dressing room is that way, pilgrim."

"Wolf, honey!" Maggie shrieked. "How's it going, Ace? Ya catch the show?"

"No, I—"

"You shoulda. I was good. Really good. Janis herself was never better. Hey, gang! Let's split, hah? Let's go somewhere and get down and boogie."

A group of twenty ended up taking over a methane-lit bar outside the zoned-for-electricity sector. Three of the band had brought along their instruments, and they talked the owner into letting them play. The music was droning and monotonous. Maggie listened appreciatively, grinning and moving her head to the music.

"Whatcha think of that, Ace? Pretty good, hey? That's what we call Dead music."

Wolf shook his head. "I think it's well named."

"Hey, guys, you hear that? Wolf here just made a funny. There's hope for you yet, honey." Then she sighed. "Can't get behind it, huh? That's really sad, man. I mean they played *good* music back then; it was real. We're just echoes, man. Just playing away at them old songs. Got none of our own worth singing."

"Is that why you're doing the show, then?" Wolf asked, curious.

Maggie laughed. "Hell, no. I do it because I got the chance. DiStephano got in touch with me—"

"DiStephano? The comptroller?"

"One of his guys, anyway. They had this gig all set up, and they needed someone to play Janis. So they ran a computer search and came up with my name. And they offered me money, and I spent a month or two in Hopkins being worked over, and here I am. On the road to fame and glory." Her voice rose and warbled and mocked itself on the last phrase.

"Why did you have to go to Hopkins?"

"You don't think I was *born* looking like this? They had to change my face around. Changed my voice too, for which God bless. They brought it down lower, widened out my range, gave it the strength to hold on to them high notes and push 'em around."

"Not to mention the mental implants," Cynthia said.

"Oh, yeah, and the 'plants so I could talk in a bluesy sorta way without falling out of character," Maggie said. "But that was minor."

Wolf was impressed. He had known that Hopkins was good, but this—! "What possible benefit is there for them?"

"Beats the living hell out of me, lover-boy. Don't know, don't care, and don't ask. That's my motto."

A long-haired pale young man sitting nearby said, "The government is all hacked up on social engineering. They do a lot of weird things, and you never find out why. You learn not to ask questions."

"Hey, listen, Hawk, bringing Janis back to life isn't weird. It's a beautiful thing to do," Maggie objected. "Yeah. I only wish they could *really* bring her back. Sit her down next to me. Love to talk with that lady."

"You two would tear each other's eyes out," Cynthia said.

"What? Why?"

"Neither one of you'd be willing to give up the spotlight to the other."

Maggie cackled. "Ain't it the truth? Still, she's one broad I'd love to have met. A *real* star, see? Not a goddamned echo like me."

Hawk broke in, said, "You, Wolf. Where does your pilgrimage take you now? The group goes on tour the day after tomorrow; what are your plans?"

"I don't really have any," Wolf said. He explained his situation. "I'll probably stay in Baltimore until it's time to go up north. Maybe I'll take a side trip or two."

"Why don't you join the group, then?" Hawk asked. "We're planning to make the trip one long party. And we'll slam into Boston in just less than a month. The tour ends there."

"That," said Cynthia, "is a real bright idea. All we need is another nonproductive person on board the train."

Maggie bristled. "So what's wrong with it?"

"Nothing's wrong with it. It's just a dumb idea."

"Well, *I* like it. How about it, Ace? You on the train or off?"

"I—" He stopped. Well, why not? "Yes. I would be pleased to go along."

"Good." She turned to Cynthia. "*Your* problem, sweets, is that you're just plain jealous."

"Oh, Christ, here we go again."

"Well, don't bother. It won't do you any good. Hey, you see that piece of talent at the far end of the bar?"

"Maggie, that 'piece of talent,' as you call him, is eighteen years old. At most."

"Yeah. Nice though." Maggie stared wistfully down the bar. "He's kinda pretty, ya know?"

Wolf spent the next day clearing up his affairs and arranging for the letters of credit. The morning of departure day, he rose early and made his way to Baltimore Station. A brief exchange with the guards let him into the walled train yard.

The train was an ungainly steam locomotive with a string of rehabilitated cars behind it. The last car had the word PEARL painted on it, in antique psychedelic lettering.

"Hey, Wolf! Come lookit this mother." A lone figure waved at him from the far end of the train. Maggie.

Wolf joined her. "What do you think of it, hah?"

He searched for something polite to say. "It is very impressive," he said finally. The word that leapt to mind was *grotesque.*

"Yeah, there's a methane processing plant nearby. Hey, lookit me! Up and awake at eight in the morning. Can ya take it? Had to get behind a little speed to do it, though."

The idiom was beyond him. "You mean—you were late waking up?"

"What? Oh, hey, man, you can be—look, forget I said a thing. No." She pondered a second. "Look, Wolf. There's this stuff called 'speed,' it can wake you up in the morning, give you a little boost, get you going. Ya know?"

Awareness dawned. "You mean amphetamines."

"Yeah, well this stuff ain't exactly legal, dig? So I'd just as soon you didn't spread the word around. I mean, I trust you man, but I wanna be sure you know what's happening before you go shooting off your mouth."

"I understand," Wolf said. "I won't say anything. But you know that amphetamines are—"

"Gotcha, Ace. Hey, you gotta meet the piece of talent I picked up last night. Hey, Dave! Get your ass over here, lover."

A young sleepy-eyed blond shuffled around the edge of the train. He wore white shorts, defiantly it seemed to Wolf, and a loose blouse buttoned up to his neck. Giving Maggie a weak hug around the waist, he nodded to Wolf.

"Davie's got four nipples, just like me. How about that? I mean, it's gotta be a pretty rare mutation, hah?"

Dave hung his head, half blushing. "Aw, Janis," he mumbled. Wolf waited for Maggie to correct the boy, but she didn't. Instead she led them around and around the train chatting away madly, pointing out this, that, and the other thing.

Finally, Wolf excused himself, and returned to his hostel. He left Maggie prowling about the train, dragging her pretty-boy after her. Wolf went out for a long lunch, picked up his bags, and showed up at the train earlier than most of the entourage.

The train lurched, and pulled out of the station. Maggie was in constant motion, talking, laughing, directing the placement of luggage. She darted from car to car, never still. Wolf found a seat and stared out the window. Children dressed in rags ran alongside the tracks, holding out hands and begging for money. One or two of the party threw coins; more laughed and threw bits of garbage.

Then the children were gone, and the train was passing through endless miles of weathered ruins. Hawk sat down beside Wolf. "It'll be a slow trip," he said. "The train has to go around large sections of land it's better not to go through." He started moodily at the broken-windowed shells that were once factories and warehouses. "Look out there, pilgrim, *that's* my country," he said in a disgusted voice. "Or the corpse of it."

"Hawk, you're close to Maggie."

"Now if you go out to the center of the continent . . . " Hawk's voice grew distant. "There's a cavern out there, where they housed radioactive waste. It was formed into slugs and covered with solid gold—anything else deteriorates too fast. The way I figure it, a man with a lead suit could go into the cavern and shave off a fortune. There's tons of the stuff there." He sighed. "Someday I'm going to rummage through a few archives and go."

"Hawk, you've got to *listen* to me."

Hawk held up a hand for silence. "It's about the drugs, right? You just found out, and you want me to warn her."

"Warning her isn't good enough. Someone has to stop her."

"Yes, well. Try to understand, Maggie was in Hopkins for *three months* while they performed some very drastic surgery on her. She didn't look a thing like she does now, and she could sing but her voice wasn't anything to rave about. Not to mention the mental implants.

"Imagine the pain she went through. Now ask yourself what are the two most effective painkillers in existence?"

"Morphine and heroin. But in my country, when drugs are resorted to, the doctors wean the patients off them before their release."

"That's not the point. Consider this—Maggie could have had Hopkins remove the extra nipples. They could have done it. But she wasn't willing to go through the pain."

"She seems proud of them."

"She talks about them a lot, at least."

The train lurched and stumbled. Three of the musicians had uncrated their guitars and were playing more "Dead" music. Wolf chewed his lip in silence for a time, then said, "So what is the point you're making?"

"Simply that Maggie was willing to undergo the greater pain so that she could become Janis. So when I tell you she only uses drugs as painkillers, you have to understand that I'm not necessarily talking about physical pain." Hawk got up and left.

Maggie danced into the car. "Big time!" she whooped. "We made it into the big time, boys and girls. Hey, let's party!"

The next ten days were one extended party, interspersed with concerts. The reception in Wilmington was phenomenal. Thousands came to see the show; many were turned away. Maggie was unsteady before the first concert, achingly afraid of failure. But she played a rousing set, and was called back time and time again. Finally, exhausted and limp, her hair sticking to a sweaty forehead, she stood up front and gasped, "That's all there is, boys and girls. I love ya and I wish there was more to give ya, but there ain't. You used it all up." And the applause went on and on . . .

The four shows in Philadelphia began slowly, but built up big. A few seats were unsold at the first concert; people were turned away for the second. The last two were near-riots. The group entrained to Newark for a day's rest and put on a Labor Day concert that made the previous efforts look pale. They stayed in an obscure hostel for an extra day's rest.

Wolf spent his rest day sight-seeing. While in Philadelphia he had hired a native guide and prowled through the rusting refinery buildings at Point Breeze. They rose to the sky forever in tragic magnificence, and it was hard to believe there had ever been enough oil in the world to fill the holding tanks there. In Wilmington, he let the local guide lead him to a small Italian neighborhood to watch a religious festival.

The festival was a parade, led first by a priest trailed by eight altar girls, with incense burners and fans. Then came twelve burly men carrying the flower-draped body of an ancient Cadillac. After them came the faithful, in coveralls and chador, singing.

Wolf followed the procession to the river, where the car was placed in a hole in the ground, sprinkled with holy water, and set afire. He asked the guide what story lay behind the ritual, and the boy shrugged. It was old, he was told, very very old.

It was late when Wolf returned to the hostel. He was expecting a party, but found it dark and empty. Cynthia stood in the foyer, hands behind her back, staring out a barred window at black nothingness.

"Where is everybody?" Wolf asked. It was hot. Insects buzzed about the coal-oil lamp, batting against it frenziedly.

Cynthia turned, studied him oddly. Her forehead was beaded with sweat. "Maggie's gone home—she's attending a midschool reunion. She's going to show her old friends what a hacking big star she's become. The others?" She shrugged. "Off wherever puppets go when there's no one to bring them to life. Their rooms, probably."

"Oh." Cynthia's dress clung damply to her legs and sides. Dark stains spread out form under her armpits. "Would you like to play a game of chess or—something?"

Cynthia's eyes were strangely intense. She took a step closer to him. "Wolf, I've been wondering. You've been celibate on this trip. Is there a problem? No? Maybe a girlfriend back home?"

"There was, but she won't wait for me." Wolf made a deprecating gesture. "Maybe that was part of the reason I took this trip."

She took one of his hands, placed it on her breast. "But you *are* interested in girls?" Then, before he could shape his answer into clumsy words, she whispered, "Come on," and led him to her room.

Once inside, Wolf seized Cynthia and kissed her, deeply and long. She responded with passion, then drew away and with a little shove toppled them onto the bed. "Off with your clothes," she said. She shucked her blouse in a complex fluid motion. Pale breasts bobbled, catching vague moonlight from the window.

After an instant's hesitation, Wolf doffed his own clothing. By contrast with Cynthia he felt weak and irresolute, and it irked him to feel that way. Determined to prove he was nothing of the kind, he reached for Cynthia as she dropped onto the bed beside him. She evaded his grasp.

"Just a moment, pilgrim." She rummaged through a bag by the headboard. "Ah. Care for a little treat first? It'll enhance the sensations."

"Drugs?" Wolf asked, feeling an involuntary horror.

"Oh, come down off your high horse. Once won't melt your genes. Give a gander at what you're being so critical of."

"What is it?"

"Vanilla ice cream," she snapped. She unstoppered a small vial and meticulously dribbled a few grains of white powder onto a thumbnail. "This is expensive, so pay attention. You want to breathe it all in with one snort. Got that? So by the numbers: take a deep breath and breathe out slowly. That's it. Now in. Now out and hold."

Cynthia laid her thumbnail beneath Wolf's nose, pinched one nostril shut with her free hand. "Now in fast. Yeah!"

He inhaled convulsively and was flooded with sensations. A

crisp, clean taste filled his mouth, and a spray of fine white powder hit the back of his throat. It tingled pleasantly. His head felt spacious. He moved his jaw, suspiciously searching about with his tongue.

Cynthia quickly snorted some of the powder herself, restoppering the vial.

"Now," she said. "Touch me. Slowly, slowly, we've got all night. That's the way. Ahhhh." She shivered. "I think you've got the idea."

They worked the bed for hours. The drug, whatever it was, made Wolf feel strangely clearheaded and rational, more playful and more prone to linger. There was no urgency to their lovemaking; they took their time. Three, perhaps four times they halted for more of the powder, which Cynthia doled out with careful ceremony. Each time they returned to their lovemaking with renewed interest and resolution to take it slowly, to postpone each climax to the last possible instant.

The evening grew old. Finally, they lay on the sheets, not touching, weak and exhausted. Wolf's body was covered with a fine sheen of sweat. He did not care to even think of making love yet another time. He refrained from saying this.

"Not bad," Cynthia said softly. "I must remember to recommend you to Maggie."

"Sin, why do you do that?"

"Do what?"

"We've just—been as intimate as two human beings can be. But as soon as it's over, you say something cold. Is it that you're afraid of contact?"

"Christ." It was an empty syllable, devoid of religious content, and flat. Cynthia fumbled in her bag, found a metal case, pulled a cigarette out, and lit it. Wolf flinched inwardly. "Look, pilgrim, what are you asking for? You planning to marry me and take me away to your big, clean African cities to meet your momma? Hah?

"Didn't think so. So what do you want from me? Mental souvenirs to take home and tell your friends about? I'll give you one; I spent years saving up enough to go see a doctor, find out if I could have any brats. Went to one last year, and what do you think he tells me? I've got red-cell dyscrasia, too far gone for treatment, there's nothing to do but wait. Lovely, hah? So one of these days it'll just stop working and I'll die. Nothing to be done. So long as I eat right, I won't start wasting away, so I can keep my looks up to the end. I could buy a little time if I gave up drugs like this"—she waved the cigarette, and an ash fell on Wolf's chest. He brushed it away quickly—"and the white powder, and anything else that makes life worth living. But it wouldn't buy me enough time to do anything worth doing." She fell silent. "Hey. What time is it?"

Wolf climbed out of bed, rummaged through his clothing until he found his timepiece. He held it up to the window, squinted. "Um. Twelve . . . fourteen."

"Oh, *nukes*." Cynthia was up and scrabbling for her clothes. "Come on, get dressed. Don't just stand there."

Wolf dressed himself slowly. "What's the problem?"

"I promised Maggie I'd get some people together to walk her back from that damned reunion. It ended *hours* ago, and I lost track of the time." She ignored his grin. "Ready? Come on, we'll check her room first and then the foyer. God, is she going to be mad."

They found Maggie in the foyer. She stood in the center of the room, haggard and bedraggled, her handbag hanging loosely from one hand. Her face was livid with rage. The sputtering lamp made her face look old and evil.

"Well!" she snarled. "Where have you two been?"

"In my room, balling," Cynthia said calmly. Wolf stared at her, appalled.

"Well, that's just beautiful. That's really beautiful, isn't it? Do you know where I've been while my two best friends were upstairs humping their brains out? Hey? Do you want to know?" Her voice reached hysterical peak. "I was being *raped by two jennie-deafs*, that's where!"

She stormed past them, half-cocking her arm as if she were

going to assault them with her purse, then thinking better of it. They heard her run down the hall. Her door slammed.

Bewildered, Wolf said, "But I—"

"Don't let her dance on your head," Cynthia said. "She's lying."

"Are you certain?"

"Look, we've lived together, bedded the same men—I know her. She's all hacked off at not having an escort home. And Little Miss Sunshine has to spread the gloom."

"We should have been there," Wolf said dubiously. "She could have been killed, walking home alone."

"Whether Maggie dies a month early or not doesn't make a bit of difference to me, pilgrim. I've got my own problems."

"A month—? Is Maggie suffering from a disease too?"

"We're all suffering, we all—Ah, the hell with you too." Cynthia spat on the floor, spun on her heel, and disappeared down the hallway. It had the rhythm and inevitability of a witch's curse.

The half-day trip to New York left the troupe with playtime before the first concert, but Maggie stayed in seclusion, drinking. There was talk about her use of drugs, and this alarmed Wolf, for they were all users of drugs themselves.

There was also gossip about the reunion. Some held that Maggie had dazzled her former friends—who had not treated her well in her younger years-had been glamorous and gracious. The predominant view, however, was that she had been soundly snubbed, that she was still a freak and an oddity in the eyes of her former contemporaries. That she had left the reunion alone.

Rumors flew about the liaison between Wolf and Cynthia too. The fact that she avoided him only fed the speculation.

Despite everything the New York City concerts were a roaring success. All four shows were sold out as soon as tickets went on sale. Scalpers made small fortunes that week, and for the first time the concerts were allowed to run into the evening.

Power was diverted from a section of the city to allow for the lighjting and amplification. And Maggie sang as she had never sung before. Her voice roused the audience to a frenzy, and her blues were enough to break a hermit's heart.

They left for Hartford on the tenth, Maggie sequestered in her compartment in the last car. Crew members lounged about idly. Some strummed guitars, never quite breaking into a recognizable tune. Others talked quietly. Hawk flipped tarot cards into a heap, one at a time.

"Hey, this place is fucking *dead!*" Maggie was suddenly in the car, her expression an odd combination of defiance and guilt. "Let's party! Hey? Let's hear some music." She fell into Hawk's lap and nibbled on an ear.

"Welcome back, Maggie," somebody said.

"Janis!" she shouted happily. "The lady's name is Janis!"

Like a rusty machine starting up, the party came to life. Music jelled. Voices became animated. Bottles of alcohol appeared and were passed around. And for the remainder of the two days that the train spent making wide looping detours to avoid the dangerous stretches of Connecticut and New York, the party never died.

There were tense undertones to the party, however, a desperate quality in Maggie's gaiety. For the first time, Wolf began to feel trapped, to count the days that separated him from Boston and the end of the tour.

The dressing room for the first Hartford concert was cramped, small, badly lit—like every other dressing room they'd encountered. "Get your ass over here, Sin," Maggie yelled. "You've gotta make me up so I look strung out, like Janis did."

Cynthia held Maggie's chin, twisted it to the left, to the right. "Maggie, you don't *need* makeup to look strung out."

"Goddammit, yes I *do.* Let's get it on. Come on, come on— I'm a star, I shouldn't have to put up with this shit."

Cynthia hesitated, then began dabbing at Maggie's face, lightly accentuating the lines, the bags under her eyes.

Maggie studied the mirror. "Now *that's* grim," she said.

"That's really grotesque."

"That's what you look like, Maggie."

"You cheap bitch! You'd think *I* was the one who nodded out last night before we could get it on." There was an awkward silence. "Hey, Wolf!" She spun to face him. "What do *you* say?"

"Well," Wolf began, embarrassed, "I'm afraid Cynthia's . . . "

"You see? Let's get this show on the road." She grabbed her cherished Southern Comfort bottle and upended it.

"That's not doing you any good either."

Maggie smiled coldly. "Shows what *you* know. Janis always gets smashed before a concert. Helps her voice." She stood, made her way to the curtains. The emcee was winding up his pitch.

"Ladies and gentlemen . . . Janis!"

Screams arose. Maggie sashayed up to the mike, lifted it, laughed into it.

"Heyyy. Good ta see ya." She swayed and squinted at the crowd, and was off and into her rap. "Ya know, I went ta see a doctor the other week. Told him I was worried about how much drinking I was doing. Told him I'd been drinkin' heavy since I was twelve. Get up in the morning and have a few Bloody Marys with breakfast. Polish off a fifth before lunch. Have a few drinks at dinner, and really get into it when the partying begins. Told him how much I drank for how many years. So I said, 'Look, Doc, none of this ever hurt me any, but I'm kinda worried, ya know? Give it to me straight, have I got a problem?' And he said, 'Man, I don't think you've got a problem. *I* think you're doing just *fine!*' " Cheers from the audience. Maggie smiled smugly. "Well, honey, *everybody's* got problems, and I'm no exception." The music came up. "But when I got problems, I got an answer, 'cause I can sing dem ole-time blues. Just sing my problems away." She launched into "Ball and Chain," and the audience went wild.

Backstage, Wolf was sitting on a stepladder. He had bought a cup of water from a vendor and was nursing it, taking small sips. Cynthia came up and stood beside him. They both watched Maggie strutting on stage, stamping and sweating, writhing and howling.

"I can never get over the contrast," Wolf said, not looking at Cynthia. "Out there everybody is excited. Back here, it's calm and peaceful. Sometimes I wonder if we're seeing the same thing the audience does."

"Sometimes it's hard to see what's right in front of your face." Cynthia smiled a sad cryptic smile and left. Wolf had grown used to such statements, and gave it no more thought.

The second and final Hartford show went well. However, the first two concerts in Providence were bad. Maggie's voice and timing were off, and she had to cover with theatrics. At the second show she had to order the audience to dance—something that had never been necessary before. Her onstage raps became bawdier and more graphic. She moved her body as suggestively as a stripper, employing bumps and grinds. The third show was better, but the earthy elements remained.

The cast wound up in a bar in a bad section of town, where guards with guns covered the doorway from fortified booths. Maggie got drunk and ended up crying. "Man, I was so blitzed when I went onstage—you say I was good?"

"Sure, Maggie," Hawk mumbled. Cynthia snorted.

"You were very good," Wolf assured her.

"I don't remember a goddamned thing," she wailed. "You say I was good? It ain't fair, man. If I was good, I deserve to be able to remember it. I mean, what's the point otherwise? Hey?"

Wolf patted her shoulder clumsily. She grabbed the front of his dashiki and buried her face in his chest. "Wolf, Wolf, what's gonna *happen* to me?" she sobbed.

"Don't cry," he said. Patting her hair.

Finally, Wolf and Hawk had to lead her back to the hostel. No one else was willing to quit the bar.

They skirted an area where all the buildings had been torn down but one. It stood alone, with great gaping holes where plate glass had been, and large nonfunctional arches on one side.

"It was a fast-food building," Hawk explained when Wolf asked. He sounded embarrassed.

"Why is it still standing?"

"Because there are ignorant and superstitious people every-where," Hawk muttered. Wolf dropped the subject.

The streets were dark and empty. They went back into the denser areas of town, and the sound of their footsteps bounced off the buildings. Maggie was leaning half-conscious on Hawk's shoulder, and he almost had to carry her.

There was a stirring in the shadows. Hawk tensed. "Speed up a bit, if you can," he whispered.

Something shuffled out of the darkness. It was large and only vaguely human. It moved toward them. "What—?" Wolf whispered.

"Jennie-deaf," Hawk whispered back. "If you know any clever tricks, this is the time to use 'em." The thing broke into a shambling run.

Wolf thrust a hand into a pocket and whirled to face Hawk. "Look," he said in a loud, angry voice. "I've taken *enough* from you! I've got a *knife,* and I don't care *what* I do!" The jennie-deaf halted. From the corner of his eye, Wolf saw it slide back into the shadows.

Maggie looked up with sleepy, quizzical expression. "Hey, what . . . "

"Never mind," Hawk muttered. He upped his pace, half dragging Maggie after him. "That was arrogant," he said approvingly.

Wolf forced his hand from his pocket. He found he was shivering from the aftershock. *"Nada,"* he said. Then: "That is the correct term?"

"Yeah."

"I wasn't certain that jennie-deafs really existed."

"Just some poor mute with gland trouble. Don't think about it."

Autumn was just breaking out when the troupe hit Boston. They arrived to find the final touches being put on the stage on

Boston Commons. A mammoth concert was planned; dozens of people swarmed about making preparations.

"This must be how America was all the time before the Collapse," Wolf said, impressed. He was ignored.

The morning of the concert, Wolf was watching canvas being hoisted above the stage, against the chance of rain, when a gripper ran up and said, "You, pilgrim, have you seen Janis?"

"Maggie," he corrected automatically, "No, not recently."

"Thanks," the man gasped, and ran off. Not long after, Hawk hurried by and asked, "Seen Maggie lagging about?"

"No. Wait, Hawk, what's going on? You're the second person to ask me that."

Hawk shrugged. "Maggie's disappeared. Nothing to scream about."

"I hope she'll be back in time for the show."

"The local police are hunting for her. Anyway, she's got the implants; if she can move she'll be onstage. Never doubt it." He hurried away.

The final checks were being run, and the first concertgoers beginning to straggle in, when Maggie finally appeared. Uniformed men held each arm; she looked sober and angry. Cynthia took charge, dismissed the police, and took Maggie to the trailer that served as a dressing room.

Wolf watched from a distance, decided he could be of no use. He ambled about the Commons aimlessly, watching the crowd grow. The people coming in found places to sit, took them, and waited. There was little talk among them, and what there was was quiet. They were dressed brightly, but not in their best. Some carried winejugs or blankets.

They were an odd crew. They did not look each other in the eye; their mouths were grim, their faces without expression. Their speech was low, but with an undercurrent of tension. Wolf wandered among them, eavesdropping, listening to fragments of their talk.

"Said that her child was going to . . . "

". . . needed that. Nobody needed that."

"Couldn't have paid it away . . . "

" . . . tasted odd, so I didn't . . . "

"Had to tear down three blocks . . . "

" . . . blood."

Wolf became increasingly uneasy. There was something about their expressions, their tones of voice. He bumped into Hawk, who tried to hurry past.

"Hawk, there is something very wrong happening."

Hawk's face twisted. He gestured toward the light tower. "No time," he said, "the show's beginning. I've got to be at my station." Wolf hesitated, then followed the man up the ladders of the light tower.

All of the Commons was visible from the tower. The ground was thick with people, hordes of ant-specks against the brown of trampled earth. Not a child among them, and that felt wrong too. A gold-and-purple sunset smeared itself three-quarters of the way around the horizon.

Hawk flicked lights on and off, one by one, referring to a sheet of paper he held in one hand. Sometimes he cursed and respliced wires. Wolf waited. A light breeze ruffled his hair, though there was no hint of wind below.

"This is a sick country," Hawk said. He slipped a headset on, played a red spot on the stage, let it wink out. "You there, Patrick? The kliegs go on in two." He ran a check on all the locals manning lights, addressing them by name. "Average life span is something like forty-two—*if* you get out of the delivery room alive. The birth-rate has to be very high to keep the population from dwindling away to nothing." He brought up all the red and blue spots. The stage was bathed in purple light. The canvas above looked black in contrast. An obscure figure strolled to the center mike.

"Hit it, Patrick." A bright pool of light illuminated the emcee. He coughed, went into his spiel. His voice boomed over the crowd, relayed away from the stage by a series of amps with timed delay synchronization with the further amplification. The crowd moved sluggishly about the foot of the tower, set in motion by latecomers straggling in. "So the question you should ask yourself is why the government is wasting its resources on a goddamned show."

"All right," Wolf said. "Why?" He was very tense, very still. The breeze swept away his sweat, and he wished he had brought along a jacket. He might need one later.

"Because their wizards said to—the damn social engineers and their machines," Hawk answered. "Watch the crowd."

". . . *Janis!*" the loudspeakers boomed. And Maggie was onstage, rapping away, handling the microphone suggestively, obviously at the peak of her form. The crowd exploded into applause. Offerings of flowers were thrown through the air. Bottles of liquor were passed hand over hand and deposited on the stage.

From above it could not be seen how the previous month had taken its toll on Maggie. The lines on her face, the waxy skin, were hidden by the colored light. The kliegs bounced off her sequined dress dazzlingly.

Halfway through her second song, Maggie came to an instrumental break and squinted out at the audience. "Hey, what the fuck's the matter with you guys? Why ain't you *dancing?*" At her cue, scattered couples rose to their feet. "Ready on the kliegs," Hawk murmured into his headset. "Three, four, and five on the police." Bright lights pinpointed three widely separated parts of the audience, where uniformed men were struggling with dancers. A single klieg stayed on Maggie, who pointed an imperious finger at one struggling group and shrieked, "Why are you trying to stop them from dancing? I want them to dance. I *command* them to dance!"

With a roar, half the audience were on their feet. "Shut down three. Hold four and five to the count of three, then off. One—Two—Three! Good" The police faded away, lost among the dancers.

"That was prearranged," Wolf said. Hawk didn't so much as glance at him.

"It's part of the legend. You, Wolf, over to your right." Wolf

looked where Hawk was pointing, saw a few couples at the edge
of the crowd slip from the light into the deeper shadows.

"What am I seeing?"

"Just the beginning." Hawk bent over his control board.

By slow degrees the audience became drunk and then
rowdy. As the concert wore on, an ugly, excited mood grew. Sitting far above it all, Wolf could still feel the hysteria grow, as
well as see it. Women shed chador and danced atop it, not fully
dressed. Men ripped free of their coveralls. Here and there,
spotted through the crowd, couples made love. Hawk directed
lights onto a few, held them briefly; in most cases the couples
went on, unheeding.

Small fights broke out, and were quelled by police. Bits of
trash were gathered up and set ablaze, so that small fires dot-
ted the landscape. Wisps of smoke floated up. Hawk played colored spots on the crowd. By the time darkness was total, the
lights and the bestial noise of the revelers combined to create
the feel of a witches' Sabbath.

"Pretty nasty down there," Hawk observed. "And all most
deliberately engineered by government wizards."

"But there is no true feeling involved," Wolf objected. "It is
nothing but animal lust. No—no involvement."

"Yeah." Onstage, Maggie was building herself up into a frenzy. And yet her blues were brilliant—she had never been better. "Not so much different from the other concerts. The only
difference is that tonight nobody waits until they go home."

"Your government can't believe that enough births will
result from this night to make a difference."

"Not tonight, no. But all these people will have memories to
keep them warm over the winter." Then he spat over the edge
of the platform. "Ahhh, why should I spout their lies for them?
It's just bread and circuses is all, just a goddamned release for
the masses."

Maggie howled with delight. "Whee-ew, man! I'm gettin'
horny just looking at you. Yeah, baby, get it on, that's right!"
She was strutting up and down the stage, a creature of bound-

less energy, while the band filled the night with music, fast and urgent.

"Love it!" She stuck her tongue out at the audience and received howls of approval. She lifted her Southern Comfort bottle, took a gigantic swig, her hips bouncing to music. More howls. She caressed the neck of the bottle with her tongue.

"Yeah! Makes me horny as sin, 'deed it does. Ya know," she paused a beat, then continued, "that's something I can really understand man. 'Cause I'm just a horny little hippie chick myself. Yeah." Wolf suddenly realized that she was competing against the audience itself for its attention, that she was going to try to outdo everybody present.

Maggie stroked her hand down the front of her dress, lingering between her breasts, then between her legs. She shook her hair back from her eyes, the personification of animal lust. "I mean, shit. I mean, hippie chicks don't even wear no underwear." More ribald howls of applause. "Don't believe me, do ya?"

Wolf stared, was unable to look away as Maggie slowly spread her legs wide and squatted, giving the audience a good look up her skirt. Her frog face leered, and it was an ugly, lustful thing. She lowered a hand to the stage behind her for support, and beckoned. "Come to momma," she crooned.

It was like knocking the chocks out from a dam. There was an instant of absolute stillness, and then the crowd roared and surged forward. An ocean of humanity converged on the stage, smashing through the police lines, climbing up on the wooden platform. Wolf had a brief glimpse of Maggie trying to struggle to her feet, before she was overrun. There was a dazed, disbelieving expression on her face.

"Mother of Sin," Wolf whispered. He stared at the mindless, evil mob below. They were in furious motion, straining, forcing each other in great swirling eddies. He waited for the stage to collapse, but it did not. The audience kept climbing atop it, pushing one another off its edge, and it did not collapse. It would have been a mercy if it had.

A hand waved above the crowd, clutching something that sparkled. Wolf could not make it out at first. Then another hand waved a glittering rag, and then another, and he realized that these were shreds of Maggie's dress.

Wolf wrapped his arms around a support to keep from falling into the horror below. The howling of the crowd was a single chaotic noise; he squeezed his eyes shut, vainly trying to fend it off. "Right on cue," Hawk muttered. "Right on god-damned cue." He cut off all the lights, and placed a hand on Wolf's shoulder.

"Come on. Our job is done here."

Wolf twisted to face Hawk. The act of opening his eyes brought on a wave of vertigo, and he slumped to the platform floor, still clutching the support desperately. He wanted to vomit, and couldn't. "It's—they—Hawk, did you *see* it? Did you see what they did? Why didn't someone—?" He choked on his words.

"Don't ask me," Hawk said bitterly. "I just play the part of Judas Iscariot in this little drama." He tugged at Wolf's shoul-ders. "Let's go, pilgrim. We've got to go down now." Wolf slowly weaned himself of the support, allowed himself to be coaxed down from the tower.

There were men in black uniforms at the foot of the tower. One of them addressed Hawk. "Is this the African national?" Then, to Wolf: "Please come with us, sir. We have orders to see you safely to your hostel."

Tears flooded Wolf's eyes, and he could not see the crowd, the Commons, the men before him. He allowed himself to be led away, as helpless and as trusting as a small child.

In the morning, Wolf lay in bed staring at the ceiling. A fly buzzed somewhere in the room, and he did not look for it. In the streets iron-wheeled carts rumbled by, and children chanted a counting out game.

After a time he rose, dressed, and washed his face. He went to the hostel's dining room for breakfast.

There, finishing off a piece of toast, was DiStephano.

"Good morning, Mr. Mbikana. I was beginning to think I'd have to send for you." He gestured to a chair. Wolf looked about, took it. There were at least three of the political police seated nearby.

DiStephano removed some documents from his jacket pocket handed them to Wolf. "Signed, sealed, and delivered. We made some minor changes in the terms, but nothing your superiors will object to." He placed the last corner of toast in the side of his mouth. "I'd say this was a rather bright beginning to your professional career."

"Thank you," Wolf said automatically. He glanced at the documents, could make no sense of them, dropped them in his lap.

"If you're interested, the *African Genesis* leaves port tomorrow morning. I've made arrangements that a berth be ready for you, should you care to take it. Of course, there will be another passenger ship in three weeks if you wish to see more of our country."

"No," Wolf said hastily. Then, because that seemed rude, "I'm most anxious to see my home again. I've been away far too long."

DiStephano dabbed at the corners of his mouth with a napkin, let it fall to the tablecloth. "Then that's that." He started to rise.

"Wait," Wolf said. "Mr. DiStephano, I . . . I would very much like an explanation."

DiStephano sat back down. He did not pretend not to understand the request. "The first thing you must know," he said, "is that Ms. Horowitz was not our first Janis Joplin."

"No," Wolf said.

"Nor the second."

Wolf looked up.

"She was the twenty-third, not counting the original. The show is sponsored every year, always ending in Boston on the equinox. So far, it has always ended in the same fashion."

Wolf wondered if he should try to stab the man with a fork, if he should rise up and attempt to strangle him. There should be rage, he knew. He felt nothing. "Because of the brain implants."

"No. You must believe me when I say that I wish she had lived. The implants helped her keep in character, nothing more. It's true that she did not recall the previous women who played the part of Janis. But her death was not planned. It's simply something that—happens."

"Every year."

"Yes. Every year Janis offers herself to the crowd. And every year they tear her apart. A sane woman would not make the offer; a sane people would not respond in that fashion. I'll know that my country is on the road to recovery come the day that Janis lives to make a second tour." He paused. "Or the day we can't find a woman willing to play the role, knowing how it ends."

Wolf tried to think. His head felt dull and heavy. He heard the words, and he could not guess whether they made sense or not. "One last question," he said. "Why me?"

DiStephano rose. "One day you may return to our nation," he said. "Or perhaps not. But you will certainly rise to a responsible position within the Southwest Africa Trade Company. Your decisions will affect our economy." Four men in uniform also rose from their chairs. "When that happens, I want you to understand one thing about your land: *We have nothing to lose.* Good day, and a long life to you, sir."

DiStephano's guards followed him out.

It was evening. Wolf's ship rode in Boston harbor, waiting to carry him home. Away from this magic nightmare land, with its ghosts and walking dead. He stared at it and he could not make it real; he had lost all capacity for belief.

The ship's dinghy was approaching. Wolf picked up his bags.

The Blind Minotaur

IT WAS LATE AFTERNOON when the blinded Minotaur was led through the waterfront. He cried openly, without shame, lost in his helplessness.

The sun cast shadows as crisp and black as an obsidian knife. Fisherfolk looked up from their nets or down from the masts of their boats, mild sympathy in their eyes. But not pity; memory of the Wars was too fresh for that. They were mortals and not subject to his tragedy.

Longshoremen stepped aside, fell silent at the passing of this shaggy bull-headed man. Offworld tourists stared down from their restaurant balconies at the serenely grave little girl who led him by the hand.

His sight stolen away, a new universe of sound, scent, and touch crashed about the Minotaur. It threatened to swallow him up, to drown him in its complexity.

There was the sea, always the sea, its endless crash and whisper on the beach, and quicker irregular slap at the docks. The sting of salt on his tongue. His callused feet fell clumsily on slick cobblestones, and one staggered briefly into a shallow puddle, muddy at its bottom, heated piss-warm by the sun.

He smelled creosoted pilings, exhaust fumes from the great shuttles bellowing skyward from the Starport, a horse sweating as it clipclopped by, pulling a groaning cart that reeked of the day's catch. From a nearby garage, there was the *snap* and ozone crackle of an arc-welding rig. Fishmongers' cries and the creaking of pitch-stained tackle overlaid rattling silverware from the terrace cafes, and fan-vented air rich with stews and squid and grease. And, of course, the flowers the little girl—was she really his daughter?—held crushed to her body with one arm. And the feel of her small hand in his, now going slightly slippery with sweat, but still cool, yes, and innocent.

This was not the replacement world spoken of and promised to the blind. It was chaotic and bewildering, rich and contradictory in detail. The universe had grown huge and infinitely complex with the dying of the light, and had made him small and helpless in the process.

The girl led him away from the sea, to the shabby buildings near the city's hot center. They passed though an alleyway between crumbling sheetbrick walls—he felt their roughness graze lightly against his flanks—and through a small yard ripe with fermenting garbage. The Minotaur stumbled down three wooden steps and into a room that smelled of sad, ancient paint. The floor was slightly gritty underfoot.

She walked him around the room. "This was built by expatriate Centaurimen," she explained. "So it's laid out around the kitchen in the center, *my* space to this side"—she let go of him briefly, rattled a vase, adding her flowers to those he could smell as already present, took his hand again—"and yours to this side."

He let himself be sat down on a pile of blankets, buried his head in his arms while she puttered about, raising a wall, laying out a mat for him under the window. "We'll get you some cleaner bedding in the morning, okay?" she said. He did not answer. She touched a cheek with her tiny hand, moved away.

"Wait," he said. She turned, he could hear her. "What—what is your name?"

"Yarrow," she said.

He nodded, curled about himself.

By the time evening had taken the edge off the day, the Minotaur was cried out. He stirred himself enough to strip off his loincloth and pull a sheet over himself, and tried to sleep.

Through the open window the night city was coming to life. The Minotaur shifted as his sharp ears picked up drunken laughter, the calls of streetwalkers, the wail of jazz saxophone from a folk club, and music of a more contemporary nature, hot and sinful.

His cock moved softly against one thigh, and he tossed and turned, kicking off the crisp sheet (it was linen, and it had to be white), agonized, remembering similar nights when he was whole.

The city called to him to come out and prowl, to seek out women who were heavy and slatternly in the *tavernas*, cool and crisp in white, gazing out from the balconies of their husbands' *casavillas*. But the power was gone from him. He was no longer that creature that, strong and confident, had quested into the night. He twisted and turned in the warm summer air.

One hand moved down his body, closed about his cock. The other joined it. Squeezing tight his useless eyes, he conjured up women who had opened to him, coral-pink and warm, as beautiful as orchids. Tears rolled down his shaggy cheeks.

He came with great snorts and grunts.

Later he dreamed of being in a cool white *casavilla* by the sea, salt breeze wafting in through open windowspaces. He knelt at the edge of a bed and wonderingly lifted the sheet—it billowed slightly as he did—from his sleeping lover. Crouching before her naked body, his face was gentle as he marveled at her beauty.

It was strange to wake to darkness. For a time he was not even certain he *was* awake. And this was a problem, this unsureness,

that would haunt him for all his life. Today, though, it was comforting to think it all a dream, and he wrapped the uncertainty
around himself like a cloak.

The Minotaur found a crank recessed into the floor, and lowered the wall. He groped his way to the kitchen, and sat by the
cookfire.

"You jerked off three times last night," Yarrow said. "I could
hear you." He imagined that her small eyes were staring at him
accusingly. But apparently not, for she took something from
the fire, set it before him, and innocently asked, "When are you
going to get your eyes replaced?"

The Minotaur felt around the platedough, and broke off a bit
from the edge. "Immortals don't heal," he mumbled. He dipped
the fragment into the paste she ladled onto the dough's center,
stirred it about, let the bread drop. "New eyes would be rejected,
didn't your mother tell you that?"

She chose not to answer. "While you were asleep, a new-
shawk came snooping around with that damned machine
grafted to his shoulder. I told him he had the wrong place."
Then, harshly, urgently, "Why won't they just leave you *alone?*"

"I'm an immortal," he said. "I'm not supposed to be left
alone." Her mother really *should* have explained all this, if she
was really what she claimed to be. Perhaps she wasn't; he
would have sworn he had never bedded another of his kind,
had in fact scrupulously avoided doing so. It was part of the
plan of evasion that had served him well for so many years,
and yet ended with his best friend dying in the sand at his feet.

Yarrow put some fragment of foodstuff in his hand, and he
automatically placed it in his mouth. It was gummy and tasteless, and took forever to disappear. She was silent until he
swallowed, and then asked, "Am I going to die?"

"What kind of question is that?" he asked angrily.

"Well, I just thought—my mother said that I was an immortal like her, and I thought . . . Isn't an immortal supposed to be
someone who never dies?"

He opened his mouth to tell her that her mother should be

hung up by her hair—and in that instant the day became inarguably, inalterably real. He wanted to cling to the possibility that it was all a dream for just a while longer, but it was gone. Wearily, he said, "Yarrow, I want you to go get me a robe. And a stick"—he raised a hand above his head—"so high. Got that?"

"Yes, but—"

"Go!"

A glimmering of his old presence must have still clung to him, for the child obeyed. The Minotaur leaned back, and—involuntarily—was flooded with memories.

He was young, less than a year released from the crèche by gracious permission of the ministries of the Lords. The Wars were less than a year away, but the Lords had no way of knowing that—the cabarets were full, and the starlanes swollen with the fruits of a thousand remarkable harvests. There had never been such a rich or peaceful time.

The Minotaur was drunk, and at the end of his nightly round of bars. He had wound up in a *taverna* where the patrons removed their shirts to dance and sweet-smelling sweat glistened on their chests. The music was fast and heavy and sensual. Women eyed him as he entered, but could not politely approach him, for he still wore his blouse.

He bellied up to the bar, and ordered a jarful of the local beer. The barkeep frowned when he did not volunteer money, but that was his right as an immortal.

Crouched on their ledge above the bar, the musicians were playing hot and furious. The Minotaur paid them no attention. Nor did he notice the Harlequin, limbs long and impossibly thin, among them, nor how the Harlequin's eyes followed his every move.

The Minotaur was entranced by the variety of women in the crowd, the differences in their movements. He had been told that one could judge how well a woman made love by how well she danced, but it seemed to him, watching, that there must be a thousand styles of making love, and he would be hard put to choose among them, were the choice his.

One woman with flashing brown feet stared at him, ignoring her partner. She wore a bright red skirt that flew up to her knees when she whirled around, and her nipples were hard and black. He smiled in friendly cognizance of her glance, and her answering grin was a razor-crisp flash of teeth that took his breath away, a predatory look that said: *You're* mine *tonight.*

Laughing, the Minotaur flung his shirt into the air. He plunged into the dancers and stooped at the woman's feet. In a rush he lifted her into the air, away from her partner, one hand closing about her ankles, the other supporting her by the small of her back. She gasped, and laughed, and balanced herself, so that he could remove one hand and lift her still higher, poised with one foot on the palm of his great hairy hand.

"I am strong!" he shouted. The crowd—even the woman's abandoned partner—cheered and stamped their feet. The Harlequin stepped up the band. The woman lifted her skirts and kicked her free leg high, so that one toe grazed the ceiling beams. She threw her head back and laughed.

The dancers swirled about them. For a single pure moment, life was bright and full and good. And then . . .

A touch of cool air passed through the crowd. A chance movement, a subtle shifting of colors, brought the Minotaur's eyes around to the door. A flash of artificial streetlight dazzled and was gone as the door swung shut.

The Woman entered.

She was masked in silver filigree, and her breasts were covered. Red silk washed from shoulder to ankle, now caressing a thigh, now releasing it. Her eyes were a drenched, saturated green. She walked with a sure and sensual authority, knowing the dancers would part for her. No one could mistake her for a mortal.

The Minotaur was stunned. Chemical and hormonal balances shifted in preparation for the bonding to come. Nerveless, his arms fell to his sides. With an angry squawk, the woman he had hoisted into the air leapt, arms waving, to avoid falling. The

Minotaur did not notice. He stepped forward, eyes wide and helpless, toward the immortal.

The silver mask headed straight for him. Green eyes mocked, challenged, promised.

Behind him, unnoticed, the Harlequin slipped to the floor. He wrapped long fingers lovingly around a length of granite pipe, and brought it down fast and surprisingly forcefully, into the back of the Minotaur's neck.

Bright shards of light flashed before the Minotaur's eyes. The dance floor washed out and faded to white. He fell.

At the Minotaur's direction, Yarrow led him out to the bluffs on the outskirts of the city. There was a plaza there, overlooking the ocean. He sent the child away.

Though his every bone protested, he slowly crouched, and then carefully spread out a small white cloth before him. He was a beggar now.

Salt breezes gusted up from the ocean, and he could feel the cobalt sky above, and the cool cumulus clouds that raced across the sun. There were few passersby, mostly dirt farmers who were not likely to be generous. Perhaps once an hour a small ceramic coin fell on his cloth.

But that was how he preferred it. He had no interest in money, was a beggar only because his being demanded a role to play. He had come to remember, and to prepare himself for death by saying farewell to the things of life.

Times had changed. There was a stone altar set in the center of this very plaza where children had been sacrificed. He had seen it himself, the young ones taken from their homes or schooling-places by random selection of the cruel Lords. They had shrieked like stuck pigs when the gold-masked priests raised their bronze knives to the noonday sun. The crowds were always large at these events. The Minotaur was never able to determine whether the parents were present or not.

This was only one of the means the Lords had of reminding their subjects that to be human was often painful or tragic.

"Let's not sleep the day away, eh? Time to start rehearsing."

The Minotaur awoke to find himself sprawled on the wooden floor of a small caravan. The Harlequin, sitting cross-legged beside him, thrust a jar of wine into his hand.

Groggily, the Minotaur focused his eyes on the Harlequin. He reached for the man's neck, only to find one hand taken up by the winejar. He squinted at it. The day was already hot, and his throat as dry as the Severna. His body trembled from the aftereffects of its raging hormonal storm. He lifted the wine to his lips.

Chemical imbalances shifted, found a new equilibrium.

"Bravo!" The Harlequin hauled the Minotaur to his feet, clapped him on the back. "We'll be famous friends, you and I. With luck, we may even keep each other alive, eh?"

It was a new idea to the Minotaur, and a disquieting, perhaps even blasphemous, one. But he grinned shyly, and dipped his head. He *liked* the little fellow. "Sure," he said.

The sun was setting. The Minotaur felt the coolness coming off of the sea, heard the people scurrying to their homes. He carefully tied the ceramics into his cloth, and knotted it onto his belt. He stood, leaning wearily on his staff. Yarrow had not yet come for him, and he was glad; he hoped she had gone off on her own, forgotten him, left him behind forever. But the city's rhythms demanded that he leave, though he had nowhere to go, and he obeyed.

He went down into the city, taking the turns by random whim. He could not be said to be lost, for one place was as good as another to him.

It was by mistake, though, that he found himself in a building whose doors were never shut, whose windows were not shuttered. He had entered, thinking the way yet another alley. No doors barred progress down halls or into rooms. Still, he felt closed in. The corridors smelled—there was the male stench and the female, and intermingled with them, almost overpowering, an insect smell, the odor of something large and larval.

He stopped. Things stirred about him. There was the pat of bare feet on stone, the slow breathing of many people, and—again—a sluggish movement of creatures larger than anything smelling thus should be. People were gathering; twelve, eighteen, more. They surrounded him. He could tell they were all naked, for there was not the whisper of cloth on cloth. Some walked as if they had almost forgotten how. In the distance, he thought he could hear someone crawling.

"Who are you?" Panic touched him lightly; sourceless, pure.

"Whrrarrwr," began one of the people. He stopped, swallowed, tried again. "Why are you in the Hive?" His voice sounded forced, as if he were unused to speech. "Why are you here? You are a creature of the old days, of the Lords. This is no place for you."

"I took a wrong turn," the Minotaur said simply. Then, when there was no reply, "Who are you people? Why do you cohabit with insects?"

Someone coughed and sputtered and made hacking noises. A second joined her, making the same sounds, and then others, and yet more. With a start, the Minotaur realized they were laughing at him. "Is it religious or political?" he demanded. "Are you seeking transcendence?"

"We are trying to become victims," the speaker said. "Does that help you understand?" He was growing angry. "How can we explain ourselves to you, Old Fossil? You never performed a free act in your life."

Some whim, then, of internal chemistry made him want these strangers, these creatures, to understand him. It was the same compulsion that had forced him to empty himself to the newshawks before Yarrow appeared to lead him out of the arena.

"I had a friend, another immortal," the Minotaur said. "Together, we cheated the patterning instinct by making our own pattern, a safe, strong one, we were like"—his short, powerful fingers joined, closing around the staff, intermeshing—"like *this*, you see. And it worked, it worked for years. It was only when our predators worked *within* the patterns we formed that we were destroyed." The words gushed out, and he trembled as the hormones that might give him the power to explain *almost* keyed in.

But the communards did not want to understand. They closed in on him, their laughter growing sharper, with more of a bark, more of a bite to it. Their feeble footsteps paltered closer, and behind him the chitinous whine grew louder, was joined by that of more insects, and more, until all the world seemed to buzz. The Minotaur flinched back.

And then they seemed to hesitate in confusion. They milled about uncertainly for a moment, then parted, and quick, small footsteps passed through them, ran to his side. A cool, smooth hand took his.

"Come with me," Yarrow said. And he followed.

He dreamed of the arena that night, of the hot white sands underfoot that drank up his friend's blood. The Harlequin's body lay limp at his feet, and the bronze knife was a heavy as guilt in his hands.

It was as if his eyes had opened, as if he were seeing clearly for the first time. He stared around the encircling bleachers, and every detail burned into his brain.

The people were graceful and well-dressed; they might almost have been the old Lords, deposed these many years ago in violent public revulsion. The Woman sat ringside. Her silver mask rested lightly on the lip of the white limestone wall, beside a small bowl of orange ices. She held a spoon in her hand, cocked lightly upward.

The Minotaur stared into her blazing green eyes, and read in them a fierce triumph, an obscene gloating, a very specific and direct lust. She had hunted him out of hiding, stripped him of his protection, and chivvied him into the open. She had forced him to rise to his destiny. To enter the arena.

Try though he might, the Minotaur could not awaken. If he had not known all this to be a dream, he would have gone mad.

Waking, he found himself already dressed, the last bit of breakfast in his hand. He dropped it, unnerved by this transition. Yarrow was cleaning the kitchen walls, singing an almost tuneless made-up song under her breath.

"Why aren't you out being taught?" he demanded, trying to cover over his unease with words. She stopped singing. "Well? Answer me!"

"I'm learning from you," she said quietly.

"Learning what?" She did not answer. "Learning how to tend to a cripple? Or maybe how a beggar lives? Hey? What could you possibly learn from me?"

She flung a wet cloth to the floor. "You won't tell me anything," she cried. "I ask you and you won't tell me."

"Go home to your mother," he said.

"I can't." She was crying now. "She told me to take care of you. She said not to come back until my task was done."

The Minotaur bowed his head. Whatever else she might or might not be, the mother had the casual arrogance of an immortal. Even he could be surprised by it.

"Why won't you tell me anything?"

"Go and fetch me my stick."

Bleak plains dominated the southern continent, and the Minotaur came to know them well. The carnival worked the long route, the four-year circuit of small towns running up the coast and then inland to the fringes of the Severna Desert.

Creeping across the plains, the carnival was small, never more than eight hands of wagons and often fewer. But when the paper lanterns had been lit, the fairway laid out, the holographic-woven canvases blazing neon-bright, they created a fantasy city that stretched to the edge of forever.

The Minotaur grunted. Muscles glistening, he bent the metal bar across his chest. Portions of the audience were breathing heavily.

It was the last performance of the evening. Outside the hot, crowded tent, the fairgoers were thinning, growing quieter. The Minotaur was clad only in a stained white loincloth. He liked to have room to sweat.

Applause. He threw the bar to the stage and shouted: "My last stunt! I'll need five volunteers!" He chose the four heaviest, and the one who blushed most prettily. Her he helped up on the stage, and set in the middle of the lifting bench, a pair of hefty *bouergers* to either side.

The Minotaur slid his head under the bench. His face emerged between the young woman's legs, and she shrieked and drew them up on the bench. The audience howled. He rolled his eyes, flared his nostrils. And indeed, she did have a pleasant scent.

He dug into the stage with naked toes, placed his hands carefully. With a grunt, the Minotaur lifted the bench a handsbreadth off the floor. It wobbled slightly, and he shifted his weight in compensation. A surge—he was crouching.

Sweat poured down the Minotaur's face, and ran in rivulets from his armpits. The tent was saturated with the sweet smell, redolent with his pheromones. He felt a light touch on his muzzle. The woman on the bench had reached down to caress his nose with quick, shy fingertips. The Minotaur quirked a half-grin on one side of his mouth.

By the tent flap, the Harlequin lounged on a wooden crate, cleaning his toenails with a knife. They had a date with a sculptor in town after the show.

The Minotaur awoke suddenly, reached out and touched the cloth laid out before him. There was nothing on it, though he distinctly remembered having heard ceramics fall earlier. He swept his hands in great arcs in the dust, finding nothing.

Snickers and derisive jeers sounded from the stone in the

plaza's center. Small feet scurried away—children running to deliver the swag to their masters. "Little snots," the Minotaur grumbled. They were an ever-present nuisance, like sparrows. He fell back into his daydreaming.

The sculptor had had stone jugs of wine sent up. By orgy's end they were empty, and the women lay languid on the sheets of their couches. They all stared upward, watching the bright explosions in space, like slow-blossoming flowers. "What do they hope to accomplish, these rebels?" the Minotaur asked wonderingly. "I can see no pattern to their destruction."

"Why should a man like you—a *real* man—look any higher than his waist?" the sculptor asked coarsely. He laid a hand on the Minotaur's knee. His lady of the moment laughed throatily, reached back over her head to caress his beard.

"I'd just like to know."

The Harlequin had been perched on the wall. He leapt down now, and tossed the Minotaur his clothes. "Time we went home," he said.

The streets were dark and still, but there were people in the shadows, silently watching the skies. The sidestreet cabarets were uncharacteristically crowded. They stopped in several on their way back to the carnival.

The Minotaur was never sure at exactly what point they picked up the woman with skin the color of orange brick. She was from offworld, she said, and needed a place to hide. Her hands were callused and beautiful from work. The Minotaur liked her strong, simple dignity.

Back at the carnival, the Harlequin offered their wagon, and the woman refused. The Minotaur said that he would sleep on the ground, it didn't bother him, and she changed her mind.

Still, he was not surprised when sometime later, she joined him under the wagon.

The sun hot on his forehead, the Minotaur again dreamed of the arena. He did not relive the murder—that memory had been driven from his mind, irretrievably burned away, even in dream. But he remembered the killing rage that drove the knife upward, the insane fury that propelled his hand. And afterward he stood staring into the Woman's eyes.

Her eyes were as green as oceans, and as complex, but easy to read for all that. The lusts and rages, and fears and evil, grasping desire that had brought them all to this point—they were all there, and they were . . . insignificant. For the true poisoned knowledge was that she was lost in her own chemical-hormonal storm, her body trembling almost imperceptibly, all-but-invisible flecks of foam on her lips. She had run not only him, but herself as well, to the blind end of a tangled and malignant fate. She was as much a puppet as he or the Harlequin.

There, on the burning sands, he tore out his eyes.

The newshawks vaulted the fence to get at him. His drama completed, he was fair game. They probed, scanned, recorded—prodded to find the least significant detail of a story that might be told over campfires a thousand years hence, in theatrical productions on worlds not yet discovered, in uninvented media, or possibly merely remembered in times of stress. Trying to get in on a story that might have meaning to the human race as it grew away from its homeworld, forgot its origins, expanded and evolved and changed in ways that could not be predicted or prepared for.

They questioned the Minotaur for hot grueling hours. The corpse of his friend began to rot, or perhaps that was only olfactory hallucination, a side effect of his mind telling his body that it had no further purpose. He felt dizzy and without hope, and he *could not* express his grief, *could not* cry, *could not* scream or rage or refuse their question or even move away until they were done with him.

And then a cool hand slipped into his, and tugged him away. A small voice said, "Come home, Papa," and he went.

Yarrow was screaming. The Minotaur awoke suddenly, on his feet and slashing his stick before him, back and forth in pure undirected reaction. "Yarrow?" he cried.

"No!" the child shrieked in anger and panic. Someone slapped her face so hard she fell. The sound echoed from the building walls. "Fuckpigs!" she swore from the ground.

The Minotaur lurched toward her, and someone tripped him up, so that he crashed onto the road. He heard a rib crack. He felt a trickle of blood from one nostril. And he heard laughter, the laughter of madwomen. And under that he heard the creaking of leather harness, the whirring of tiny pumps, the metal snicks of complex machinery.

There was no name for them, these madwomen, though their vice was not rare. They pumped themselves full of the hormone drugs that had once been the exclusive tools of the Lords, but they used them randomly, to no purpose. Perhaps—the Minotaur could not imagine, did not care—they enjoyed the jolts of power and importance, of sheer godlike caprice.

He was on his feet. The insane ones—there were three, he could tell by their sick laugher—ignored him. "What are you doing?" he cried. "Why are you doing it?" They were dancing, arms linked, about the huddled child. She was breathing shallowly, like a hypnotized animal.

"Why?" asked the one. "Why do you ask why?" and convulsed in giggles.

"We are all frogs!" laughed the second.

Yarrow lay quietly now, intimidated not so much by the women's hyperadrenal strength as by the pattern of victim laid out for her. There were microtraces of hormones in the air, leaks from the chemical pumps.

"She has interesting glands," said the third. "We can put their secretions to good use."

The Minotaur roared and rushed forward. They yanked the stick from his hand and broke it over his head. He fell against the altar stone, hard, nearly stunning himself.

"We need to use that stone," said the madwoman. And when he did not move away, said, "Well, we'll wait."

But again the Minotaur forced himself to stand. He stepped

atop the stone. Something profound was happening deep within him, something beyond his understanding. Chemical keys were locking into place, hormones shifting into balance. Out of nowhere his head was filled with eloquence.

"Citizens!" he cried. He could hear the people at their windows, in their doorways, watching and listening, though with no great interest. They had not interfered to save Yarrow. The Lords would have interfered, and human society was still in reaction to the rule of the Lords. "Awake! Your freedom is being stolen from you!"

A lizard, startled, ran over the Minotaur's foot, as quick and soft as a shiver. The words poured from him in a cold fever, and he could hear the householders straighten, lean forward, step hesitantly out onto the cobblestones. "No one is above you now," he shouted. "But I still see the dead hands of the Lords on your shoulders."

That got to them—he could smell their anger. His throat was dry, but he dared not spare the time to cough. His head was light, and a cool breeze stirred his curls. He spoke, but did not listen to the words.

Yarrow was lost, somewhere on the plaza. As he spoke, the Minotaur listened for her, sniffed the air, felt for vibrations through the stone—and could not find her. "Inaction is a greater tyrant than error ever was!" he cried, listening to heads nodding agreement with the old familiar homily. He could hear the frantic hopping motions the madwomen made, forward and back again, baffled and half-fascinated by the hormones he was generating, by the cadences and odd rhythms of his words.

The speech was a compulsion, and the Minotaur paid it no more mind than he did to the sliding of muscles under skin that went into his gestures, some wide and sweeping, others short and blunt. A whiff of girlish scent finally located Yarrow, not two arm's lengths away, but he could not go to her. The words would not release him, not until he had spoken them all.

And when, finally, he lowered his arms, the plaza was filled with people, and the madwomen's harnesses had been ripped from them, the drug pumps smashed underfoot, their necks snapped quickly and without malice.

He turned to Yarrow, offered his hand. "Come," he said. "It's time to go home."

The Minotaur lay belly-down on the earth under the wagon. He stared down his muzzle at a slice of early-morning sky framed by two wheel spokes. The clouds of energy were still slowly dissipating, "I'd love to go out there," he said. "To see other worlds."

The orange-skinned woman scratched him above the ears, at the base of his small ivory horns. Her hands were strong and sure. "They couldn't refuse you passage. What's stopping you?"

He nodded upward. "He gets sick—I'd have to go alone."

A triceratops beetle crept laboriously past his nose. He exhaled sharply, trying to turn it over, failed. "You two are inseparable, aren't you?" the woman asked.

The beetle was getting away. He snorted sharply again, twice. "I guess."

"Won't he be upset that I chose you over him?"

It took the Minotaur a moment to puzzle out her meaning. "Ah! You mean—I see. Good joke, very good joke!" He laughed without taking his eyes away from the beetle, watched it escape into the grass. "No, the Harlequin doesn't know that women are important."

It did not take long to gather belongings: the Minotaur had none and Yarrow few. "You can find your mother?" he asked her. They left the door open behind them, an old Centaurimen custom at final partings.

"I can always find my mother," Yarrow said.

"Good." Still, he did not let her go. He led her by the hand back along the waterfront. There, among the sounds and smells, the subliminal tastes and touches that had grown familiar to him, he leaned forward to kiss her tenderly on the cheeks and forehead.

"Good-bye," he said. "I am proud that you are my daughter."

Yarrow did not move away. There was a slight tremble in her

voice when she spoke. "You still haven't *told* me anything."

"Ah," the Minotaur said. For a moment he was silent, mentally cataloging what she would need to know. The history of the Lords, to begin with. Their rise to power, how they had shaped and orchestrated the human psyche, and why they thought the human race had to be held back. She needed to know of the crèches, of their bioprogramming chemicals, and of those immortals released from them who had gone on to become legend. She needed to know everything about the immortals, in fact, for the race had been all but exterminated in the Wars. And how the Lords had endured as long as they had. How their enemies had turned their toys against them. All the history of the Wars. It would not be a short telling.

"Sit down," he commanded. There, in the center of the thoroughfare, he sat, and Yarrow followed.

The Minotaur opened his mouth to speak. At the sound of his words, resonant and deep, people would stop to listen for the briefest second . . . for just a moment longer . . . they would sit down in the road. The hormonal combinations that enforced strictest truth before the newshawks were to be in his voice, but combined with the strong eloquence of earlier in the day. He would speak plainly, with a fine parsimony of syllables. He would speak in strict accord with the ancient traditions. H would speak with tongues of fire.

The waterfront would fill and then overflow as people entered and did not leave, as they joined the widening circle of hushed listeners, as the fisherfolk came up from their boats and down from their masts, the boy prostitutes came out from the brothels, the offworld *tourista* joined with the kitchen help to lean over the edges of their terraces.

In future years this same telling, fined down and refined, elaborated and simplified, would become the epic that was to mark this age—his age—as great for its genesis. But what was to come in just a moment was only a first draft. A prototype. A seed. But it was to be beautiful and moving beyond all possible imagining of its listeners, for it was new, an absolutely new word, a clear new understanding. It was to sum up an age that most people did not realize was over.

"Listen," said the Minotaur.

He spoke.

The Transmigration
of Philip K

PHILIP K WAS BURIED in the grave that had been waiting for him all his life. It was one half of a twin plot, and in the other half was buried his twin sister, who had died at birth.

Through all his life, she had awaited him with the eerie patience of the dead. Now, as the last shovel of earth was thrown over his coffin, the last prayer faded into air, the last mourner gone back to the city, the circuit was complete. Energy passed between brother and sister.

At last, it could begin.

Whirr-buzz-click.

The robot came walking down the street. A chromed knee peeked regularly from the wrinkled trench coat, flashing in the sunlight. Highly polished steel shone above the clumsily tied-up Adidas. Its face was a smooth ovoid, broken only by two telescoping camera lenses where the eyes might be, and a round speaker grill for the mouth. It wore a broken-down slouch hat, pulled low over its camera eyes for further concealment.

From his living room, Sandy Pankopf stared in terror as the

thing approached. It nodded as it passed by the milkman, and the milkman in response grinned and touched his cap. This can't be happening, Pankopf thought. Not again. Not for the fifth day in a row.

The robot walked up to his house. Peering from behind the drapes, Pankopf wondered if the device knew he was there. It had never given any sign that it did. But who knew what powers it might have? Infrared or ultraviolet detectors. X-ray vision.

Now Mrs. McMurtry, his next-door neighbor, straightened up from her flower bed, brushing dirt from her hands, turning to pick up the next pansy in the tray alongside her. She saw the robot, and smiled. The robot turned to face her, and must have offered some pleasantry—from where he cowered, Sandy couldn't hear—for she threw her head back and laughed.

Now the robot had reached his front walk. It paused at the mailbox. Using a metal hand as carefully articulated as any of flesh, it rummaged within. It removed a fistful of mail that Pankopf had left for the mailman, and scrutinized it letter by letter, holding each piece up to its camera eyes for a long and careful scanning. At last it returned every piece but one to the box, closed the door, and raised the flag signaling the mailman there was mail within to be picked up.

Then—servomotors humming gently to themselves—it turned and went away, striding down the sidewalk as if it owned the town.

Just before it turned the corner and disappeared from sight, Pankopf's dog, Spot, came bounding up from the backyard. The robot paused to pat the mongrel on the head. Spot lolled out his tongue and wagged his tail.

Whirr-buzz-click.

The grey fog was creeping in again. Just a wisp or two to begin with, coming in through the doorway and seeping under the windowsill, but there would be more soon, Dorff knew. The way things were going.

"I've got Pankopf on the phone," Miss Goodbody said.

"Thank you." Dorff picked up the receiver, and glared into the cathode-ray tube. "Pankopf, you putz, why aren't you at work?"

On the screen, Pankopf looked positively green. "I'm running a little late today, boss. I was just heading out the door."

"Well, you'd better," Dorff growled. "Your job is none too secure here. It's hanging by a thread." He hung up and the screen went dead. "Jesus. Did you see the phone he was holding? One of those black jobbies, without any buttons, just—what do you call it?—a dial."

More of the grey fog floated in. Sometimes the entire office seemed to fill up with it. The employees in their cubicles were degenerating now—he could see them through the open door, their flesh turning grey and peeling away from the skull, their clothing rotting on bodies gone suddenly gaunt. They looked like the drawings of ghouls in the old EC comics.

"I don't see why you keep coddling that twerp," Miss Goodbody said. "If it were up to me, I'd have given him the old heave-ho a year ago."

Dorff looked at her. She was changing in some subtle way he couldn't quite put a finger on yet. Sometimes the fog made people mutate into pig-creatures, or tentacular monstrosities. Sometimes it devolved them into prehuman brutes. "That 'twerp,' as you call him," he said coldly, "is all that stands between us and chaos. He may think he's living in 1956, with Eisenhower in the White House and Howdy Doody on the silver screen, but he has a firmer grasp on reality than anyone I know. Do you know how many cancellations his neighborhood has had this year? None. Half of them aren't even fully aware of the problem. They think it's something that only happens in Cambodia or Nebraska or someplace, for Chrissake."

The fog wrapped itself about Miss Goodbody. She leaned forward, a shadowy, secretive shape. Her eyes were two red coals. "You don't need him," she said. "Drop him. Let him twissst in the wind." She leaned closer, and her breath was a cold wind from out of the grave. "Cassst him assside. Cut hisss abdomen open, and let me eat hisss entrails for you."

"That's completely out of line, Miss Goodbody!" Dorff snapped. He gestured to the door. "I believe you have typing to do."

When she left, he sighed and removed his glasses, pinching the bridge of his nose between two fingers, It was all going to hell, and he only had Pankopf left. With Philip Kingsley dead, the whole megillah rested on the shoulders of a lone, paranoid little twerp.

There was a rap on the door, and a robot came in. "I retrieved this item as per your instructions, sir," it said, depositing a letter on his desk.

"Good, good." Dorff glanced at the thing—another letter of resignation. He placed it in his desk drawer, along with the others. "We're safe for another day, at least." He glanced up sharply. "You don't suppose he'll have the nerve to quit in person, do you?"

"No, sir," the robot said. "It is my considered opinion that he will not. He is not what you'd call a confident man, and you're something of a father figure to him. Before he could bring himself to defy you to your face, he'd first have to resolve the inner torments he suffers."

Terrific, thought Dorff. Pankopf saves the world, and I keep him scared and neurotic. That's my job. To make sure he doesn't develop the backbone to throw his rotten little job in my face.

He dismissed the robot. It was bright and gleaming. The fog did not seem to affect mechanicals the way it did humans. Maybe because they were inorganic life, and not subject to the inevitable entropic decay of protoplasm. Or possibly it was because humans felt doubt and pain and guilt, while inorgs did not.

It was certainly something to think about.

But when he opened the desk for another glimpse at the letters, they had already disintegrated to moldy debris at the bottom of the drawer. Dorff shut the drawer hastily, with a pale hand grown suddenly leprous and thin. The grey fog closed about him.

It was getting harder and harder to hold it all together.

"I sure do miss old Phil," Pankopf said.

"Don't you have any work to do?" Milligan grumbled. But he pushed his chair away from his desk and leaned back, with an Irishman's readiness to talk. Even though he was fifth-generation American or something. "I didn't know Phil Karlton. He wrote those little jingles for the bubble-gum inserts, like you do, didn't he?"

"Chewsy Rhymes," Pankopf said. "That's what we call them. Chewsy Rhymes for Chewsy People. It's not as easy as it sounds. Dorff has got all these weird theories about what sells bubble-gum cards, and he'll want six disparate words all put into the same limerick. You haven't lived until you've tried to fit 'Chevrolet Cordoba' and 'cirque glacier' into the same couplet."

"Oops." Milligan bent hastily over his work. "Her nibs is coming."

Miss Goodbody strode up to Pankopf, a sheath of papers in her hand. "You weren't at your desk," she said accusingly. Then, "These will all have to be done over. Mr. Dorff found them unsatisfactory."

Unhappily, Pankopf leafed through the papers. He stopped at one that began *A ferris-wheel addict, Marie . . .* "What's wrong with this one? It scans perfectly."

"It also rhymes Marie with Paris. Mr. Dorff does not want the French pronunciation. He wants Paris to rhyme with ferris."

"But if I do that, the word wheel drops down to the next line and screws up the scansion!"

"That's your problem," Miss Goodbody said coldly. "They're *all* your problem. And I might state confidentially that Mr. Dorff is none too pleased with your work of late. I'd suggest you buckle down. You can be replaced by a rhyming dictionary, you know."

"Cripes," Pankopf muttered as she walked away. Milligan studied her departing posterior with interest.

"How'd you like to take a bite out of that?" he grinned. Then, grabbing his hat, "Come on. She's not going to check up on you for hours. Let's skip across the street for a beer."

Several hours later, they were still drinking. Empty Iron City bottles littered their table. Pankopf glanced out the window. "Sure is foggy out there."

Milligan merely shivered, and hunched down over his stein. As the fog had grown, Bob Milligan had gotten more and more morose and uncommunicative, until now he was sunken in Celtic gloom. It made him dull company; if Pankopf hadn't been half-plastered, he'd have left long ago.

A man stepped in out of the fog. He was tall and thin, and wore a Burberry overcoat with a snap-brim hat. In the dim light, he looked a lot like Humphrey Bogart. The door closed quietly behind him, and he walked toward their table. As he passed by a neon Budweiser sign, his face was briefly illumined in red.

"Phil!" Pankopf cried in astonishment. "Phil Korzinski!"

Milligan's head jerked up. Skin pale, he twisted around in his chair.

"Jesus, Phil, we all thought you were dead," Pankopf said happily. But Korzinski ignored him. He slipped a hand into his trench coat and quietly said, "Stand up, Milligan. The day of reckoning is at hand."

With a despairing croak, Milligan lurched to his feet, and tried to flee. His chair clattered to the floor.

Korzinski's hand whipped out, holding a small white card. He thrust it at Milligan, who fearfully took it with both hands. Slowly, Milligan bent his head to reach the card. His eyes opened wide in horror, and a convulsive shudder ran through his body.

He fell dead at Korzinski's feet.

Now Korzinski stepped forward and pressed something into Pankopf's hands—a pair of pills, white, with PK-47 embossed into the surface of each. Sandy looked up into the eyes of his old friend. There was an odd look in those eyes. Compassion, maybe.

Korzinski smiled gently. "Things are seldom what they seem," he said. Then he turned away, and walked back out into the fog.

Pankopf stared down at the corpse. There was no blood. But the fall had cracked Milligan's skull, and through that crack there gleamed tiny wheatseed lights, and slow-moving silver cogs.

Bob Milligan was a robot.

For a moment Pankopf stood stunned. Then, transferring the PK-47s to his pocket, he bent over and picked up the small white card that Korzinski had used to kill Milligan. It was resting on the robot's chest, printed side down. He turned it over. It read:

BANG
You're Dead

A pattern was beginning to emerge.

An instant after Dorff's orgasm, Miss Goodbody raised herself from the supine body of her superior, and abruptly announced, "Milligan's dead."

It took Dorff a moment to realize what she was talking about. Then he remembered the telemetry. Even here, in the privacy of his luxury penthouse, Miss Goodbody was wired into the workings of his business empire. "We've got bigger things to worry about," he said. "We almost lost Paris today. Not to mention ferris wheels. Milligan is only a robot. He can be repaired and back on the job tomorrow."

"It won't be the same," Miss Goodbody said. She left Dorff on the bed, picked up her bra and snapped it around her body, clasp to the front. Then she twisted it around and slipped her arms into the straps. She shrugged it on, adjusted the fit. "If there's any discontinuity of mental function, the personality dies. The mind that's reawakened might think the same, act the same, have the same memories. But that's no consolation to the personality that died."

"Mere sophistry," Dorff scoffed. "A difference that makes no difference is no difference at all."

"Isn't it?" She stalked toward him, still wearing only the brassiere. "Let's put you in his place. Let's imagine that you've been cloned and that your exact physical double exists, alive but un-awakened. Let's further imagine that it is possible to record all your memories and program them into this hypothetical clone of yourself. Suppose then that I strangled you"—she placed her hands around his neck, touching thumb to thumb and index finger to index finger—"and ordered the clone programmed with your memories and awakened. To the rest of the world, this would be the same person you had always been. But to you—the *dead* you—it would make a very big difference."

Dorff did not respond. He could not. After a moment, Miss Goodbody opened her hands, and his dead body slumped down to the bed. She lit a cigarette, but made no move to get dressed.

Shortly, the robots she had summoned earlier entered the room with Dorff's clone on a gurney. They deftly traded clone and corpse, and flash-recorded the memories of the dead industrialist. Miss Goodbody examined the tape, snipped a least fraction off with her long nails, and supervised the programming.

A moment later they were gone. Miss Goodbody snubbed out her cigarette, found her position. A vein in the clone's forehead throbbed. It came alive.

"Milligan is only a robot," Dorff said. "He can be repaired and back on the job tomorrow."

Miss Goodbody shrugged. "Don't forget that *I* am a robot too." She smiled oddly.

A strange sourceless shiver ran up Dorff's spine. No, he thought. No, you're not a robot. You're something else entirely.

But he was afraid to ask himself what.

Whirr-buzz-click.

I'm almost getting used to this, Pankopf thought, as the

robot disappeared around the corner, his latest letter of resignation held fast in its mechanical fist. He unfolded his newspaper, glanced down the front page—something Dulles had said about nuclear brinksmanship, a photo of Ike at the golf course—and the phone rang. Pankopf moved to answer it, then stopped himself.

The hell with it, he thought. It's just Dorff again. I'll leave now and if he asks, I'll say I'd just left when I heard the phone ring. Feeling rather daring, he put the paper down and stepped out the door.

Mrs. McMurtry was at work in her front-yard flower bed. "Good morning, Mr. Pankopf," she said brightly. Then she frowned, and yanked up a tangle of blue-and-red threads from the ground. "Have you ever seen anything like these? They're all through the soil." She *tsked*. "And just since this morning, too." Unaccountably, the thin wirelike roots made him feel uncomfortable. Pankopf shook his head.

"Oh, and I have this for you." Mrs. McMurtry pulled an envelope from her gardening apron. "A Mr. Phillip Kamin asked me to pass this on to you."

Hands trembling, he tore open the envelope. The letter inside read, *You'd better wake up soon, Sandy! You're in grave danger. Don't trust Goodbody or Milligan. Dorff is okay, but he's badly misinformed. I'll do what I can for you, but ultimately we're all in this alone. Right? I'd advise you to do up those drugs immediately.* It was signed *Phil*.

Phil, he thought. His old dead friend. But Milligan had been his friend too. If Phil really was still on his side, reaching out from beyond the grave to give him a shot of the straight truth, why had he killed Milligan?

He turned the letter over. On the other side was a postscript. It read, *P.S. Oh, wise up, Sandy. Milligan isn't your friend. He and Miss Goodbody are playing good cop/bad cop with you. Don't fall for it. And cheer up—things are bad enough without you mooning about like this.—PK*

Mrs. McMurtry was watching him carefully. "Is something wrong, dear?" she asked in a motherly tone.

"No, no," he said hastily, folding the letter. "Everything's fine." The PK-47s were heavy in his pocket, but he wasn't ready to take them yet.

Phil wants me to cheer up, he thought. He's *dead* and he thinks I'm taking too pessimistic a view of things.

It was a depressing thought.

Dorff had a teleconference first thing that morning. He was seated at the head of the conference table when the telerobots—big burly inorgs with visor screens in place of their heads—lumbered in and took their seats. The images of their distant managers, forwarded by satellite from their native lands, flickered blue on the screens.

Present today were Señor Velasquez of Argentina, Herr Altemeister from the Deutscherepublik, and Jerome Hunt of South Africa. Absent was Kommisar Gavronsky, who managed the *two* maintainers in the Soviet Socialist Republics. There were rumors of another maintainer in China, but the Communist bureaucracy there refused to confirm or communicate.

Jerome Hunt kicked off the discussion by clearing his throat, and announcing, "I have more on the parallels between our maintainers and the kabbalistic notion of the seven just men who maintain the world in the sight of God."

A chorus of groans went around the telerobots. Hunt was a thin, starved-looking man with the pinched soul of an academic. Dorff often thought the South African viewed his country's maintainer primarily as an opportunity to deliver an endless series of lectures on phenomenology.

Then again, perhaps he was simply embarrassed that their maintainer—a fat, jovial woman in her early fifties—was black. This might be his way of avoiding dealing with the implications of the fact.

"Go on," Dorff said.

Hunt's telerobot picked up an imaginary bundle of papers,

and leafed through them. "If we accept as a working hypothesis that reality is maintained through consensus, i.e., through our *perception* of it, then we must also accept that it is the job not only of the select few—our maintainers—but of each and every one of us to maintain reality. In much the same way the Medievals held that virtue was the duty of all, no matter that it was displayed in pure form only by the select few. By 'saints,' if you will.

"Thus, in relinquishing control to a handful of maintainers, we are experiencing a collective failure of nerve. A wholesale backing away from the responsibility of existence."

As Hunt droned on, Dorff found his attention wandering. He noted that Velasquez's telerobot was already going through his characteristic fidget. It was impossible to say what was actually going on, but it looked like the man was picking up and snapping pencils, one after another. Hundreds of them per session.

"The teleological imperatives are . . . "

Dorff wondered idly if it was possible that Velaquez *was* snapping pencils. Perhaps there was an undersecretary of stationery who kept him supplied with endless boxes of perfectly sharpened number-two leadeds.

His train of thought was shattered when the conference-room door suddenly slammed open. A new telerobot bulled its way into the room, Kommisar Gavronsky's face flickering on its screen. The other telerobots looked up, annoyed and muttering. But Gavronsky silenced them all with a wave of his metal hand. "Olga is dying!" he announced.

A chorus of protest arose. Impossible, Dorff thought. Olga was young and healthy, even athletic, and she was the most perceptive of the known maintainers. Her eyes were a clear and limpid blue that missed nothing. How could she be dying?

"Soviet medicine is the best in the world," Gavronsky was angrily retorting to some accusation. "It is not a matter of the body. She has lost confidence in herself. A matter of an unfortunate love affair. The people responsible have—"

His telerobot disintegrated into dust.

"So," Jeremy Hunt said with gloomy satisfaction. "There are now only *six* just men left in the world. And seven are needed to keep it from destruction." Grey fog began creeping into the room.

The meeting broke up in disarray.

First thing at work, Milligan came by his desk and with a big grin said, "Some night last night, huh? Have I got a head this morning!"

Pankopf flinched back from the man. He looked different. It wasn't just that he ought to be dead. That wasn't his old roguish devil-may-care Irish grin. It was a mean grin now, and malice sparkled in his eyes.

"I think I need an aspirin," Pankopf said. He opened his deck drawer and began searching through it, deliberately keeping his eyes averted from Milligan's.

"Have you ever noticed," Milligan said casually, "how if you say a common everyday word—aspirin, for example—often enough it loses all meaning? You think aspirin, and you can't even picture it. It's just a funny combination of syllables. Aspirin."

"No, I never did," Pankopf said. But he did now. He kept searching for and not finding the pills. Aspirins.

"Or pens," Milligan said. "Or pencils, for that matter. Paper. Say it over a few times to yourself. Paper. What does it mean? Nothing. How could it mean anything? Paper."

The drawer was strangely empty now, and growing emptier as Milligan droned on and on, naming things that Pankopf seemed to forget as soon as they were mentioned. And yet, in spite of the fact the drawer contained so little, Pankopf was still unable to find the—whatever it was he was looking for. It must not be in the drawer. Numbly, as if he were reaching through a haze of pain, he began searching through his pockets.

"Park benches," Milligan said. "Pears, peacocks, and piggy banks. All meaningless. Parachutes."

There was something in his shirt pocket. Pankopf took it out and unfolded it, hoping against hope that the . . . whatever, was in there.

It was a letter, the one he had gotten from Philip Korman. It seemed to be made of metal foil now, rather than of that stuff he couldn't seem to put a name to but that letters were normally written on. By turning it side to side, he could read the embossed letters as light flashed silver on them: *For the love of God, Sandy! Assert yourself!—K*

"For that matter, what in the world is a Pankopf!" Milligan said, his grin growing wider and more malicious by the second. "Pan-kopf. Say it over to yourself a few times slowly. Pan—"

Pankopf broke and ran.

The grey mists parted and Dorff came to. For a moment he lay motionless, eyes closed. I'm in a hospital, he thought. Something is seriously wrong. The last thing he remembered, he was in his penthouse with Miss Goodbody. Discussing the nature of identity. Then, without the least sense of transition—here. He hoped he wasn't dying.

He opened his eyes, and found himself staring into his own face.

"Come on, Dorff, get up," Dorff said, hauling himself roughly to his feet. "No time to lollygag about."

Dorff sat up and stared about, blinking. He was in a vast room with row upon row of cryogenic clone tanks. A good half of them were already open. Not far away, a cluster of some twenty Dorffs talked quietly to himself. Here and there in the room he walked alone, thinking.

"What's going on?" he asked.

"Oh, God, I don't think I can stomach going through the explanations one more time." Dorff made a disgusted face, then thrust a bundle of clothing into his arms. "Get dressed. We've got to get moving. Phil tipped me off to what's happening—"

"Phil? You mean Phil Kavanaugh? But he's dead."

"That's the one," Dorff said. "Snap it up, will you? We're in trouble. Real bad trouble. Pankopf's ready to break."

The world was falling apart. Probably this was nothing new, but Pankopf was finally coming to accept it now. So he was startled, but not really surprised, when the cab he got into lifted straight up into the air, angled forward, and soared west.

"Where to, Mac?" The cabbie threw a chromed elbow over the back of the front seat and twisted around to face him. Another robot.

It was too much. Pankopf no longer cared. "Mount Pleasant Avenue," he said, and the robot banked his crate, heading for the suburbs. They drove in silence, the land below flat and misty blue, while Pankopf tried to collect his thoughts.

At last he asked, "What does the phrase 'Things are seldom what they seem' mean to you?"

"It's from Gilbert and Sullivan's *H.M.S. Pinafore,* sir," the robot said politely. "The next line is 'Skim milk masquerades as cream.'"

"My problem is I don't know who to trust," Pankopf said. "I mean everybody claims to be my friend, but all I have to go on is appearances. I had hoped that phrase might give me a clue. Obviously, I was wrong."

"On the contrary, sir. The difference between skim milk and cream is not great, more a matter of degree than of kind. I would say that in the same way the difference between perception and reality is most likely slight. One might not trust appearances, but in the absence of reliable information to the contrary, one must act *as if* surface appearances were reliable."

"Maybe you're right." Pankopf said thoughtfully.

The hack dropped him off before his house, and lifted away. Ignoring Mrs. McMurtry's cheery wave, Pankopf hurried down the walk. He quickly stepped inside, turned and locked the door behind himself. For the first time in ages, he felt safe.

"Got you!" Miss Goodbody said with satisfaction.

"I feel silly," Dorff said.

"Shut up!" the Dorff-in-command snapped. "Straighten those ranks!" They were marching up Mount Pleasant Avenue in locked-step formation, hundreds of Dorffs all dressed in identical jumpsuits. The grey fog parted for them in front, and closed in behind them as they passed. Inside the mists, large shadowy shapes moved. A chittering insect noise sounded. Dorff was not the only one to shudder.

But even facing enemies as horrific as these, this kind of regimentation is wrong, Dorff thought. You shouldn't be forced to conform, to be just like everyone else in the crowd. Not even if everyone else in the crowd was you, too.

But as Dorff advanced in even columns, the neatly mowed lawns before them began to stir. Black holes appeared in the green, small at first, but growing larger.

"Prepare for combat!" Lieutenant Dorffs broke him into squadrons.

With what? Dorff wondered suddenly. None of him had been issued weapons.

Things came burrowing up out of the ground.

"Kumquat," Milligan said. He held the fruit out in his palm, and frowned when it didn't disappear. "He's not cooperating," he complained.

Miss Goodbody took a sip of her tea, looked down at Pankopf, tied to his own easy chair. "Tepid," she said. Very deliberately she turned the cup over, pouring the lukewarm tea into Pankopf's lap. "He has nice eyes. Heat up a few butter knives on the kitchen range."

Just then there was a knock at the door. It opened a crack, and Mrs. McMurtry peeked in.

"Yoo hoo!" she cried, holding a rolled-up newspaper before her. "Is Mr. Pankopf here? His dog just dropped his paper on my stoop." She peered about, saw him tied to his chair. "Oh, there you are!"

"Grab her!" Miss Goodbody screamed.

She and Milligan had just grabbed the old woman's arms when Dorff stepped out from his hiding place outside the door, automatic weapon in hand. He was wearing a beret set at a jaunty angle on his head. "Didn't think any of me would make it through, did you?" he grinned. He herded the two abductors to the back of the room, while Mrs. McMurtry untied Pankopf. "You okay, Sandy?"

"I suppose so. What's going on?"

Dorff looked to Mrs. McMurtry, who nodded curtly. "Reality is falling apart," he said. "The scientists think that some of the weapons used in World War VII have permanently damaged the fabric of reality. People and places have been simply winking out of existence. Or else they change into . . . something else.

"But there are little islands of sanity here and there, places where people don't disappear or change. We investigated, and found that a few scattered individuals were maintaining reality about them. You're one of them, Sandy. Even if you do think you're living a hundred years in the past. That's why we moved Mrs. McMurtry in next door to you. As President of the United States, her welfare is second only to yours."

Jesus, Pankopf thought. A woman President.

"Cover me while I tie these two up," Mrs. McMurtry ordered Dorff. Ignored, Pankopf glanced down at the newspaper the president had brought with her. There was a picture of Phil on the front page. Wonderingly, he picked it up, and began reading the article beneath the photo:

> CAMDEN (UPI)-Phillip Kirby today expressed doubt that Sanford Pankopf would ever see through to the true nature of reality. "Sandy's a good guy," he told the reporters, "but he's got to learn to think for himself. Right now it looks like he's going to buy Dorff's version of things. And that would be a big mistake." Pankopf was recently rescued from two assailants by Lemuel Dorff and President Helen McMurtry. In a daring daytime raid—

Pankopf put down the paper. Even Phil's given up on me, he thought. I guess I've really made a mess of things. He didn't for an instant think that he'd worked through to the truth yet. It was like an onion, where you peel off layer after layer until you're left with—what? Maybe nothing. But he still had the duty to search for that ultimate center.

He dug out the PK-47s and looked at the small white pharmaceuticals. Maybe they'd burn out his brain, and leave him a helpless drooling addict for the rest of his life. But it was a risk he had to take. One after the other, he popped the pills, without water. For an instant his head swam dizzily. Then he was left feeling calm and lucid. The air seemed preternaturally clear. And he knew what he had to do.

"Milligan," he said suddenly, "what are you really? Are you a robot or what?"

The bound man twisted his head away from Pankopf's stare. But Pankopf kept looking anyway, not blinking, willing himself to see. Milligan shimmered. His shape went vague, then melted, shifting and re-forming at random, until at last he stabilized into a gigantic insect.

It was a beetle. It stood taller than Pankopf did, and its hard carapace was shiny black. Milligan shifted slightly, and iridescent rainbows danced over his shell. He was beautiful, in the way that a bulgy black landcar can be beautiful. "Milligan?" Pankopf said hesitantly. The creature clacked its pincers. Beyond it, Miss Goodbody smiled scornfully.

Dorff backed away from the beetle. The President followed, not as quickly, a look of shrewd surmise on her face.

"And you?" Pankopf demanded of Miss Goodbody. "What do you really look like?" As if by magic, she too turned into an insect.

"My God, Pankopf!" Dorff cried. "What are you doing?"

"Something I have to. To retain my self-respect." He looked directly at Dorff. His boss. "What are *you* really like?"

Dorff froze. His eyes closed, and his lips turned pale. Whiteness spread, like rimefrost, across his face. At his elbow, President McMurtry was also struck motionless, her skin the blue-white hue of a corpse.

Don't stop there, Pankopf thought through his horror and nausea. There's more to go. He gazed around the comfortably furnished room and through the window at the green lawns outside, the flower beds, the tidy little houses. The sky above, the clouds, and the earth below.

He addressed them all: "The masquerade's over. Show yourselves!"

"Bravo," Phil said. "I was beginning to have my doubts, but you came through with flying colors."

Slowly Pankopf lifted his head from the mass of blue-and-red wires nested about him. He looked at the paper walls, the endless line of occupied therapy couches. "Where am I?" he asked. But already he remembered some of it.

The couches came from the colonizing starship *Rasputin*. Of which he was the astrogator. And Phil—Phil and the woman at his elbow, his twin sister, were the co-captains.

A gigantic black beetle wearing a nurse's cap scuttled up and thrust a thermometer in his mouth. It took his wrist in its pincers. "No fever," it declared. "His pulse is a little fast."

"I'm not surprised," Phil said. He and his sister eased Pankopf to his feet. "We're on New Camden. Do you remember landing on this planet?"

"No—I . . . yes. There was intelligent life here already. Big black insects." Pankopf shook his head. He felt muzzy.

"That's fine. What else can you remember?"

"We were . . . were going to colonize New Camden. The probes said it would sustain life. But the . . . insects were here already."

"They have a highly developed civilization," Phil said. "One we can be jealous of. And their city-nests cover all the continents. There isn't any land left unspoken for. Fortunately, they offered us a place within their society. We can share their nests as equals, but we have to live *among* them. Do you remember that?"

Pankopf shuddered. "Yes," he said at last. "I remember. And

I remember that I . . . couldn't take it."

"A lot of us couldn't take it. I was one, you were another. That's why we had to work through the trauma with the therapy couches."

Pankopf looked at the tangle of wires about him, remembered the dreams. "You were healing me." Working through trauma fantasies was a long and involved process, even with tools like the couches. There was still a headset dangling from the couch. "You were helping guide me back to sanity."

"To acceptance of your world," the co-captain said. "Yes. I did that. With a little help from our fellow citizens." He glanced significantly at the beetles scurrying about the ward. Others wore headsets and sat motionless by the couches.

"Miss Goodbody?" Pankopf suspected, though with a layman's ignorance, that her behavior had not been all that one might desire of a therapist.

"She's a patriot." Phill looked embarrassed. "Not everybody welcomes us on New Camden. There's a small militant group that doesn't want their racial purity tainted by our presence. Usually we manage to screen them out."

Pankopf took a deep breath. "What now? Do I just go live among the beetles?" He found that the idea no longer troubled him. He must be healed.

"That too," Phil said. "But I need your help if you'll give it. We're desperately short of guides, and there are still a lot of others left in the therapy couches. Dorff for one. He's coming along nicely, but he still needs help." Then he smiled, and gestured toward a freshly made hospital bed. Pankopf sat down on it. He felt physically drained. "But that's for later. Right now, I just want you to rest. We'll talk about the future afterward." He winked reassuringly, and strolled away.

Pankopf was about to lie down when he noticed the small white card on the pillow. It had printing on it: *Don't believe them, Sandy. They're just blinding you with science. Keep up the search for the truth.* It was signed *Phillip K.*

Jesus, Pankopf thought. It never ends.

A metal hand reached over his shoulder and took the card. He whirled around and, dumbfounded, saw a robot striding away, down the corridor. It was dressed in a baggy old overcoat and a pulled-down slouch hat. A pair of Adidas were tied up at its chromed ankles.

Just before it disappeared from sight it tipped its hat to a gigantic beetle-nurse. The insect curtsied back.

Whirr-buzz-click.

Covenant of Souls

SOMETHING UGLY WAS growing in the air above the altar. Peter Wieland didn't notice it at first. He'd entered the sanctuary from the rear, through the Thirty-seventh Street narthex, and gone to the front pew without once glancing at the altar. He set his brown paper bag down beside him and removed a Styrofoam cup of black coffee, a bottle of grapefruit juice, and an egg-and-sausage sandwich. He flattened the bag and carefully set the bottle and cup atop it. Stray drops of coffee and juice mingled in its folds.

Downstairs the nursery school was coming in from the play yard—Peter could hear the children's voices. He loosened his coat and reached into his shirt pocket for the leads to his Sony-Toshiba "Soundless." The magazine was loaded to capacity with forty-some thumbnail disks. He looped the bone-inductor mike around his neck and, eyes closed, switched it on.

Full, rich music flooded his body—Peter had set the *Worcester Fragments* first in the stack, so he could have Gregorian chants to go with breakfast and the beginning of the workday. He leaned back and let the noiseless sound thunder up his spine. Then slowly, lazily, he opened his eyes.

Light through the east rose window glinted yellow off a carved wooden angel at the tip of one rafter support. Peter's

gaze wandered to the front of the chancel, and down the arch
of organ pipes recessed into the stone behind the darkly shadowed presbytery.

He saw the thing.

Peter squinted, shook his head in an involuntary shiver. He
saw . . . *something,* he was not sure what. It was as if he'd
stared into the sun until the rods and cones of his eyes began
to burn out. It shimmered. Gingerly, he stretched out a thumb
at arm's length, and found he could hide it from view. But it
was still there when he lowered his arm, a small crawling . . .
nothingness in the air.

He shifted his head, forcing his gaze away. The thing did not
move. It remained over the altar, whether he was looking that
way or not.

Peter's mouth tasted sour. He wrapped his unfinished sandwich in a paper napkin, shoved it into his pocket, and gathered
up the trash. He left the sanctuary with only one backward
glance at the strange presence he was *not quite* sure was there.

Peter dumped the trash in a basket in the parish hall, and then
paused to reset the thermostat timer for the Social Action Com-
mittee meeting that night. He went downstairs to the smaller
furnace room off the kitchen, to check the boiler's water level.
It was low today, and he ran a few gallons in.

Back through the staircase landing, with its line of padlocked
storage cabinets, Peter climbed the four wood steps to the dirt-
floored half-basement under the sanctuary. He unlocked the
door. The *Fragments* were still playing within him, though he
had long forgotten their presence.

Peter peered into the dark, cold basement. A few miserly
glints of light seeped from windows inadequately boarded-up.
He flicked the light switch, and a string of bare electric bulbs
lit up in a sparse line to the sanctuary boiler in the far rear.
Their light barely seemed to reach the ground; darkness huddled in around them.

Taking the unfinished sandwich from his pocket, Peter

unwrapped it and set it down on the dirt, atop his napkin. "Listen," he called into the darkness. "There's a bite of food here, and if you stop by the church office, I'll write you out a meal letter. You can take it to the Emergency Center down the street and they'll give you a meal, you understand? But I want you out of here or I'll call the cops. You understand that? Do you?"

There was no answer.

He locked the door behind him and took the steps in two leaps. The momentum stayed with him, and when Sheila from the nursery stepped into the landing, he almost collided with her. She flinched away with a small shriek.

"Jesus!" he said, "you startled me." The music switched off, and suddenly the world seemed empty and silent.

Dark curly hair framed Sheila's thin face. "I'm sorry." She laughed and made a clutching motion at her heart. Then, serious again, she nodded toward the door. "So what's the verdict? Do you still think there's someone living in there?"

"Yeah, one of the vent people, I think." He moved away from the door so the possible squatter couldn't overhear. "I mean, probably just some harmless old wino who kicked in a window, but I'd hate to go wandering through there looking for him. It's like a maze, all broken furniture and old walls for rooms that don't exist anymore."

"Well, couldn't we just call the police and let *them* throw this guy out?"

Peter shook his head. "I wouldn't want to unless I was absolutely sure. You realize that they're charging fifty bucks for a false call?"

"I can remember when the police would come for free."

"You should—they only started charging six months ago."

Sheila looked at him reproachfully. "That was a joke."

"Oh." There was something terribly woebegone about her expression, her tone of voice, that was completely out of sync with their conversation. Peter looked more carefully at Sheila, and saw that she was actually trembling at the brink of tears. "What's the matter, then?" he asked gently.

"Have you seen Sam lately?"

The question took him by surprise. "No, not lately—I'd assumed he was mostly working in this part of the building."

"Oh, Peter, I just talked with Sam yesterday, and I think he's dying!"

Jennifer came out from the coal bin, where she had made a nest for herself. Furtively, she made her way to first the one door (sniffing at the sandwich there, but not touching it), then the other. The second door's frame was weak. She put a shoulder to it and heaved, and gave the door a shove with one hand. Still locked, it popped open.

She was in the children's bathroom now, all yellow-painted stalls and a single sink. It was warm in here, and smelled pleasantly of decay. She paused at the back landing to listen before going through the main room and into the kitchen. The children and their attendant teachers were out in the play yard again, their voices muffled by thick stone walls.

Jennifer hit up the refrigerator first, stealing a swallow of milk from a plastic gallon there, and an open jar of spaghetti sauce with a circle of blue-green mold growing atop it. In one of the cupboards was a tin of cookies, sealed against the mice and she lifted a handful of cookies from it.

With a spoon she found in the stainless-steel sink, Jennifer carefully scraped off the mold. She retreated back to her nest, temporarily satisfied, alternating butter cookies with spoonfuls of sauce.

She still could not remember coming to the church or what— if anything—had come before. Her mind was like a body coming out of surgery, numb but with unfamiliar pains waiting under the anesthetic. She was not consciously aware that her memories had fled, and she was driven by no desires, aims, or goals.

But she knew that she had to eat.

When Peter arrived at his office in the old manse (which was attached *to* the church, but had no connecting passage *with* it), he found a note from the pastor on a piece of Covenant letterhead: "On study leave thru Tues week—will leve typing, take mssges eves." Beside it was a stack of work: routine correspondence, the November Peace Letter, next Sunday's service, last month's Council minutes.

With a disgusted sigh, Peter slapped on the typewriter. His Toshiba began playing a decade-old Touchstone album: hard-driving electric folk. He set the Council notes to one side of the typewriter and an ashtray to the other, lit up, and began typing:

> Council APPROVED the Trustees' recommenda-
> tions that (1) we will need to terminate our exist-
> ing contract with the sexton effective January 1 of
> the new year. We will provide positive letters of
> recommendation and provide assistance in seek-
> ing out other churches for Sam, if he is interested.

Peter let the cigarette dangle from his mouth, like Bogart, occasionally drawing it up with his lips and sucking in a long drag. He paid little attention to what he was typing, still worried about the thing over the altar, still wondering whether he'd gotten caught in the weekend drugs trap and taken his hallucinations home with him into the workweek.

The outer door slammed, the office door flew open, and Sam stormed into the office. "Listen," he said, "you call the curator, call Mr. Alverson, and tell him that the coffee urn in the kitchen is broke. It's broke and *I* can't fix it, 'cause I don't got the parts. Now I've shut off the water to the urn and I've disconnected the pipes, but I don't know whether I can lift it down or not. I can't move this arm too well, 'cause they just operated on it."

The old sexton's face and neck were swelled and puffy, and his skin was unnaturally grey. His breathing was harsh.

"I could help you take the urn down," Peter offered.

"I didn't ask for no help!" the man snapped. "I can do it. Never said I couldn't. I just want you to call Mr. Alverson and tell him I'll need me some money for parts."

A quick flip through the Rolodex brought up Alverson's work

number, and he punched it into his phone. A secretarial voice said, "Rosen and Weiss," and Peter said, "Yes. Hello. I'm calling from Midlands Investment Corporation, and I'd like to speak with Mr. Alverson."

A moment later, Alverson's voice said, "Hello, Mr. Wexburg? I—"

"No, this is the church," Peter said. "The reason I'm calling is . . ."

"Peter," Alverson said tiredly, "there is not the *money* for whatever it is. How can I make you understand that?"

"Look," Peter said. "I'm not calling you about the roof or the toilets or the pipes that are going to burst one of these days and take out half the church with them. I just want you to talk with Sam." He thrust the receiver at the sexton. "Here."

He snatched up the Peace Letter and scanned a pious rant on radiation-burn victims for grammatical errors. When Sam was gone, he reread the last paragraph on the typewriter. *I'll bet that nobody's actually told Sam any of this,* he thought. He went on to the next paragraph.

> (2) When a new sexton is hired, a warm, sensitive supervisory relationship should be developed which has not existed in recent years with Sam.

It was night when Jennifer next came out, and because she dared not return to the refrigerator so soon, food was harder to find. The kitchen cupboards yielded only a chunk of old cheese, hard as a rock and ignored even by the mice. Gnawing off one tasteless flake at a time, Jennifer went up the back-stairs to the top floor.

The room was over the parish hall was originally a chapel, and it still retained the rose windows and oak balconies. But the floor space had been partitioned into three rooms at a time when the nursery school had been larger. Now they were used exclusively for storage. Jennifer climbed over a partition and systematically rifled old supply cabinets until finally she found a box of noodles among the crayons, paper scissors, and glue.

She took two handsful down to the kitchen and threw them into a pot, which she filled with water and set on the ancient black gas stove to boil.

The nursery room across from the kitchen had been left unlocked, and Jennifer peeked within. It was a room for hobbits, filled with child-scaled tables and chairs, and lit only by a fluorescent bulb over the fish tank. Chains of paper loops and shadowy crayoned pictures festooned the walls. Low shelves were tumbleful of toys. She tapped a bit of fish food to the guppies and watched them flurry over it.

There was a plastic brush on one table. She picked it up and sat down in a munchkin-sized chair and began combing out her straight midback-length hair. It glinted auburn in the fishlight.

She was about to go check on the noodles when the lights blazed on, and an old black man walked in the door.

Jennifer flinched back in the chair, half-blinded and afraid. Her heart scudded wildly, and her large-knuckled hands clenched white. The sexton stopped when he saw her. "I got to clean this room *tonight,* Missy," he said defiantly.

But when Jennifer started to stand, the man waved her down. "No, don't you get up, that's all *right*—I'll mop around you. No need for you to get up."

He lifted a bucket of soapy water into the room and shifted a few chairs and toys, shaking his head at their being in his way. He plunged the mop into the bucket and began swabbing.

"You with the nursery school?" Sam asked. When she said nothing, he nodded, taking her silence for assent. He mopped vigorously, with the habit of years. But the effort it cost him was obvious, and his breathing soon grew ragged and harsh. He took a gulping breath and leaned against the mop, closing his eyes for strength. "Then you ought to know that I can't come in during the day," he said. "A little bit in the morning, but I got chemotherapy and radiotherapy during the day. I don't *want* to come in at night, but I got no choice."

"Why?" She was startled by her voice—it was totally new to her. It frightened her, and yet almost immediately she wanted to say something again, for the question had caught her by surprise, and she still had no sense of how her voice sounded.

"There's a mass on my lungs," he said, "but that's not all. There's more wrong than that. They found the mass, but they're not sure about the other." Gingerly, he sat down on one of the low tables. "There's something the matter with my heart."

Jennifer searched for words, found some: "You'll get better." Their sound thrilled and elated her.

The old man opened his eyes, stared off into the middle distance sightlessly. "I'm not going to get no better, young miss, I'm going to die." Tears trembled at the corners of his eyes, and he shook his head, sending them flying. "But you know what, I don't *want* to die. I realize that everybody got to die *some*time, but that don't make it any easier. I don't *want* to die!"

"You won't die," Jennifer said.

Sam clutched the mop handle, staring bitterly at the floor. The tears began falling, large, slow, one at a time.

Quietly, Jennifer left. In the kitchen she found the noodles had overboiled and the water had put out the flame in the gas burner.

Before she returned to her nest, though, she saw Sam put his key ring away in one of the cupboards in the front basement landing. He covered them over with an old rag, but she knew where they were.

Coming up the walk to his office, Peter tripped and dropped his breakfast. The bottle of juice shattered into the sandwich, and he was only able to save half the coffee. He entered his office in a foul mood, dumped the food into the trash, and plugged in the electric heater he kept in the leg well of his desk.

He pulled the paperback copy of *Moby Dick* from his hip pocket (he was one-third through this time, his usual bog-down point), and slammed it onto the desktop. Impatiently he drew up his chair.

Among the papers on his desk was the Xeroxed Council

minutes sheet he'd left in the pastor's mail slot the night before. He'd circled the sexton items and written "Has anybody told Sam?" in the margin. Now it had been returned with "No, do it please" printed below in the pastor's calm, neat lettering.

Angrily, Peter scrawled "Are you aware that Sam is *dying?*" below the pastor's note and returned the minutes to the slot. That bought him a day, anyway. He picked up his paperback, ignoring the phone that started ringing just then, since he wasn't yet officially in. Then the doorbell buzzed and *that* he couldn't possibly ignore.

"Yes?" He opened the door partway, blocking entry with his body. It was one of the vent people, a short, fat man with his hair done up in greasy dreadlocks. His clothes were rotting on his body. Peter could smell them. The man was the color of the city—clothes, skin, hair, all were the same grimy industrial grey—and Peter recognized him. "Oh, it's you, Ashod."

Ashod clutched a broken plastic rosary in one fist, held up before him, crucifix dangling at the end of a single string. It was bright pink. "I gave you a meal letter two weeks ago," Peter said. "I can't give you another for at least a month. Come back when it gets really cold and nobody'll mind."

Ashod waved his fist back and forth in negation, the crucifix swinging wildly. "No, no, it's not that," he said. "I want to see the lady."

"Lady? Somebody in the nursery school?"

Ashod nodded his head vigorously. "No. I want to see the *lady.* I want her to make the voices go away."

The telephone was ringing again, and by now it was almost certainly time he was at work. "Come back when it's cold," Peter said, closing the door. "Understand—*cold?*"

Jennifer was learning the building's rhythms, the daily ebb and flow of people. She emerged when the nursery school children were outside in the yard. Moving quickly, efficiently, she stole another handful of noodles and set them to boiling. Then she took a double handful of colored crayons, being careful to choose only the largest, near-unused ones, and husked them of their paper shells.

She set a second pot of water to boil and placed a slightly smaller pot within to make a double-boiler. She dumped the crayons into the smaller pot and watched them soften and wilt, periwinkle blue folding over aquamarine, goldenrod yellow over bittersweet brown.

When the noodles were done, she strained them and dumped them onto a plate. The crayons were all melted by then, and she briskly stirred them into a brown swirl, and then a chocolate mess. She poured the crayons over the noodles, took up a spoon, and began eating.

She found Peter just inside the sanctuary door. One hand rested on a stone arch, and a trace of steam curled up from his nostrils. "Peter," she said, "the nursery rooms are *freezing*. Isn't there anything you can do about it?"

"Already taken care of," he answered abstractedly. "The water was low in the boiler so the automatic shutoff cut in. I bled in water, and the radiators should be heating up soon."

"Everything seems to be going wrong now that Sam isn't here in the daytime anymore. Why does the heat keep going off?"

"Well, you could say it's because there's a leak where the radiator pipes loop under the sanctuary. When the water heats up, the pipe expands and dumps into the dirt floor there until the system shuts itself off. Or you could say it's because most apprentice plumbers were of draft age, so the master plumbers have to do the scut work themselves, so there's more demand than they have time for, and they charge accordingly. Or you could say that as long as I can correct it by adding water, it's not an emergency, and they won't allocate money to fix it."

"But—"

"The thing to keep in mind," Peter said, "is that this kind of problem is normal with a system this old."

"I guess so, but—oh! Do you want to hear the latest? The children have seen a ghost!"

"A ghost?" Peter said blankly.

"Yes, a girl ghost—they say she's very pretty. They're all excited, and now they're trying to set up ghost traps. They're all so cute!"

Peter was giving her his undivided attention now, and Sheila found his steady green gaze disconcerting. He said nothing, but she had no difficulty following his thoughts.

"Oh," she said. "You think the person in the basement . . . Peter, you've got to call the police and get her *out* of there!"

"As long as the nursery school guarantees the false-call fee."

"They wouldn't hurt her, would they?" Sheila asked, suddenly apprehensive.

Peter smiled cynically. "They'd beat the crap out of her for sure. The police have been taking a real tough line on street people lately."

"Then there must be some other way!"

"No," Peter said calmly, "it's the police or else let her stay." His expression was distant, abstracted, again. He reached out and took her hand, placed it against the stone arch. "Feel this, would you?"

The stone was as cold as ice. It throbbed ever so slightly under her touch. Now that she was aware of it, too, it hummed subliminally, like a machine or a high-tension power line. Attuned, it seemed as if the entire building were full of the almost inaudible vibration. "What is it?" she asked.

Peter shrugged.

"It must have something to do with how cold it is," she decided.

Peter turned from locking up the church to see that someone was standing before the manse door, futilely waiting for someone to come answer the bell. He walked up behind the man, keys out, said, "Can I help you?" in a tone that implied he couldn't, and began unlocking the door.

"Yes," the man said. "I'd like to see the inside of your church."

He was well dressed and clean-shaven and good-looking in a perfectly forgettable sort of way. There was something cold about him.

"Services are ten-thirty Sunday mornings," Peter said, stepping inside and preparing to close the door.

"It's not about that, sir!" the man said quickly, bringing his hands up before him. He proffered a wallet badge—badly printed allegorical figures with a shield, Latin slogan, space for name typed in and signature squiggle—and put it away when Peter shrugged. "I'm from the Cancer Research Center at Philadelphia Medical College—perhaps you've heard of us?" Of course Peter had; the College was only a few blocks distant. "We're doing a building-to-building canvass in this area."

"We give through the church's national headquarters."

"Oh, it's not that sir." The man gave a short, insincere laugh. "We're searching for some stolen—and very valuable—research materials, and we have good reason to believe hat the thief had hidden them in this area. If you could only—"

"No," Peter said.

The man smiled plausibly, "I believe you will find it *easier,* sir, if you—"

"I'm halfway through the week, and already I'm two days behind schedule. I've got a bulletin and two mailings to get out, and I can't spare the time to nursemaid visitors. Now if you want to go through channels, the pastor here is associated with PMC through the chaplain's office. If you can get him to agree that you are more important than my usual work—fine. If not, you can always come to services. Ten-thirty Sunday mornings." He shut the door in the man's face.

But my God, that man's eyes were cold.

Jeremy was playing hide-and-go-seek. Normally it was hard to get away from the teachers, but today Debbie was sick and the substitute never showed up, and neither did one of the parent volunteers, so they were short on adults. And then Gregory's mother had called because he'd forgotten his lunch, and Ming-su had started crying because she always cried at that time of day, and there was someone banging on the door to get in, so for a minute there was no one in the room but kids. So Jeremy told Heather, who was his girlfriend and who was going to marry him when they grew up, to close her eyes and count real slow, and he ran into the kitchen looking for a place to hide.

The kitchen was full of cupboards and stuff, but they were either locked or else the knobs were too high to reach. It was too narrow behind the refrigerator and too open under the sinks. Then he noticed that someone had left the oven door open.

Jeremy knew that ovens were dangerous, so he put his hand in first to make sure it was off and not hot. Then he crawled in. It was roomy inside, and easy to shut the door after him, because it was springy and light. You just tapped it and it closed on its own.

It was dark inside the oven. Lying on the floor, Jeremy stifled a giggle at the thought of Heather looking for him. There was a little hole near his nose, and a funny smell came out of it that made him feel sleepy.

He had just closed his eyes for a minute or two when the oven door opened and the ghost looked in. She was real pretty and real skinny too. She did not look surprised to see Jeremy, and he was too sleepy to be surprised himself. "Shhh," he said, "I'm hiding."

"Oh," the ghost said. Then, "Is it fun?"

Jeremy thought that for a moment, then said, "No." It had been fun, but now it was mostly dull.

The ghost smiled then, and said, "Well, why don't you come out?" She reached in her arm—a long, long way—and gently tugged him out.

For an instant, he felt dizzy and funny and cold, but then he was standing blinking on the kitchen floor and the ghost was gone. The kitchen looked funny, because the shadows had shifted and the light had changed since he had crawled inside. It was all of a sudden a lot later in the day.

He ran off to find Heather.

Peter was the only attendee from the church staff at the monthly tenants' meeting. They sat around a table in the old manse's conference room, in front of the fireplace with its glacé tile and tinned-up front, swapping gossip and sharing news. Peter listened and nodded and answered questions and constructed the month's complaint list:

> 1. Heat!!! (Leak under sacristy—fix?)
> 2. Mice
> —more traps?
> —poison not working?
> 3. Light bulbs ((*if* can find source will extend credit))
> 4. Toilet paper (tell Sam)
> 5. Building Security
> —more padlocks
> —everyone more care
> 6. Dupe key for Womens Rights
> 7. Rent Schedule
> —can wait another week, nursery school?
> —can wait another *month*, STPPRCDC?

The afternoon volunteer for the Stop the Point Pleasant Radio-Chemical Dump Coalition complained that the Latin American campaign was drawing off most of their volunteer labor, and wanted to know why there were so many derelicts around the building of late. Peter shrugged, promised to find out, and made a note:

> 8. Why winos?

Mrs. Untiedt, of Womens Rights—a relatively successful organization that rented the entire basement floor of the old manse, and mostly used the door directly out through the nursery-school play yard—asked why they hadn't gotten their doorbell fixed yet. Peter explained that their usual handyman didn't like working for churches, which were notoriously slow to pay, and made another note:

9. Nudge Jack—doorbell!

Sheila told about one of the nursery school children who had been lost for several hours that morning, and who claimed to've hidden in the kitchen oven. "He couldn't have hidden there," she said, "or he'd have suffocated. So we don't know where he was hiding for most of that time." Then, thoughtfully, "I don't think that oven is safe, though, Peter. You've really got to *do* something."

"Do you want the door welded shut?" Peter asked.

"No, don't do *that*," Sheila said. "We need the oven because sometimes we bake for the children."

Peter nodded, and wrote:

10. Make oven safe for children.

Before Sheila could think to ask how he intended doing this, he rose and broke up the meeting.

Sam was waiting at the desk. "Listen," he said, "I got to talk with Mr. Alverson." His neck was still puffed out beyond his chin, and his skin was a gruesome color grey. Peter nodded, dialed, and told the secretary: "This is Harry's brother—Fred Alverson? I'm in town unexpectedly, and thought I could have lunch with Harry."

When Alverson's voice cried, "Fred! You old son of a bitch, what are you—" Peter handed the phone over to Sam and walked out of the room.

Sheila was waiting in the hallway. She nodded toward the room and in a low voice said, "How is he?"

Peter shook his head. "He's going to die."

"Don't say that!"

"He's going to die," Peter said stubbornly, "And he's going to keep working here until he drops. Every time I go to the bathroom I expect to open the stall door and find him sitting dead on the crapper."

There were a lot of different paints in the cabinet, and some were good to drink and others were not. There was a thunderstorm going on, and as Jennifer crouched in the dark and tasted, she could hear distant rumblings and stone-rattling *cracks* in the air overhead. There was also the sound of pouring water and a few snaps of blue electricity from the steel cable of one lightning rod that ran through the cellar into the earth.

Sated at last, she fetched the sexton's keys and went exploring.

The door to the organ room was off the sacristy, and it didn't open all the way. Jennifer slid inside, closing the door after her, and waited for her eyes to adjust. Outside, the storm still raged.

Everything was grey and dark and dusty. The organ workings were mostly tier upon tier of wood pipes and electrical fixtures, with two long rows of leather bellows-hinges, all hammered together a lot looser and more haphazardly than one would expect. They towered up and up, behind the metal arch of the treble pipes, and Jennifer found a wooden ladder nailed to the works and clambered up to the first landing.

The dust was finger-thick there, and other than a half-burnt candle stub or two, there was nothing of interest. She found the next set of rungs off to one side, and went up.

As she climbed, she became aware of a strange expectant feeling in the air, a crackly sense of static electricity. Glancing over a shoulder, she saw pale pastel lights shimmer on the treble pipes—St. Elmo's fire.

With a surge, she heaved herself onto the top level. She could see all of the sanctuary from here, through the pipes, and the electrical fires blazed up brighter, shifting in quicksilver fashion. She saw the thing afloat over the altar too, but to her untutored eye it was no greater interest than any other part of the building.

Jennifer's hair lifted lightly upward, the ends trailing blue sparks, so that it formed an aura about her face. Fata morganas drifted through the floating mass.

The flames leaped from organ pipe to organ pipe, blazing up and subsiding like one of Bach's fugues played on a color organ. There was sparkling electricity everywhere, in the cables and fixtures and wires, and the stops began opening and shutting on their own accord, in a silent electric symphony.

Jennifer stretched up on her toes. Her auburn hair afloat, the world crackling with color and energy, thin electrical flames sizzling about her, she danced.

Later she found a burnt-out light bulb there, on the upper catwalk, and ate the filament at its heart. She had to break the inside to get at it, but she fixed it up afterward, as good as new.

The minutes were waiting for Peter on his desk, with a new notation in the pastor's hand: "Salaries must be cut *some*-where—please notify Sam." It was close to an explicit threat as he was going to get.

Peter lit up a cigarette, realized that he already had one going in the ashtray, and stubbed it out. He rubbed the back of his neck, then restlessly strode to the chancel kitchen off of the conference room. It was tiny, and contained a broken refrigerator, a rusting gas stove that no one dared fire up, and a dozen empty cupboards. The linoleum was browned and buckling.

Taking a glass from the strainer, Peter washed it thoroughly under the tap and drew a drink of water. He tapped his cigarette's ashes into the sink, and washed them down the drain with a long spurt of water. Then, back at his desk, he rummaged through the small emergencies drawer until he found a bottle of aspirin among the tampons and the lollipops.

Where, he asked himself, was the loophole? He popped the aspirin dry, thought a minute, took a sip of water. Finally, he slapped on the typewriter. The pastor hadn't actually ordered him to fire Sam in person.

It took three tries to come up with a final draft of the memo. He typed up a clean copy, read it through, and was satisfied. He forged the pastor's signature to it and dropped it in Sam's mail slot.

Done, he lit up a cigarette, noticed the previous one burning in the ashtray, and exasperated, let them both burn. He was too wired to type now, so he scooped up a box of old clothing that had been donated to the church weeks ago, and which he'd been meaning to store in the church with the rest.

Outside, en route to the church, he noticed several clutches of wine bottles against the church wall, and made a mental note to lift some more padlocks from the hardware store, to firm up security. He passed through the sanctuary without once looking at the altar, and went to the front narthex, where the staircases to the balcony were.

He was halfway up one set of stairs when a pale face appeared at the top. A slender young woman in denim—a redhead. "The church is closed, miss," he called to her, and the face disappeared.

A cold touch of fear in his stomach, he jogged up the stairs, looked around. "If you need help . . . " he called. Something stirred off to one side, a ripple of stained-glass light over red hair, and the woman shifted into the shadows of the far stairway.

"Hey!" He dropped the box and stumbled over piles of dusty cartons crammed with donations for the annual rummage sale. At the foot of the stairs, the door between the narthex and the sanctuary was swinging shut. He pushed through.

He was just in time to see the woman disappear behind the presbytery beyond the altar. A door closed gently.

Peter didn't try to follow. The thing over the altar was swirling madly, like a pinwheel. He couldn't understand how the woman could have moved so quickly, and he yelled after her. *"I wasn't going to hurt you! What do you think I am, some kind of fucking monster?"*

The children were playing a run-around game, so Sheila felt secure in leaving them to the supervision of parent volunteers while she went up to the old chapel for supplies. She retrieved the library paste first, paused, then went into the Toddlers' Room for the construction paper.

The Toddlers' Room had been part of the Sunday School program when Covenant was still an expanding congregation. A good dozen cribs stood serene in the soft light. They were arranged neatly against the walls, sidebars up and plasticized mattress growing dusty. To the near corner a stairway rose to the west balcony. The stairs were so cluttered with broken furniture and toys that only a narrow, twisting pathway led upward.

Sam sat on the third step up. His eyes were dry and hard, and he was staring sightlessly at the cribs.

"Sam?" Sheila said. "Is everything all right—why aren't you at the hospital?"

He didn't answer, didn't even move.

"Sam!" She was genuinely alarmed now, and reached out to touch his arm.

It was as if her touch broke a spell. Sam snapped his head her way, eyes startled, and scrambled awkwardly to his feet. "I was just taking some things upstairs," he said defensively. "That's all I was doing."

"I believe you, I believe you!" Sheila protested. The old man scooped up a broken hobbyhorse, cradled it in his arms.

"It ain't no question of believing or not believing," he said. "I was just going upstairs." He turned and ascended.

Sheila stared after him for a long moment before hoisting her supplies and turning to go. As soon as she was far down the stairs enough that he wouldn't hear her, she threw back her head and said aloud, "I do not believe that man! He is so *exasperating.*" It made her feel a lot better.

Halfway down the stairs she was stopped again, this time by a near-subliminal noise. She cocked her head. It was almost like the vibration in the sanctuary the other day, or—she raced

down the stairs, cut across the parish hall, and out to the Thirty-seventh Street narthex. Someone was outside, leaning on
the buzzer.

"Who is it?" she called. Putting down her supplies, she
peered through the peephole. There was a man outside,
dressed in a suit. He was none of the nursery school parents.
"You'll have to speak up," she yelled.

" . . . from the hospital," the man was saying. "We're running
a canvass of all the buildings—"

"You'll have to go to the church office," she called back. "We
don't open this door during school hours." She picked up her
box and headed downstairs.

Almost to her surprise, the man went away.

The acid was in the glue backing of a Mickey Mouse decal.
Mickey was dressed as the Sorcerer's Apprentice, gesturing up
stars, and you were supposed to lick off the LSD and then slap
the decal onto your forehead. Too cute by half, Peter thought,
and when he'd done up the tab, he crumpled the little mouse
and swallowed it.

While waiting for the drug to pass into his bloodstream,
Peter did first some typing, and then some filing. When he
found himself obsessively going back to each piece of filing to
be sure it was retrievable and not placed away in some non-
sensical drug-generated location, he quit and went up the
stairs to the second floor.

Hands behind his back, Peter stood before the hall window,
looking down into the play yard. Children were scurrying about
busily, swinging on the old tire hung from the oak tree, scrambling over the wooden monkey bars some parent had built
years ago. Foam-rubber mattresses had been tied around the
oak's trunk, to protect the children.

As he watched, a sudden wind blew through the tree and
filled the air with yellow leaves. For an instant they hung
motionless, defining the space between ground and sky, reced-
ing into infinite perspective. Then they swirled away.

Years before he'd worked for an inner-city corporation, in a room with a window view of a church's slate roof and nothing else. Ordinarily the roof was a barren featureless stretch, but this one time it had snowed the night before, and the snow was loosened by a warm winter sun so that occasionally patches would let go and slide away in a puff of powdery white. Kim Soong—the only other typist in the room at that moment—leaned over her machine and stared, entranced. The room filled with silence.

The acid was hitting. He felt a painful twinge in his stomach, from the minute trace of strychnine that was a by-product of the drug's manufacture. Slowly he descended the newly challenging stairway and, remembering to lock up behind him, went outside and to the church door.

Two men lay across the step, passing a paper-bagged bottle back and forth. The dark one beamed at Peter's appearance, and they both scrambled to their feet.

"This is my friend Walter," Ashod said. His companion, a sallow half-shaven beanpole of a man, nodded several times. He had haunted eyes, with ring upon ring of darkness beneath them. "He's come to meet the lady too."

Peter looked blankly first at the one man, then the other, and then away from both. He saw that there were a dozen or so more vent people—shopping-bag ladies among them—scattered about the churchyard. Some wandered slowly, aimlessly about, and others sat huddled in decaying blankets and chunks of squashed-down cardboard boxes. One was pissing against the wall. It was a regular little Reaganville, and they looked as though they had come to stay. *Fuck it*, he decided suddenly, *I'm on drugs, I don't have to cope with this.* He retreated into the church, slamming the door after him.

The stone ribs of the sanctuary were still humming softly to themselves, but now—with the acid in him—Peter was not bothered by the phenomenon. Things were *supposed* to be strange on acid. And one way or another, Peter was determined to return things to the way they were supposed to be.

The sanctuary was cold. Peter shivered, convulsively stared upward, and was shocked motionless by the wooden angels above. They glinted gold and then silver shards of ice. They multiplied, like the leaves had earlier, and filled the church, angel upon angel, as regular and unvarying as an Escher print.

The empty spaces were angels too, and the images flashed from solid angels to negative angels and back in a flickering dance. The air was filled with music, words and notes transformed into a solid calligraphic tracery in an alphabet he did not know. There was something familiar about the music, and with a start, Peter recognized it as Vangelis's *Heaven and Hell.* His Toshiba was still playing, and that realization was a jarring intrusion of reality.

The thing over the altar was larger now, much larger, the size of a clenched fist or of a coiled snake. The angels that intruded upon it were seized as if by overwhelming gravitational forces, crumpled to nothing, and swallowed up by it.

The angels went on dancing. In a flash of insight, Peter realized that they were all mechanical. Identical, perfect—they were machines, creatures of a purely deterministic universe, entirely devoid of free will. They danced their machine dance in the air and it meant nothing.

There were fewer angels now, as one by one they were devoured by the thing over the altar. They kept on dancing, though, and if they were aware of the thing—if they were even capable of awareness—it did not matter, for all was meaningless, all was a dance. Blind forces ground them down and, joylessly, they danced.

And the thing over the altar continued to slowly grow.

He fled—from the angels' cold dance, from the acid-etched sense of total futility, but mostly from the horrible, nasty *eating* obscenity afloat in the church. Out of the sanctuary and down, into the basement, away from the light, into obscurity and darkness.

When he had stopped, he found himself huddled into a

cold, lightless corner. The ghost was there. He could feel her breath on his face, sense a near-visual glimmering of warmth from her body.

Sam was eating lunch. He sat with the makings spread out before him in the old chapel, by the unused chimney where the rat had taken up residence. He started with an apple, chewing it slowly and thoughtfully as he considered the job he had done on the trap.

The rattrap was dark and smoky. Rats were clever; they didn't like new smells, chemical smells, human smells. He'd built a small fire of twigs and old leaves out by the trash cans in the play yard, and charred the trap over it, holding the trap in a clamp he had made of an old coat hanger.

The apple finished, Sam unscrewed the peanut butter jar, plunged a knife in, and stirred the oils around real good. He began spreading it onto a slice of Wonder Bread, paying close attention to the act, involving his whole mind in it, because the alternative was to think about what the doctors had told him that morning.

He paused and smeared a dab of peanut butter onto the trap for bait, then returned to spreading the sandwich thick. Peanut butter made good bait because rats liked that kind of greasy stuff, oily and rancid.

He was sitting in a patch of colored light from the south rose window, and for some while it had flickered gently, as if interrupted by the shadows of a lightly tossing tree branch. But there was no tree outside there, and Sam looked up automatically, puzzled, to see what was interfering with the light.

There was a girl in front of the window, glory light streaming about her, and she was sitting cross-legged in the air.

Sam could not blink, could not look away. His sandwich was frozen in front of him. He knew this girl, had met her once before in the basement. She had been wearing the same denim jeans and jacket then, and her hair was as red as it had ever been.

Footsteps sounded on the stairs, and Sam ignored them. But when the door slammed open, the suddenness of the sound made him glance without thinking back toward the hallway, and he saw Sheila enter the room. The light about him cleared, and he didn't have to look up again to know that the girl was gone.

"Sam." The nursery school teacher was before him now, and she peered into his face, concerned. "Sam, I'm very worried about you, about the way you've been acting today. Have I offended you in some way? Should I be apologizing for something?"

He looked away, could not answer. But she would not go away.

"Sam, what's *wrong* with you today?"

Sooner or later, he knew, he would have to tell somebody. "I think I'm cured," he said slowly. And burst into tears.

The vent people were roasting a dog in a window well. By pure good fortune they'd chosen one of the few wells that had been cinder-blocked up. The skinned carcass was hung on a spit, turned erratically by an enthusiastic hunchbacked individual. The church wall was black with smoke and grease. They offered Peter a leg, but he shook his head and wandered away.

There were over a hundred vent people in the churchyard, and their trash and scattered possessions made the yard as cluttered and filthy as a battlefield. One toothless old hag lifted her skirts and squatted, to the profound disinterest of her fellows. Her piss steamed as it hit the ground. A convulsive alky, looking like a skinny black spider, swooped great circles in the walkway dust with both hands, babbling of demons in his head.

And all the while there were at least five radios playing, battered and ugly things scavenged from garbage bags, but with a good decade's life left in their permablast batteries. They were turned to three separate newscasts, and the fragmentary snatches of global hysteria tumbled and cascaded one over another.

—warned that unless American troops withdraw from

Burma—escaped from the Rocky Mountain Arsenal—survivors'
reports of CBW warfare were denied—troops called up from—
martial law declared in five Midwestern states—

Peter stopped before an old scissors-grinder, who had set up
his cart on the sidewalk. I was an ancient thing, hammered
together from scraps and pushed about by hand. The whet-
stone was run by a vintage 1922 electric motor in black-enam-
eled housing, which fed off of a tangle of car batteries hooked
up in series.

—reported shot down over Sinkiang—

"You and I," shouted the scissors-grinder, "HEEDLESSLY
deserted God some MANY years ago to join vain Satan's VAIN
revolt against God's TEMPORARY laws. All TRUTHS emanate
from God and we will reap WHAT we have sown. This is WHY
we are now in human bodies. TO REAP WHAT?"

A fat woman waddled past, going "Quackquackquack,"
like a cartoon duck on amphetamines. She drew Peter's eyes
away from the operator, and he saw that the yard was as abuzz
with divergent theologies as the Middle Ages were before the
Inquisition.

—meanwhile tensions escalated in the Middle East and
Africa in a bizarre—

A deadpan little man in very clean clothes stood on the steps
and shouted, "The Bible tells of the SCARLET WHORE that is
BABYLON that is the BEAST that has put her FOOT on the ser-
pent! She has SWALLOWED UP the Seventh Seal and has
loosed the horrors of the ROCKY MOUNTAIN ARSENAL. If you
have FAITH the size—"

And somehow in the bubbling confusion of voices, Peter
realized that he did not have to be here, did not, in fact, even
know how he had gotten here, and went inside, to his office.

—limited use of tactical nuclear—

There were three cigarettes afire in the ashtray by the time
Sheila came into the office. One by one, Peter had lit them up

and put them down, unsmoked. She cheerfully waved a hand in the bluish smoke and said, "Phew! It smells like a train station in here."

Her presence was an anchor he could hang on to. "Hi," he said.

"Peter, it's wonderful," she bubbled. "Have you heard the news? Sam's doctors say he's going to be okay. He's had a spontaneous remission—isn't that wonderful? It was a miracle, they said—a one-chance-in-a-billion miracle!" She banged her fists together, and bounced up on her toes in elation.

"A miracle," Peter said numbly. He should have felt happy for Sam, and yet he didn't. All he could think of was the memo firing the old man, and that Sam wasn't going to die in time for him to avoid receiving it.

"Yes, but Peter"—her mood shifted again—"you have to do something about all these dirty, filthy vagrants that are hanging around the church. The parents are going to be coming by to pick up their children in a couple of hours, and they are going to have a *fit*. Really."

"They're not really dangerous," Peter said. "They're none of them capable enough to be dangerous."

"Peter, I want you to get rid of them! Call the police or something. If we don't get them out of here, we're going to lose half our students!" She leaned forward, examining his face. "Are you *on* something?"

"Not anymore," he said, and belatedly realized that it was true. He was perfectly straight. Just tired—extremely tired, almost stunned with weariness. There was a strange blank area in his memory, between when the acid had peaked and he'd come to among the vent people. Something flickered there, bright and ungraspable. He shrugged mentally. Chalk it up to the drugs and forget it. You could only go on as before.

Taking a deep breath to settle himself, he picked up the phone, dialed, and when Alverson's secretary refused to put him through snarled, "Listen, sister, this is Sergeant Blindwood of the Pennsylvania State Police, and I am right in the middle of a fucking *shootout.* We have a psychotic individual holding this fucker's wife and fucking kids and shouting slogans about the fucking Hard Anarchy Liberation *Army,* and you are holding me *up.* How'd you like to have your sex life investigated with a fucking *crowbar?*"

A moment later a very small hesitant voice said, "Peter . . . this is you, isn't it?"

Peter tossed the receiver to a horrified Sheila. "All yours," he said.

She held it as if it were a poisonous snake that would bite her if she let go. Then she said, "Peter, you can't evade responsibility by having someone else say the words." There was compassion in her voice.

Slowly—reluctantly—Peter reached for the phone, closed his fingers about it, took it. "Harry?" he said into the receiver. "Listen, I'm sorry about all this. I dialed the wrong number." He listened in silence for a time, said, "Yes, I know," and listened some more. The outside door closed gently as Sheila left.

When Alverson hung up, Peter jabbed down on the plunger with one finger, cutting the connection. He took a deep breath, and dialed the number for the police.

"Hello," he said, "I'm calling from the Church of the Covenant on Thirty-seventh Street . . . "

Time was short, and Jennifer was hungry again. She had scoured the church from top to bottom, passing by many things—cookie dough, Ivory Soap flakes, Brillo pads, clay— that she might normally have lingered over. But she could no longer spare the time to build from precursor elements.

The chemical dump counteradvocacy group's office was originally the choir director's, a century ago when the position was full-time. It had a skylight through the slate roof (with plastic stapled to its underside to cut down on infiltration), and a row of narrow leaded-glass windows that looked out into the storage rooms of the top floor. Jennifer had climbed through one of these and was going through a carton of bumper stickers when the thing in the sanctuary stirred.

The sense of its movement rose thorough shafts and vents left over from an early unsuccessful attempt to retrofit a forced air heating system to the church. Jennifer shuddered as if a jolt of electricity had shot up her spine.

For an instant she thought it was about to happen, and she was racked by terror and bleak despair. It was too early. She was not ready. Then the movement ceased—there was yet a chance, however slim. She was on her feet and through the window almost immediately.

Fear drove her down the stairs, running silently, wanting to hide but not daring to do so. Inspiration made her nab the key ring from the sexton's closet. As sly and furtive as a shadow, she slipped back up the stairs through the narthex and into the parish hall.

She could hear the sexton working in the chancel, but the connecting door was shut and he couldn't see her. One key of the ring fit into the communion cabinet. She opened the doors and found what she needed.

There were a lot of linen napkins, which she shoved aside, and a tray with slots for perhaps a hundred tiny little glasses to fin into. The bread was carefully wrapped in white paper. It was half-gone from the previous Sunday, and stale and hard as wood, but it would do—it would do!

Triumphantly she shoved the bread under one arm, and cradled the two bottles of communion wine in the other. She ran.

There was a dark storm gathering outside. The thunderhead piled up, charcoal blue, over the surrounding buildings. Faint lightnings shimmered within its heart. The vent people danced happily on the saturated-green lawn. To every side, the blind and featureless walls of the high rises blocked out large chunks of the sky. It felt like being enclosed in a box.

Peter stared glumly out the window, waiting, all pretense of working gone. Once, the phone rang and he let it go until someone in the nursery school picked it up on their extension.

He shifted papers to either side of his desk to make room for his elbows, and rested his chin on his arms.

Fast flashes of red-and-blue light struck and rebounded off the church walls, and Peter saw that police cars were pulling up, blocking off the surrounding streets. There were more of them than he had expected, some twenty or so, and they arrived eerily silent—flashers on and sirens mute.

Three cars—one civilian—nosed through the blockade and parked by the curb. Their inhabitants conferred, formed a party, and moved briskly up the walk. The civilian craned his neck interestedly as they passed by the scissors-grinder's old cart, which had been pulled apart and made into an altar of sorts. What might have been a crucifix canted crazily atop it, with several broken plaster Madonnas—scavenged from God knows where—lashed to its arms. Several attempts had been made to paint the assemblage, each abandoned for lack of paint or concentration. The result was an unpretty riot of mis-matched color.

Peter stood as the deputation neared the door. Outside, police lounged against their cars, the visors of their black-glass helmets flipped up. They were held in check by neocortical implants, like dogs on a leash, and several were gently tapping their truncheons into open palms.

The doorbell rang.

Answering, Peter found himself facing three police officers. Their faces were impassive, and might well have been carved from the same block of ice. With them was the smooth and plausible man from the Cancer Research Center.

"Hello," the Cancer Research man said pleasantly. "I see we're on the same team now."

The door from the chancel to the back stairway was badly warped out of shape. There were splits through the center, and it was so badly bowed that it wouldn't even shut properly. Sam had removed it from the frame and set it down on two saw-horses.

To do the job properly, he should soak the oaken door in water for a few days, and then weight it down between flat metal plates, to warp it back into shape. Lacking the time and tools, though, one did the best one could. So . . . first you move the hinges down an inch, to rehang the door lower. Then you sand down the edges where it's sticking. A little putty in the cracks, some weather-stripping around the edges, and the job is done.

Sam whistled an old Motown tune as he sanded, enjoying the shift and feel of his muscles. He felt good, stronger than he had been in years, and all the swelling around his neck had gone down. The doctors wanted him to go through another battery of tests, but under close questioning by his sister—she was a sharp-tongued woman, was Sophia!—they admitted that he didn't actually need them. They were just curious to know why he wasn't dead. He was healed, though. They said so themselves.

He could feel—subliminally—the thing growing in the sanctuary, but he felt no need to do anything about it. There was enough trouble in the world, without borrowing more. And like they always said, you don't open the oven door until the cake is done.

Fine oak dust whispered down to the floor as he handled the paper, sliding it along the door's edge in long, firm, even strokes.

The communion wine was cheap stuff, with a metal cap that unscrewed instead of a cork. Jennifer took only a taste, but that first sip went down *real* smooth. It jolted through her brain like lightning, snapping synapses open and shut, setting off a cascade of images from her past:

She was back in the hospital, strapped onto a gurney. Everything was white and smelled of disinfectant and hospital food. They had cropped her long blond hair, and were shaving the stubble that remained. When she opened her mouth to scream, someone shoved the side of his hand in, saying,

"Hush, pretty baby, we're just going to fine-tune that pretty little brain of yours." She bit down hard and his hand tasted—

His hand tasted like her husband's when they made love. He would touch her face gently, wonderingly, and she'd twist her head sideways to catch his hand in her teeth. Feeling like some kind of wild, free animal, she'd bite down into the flesh. It tasted of salt and sweat and curly black hairs. He was on leave from the Air Force, but scheduled to rotate back to Mauritania soon, to fly more bombing missions. He was an officer—

He was an officer, and when she saw him coming up the walk, stalwartly expressionless, she knew her husband wasn't coming back from Africa, and she wished so hard for it to be all a mistake that it seemed the world must shudder to its core for the sheer intensity of her desire. But the officer walked right up to her door anyway, rang the bell, delivered the news. It was only as he was turning away that the air seemed to shimmer and the young officer fell to the ground, blood gushing from his nose and mouth. Half-embedded in the walkway, he struggled. She knew that he wasn't to blame, but still the blood came out—

The blood came out the same way it did later when she left the hospital, her skull abristle with tiny silver wires and implants that were supposed to control her but did not. All the guards fell down, hemorrhaging, even those who did not try to stop her but turned to run. The red hair and the clothing formed around her because on some cunning animal level she knew she needed them to escape. She walked—

They were good memories, and they filled up the empty spaces. The pain was real and good and brought her a step closer to being human again. She tilted the bottle and chugalugged it all down. Bubbles blocked to the top, and the bottle was empty and her head was full of thoughts.

She uncapped the second bottle.

"I shouldn't be letting you in without the pastor's explicit permission," Peter fretted.

—half of Houston up in flames. We're trying to get a reporter in now to confirm—

The vent people parted for the group, stepping back a pace from the intensity of the Cancer Man's eyes, recognizing in them an insanity that even *they* had to respect. Ashod came bustling forward, and waved his pink plastic rosary in Peter's face. "Save yourself!" he shouted. "Get down on your knees—pray for forgiveness!"

One of the police escort reached out to touch Ashod gently on the chest, and he went stumbling back, face contorted with pain.

"Peter," the Cancer Man said. They were at the church door now, and Peter had his keys out. "Let me introduce myself. My name is William Oberg. I'd be pleased if you called me Bill." He shook Peter's hand. "Now," he said, not letting go, "we're friends, yes? I'm sure you wouldn't mind showing your old chum where you work, would you?" He tightened his grip, and Peter gasped in pain. The police looked on with interest.

"No," Peter said quickly. "No objection." The pain ceased.

"Good." Oberg let Peter open the door, then led the troupe through the narthex and into the sanctuary. He stopped in amazement.

"Jesus Christ," one of the cops said. Another crossed himself.

The thing over the altar had grown. It was the size of a basketball now, so large that it was almost possible for the eye to fix on it and assign it some definite shape and image. But not quite. It was oddly compelling, even hypnotic. Peter seemed to remember—

"Okay, it's pretty far gone," Oberg said, "but we can still handle it if we can get hold of the girl."

Peter started, and for the first time actually *looked* at Oberg. He could half-see into the man, see the whirling wheels and cams embedded just below the plastic flesh, the fine gold wires and wheatseed monitor lights. Oberg glanced fleetingly Peter's way, and Peter's breath froze within his throat. The man had no eyes! Only deep metal funnels that led from his face into a cold and lightless stacking of cryonic plates.

Peter exhaled, and Oberg shifted into a thin surface image, with no interior, as unsubstantial as a hologram or a soap bubble. His movements left long bright trails. *Oh God, no*, Peter thought. He was flashing back. His hallucinations were rising up again, and this was not the crowd to be in under these circumstances. These fuckers were not going to show him any mercy if they discovered he was on drugs.

Luckily, they were scurrying about like automatons, and hadn't noticed yet. Oberg was laying out elastic cords and metal restraints on the communion table. One policeman unhooked a flashlight from his belt and clambered over the presbytery. He poked the light between the organ pipes and peered within.

The two other police went into the balconies. One shimmied up a loose pew to the steeple door. From within, he called down, "Ugh. It's ankle-deep in pigeon shit here."

"The windows have been broken for years," Peter said inanely. It was harder to fake a straight response than he'd thought it would be.

"Check it all out anyway," Oberg called back. He tightened a last cinch on the communion table and stepped back, satisfied. The altar had become a restraining table, with devices to hold the legs spread wide *here*, the arms up and the side *there*. Directly above, the thing whirled madly.

The table lacked only a victim. Oberg laid a fatherly hand on Peter's shoulder. "Perhaps you have some idea where she might be?" he suggested.

The second bottle of wine was on its way to her lips when the passage suddenly convulsed. The walls turned blue and lurched over on their sides. Jennifer jerked, and the floor came smashing up into the side of her face. The empty bottle fell away, shattering into a thousand cobalt fragments. The half-eaten communion loaf burst into cold blue flames.

The surviving bottle was pouring purple wine into Jennifer's lap. Frantically, she stopped it with her thumb. The glass was scalding cold; it stung like hornets. But she clutched it to her, and did not let go.

Sick with uncertainty and pain, she stood. Her head was abuzz with blue sparks, and the carbon smoke from the burning loaf was billowing up to fill the room. All the passages were atilt; they steepened when she tried to climb them. She had to grab one-handed at pillars and moldings and doorjambs to pull herself upward, into the icy flames.

The arm cradling the bottle spasmed with cold, and the bottle fell away. It bounced twice, spraying wine, but miraculously did not break. Jennifer stretched out, trying to retrieve it. She almost fell from her fingerhold trying, but—too far! Too far! She reached again, nearly dislocating her shoulder and wrists with the effort.

Her knuckles whitened, weakened. Involuntarily, she let go of the door frame, and slid four yards down the hall. The wine bottle rested on the floor curling above her, in the center of a spreading purple stain. A full quarter of its contents remained within the bottle—she could see it.

But she could not reach it. The floor lifted away from her too steeply, and could not be scaled. It was easier—much easier—to let gravity pull her down the hall, into the redness.

Into the warmth.

"No," Peter said. "I couldn't guess."

But he was afraid of Oberg. And Oberg was a man who understood fear, knew its every touch and nuance, could read its track on the human face. "Is she on this floor?" he asked. "No? Upstairs, then? Downstairs? *Where* in the basement?"

Outside, the vent people were suddenly still. The silence was startling. Then a quick series of soft explosions went *pop-pop-pop*. Tear gas. Pandemonium broke out, shrieks of pain or rage mingling with incoherent cries of fear as the police moved in.

Like most urban dwellers, Peter had seen his share of riots in the past few years. He could picture in his mind what was happening: there would be an outer circle of police, to prevent fugitives from escaping and force them back into the fray, and two or more flying wedges to move through the mob, clubs flashing.

Oberg touched Peter gently, caressingly. His fingers scuttled up Peter's neck like a spider, and stroked softly below one ear. "Why don't you lead us there, hmmm?"

It was hard to concentrate. Peter trembled in confusion, caught between the vision of the riot and the touch of Oberg's hand. He was no longer sure which was real.

Something crashed against one of the windows, an early Tiffany the congregation had always held in reserve against final bankruptcy. It smashed a small piece of emerlald glass, sending splinters flying. The entire window echoed and reverberated with the blow.

"Shall we go?" Oberg said.

Miserably, Peter led them downward.

Sam was lifting the door into place when the call came. He paused in his work and cocked his head, listening. Outside, the vagrants were stirring up a fuss, but he ignored them. The call came from closer in, somewhere below.

He leaned the door carefully against the sheet music cabinet, jiggling it a bit from side to side to make sure it was steady, and went down the stairs. He paused at his supply closet to pick up the flashlight. It was a long heavy thing, encased in a black rubber sheath. He flicked it on and off, to make sure it worked.

He was unlocking the door to the dirt basement when a small white boy caromed into his legs. "Whoah, now," he said. "What's this?" He put his hands on the boy's shoulders.

"I got to see the ghost!" the child cried. Sam hoisted him into the air, let him rest in the crook of his arm. It had been a long time since he had held a child like this; not since his own son was a little boy, in fact. A long, long time.

They were not the only two to hear the call. Sheila joined them at the lady's side.

Peter had an awful feeling about the whole affair. He unhappily led Oberg and the policemen down. Twice he tried to turn them away, and each time Oberg had read the tension in his neck, his shoulders, and turned him back to the right path.

He didn't even know how he knew it was the right path, and yet he did. It was getting harder to keep track of what was and was not. His vision split fuzzily in two, and he glimpsed briefly through the eye of a nursery school child and then one of her teachers. Alternate scenes overlay one another.

It was an awful choking sensation. Peter was dizzied by shifting visions through the eyes of others—Sam, Jeremy, Sheila, even the police. Sometimes one, sometimes several at once. He felt their thoughts running through his head, briefly there and then gone. It confused him, made him foggily unsure as to which of these many people he actually was.

The only light in the coal bin came from Sam's flashlight, shining like an orange moon in her eyes, they were green, and Sam wanted to crouch down and raise her from the dirt but somehow (Sheila didn't know how she knew) it was understood that she was not to be moved. Jeremy stared down with large solemn eyes, and dug an elbow into Sam's ribs—the sexton understood, and put him down—and Sheila fretted because she had children to tend to, a door to rehang, and none of them knew what was actually going on.

A voice came from out of the darkness.

"Children, there is a new world growing," it said. "It was planted by mistake and it grows like a weed—without direction. But it can be tamed and pruned—it can be reclaimed by the proper authorities."

Now Oberg loomed out of the darkness, amusement predominant on his face. "What is growing," he said, "is a viewpoint more than anything else. It has been contaminated by your presence, by everyone here in the church that this young lady has met. Left alone, it would become a perfect reflection of your true selves. It would be a judgment on you."

He paused. Nobody spoke or moved. "There is a war on," he said. The police were pale blobs behind him, clustered loosely about Peter (he glimpsed himself multiplied through their eyes). "Our government is locked in a death struggle with the evil empires of the Earth. This young woman had the potential to win that war for us. Under our direction, the world can be . . . *turned*. It can be made safe for us forever."

He sauntered forward casually, in no particular hurry. "Please stand back," he said. "This woman is government property."

When Sam saw the man reach for Jennifer, he acted swiftly, without thought. His flashlight swung in a great arc at Oberg's face as Sheila shrieked and grabbed for Jeremy, who was knocked laughing to the floor. Oberg didn't even flinch. One of the police seized Sam and swung him about; another forced his hands behind his back and snapped handcuffs on them— Sheila saw them glint in the light cast by the flashlight that fell, forgotten, to the floor. There was a foot right by Jennifer's eyes; it loomed enormous and she ignored it.

Peter was with them, the boy from the church office. His face was slack and bewildered. "Why didn't you help?" Sam asked bitterly. "You could have done something!"

"Sam . . . " Peter said. "They wanted me to fire you, Sam." His eyes were all dazzled with tiny glittery stars. "I didn't, though, I wouldn't do it."

The government man was bending over the lady in the dirt. He lifted her up in his arms. A policeman yanked Sam backward, away from them. But he was staring at Peter, puzzlement in his face.

"What did you *do* to him?" Sam demanded. Then, angrily, "*Look* at him! What did you *do?*"

It was like a procession. First came Oberg, carrying the ghost, limp and helpless, in his arms. She stared vacantly upward.

Then came the first cop, pushing Sam, handcuffed, before him. Then the second, leading Peter by the arm, and the third, with both Sheila and the child.

That was not how Peter saw it. His vision was flashing from person to person, first through a patrolman's eyes, then out Oberg's then—simultaneously—his own and Sheila's. The shifting was growing faster, and multiple views more common so that—if he could only hold it in his mind—he was seeing a comprehensive gestalt view, each person through several sets of eyes and his own.

There was a wine bottle lying on the stairs, in the midst of a spreading stain, and Oberg casually kicked it aside. It went spinning, and bounced down two steps. Sam nearly stumbled over it, and Peter (seeing it happen in five overlapping viewpoints) snatched it up in an ungainly newborn-clumsy swoop.

Peter had no intention of doing anything with the bottle. He was just being automatically, obsessively neat. But his guard reached out and slapped it away, out of his hand, as a potential weapon. It flew downward, spraying the wine in all directions. Peter watched it slowly fall through several sets of vision, bounce and disappear behind them all.

He felt a strange sense of bereavement, and permanent loss.

Outside, the roaring of the riot was rising and falling, regular-irregular, like ocean waves or streams of cars on the freeway. "Almost to the sanctuary," Oberg commented lightly. There were people being beaten on the doorsill outside. Insanely, at least one still held a blaring radio.

—vehemently denied. Spokesmen said the nuclear strike was a preventative retrodestabilization effort. That's a direct quote. In other—

There were wet maroon stains on Peter's slacks and shirt, and a bit of wine still clung to his free hand. Absently, he raised it to his mouth, licked it off.

And the taste of it jolted him like an electric shock. It snapped his mind back together, reassembled it from scattered fragments, cut off the visions through the others' eyes. He was himself again.

And he remembered.

When he had stopped running, he found himself huddled into a cold lightless corner. The ghost was there. He could feel her breath on his face, sense a near-visual glimmering of warmth from her body.

What do you want? She asked him. He was not surprised that he could hear her even though she had not spoken, because he was still wearing his Toshiba, and his thoughts were not rational enough for any further reasoning.

But what *did* he want? It was a question he could never have answered straight. But in his hallucinogen-saturated state, he found that the answer came out easy and lucid and straightforward, as if it arose from the true center of his being, where there are no lies and evasions, no confusion and no mis-understanding, but simply what is.

"I want to understand what's going on," he said, "and I want to know what to do about it." The blackness waved around him, ran its fingers through his brain.

Her answer came—again—not in words, but in a sense of delighted amusement, of pleased recognition: So be it.

Standing there in the lightless cellar, amid dirt and broken furniture, his ears singing acid songs, head bowed slightly to avoid hitting it against the low overhead beams, he received his gift. It was an understanding so pure and complete, so detailed and comprehensive, undeniable and true, that no human mind could have contained a fraction of it without being destroyed completely.

Faced with this overload, his mind shut down to avoid handling it.

He found himself being dragged roughly through the narthex by a policeman. This was bewildering. He had only faint shadow-memories of the events since his visit to the lady in the basement, and they seemed . . . unconvincing. Nor did he retain his illumination; all that remained of it was three words, running like a mantra through his head.

"What was that?" Oberg paused before the sanctuary door. He cocked his head, trying to listen over the riot noises. "That sound . . ."

Children burst all around them, cascading up from the stairs, bubbling out into the narthex. As the startled cops drew their guns, they came whooping, crowding about them, shreeping and chirping with excitement.

"Shoot the little bastards!" Oberg commanded. The policemen all stared at him in horror and disbelief. "*Shoot* them!" he insisted, and still they disobeyed.

Peter was so preoccupied by the words running through his thoughts that he did not at first realize that his guard had released him. The children—and the parents and teachers that came running after—had separated him from the group; he realized now that he was leaning against the door to the outside.

Open the door. Open the door. Open the door. The words tumbled over and over one upon the other—*openthedoor*—urgent and overwhelming. Suppose, he thought, just suppose they meant something? Suppose you were supposed to take them literally.

He put his hand on the door. Outside, the riot was in progress. Hundreds of vent people were being forced against the door. Some were beating on it with their hands; it shivered and vibrated in sympathy.

Open the door.

Oberg had noticed him now. He was pointing at Peter and shouting some angry command that could not be heard over the children and the riot. One of the policemen turned toward him.

He opened the door, and stood to the side.

Vagrants and derelicts, vent men and shopping-bag ladies—the insane and confused, the outcast and discarded, and filthy and vile, the crazy and crippled and those haunted by religious or political visions that made no sense to anyone but themselves . . . all flooded through the doors, a great wish of stinking humanity, excited and fearful, some shouting cries of joy or triumph, many badly injured, at least one attempting to sing.

They swarmed over police, and captives, and children, teachers and Oberg and parents and all, and swept them into the sanctuary.

Oberg was slammed against the doorsill, his head crackling sharply against the wood. He slumped. The lady, falling from his arms, was snatched up by Sam, who carried her within. The flows of children and derelicts converged around the altar.

Jennifer's eyes were bright and alert, and serenely calm.

—advising all inhabitants of nuclear targets—that includes all residents of the BosWash corridor, any port cities, heavily—

The thing still hovered over the altar.

"It's *pretty!*" Sheila gasped, by Peter's ear.

It was. It glimmered slightly, where it floated, and there were hints of bright colors and far places in its light. It whirled and spun, as if to some unheard music. It seemed full of promise and possibility.

Just as Jennifer was lowered onto the altar, though, fierce light bloomed outside the windows. The unseen skies turned brilliant with nuclear fire, and the stained glass grew intensely, unbearably bright. It was the beginning of the war they had all been expecting for so long.

A horrified silence fell, and then—shocked by that awful hush—several of the children began to cry.

Jennifer gasped and convulsed—at last her time had come. She stretched out a hand over her head, and the thing above her pulsed. Three times it expanded and contracted, and then it exploded.

The explosion engulfed them all in an instant, swallowing up the church and expanding outward, ever more rapidly, still growing.

The last coherent thought Peter had before he was

transformed entirely was that perhaps Oberg was right. Perhaps it was a judgment on them all.

Rapid circles, of reality and light, raced one another around the globe.

The Dragon Line

DRIVING BY THE MALL in King of Prussia that night, I noticed that between the sky and earth where the horizon used to be is now a jagged-edged region, spangled with bright industrial lights. For a long yearning instant, before the car topped the rise and I had to switch lanes or else be shunted onto the expressway, I wished I could enter that dark zone, dissolve into its airless mystery and cold ethereal beauty. But of course that was impossible: Faerie is no more. It can be glimpsed, but no longer grasped.

At the light, Shikra shoved the mirror up under my nose, and held the cut-down fraction of a McDonald's straw while I did up a line. A winter flurry of tinkling white powder stung through my head to freeze up at the base of the skull, and the light changed, and off we went. "Burn that rubber, Boss-man," Shikra laughed. She drew up her knees, balancing the mirror before her chin, and snorted the rest for herself.

There was an opening to the left, and I switched lanes, injecting the Jaguar like a virus into the stream of traffic, looped around, and was headed back toward Germantown. A swirling white pattern of flat crystals grew in my left eye, until it filled my vision. I was only seeing out of the right now. I closed the left and rubbed it, bringing tears, but still the hallucination hovered,

135

floating within the orb of vision. I sniffed, bringing up my mouth to one side. Beside me, Shikra had her butterfly knife out and was chopping more coke.

"Hey, enough of that, okay? We've got work to do."

Shikra turned an angry face my way. Then she hit the window controls and threw the mirror, powder and all, into the wind. Three grams of purest Peruvian offered to the Goddess.

"Happy now, shithead?" Her eyes and teeth flashed, all sinister smile in mulatto skin, and for a second she was beautiful, this petite teenaged monstrosity, in the same way that a copperhead can be beautiful, or a wasp, even as it injects the poison under your skin. I felt a flash of desire and of tender, paternal love, and then we were at the Chemical Road turnoff, and I drifted the Jag through three lanes of traffic to make the turn. Shikra was laughing and excited, and I was too.

It was going to be a dangerous night.

Applied Standard Technologies stood away from the road, a compound of low, sprawling buildings afloat on oceanic lawns. The guard waved us through and I drove up to the Lab B lot. There were few cars there; one had British plates. I looked at that one for a long moment, then stepped out onto the tarmac desert. The sky was close, stained a dull red by reflected halogen lights. Suspended between vastnesses, I was touched by a cool breeze, and shivered. How fine, I thought, to be alive.

I followed Shikra in. She was dressed all in denim, jeans faded to white in little crescents at the creases of her buttocks, trade beads clicking softly in her cornrowed hair. The guards at the desk rose in alarm at the sight of her, eased back down as they saw she was mine.

Miss Lytton was waiting. She stubbed out a half-smoked cigarette, strode briskly forward. "He speaks modern English?" I asked as she handed us our visitors' badges. "You've brought him completely up to date on our history and technology?" I didn't want to have to deal with culture shock. I'd been present when my people had dug him, groggy and corpse-blue, sticky with white chrysalid fluids, from his cave almost a year ago. Since then, I'd been traveling, hoping I could somehow pull it all together without him.

"You'll be pleased." Miss Lytton was a lean, nervous woman, all tweed and elbows. She glanced curiously at Shikra, but was too disciplined to ask questions. "He was a quick study—especially keen on the sciences." She led us down a long corridor to an unmanned security station, slid a plastic card into the lock-slot.

"You showed him around Britain? The slums, the mines, the factories?"

"Yes." Anticipating me, she said, "He didn't seem at all perturbed. He asked quite intelligent questions."

I nodded, not listening. The first set of doors sighed open, and we stepped forward. Surveillance cameras telemetered our images to the front desk for reconfirmation. The doors behind us closed, and those before us began to cycle open. "Well, let's go see."

The airlock opened into the secure lab, a vast, overlit room filled with white enameled fermentation tanks, incubators, autoclaves, refrigerators, workbenches and enough glass plumbing for any four dairies. An ultrafuge whined softly. I had no clear idea what they did here. To me AST was just another blind cell in the maze of interlocking directorships that sheltered me from public view. The corporate labyrinth was my home now, a secure medium in which to change documentation, shift money and create new cover personalities on need. Perhaps other ancient survivals lurked within the catacombs, mermen and skinchangers, prodigies of all sorts, old Grendel himself; there was no way of telling.

"Wait here," I told Shikra. The lab manager's office was set halfway up the far wall, with wide glass windows overlooking the floor. Miss Lytton and I climbed the concrete and metal stairs. I opened the door.

He sat, flanked by two very expensive private security

operatives, in a chrome swivel chair, and the air itself felt warped out of shape by the force of his presence. The trim white beard and charcoal grey Savile Row pinstripe were petty distractions from a face as wide and solemn and cruel as the moon. I shut my eyes and still it floated before me, wise with corruption. There was a metallic taste on my tongue.

"Get out," I said to Miss Lytton, the guards.

"Sir, I—"

I shot her a look, and she backed away. Then the old man spoke, and once again I heard that wonderful voice of his, like a subway train rumbling underfoot. "Yes, Amy, allow us to talk in privacy, please."

When we were alone, the old man and I looked at each other for a long time, unblinking. Finally, I rocked back on my heels. "Well," I said. After all these centuries, I was at a loss for words. "Well, well, well."

He said nothing.

"Merlin," I said, putting a name to it.

"Mordred," he replied, and the silence closed around us again.

The silence could have gone on forever for all of me; I wanted to see how the old wizard would handle it. Eventually he realized this, and slowly stood, like a thunderhead rising up in the western sky. Bushy, expressive eyebrows clashed together. "Arthur dead, and you alive! Alas, who can trust this world?"

"Yeah, yeah, I've read Malory too."

Suddenly his left hand gripped my wrist and squeezed. Merlin leaned forward, and his face loomed up in my sight, ruthless grey eyes growing enormous as the pain washed up my arm. He seemed a natural force then, like the sun or wind, and I tumbled away before it.

I was on a nightswept field, leaning on my sword, surrounded by my dead. The veins in my forehead hammered. My ears ached with the confusion of noises, of dying horses and men. It had been butchery, a battle in the modern style in which both sides had fought until all were dead. This was the end of all causes: I stood empty on Salisbury Plain, too disheartened even to weep.

Then I saw Arthur mounted on a black horse. His face all horror and madness, he lowered his spear and charged. I raised my sword and ran to meet him.

He caught me below the shield and drove his spear through my body. The world tilted and I was thrown up into a sky black as well water. Choking, I fell deep between the stars where the shadows were aswim with all manner of serpents, dragons, and wild beasts. The creatures struggled forward to seize my limbs in their talons and claws. In wonder I realized I was about to die.

Then the wheel turned and set me down again. I forced myself up the spear, unmindful of pain. Two-handed, I swung my sword through the side of Arthur's helmet and felt it bite through bone into the brain beneath.

My sword fell from nerveless fingers, and Arthur dropped his spear. His horse reared and we fell apart. In that last instant our eyes met and in his wondering hurt and innocence I saw, as if staring into an obsidian mirror, the perfect image of myself.

"So," Merlin said, and released my hand. "He is truly dead, then. Even Arthur could not have survived the breaching of his skull."

I was horrified and elated: He could still wield power, even in this dim and disenchanted age. The danger he might have killed me out of hand was small price to pay for such knowledge. But I masked my feelings.

"That's just about fucking enough!" I cried. "You forget yourself, old man. I am still the Pen-dragon, *Dux Bellorum Britanniarum* and King of all Britain and Amorica and as such your liege lord!"

That got to him. These medieval types were all heavy on rightful authority. He lowered his head on those bullish shoulders and grumbled, "I had no right, perhaps. And yet how was I to know that? The histories all said Arthur might yet live. Were it so, my duty lay with him, and the restoration of Camelot." There was still a look, a humor, in his eye I did not trust, as if he found our confrontation essentially comic.

"You and your fucking Camelot! Your bloody holy and ideal court!" The memories were unexpectedly fresh, and they hurt as only betrayed love can. For I really had loved Camelot when I first came to court, an adolescent true believer in the new myth of the Round Table, of Christian chivalry and glorious quests. Arthur could have sent me after the Grail itself, I was that innocent.

But a castle is too narrow and strait a space for illusions. It holds no secrets. The queen, praised for her virtue by one and all, was a harlot. The king's best friend, a public paragon of chastity, was betraying him. And everyone knew! There was the heart and exemplar of it all. Those same poetasters who wrote sonnets to the purity of Lodegreaunce's daughter smirked and gossiped behind their hands. It was Hypocrisy Hall, ruled over by the smiling and genial Good King Cuckold. He knew all, but so long as no one dared speak it aloud, he did not care. And those few who were neither fools nor lackeys, those who spoke openly of what all knew, were exiled or killed. For telling the truth! That was Merlin's holy and Christian court of Camelot.

Down below, Shikra prowled the crooked aisles dividing the workbenches, prying open a fermenter to take a peek, rifling through desk drawers, elaborately bored. She had that kind of rough, destructive energy that demands she be doing something at all times.

The king's bastard is like his jester, powerless but immune from criticism. I trafficked with the high and low of the land, tinsmiths and river-gods alike, and I knew their minds. Arthur was hated by his own people. He kept the land in ruin with his constant wars. Taxes went to support the extravagant adventures of his knights. He was expanding his rule, croft by shire, a kingdom here, a chunk of Normandy there, questing after Merlin's dream of a Paneuropean Empire. All built on the blood of the peasantry; they were just war fodder to him.

I was all but screaming in Merlin's face. Below, Shikra drifted closer, straining to hear. "That's why I seized the throne while he was off warring in France—to give the land a taste of peace; as a novelty, if nothing else. To clear away the hypocrisy and cant, to open the windows and let a little fresh air in. The people had prayed for release. When Arthur returned, it was my banner they rallied around. And do you know what the real beauty of it was? It was over a year before he learned he'd been overthrown."

Merlin shook his head. "You are so like your father! He too was an idealist—I know you find that hard to appreciate—a man who burned for the Right. We should have acknowledged your claim to succession."

"You haven't been listening!"

"You have a complaint against us. No one denies that. But, Mordred, you must understand that we didn't know you were the king's son. Arthur was . . . not very fertile. He had slept with your mother only once. We thought she was trying to blackmail him." He sighed piously. "Had we only known, it all could have been different."

I was suddenly embarrassed for him. What he called my complaint was the old and ugly story of my birth. Fearing the proof of his adultery—Morgawse was nominally his sister, and incest had both religious and dynastic consequences—Arthur had ordered all noble babies born that feast of Beltaine brought to court, and then had them placed in an unmanned boat and set adrift. Days later, a peasant had found the boat run aground with six small corpses. Only I, with my unhuman vigor, survived. But, typical of him, Merlin missed the horror of the story—that six innocents were sacrificed to hide the nature of Arthur's crime—and saw it only as a denial of my rights of kinship. The sense of futility and resignation that is my curse descended once again. Without understanding between us, we could never make common cause.

"Forget it," I said. "Let's go get a drink."

I picked up 476 to the Schuylkill. Shikra hung over the back seat, fascinated, confused, and aroused by the near-subliminal scent of murder and magic that clung to us both. "You haven't introduced me to your young friend." Merlin turned and offered his hand. She didn't take it.

"Shikra, this is Merlin of the Order of Ambrose, enchanter and master politician." I found an opening to the right, went up on the shoulder to take advantage of it, and slammed back all the way left, leaving half a dozen citizens leaning on their horns. "I want you to be ready to kill him at an instant's notice. If I act strange—dazed or in any way unlike myself—slit his throat immediately. He's capable of seizing control of my mind, and yours too if you hesitate."

"How 'bout that," Shikra said.

Merlin scoffed genially. "What lies are you telling this child?"

"The first time I met her, I asked Shikra to cut off one of my fingers." I held up my little finger for him to see, fresh and pink, not quite grown to full size. "She knows there are strange things astir, and they don't impress her."

"Hum." Merlin stared out at the car lights whipping toward us. We were on the expressway now, concrete crashguards close enough to brush fingertips against. He tried again. "In my first life, I greatly wished to speak with an African, but I had duties that kept me from traveling. It was one of the delights of the modern world to find I could meet your people everywhere, and learn from them." Shikra made that bug-eyed face the young make when the old condescend; I saw it in the rear-view mirror.

"I don't have to ask what you've been doing while I was . . . asleep," Merlin said after a while. That wild undercurrent of humor was back in his voice. "You've been fighting the same old battles, eh?"

My mind wasn't wholly on our conversation. I was thinking

of the *bons hommes* of Languedoc, the gentle people today remembered (by those few who do remember) as the Albigensians. In the heart of the thirteenth century, they had reinvented Christianity, leading lives of poverty and chastity. They offered me hope, at a time when I had none. We told no lies, held no wealth, hurt neither man nor animal—we did not even eat cheese. We did not resist our enemies, nor obey them either, we had no leaders and we thought ourselves safe in our poverty. But Innocent III sent his dogs to level our cities, and on their ashes raised the Inquisition. My sweet, harmless comrades were tortured, mutilated, burnt alive. History is a laboratory in which we learn that nothing works, or ever can. "Yes."

"Why?" Merlin asked. And chuckled to himself when I did not answer.

The Top of Centre Square was your typical bar with a view, a narrow box of a room with mirrored walls and gold foil insets in the ceiling to illusion it larger, and flaccid jazz oozing from hidden speakers. "The stools in the center, by the window," I told the hostess, and tipped her accordingly. She cleared some businessmen out of our seats and dispatched a waitress to take our orders.

"Boodles martini, very dry, straight up with a twist," I said.

"Single malt Scotch. Warm."

"I'd like a Shirley Temple, please." Shikra smiled so sweetly that the waitress frowned, then raised one cheek from her stool and scratched. If the woman hadn't fled it might have gotten ugly.

Our drinks arrived. "Here's to progress," Merlin said, toasting the urban landscape. Silent traffic clogged the far-below streets with red and white beads of light. Over City Hall the buildings sprawled electric-bright from Queen Village up to the Northern Liberties. Tugs and barges crawled slowly upriver. Beyond, Camden crowded light upon light. Floating above the terrestrial galaxy, I felt the old urge to throw myself down. If only there were angels to bear me up.

"I had a hand in the founding of this city."

"Did you?"

"Yes, the City of Brotherly Love. Will Penn was a Quaker, see, and they believed religious toleration would lead to secular harmony. Very radical for the times. I forget how many times he was thrown in jail for such beliefs before he came into money and had the chance to put them into practice. The Society of Friends not only brought their own people in from England and Wales, but also Episcopalians, Baptists, Scotch-Irish Presbyterians, all kinds of crazy German sects—the city became a haven for the outcasts of all the other religious colonies." How had I gotten started on this? I was suddenly cold with dread. "The Friends formed the social elite. Their idea was that by example and by civil works, they could create a pacifistic society, one in which all men followed their best impulses. All their grand ideals were grounded in a pragmatic set of laws, too; they didn't rely on good will alone. And you know, for a Utopian scheme it was pretty successful. Most of them don't last a decade. But . . ." I was rambling, wandering further and further away from the point. I felt helpless. How could I make him understand how thoroughly the facts had betrayed the dream? "Shikra was born here."

"Ahhh." He smiled knowingly.

Then all the centuries of futility and failure, of striving for first a victory and then a peace I knew was not there to be found, collapsed down upon me like a massive barbiturate crash, and I felt the darkness descend to sink its claws in my shoulders. "Merlin, the world is dying."

He didn't look concerned. "Oh?"

"Listen, did my people teach you anything about cybernetics? Feedback mechanisms? Well, never mind. The Earth—" I gestured as if holding it cupped in my palm—"is like a living creature. Some say that it is a living creature, the only one, and all life, ourselves included, only component parts. Forget I said that. The important thing is that the Earth creates and maintains a delicate balance of gases, temperatures, and pressures that all life relies on for survival. If this balance were not maintained, the whole system would cycle out of control and . . . well, die. Us along with it." His eyes were unreadable, dark with fossil prejudices. I needed another drink. "I'm not explaining this very well."

"I follow you better than you think."

"Good. Now, you know about pollution? Okay, well now it seems that there's some that may not be reversible. You see what that means? A delicate little wisp of the atmosphere is being eaten away, and not replaced. Radiation intake increases. Meanwhile, atmospheric pollutants prevent reradiation of greater and greater amounts of infrared; total heat absorption goes up. The forests begin to die. Each bit of damage influences the whole, and leads to more damage. Earth is not balancing the new influences. Everything is cycling out of control, like a cancer.

"Merlin, I'm on the ropes. I've tried everything I can think of, and I've failed. The political obstacles to getting anything done are beyond belief. The world is dying, and I can't save it."

He looked at me as if I were crazy.

I drained my drink. "'Scuse me," I said. "Got to hit up the men's room."

In the john I got out the snuffbox and fed myself some sense of wonder. I heard a thrill of distant flutes as it iced my head with artificial calm, and I straightened slightly as the vultures on my shoulders stirred and then flapped away. They would be back, I knew. They always were.

I returned, furious with buzzing energy. Merlin was talking quietly to Shikra, a hand on her knee. "Let's go," I said. "This place is getting old."

We took Passayunk Avenue west, deep into the refineries, heading for no place in particular. A kid in an old Trans Am, painted flat black inside and out, rebel flag flying from the antenna, tried to pass me on the right. I floored the accelerator, held my nose ahead of his, and forced him into the exit lane. Brakes screaming, he drifted away. Asshole. We were surrounded by the great tanks and cracking towers now. To one side, I could make out six smoky flames, waste gases being burnt off in gouts a dozen feet long.

"Pull in there!" Merlin said abruptly, gripping my shoulder and pointing. "Up ahead, where the gate is."

"Getty Gas isn't going to let us wander around in their refinery farm."

"Let me take care of that." The wizard put his forefingers together, twisted his mouth and bit through his tongue; I heard his teeth snap together. He drew his fingertips apart—it seemed to take all his strength—and the air grew tense. Carefully, he folded open his hands, and then spat blood into the palms. The blood glowed of its own light, and began to bubble and boil. Shikra leaned almost into its steam, grimacing with excitement. When the blood was gone, Merlin closed his hands again and said, "It is done."

The car was suddenly very silent. The traffic about us made no noise; the wheels spun soundlessly on the pavement. The light shifted to a mélange of purples and reds, color dopplering away from the center of the spectrum. I felt a pervasive queasiness, as if we were moving at enormous speeds in an unperceived direction. My inner ear spun when I turned my head. "This is the wizard's world," Merlin said. "It is from here that we draw our power. There's our turn."

I had to lock brakes and spin the car about to keep from overshooting the gate. But the guards in their little hut, though they were looking straight at us, didn't notice. We drove by them, into a busy tangle of streets and accessways servicing the refineries and storage tanks. There was a nineteenth-century factory town hidden at the foot of the structures, brick warehouses and utility buildings ensnarled in metal, as if caught midway in a transformation from City to Machine. Pipes big enough to stand in looped over the road in sets of three or eight, nightmare vines that detoured over and around the worn brick buildings. A fat indigo moon shone through the clouds.

"Left." We passed an old meter house with gables, arched windows and brickwork ornate enough for a Balkan railroad station. Workmen were unloading reels of electric cable on the loading dock, forklifting them inside. "Right." Down a narrow granite block road we drove by a gothic-looking storage tank as large as a cathedral and buttressed by exterior struts with diamond-shaped cutouts. These were among the oldest structures in Point Breeze, left over from the early days of massive construction, when the industrialists weren't quite sure what they had hold of, but suspected it might be God. "Stop," Merlin commanded, and I pulled over by the earth-and-cinder containment dike. We got out of the car, doors slamming silently behind us. The road was gritty underfoot. The rich smell of hydrocarbons saturated the air. Nothing grew here, not so much as a weed. I nudged a dead pigeon with the toe of my shoe.

"Hey, what's this shit?" Shikra pointed at a glimmering grey line running down the middle of the road, cool as ice in its feverish surround. I looked at Merlin's face. The skin was flushed and I could see through it to a manically detailed lacework of tiny veins. When he blinked, his eyes peered madly through translucent flesh.

"It's the track of the groundstar," Merlin said. "In China, or so your paperbacks tell me, such lines are called *lung mei*, the path of the dragon."

The name he gave the track of slugsilver light reminded me that all of Merlin's order called themselves Children of the Sky. When I was a child an Ambrosian had told me that such lines interlaced all lands, and that an ancient race had raised stones and cairns on their interstices, each one dedicated to a specific star (and held to stand directly beneath that star) and positioned in perfect scale to one another, so that all of Europe formed a continent-wide map of the sky in reverse.

"Son of lies," Merlin said. "The time has come for there to be truth between us. We are not natural allies, and your cause is not mine." He gestured up at the tank to one side, the clusters of cracking towers, bright and phallic to the other. "Here is the triumph of my Collegium. Are you blind to the beauty of such artifice? This is the living and true symbol of Mankind victorious, and Nature lying helpless and broken at his feet—would you give it up? Would you have us again at the mercy of wolves and tempests, slaves to fear and that which walks the night?"

"For the love of pity, Merlin. If the Earth dies, then mankind dies too!"

"I am not afraid of death," Merlin said. "And if I do not fear mine, why should I dread that of others?" I said nothing. "But do you really think there will be no survivors? I believe the race will continue beyond the death of lands and oceans, in closed and perfect cities or on worlds built by art alone. It has taken the wit and skill of billions to create the technologies that can free us from dependence on Earth. Let us then thank the billions, nor throw away their good work."

"Very few of those billions would survive," I said miserably, knowing that this would not move him. "A very small elite, at best."

The old devil laughed. "So. We understand each other better now. I had dreams too, before you conspired to have me sealed in a cave. But our aims are not incompatible; my ascendancy does not require that the world die. I will save it, if that is what you wish." He shrugged as he said it as if promising an inconsequential, a trifle.

"And in return?"

His brows met like thunderstorms coming together; his eyes were glints of frozen lightning beneath. The man was pure theater. "Mordred, the time has come for you to serve. Arthur served me for the love of righteousness; but you are a patricide and cannot be trusted. You must be bound to me, my will your will, my desires yours, your very thoughts owned and controlled. You must become my familiar."

I closed my eyes, lowered my head. "Done."

He owned me now.

We walked the granite block roadway toward the line of cool silver. Under a triple arch of sullen crimson pipes, Merlin abruptly turned to Shikra and asked, "Are you bleeding?"

"Say what?"

"Setting an egg," I explained. She looked blank. What the hell did the kids say nowadays? "On the rag. That time of month."

She snorted. "No." And, "You afraid to say the word menstruation? Carl Jung would've had fun with you."

"Come." Merlin stepped on the dragon track, and I followed, Shikra after me. The instant my feet touched the silver path, I felt a compulsion to walk, as if the track were moving my legs beneath me. "We must stand in the heart of the groundstar to empower the binding ceremony." Far, far ahead, I could see a second line cross ours; they met not in a cross but in a circle. "There are requirements: We must approach the place of power on foot, and speaking only the truth. For this reason I ask that you and your bodyguard say as little as possible. Follow, and I will speak of the genesis of kings.

"I remember—listen carefully, for this is important—a stormy night long ago, when a son was born to Uther, then King and bearer of the dragon pennant. The mother was Igraine, wife to the Duke of Tintagel, Uther's chief rival and a man who, if the truth be told, had a better claim to the crown than Uther himself. Uther begot the child on Igraine while the duke was yet alive, then killed the duke, married the mother, and named that son Arthur. It was a clever piece of statecraft, for Arthur thus had a twofold claim to the throne, that of his true and also his nominal father. He was a good politician, Uther, and no mistake.

"Those were rough and unsteady times, and I convinced the king his son would be safest raised anonymously in a holding distant from the strife of civil war. We agreed he should be raised by Ector, a minor knight and very distant relation. Letters passed back and forth. Oaths were sworn. And on a night, the babe was wrapped in cloth of gold and taken by two lords and two ladies outside of the castle, where I waited disguised as a beggar. I accepted the child, turned and walked into the woods.

"And once out of sight of the castle, I strangled the brat."

I cried aloud in horror.

"I buried him in the loam, and that was the end of Uther's line. Some way farther in was a woodcutter's hut, and there were horses waiting there, and the wetnurse I had hired for my own child."

"What was the kid's name?" Shikra asked.

"I called him Arthur," Merlin said. "It seemed expedient. I took him to a priest who baptised him, and thence to Sir Ector, whose wife suckled him. And in time my son became king, and had a child whose name was Mordred, and in time this child killed his own father. I have told this story to no man or woman before this night. You are my grandson, Mordred, and this is the only reason I have not killed you outright."

We had arrived. One by one we entered the circle of light.

It was like stepping into a blast furnace. Enormous energies shot up through my body, and filled my lungs with cool, pain-less flame. My eyes overflowed with light: I looked down and the ground was a devious tangle of silver lines, like a printed circuit multiplied by a kaleidoscope. Shikra and the wizard stood at the other two corners of an equilateral triangle, burn-ing bright as gods. Outside our closed circle, the purples and crimsons had dissolved into a blackness so deep it stirred uneasily, as if great shapes were acrawl in it.

Merlin raised his arms. Was he to my right or left? I could not tell, for his figure shimmered, shifting sometimes into Shikra's, sometimes into my own, leaving me staring at her breasts, my eyes. He made an extraordinary noise, a groan that rose and fell in strong but unmetered cadence. It wasn't until he came to the antiphon that I realized he was chanting plainsong. It was a crude form of music—the Gregorian was codified slightly after his day—but one that brought back a rush of memories, of cer-emonies performed to the beat of wolfskin drums, and of the last night of boyhood before my mother initiated me into the adult mysteries.

He stopped. "In this ritual, we must each give up a portion

of our identities. Are you prepared for that?" He was matter-of-fact, not at all disturbed by our unnatural environment, the consummate technocrat of the occult.

"Yes," I said.

"Once the bargain is sealed, you will not be able to go against its terms. Your hands will not obey you if you try, your eyes will not see that which offends me, your ears will not hear the words of others, your body will rebel against you. Do you understand?"

"Yes." Shikra was swaying slightly in the uprushing power, humming to herself. It would be easy to lose oneself in that psychic blast of force.

"You will be more tightly bound than slave ever was. There will be no hope of freedom from your obligation, not ever. Only death will release you. Do you understand?"

"Yes."

The old man resumed his chant. I felt as if the back of my skull were melting and my brain softening and yeasting out into the filthy air. Merlin's words sounded louder now, booming within my bones. I licked my lips, and smelled the rotting flesh of his cynicism permeating my hindbrain. Sweat stung down my sides on millipede feet. He stopped.

"I will need blood," said Merlin. "Hand me your knife, child." Shikra looked my way, and I nodded. Her eyes were vague, half-mesmerized. One hand rose. The knife materialized in it. She waved it before her, fascinated by the colored trails it left behind, the way it pricked sparks from the air, crackling transient energies that rolled along the blade and leapt away to die, then held it out to Merlin.

Numbed by the strength of the man's will, I was too late realizing what he intended. Merlin stepped forward to accept the knife. Then he took her chin in hand and pushed it back, exposing her long, smooth neck.

"Hey!" I lunged forward, and the light rose up blindingly. Merlin chopped the knife high, swung it down in a flattening curve. Sparks stung through ionized air. The knife giggled and sang.

I was too late. The groundstar fought me, warping up underfoot in a narrowing cone that asymptotically fined down to a
slim line yearning infinitely outward toward its unseen patron
star. I flung out an arm and saw it foreshorten before me, my
body flattening, ribs splaying out in extended fans to either
side, stretching tautly vectored membranes made of less than
nothing. Lofted up, hesitating, I hung timeless a nanosecond
above the conflict and knew it was hopeless, that I could never
cross that unreachable center. Beyond our faint circle of
warmth and life, the outer darkness was in motion, mouths
opening in the void.

But before the knife could taste Shikra's throat, she inter-
cepted it with an outthrust hand. The blade transfixed her palm,
and she yanked down, jerking it free of Merlin's grip. Faster than
eye could follow, she had the knife in her good hand and—the
keen thrill of her smile!—stabbed low into his groin.

The wizard roared in an ecstasy of rage. I felt the skirling
agony of the knife as it pierced him. He tried to seize the girl,
but she danced back from him. Blood rose like serpents from
their wounds, twisting upward and swept away by unseen currents of power. The darkness stooped and banked, air bulging
inward, and for an instant I held all the cold formless shapes
in my mind and I screamed in terror. Merlin looked up and
stumbled backward, breaking the circle.

And all was normal.

We stood in the shadow of an oil tank, under normal evening
light, the sound of traffic on Passayunk a gentle background
surf. The groundstar had disappeared, and the dragon lines with
it. Merlin was clutching his manhood, blood oozing between his
fingers. When he straightened, he did so slowly, painfully.

Warily, Shikra eased up from her fighter's crouch. By degrees
she relaxed, then hid away her weapon. I took out my handkerchief and bound up her hand. It wasn't a serious wound;
already the flesh was closing.

For a miracle, the snuffbox was intact. I crushed a crumb on the back of a thumbnail, did it up. A muscle in my lower back was trembling. I'd been up days too long. Shikra shook her head when I offered her some, but Merlin extended a hand and I gave him the box. He took a healthy snort and shuddered.

"I wish you'd told me what you intended," I said. "We could have worked something out. Something else out."

"I am unmade," Merlin groaned. "Your hireling has destroyed me as a wizard."

It was as a politician that he was needed, but I didn't point that out. "Oh come on, a little wound like that. It's already stopped bleeding."

"No," Shikra said. "You told me that a magician's power is grounded in his mental somatype, remember? So a wound to his generative organs renders him impotent on symbolic and magical levels as well. That's why I tried to lop his balls off." She winced and stuck her injured hand under its opposite arm. "Shit, this sucker stings!"

Merlin stared. He'd caught me out in an evil he'd not thought me capable of. "You've taught this . . . chit the inner mysteries of my tradition? In the name of all that the amber rose represents, why?"

"Because she's my daughter, you dumb fuck!"

Shocked, Merlin said, "When—?"

Shikra put an arm around my waist, laid her head on my shoulder, smiled. "She's seventeen," I said. "But I only found out a year ago."

We drove unchallenged through the main gate, and headed back into town. Then I remembered there was nothing there for me anymore, cut across the median strip and headed out for the airport. Time to go somewhere. I snapped on the radio, tuned it to 'XPN and turned up the volume. Wagner's valkyries soared and swooped low over my soul, dead meat cast down for their judgment.

Merlin was just charming the pants off his great-grand-daughter. It shamed reason how he made her blush, so soon after trying to slice her open. "—make you Empress," he was saying.

"Shit, I'm not political. I'm some kind of anarchist, if anything."

"You'll outgrow that," he said. "Tell me, sweet child, this dream of your father's—do you share it?"

"Well, I ain't here for the food."

"Then we'll save your world for you." He laughed that enormously confident laugh of his that says that nothing is impossible, not if you have the skills and the cunning and the will to use them. "The three of us together."

Listening to their cheery prattle, I felt so vile and corrupt. The world is sick beyond salvation; I've seen the projections. People aren't going to give up their cars and factories, their VCRs and Styrofoam-packaged hamburgers. No one, not Merlin himself, can pull off that kind of miracle. But I said nothing. When I die and am called to account, I will not be found wanting. "Mordred did his devoir"—even Malory gave me that. I did everything but dig up Merlin, and then I did that too. Because even if the world can't be saved, we have to try. We have to try.

I floored the accelerator

For the sake of the children, we must act as if there is hope, though we know there is not. We are under an obligation to do our mortal best, and will not be freed from that obligation while we yet live. We will never be freed until that day when Heaven, like some vast and unimaginable mall, opens her legs to receive us all.

Mummer Kiss

IT WAS MUMMERS EVE morning, and a cold north wind was
blowing out of the Drift. Keith Piotrowicz eased the tanker
truck through the blockade, his nucleopore mask hanging
loosely around his neck. Jimmy Bowles dozed lightly in the
seat beside him, dark face at ease.

The guard waved his clipboard overhead. Keith nodded, fed
the engine more alcohol, shifted gears. With a low growl, the
truck surged forward. The guard, stationhouse, and red-and-
white signs marked DRIFT with radiation logos went bounce,
bounce, and were gone from the rearview mirror.

"Hey!" Keith jabbed his coworker's shoulder. "Get out that
map; tell me where we're supposed to be going."

Bowles snorted, and his eyes jerked open. He fumbled out a
map, unfolded it across two-thirds of the cab, and said: "Out
past King of Prussia. You've been that way before, right?" The
truck jolted roughly over untended highway.

"Yeah."

"Then don't wake me up again till we get there."

They back-ended the truck to the edge of a short cliff, a drop of
perhaps ten feet, and donning protective garb, climbed out.

Keith undogged the hose and pulled it loose while Bowles

took a wrench and started to mate the connectors. He stood near the lip of the cliff, feet wide, bracing himself. A century-old division of tract houses lay below, silent among small patches of snow. Gently rolling hills slowly rose to the horizon, covered with a black stubble of stunted, sometimes twisted, trees.

Bowles cursed as the cold hindered his efforts to open the master valve.

The hose was thick and filled Keith's gloved hands; together they barely circled it. There was a sharp clank as the valve unfroze under Bowles's wrench. The hose throbbed and moved. Keith staggered and quickly recovered as milky-white industrial waste spurted from the nozzle.

The liquid flew out in a long shallow arc to the frozen ground. It flowed sluggishly, covering sere brown grasses in an ever-widening puddle. Yellowish crystals formed, then were partially redissolved as new liquid overran them. They were supposed to find a new site each time out; it was usually easier to reuse the old dumps.

The land was bleak and dreary. It depressed Keith, left him feeling dull and nihilistic. He remembered stories told of how sometimes the toxic chemical wastes from one dumping would combine with those from previous dumps, and strange alchemical interactions would take place. The ground would burst into flames or weird orange worms would crawl out of the earth. There was a site he had seen in upper Bucks County where the ground actually *crawled,* boiling and bubbling year-round.

Burst into flames, he thought at the ground. But nothing happened. The last lucid drops of waste fell from the hose. He shook it, then started to reel it back up.

Back in the cab, Bowles had pulled down his cleansuit's orange hood, and slipped off his nucleopore before Keith could get the air-recycler going. Like most old-timers, he didn't wear his mask much, didn't believe that something he couldn't smell, taste, feel, or see could possibly hurt him. Bowles, taking his turn at the wheel, eased the tanker onto the highway.

"Looking forward to the parade, hey, boy?" Bowles asked.

"I guess. Hey, watch the road." The cab lurched as they ran full-tilt over a mudslide that had obliterated twenty yards of roadway. Bowles cackled.

Bowles was the only black on Quaker City Industrial Disposal's payroll. Politics had gotten him the job, and it was politics that kept it for him; he was out "sick" more often than any man Keith knew. But Bowles played for a second-rate North Philly string band, and even a black man could swing a job with *that* kind of pull. "Don't start talking like my maiden aunt," he said. "Not much traffic out here, is there?"

"Yeah, well. I'd still feel better if . . . " Bowles swung the truck through a figure-S, grazing both sides of the road, and Keith shut up. They roared past the ruins of a bank, and the wind kicked up a white spume of powder from a mound of asbestos tailings that had been dumped in its parking lot.

"There's some nice land out back, away from dump sites," Bowles said reflectively. "If I was young like you, I'd take over an old farmhouse, do a little homesteading. You don't really believe it's dangerous out here, do you, son?"

I've heard this rap before, Keith thought. That was the trouble with Philadelphia: it was all Irish and Italian. So naturally the mick dispatcher always puts the nigger and the Polack together. Gives you a chance to learn how tired you can get of one man.

"You set up a farm out here, and your privates will mutate into green fungus," he said, instantly hating himself for the words, for playing down to Bowles's level.

Bowles laughed, showing a meager scattering of eroded yellow teeth. He swerved to avoid the trunk of a mutated tree that crawled along the ground like a vine, intruding onto the highway. "Then you should join the Mummers. Good thing for an ambitious young man to do."

If he pointed out that he didn't have the pull to get into the Mummers, Bowles would sneer and lecture him that if a *black* boy could join, then a *white* boy certainly could, having natural advantages of skin tone and ancestry. Instead he said, "I don't have the money, and I'd look funny wearing feathers. Anyway, I'm not interested in politics."

Keith's father had been in the Mummers, the bottom rung anyway, more gofer than marcher, and much good it had done him. Kept him poor paying for the costumes, and all the medical benefits hadn't stopped his wife from dying of leukemia. It had probably killed him in the end, too. The old man had died of *something* funny, anyway, which Keith had always suspected he'd picked up on the job the Mummers had gotten him. The job that was all he'd had to leave to his son . . .

Bowles, swinging wide around a blind corner, turned and said, "I'm talking serious. If you—"

"Jesus, look out!"

Bowles, startled, cut the wheel hard. The front wheels hit a patch of ice, and the truck skidded out of control. Keith was slammed against the door, his nucleopore swinging wildly.

Something flashed by the windshield, a woman riding a dirt bike. She had been cutting across the road when the truck rounded the corner, and its tires lost traction. She leaned over the handlebars, coaxing the last bit of speed from her machine. "Dear God," Keith prayed as the bike slipped past the front fender, barely evading collision.

Before the motorcyclist could clear the road, the tank slewed around, catching the bike a glancing bow on its rear tire. There was a sickening loud *crunch.* Keith caught a glimpse of something flying through the air.

Bowles leaped from the truck, his door swinging loosely on its hinges behind him. Keith automatically cut the motor, pulled on his mask, and followed.

The woman's fall had been broken by a tangle of dead brush. She lay still and crumpled, looking like a bundle of discarded clothing. Some way beyond her lay the dirt bike, bent and twisted, clearly beyond repair.

"You know any first aid?" Bowles asked.

"A little," Keith said. "Jesus." He stared at a trickle of blood creeping out of the woman's nostril. It was paralyzing, this livid, glistening red. He shook off the feeling, bent to examine her.

"First we look for any obvious broken bones, um, severe bleeding—it's been a long time since I learned this stuff." She was a lean, muscular woman, somewhere in her late thirties or early forties. Slavic cheekbones, a fierce set to her face, even unconscious. A heavy kaftanlike robe had fallen partially open, revealing khaki fatigues, the light green kind that the Northern Liberation Front had worn two decades ago. Her nucleopore was knocked half off her face. He checked to see that she was still breathing, reset it. "Well, *I* don't see anything."

"What's next?"

"Um, we treat her for shock. Cushion the head, raise the feet." He started to take off his jacket to form a pillow, stopped. "This is no good. We've go to get her into town."

They carried her to the cab, awkwardly distributing her weight across their laps. Keith took the wheel, carefully started the truck rolling.

"What's this tangled around her neck?" Bowles asked. He unstrapped a leather case, looked inside. "Binoculars." He set them carefully on the dashboard, began going through her pockets. "Passport here, stamped in Philadelphia. Occupation: Scholar." He paused. "Didn't know you could make a living at that. Special Drift clearance to visit Souderton."

"Souderton's nowhere near here," Keith said. "It's hardly in the Drift at all."

"Do tell." Bowles replaced the document, continued rummaging. "Hello. She's got *two* of them." He pulled a second passport from an inner pocket.

"Hey, maybe you shouldn't be going through her things like that," Keith said uneasily. Bowles ignored him.

"Says Suzette Fletcher on both of them. Same name, same height. Age: Forty-two. That's the same. Occupation: Reporter. Now isn't that funny? She's a reporter for the *Boston Globe*, up north. And it's not stamped in Philadelphia at all."

"Hey, really, man. I'd feel a lot better if you didn't do that."

"Yeah, okay, okay." Bowles replaced the passport, smoothed the kaftan shut again. He studied the woman's face, nested in a mass of dirty blond hair in Keith's lap. "This is one damn handsome woman," he said. "How's it feel, having that face in your crotch?"

Keith slowed to negotiate a tricky patch of road, where a careless dumping had let a frozen chemical slick form on the concrete. "Aw, come on," he mumbled, involuntary embarrassed. "She's old enough to be my mother."

"Looks like she's still got bright eyes, though," Bowles said cheerily. "Bet she's got a bushy tail, too. A young man like you could *learn* something from an older woman."

The woman stirred and groaned as the truck crossed Two Street. The sun was a red smear against the horizon, weakly echoed in the rearview mirror's grimy streaks. Scattered sweepers cleaning the streets for tomorrow's parade brushed the ancient asphalt free of any lingering hot particles blown in from the Drift. They were the hard-core unemployed, unable to pay the Mummers Gift in cash, with only their services to offer. They had been working all day and would go on working until the job was done. Then they would be given a hot meal, with maybe a cup of alky-laced hot cider, and the stupid asses would be grateful.

The woman opened her eyes, painfully drew herself into a sitting position. "Philadelphia," Bowles said. "My name's Jimmy Bowles, and my partner's Keith Piotrowicz."

She bent forward, gingerly touched her forehead. "God, that smarts." She snuffled slightly, accepted a handkerchief from Bowles, held it to her nose.

"Jimmy's the first man ever to create a traffic accident in the Drift," Keith said with a touch of malice. Bowles glared at him wordlessly.

The woman straightened a bit. A corner of her faded blond

hair caught the sun, glinted red. "Oh, yes, it all comes back to me now." She forced a grin. "S.J. Fletcher. Everybody calls me Fletch."

"Pleased to meet you, Fletch," Keith said. Almost simultaneously, Bowles asked, "What were you doing out in the Drift?"

Fletch watched the tall buildings of Philadelphia glide by. In an abstracted tone, she said, "Some private genealogy. I was researching the records in Souderton—they're almost untouched, you know—and I found my grandmother's marriage license. It said she was born in King of Prussia, so . . . " She shrugged. "I was hoping for the family Bible, but it looks like a lost cause. Hey, you guys *did* pick up my stuff, didn't you?"

"On the ledge," Bowles said. The truck had slowed to a crawl as Keith eased it through the narrow riverfront streets. It was a tight turn into the company parking lot, and he nearly scraped two buildings negotiating it.

"Not that!" Fletch snapped. "My goddamn saddlebags. They've got all my . . . supplies and stuff. All my money."

All but a handful of drivers had come in ahead of Keith and his partner. The lot was choked, all the good slots gone. He eased the truck into Slot 97. "Must be with the bike," Bowles said. "We didn't go look at it."

She slammed a fist into her thigh. "Damn damn damn," she muttered to herself. Then, abruptly authoritative, "You'll just have to take me back there to get them."

"Hey now," Bowles objected.

"Look around you," Keith said. The trucks stretched in long even rows, their biohazard logos dull in the failing sunset. "The Company isn't going to let us take this thing out into the Drift again tonight." He cut the engine, yanked the key.

Bowles hopped out of the cab. "Keith, you come out back and read the meters for me," he said. "Then I'll go log us in, and you two can hash this thing out between yourselves."

"Okay." Keith pulled his door open, inhaled deeply, savoring the clean city air. He strolled around to the back of the truck, wondering what Bowles wanted to say. There were no meters, of course; either the truck was empty or it was full. He opened his jacket, letting in a hit of cold air.

"Listen," Bowles hissed fiercely. "You can do what you want with that woman; tell her anything you like. But you will keep you mouth *shut* about me looking at her papers. You got that? This is Mummer business, boy, and you'd best keep that in mind." He waited for Keith's nod, then began the long walk to the dispatcher's shed.

Keith shrugged to himself, returned to the cab. If Bowles wanted to play secret agent, that was nothing to him.

"I've been thinking," he said to Fletch. "We can take you out the day after tomorrow, if you're willing to spend the day in the truck. The dispatcher won't like it, but Jimmy can work it for you. He's got influence."

"Why not tomorrow?"

"It's the first of January," Keith explained. "Mummers Day. Everything will be closed down."

"And just what the hell am I supposed to do with myself between then and now? Sleep in the gutter?"

"I'll put you up," Keith said unhappily. "I've got a spare couch." He wasn't sure he liked this woman, and he had a sick feeling he was going to regret the offer. But for the life of him he couldn't see any alternative.

When Bowles returned, Keith briefed him on the situation. The old man slapped Keith's back. "Behave yourselves," he said with a smirk.

Keith led Fletch into his fourth-floor walk-up, and hung his nucleopore on a hook by the door. "You can take the bed," he said. "I'll sleep on the couch, I guess."

She wrinkled her nose. "This place is a dump. Don't you ever clean up in here?"

"Well . . . " Keith lifted a clutter of dirty clothes from the floor, dumped them into an already crowded closet. Fletch wandered over to the only window that wasn't boarded over for the winter, jerked the shutters open.

"Nice view of the harbor if you squint between the buildings on the left," she said wryly. Keith fed a miserly few lumps of coal into the stove, starting a fire with twists of papers from last week's *Inquirer.*

Fletch unslung her binoculars, peered through them. "It's too dark to make out," she muttered. "But I could swear that some of those ships are coal burners. Even—Good Lord! That looks like a converted oil tanker."

"Oh, yeah, we get all kinds." He blew gently on the fire, anticipating its warmth. Another few minutes and he'd be able to shed his coat.

"But those things are *old!* Single-hull construction, with the bottom rusting out and the rivets popping loose. How can you people allow that garbage in your harbor?"

"What harm could it do?" Keith asked. "Any spill would just wash downriver and out to sea. Living this close to the Drift, you learn to appreciate what you've got."

The dinner plates were piled in the sink, waiting for the night-time water rates, when there was a knock at the door. Fletch, wearing one of Keith's old sweaters over her fatigues, answered it.

A dozen or so tenants stood in the hallway. "Mummers Gift, Mummers Gift," they chanted. A single Mummer, still in street clothes, stood to the fore, holding a muslin sack in one hand.

"Mummers Gift," Keith mumbled to Fletch by way of explanation. He scooped two rolls of silver dollars from a dresser drawer and gave them to the Mummer. The man broke them open, poured them into the sack. Keith ruefully watched his year's savings disappear, and smiled dutifully.

As was customary, the Mummer had started drinking early. He was a small man, with a slightly bloated face, and the flush of alcohol accentuated the broken veins in his nose. "Paid in full," he announced. "Let the revels continue!"

The tenants cheered and poured into the room. Like the

drinking, the floating party was an ancient and hallowed custom. Somebody shoveled coal into the stove, and somebody else waved a jug of grain alcohol in the air. Keith hastened to dig out his last gallon of cider for mixer.

Jerry from the third floor grabbed Keith's sleeve and demanded an introduction to Fletch. Keith apologized, and complied. When they heard that she had come out of the Drift, several of his more superstitious friends made the sign of the horns to ward off mutation.

"No, she didn't!"

"Really?"

"Come off it—she'd be dead."

Fletch smiled politely. "You only have to worry about radiation exposure if you're right on top of the Meltdown site. For most of the Drift, the only thing to contend with is particulate matter. As long as you don't eat, drink, or breathe, you're safe."

They laughed, but there was an uneasy edge to their laughter. The rich kid from the ground floor—her father had money, and reputedly she only worked three days a week—tried to change the subject. "Keith said that you're a scholar, Ms. Fletcher," she said.

"Yes, I was mining the records in Souderton and—"

"Next tenant!" the Mummer bellowed. "Time to move the party on, we can't hang around here all night!" He bullied the party out into the hallway. They went willingly, even anxiously. Contrary to custom, Keith and Fletch were not invited along.

"Was it something I said?" Fletch wondered.

"Yes," Keith said. And tried to explain.

Souderton was the last city within the Drift to die. Its contamination levels were low, and the city had strong and determined leaders. For almost twenty years after the Meltdown, Souderton had thrived after a fashion. But after two decades of water and foodstuff laced with radioactive isotopes, the cancers and birth defects and leukemia's became too widespread, too common to be ignored.

By popular account, the panic started at a mass town assembly to discuss the problems. An alternative version was that an old woman suffering a heart attack triggered the hysteria. However it began, it turned into a wholesale evacuation of the city, a mob of thousands that fled like lemmings toward Philadelphia.

They were met at the city limits by a horde of self-appointed vigilantes, men who were afraid of mutation, of radiation poisoning, of anything that came out of the Drift.

Masked and hooded men with filters and rebreathers went into Souderton the next day with rifles and mopped things up.

"See, I go out there almost every day so it doesn't bother *me*, I tend to forget how everybody feels about the Drift, though," Keith said. "And I guess there's kind of inherited fear of Souderton itself, of what might have happened if the refugees had gotten through."

"More likely it's inherited guilt." Fletch sat down on the edge of the bed, unlaced her boots, let them drop. "Time for me to hit the sack." She pulled off the sweater.

Her breasts bounced once beneath her shirt. They sagged slightly, not much for a woman her age. Keith found himself trying to picture them in his mind. The room was uncomfortable warm, even stuffy. The single drink he had had made him almost dizzy.

"Uh, listen," he said. "The bed's big enough for two."

Fletch smiled scornfully. "Back off, sonny," she said. "You can sleep on the couch for one night without rupturing anything."

At dawn they were awakened by the sound of children running gleefully through the streets, beating on pots and pans with sticks, and shrieking with all the power in their young lungs. Keith trudged down the hall to the bathroom and returned to find Fletch up and dressed. "How you doing this morning?" he forced himself to say.

"Oh, a little stiff and creaky around the joints, but not bad for a woman who's just been run over by a truck."

After breakfast they lingered for a few hours over cups of mixed chicory and coffee—the only luxury Keith allowed himself—before going to watch the parade. Fletch made no reference to previous night, and Keith found himself almost liking her again. They were out on Two Street by late morning, in time to see the last several Comic bands.

Fletch watched with fierce interest as men in feathers, in sequins, dressed as clowns, as Indians, as playing cards, strutted by in organized disarray. A female impersonator tagging after one brigade waggled enormous mock-breasts at her, turned around, and flipped up frilly petticoats to reveal grossly overstuffed under-things. She threw back her head and laughed.

"Do women participate in this?" she asked. "All I've seen are men."

"They used to. They were banned a long time ago, just after the Meltdown."

The brass band for the Comic troupe, resplendent in feathers, mirrors, and cheap glitter, was playing "The Bummers Reel." Behind them a ragtag batch of clowns pulled a wagon float labeled CHRISTMAS WITH TRUESDUEL. Atop it stood a skinny man in baggy Santa Claus suit, who handed wrapped presents to blindfolded policemen. "What does that mean?" Fletch asked.

"There's a city councilman named Scott Truesdale, and there was an incident last May . . . um, it's kind of hard to explain if you're not familiar with local politics."

"I get the general picture," Fletch said. "I imagine your Mr. Truesdale won't be too amused by this, however."

"No." It was the end of Truesdale's career, in fact, but Keith didn't bother saying that.

The Comics, with their brass bands, floats, and slapstick anarchy, continued to strut by. At one point Keith bought two soft pretzels from a vendor and introduced Fletch to that old Philadelphia tradition. They were barely warm and cost three cents for the two, a price the vendor could never have gotten away with any other day.

The groups ranged from the bright and gaudy to the bright and gaudy and inventive. Some, obviously, took themselves more seriously than others. By the same token, these were not always more fun to watch.

"Who's next?" Keith asked. The last Comic band was strutting away, strewing confusion and firecrackers in its midst.

Through her glasses, Fletch studied the banner that led off the group. "Looks like . . . Center City Club. Would that be right?"

"Yeah. That's the first of the Fancies. After them come the String Bands."

"How did all this begin?" Fletch asked. "How did it get organized? What's it all for?"

Keith started to answer, stopped, tried again: "Uh. I don't think anybody can answer those questions. My old man used to talk a lot about the history of the Mummers. You can trace them back for centuries, back to Colonial times when they were just random gangs of men wandering around on the First, shooting off guns and raising hell. But you can't say when they became *Mummers.* They just kind of evolved."

"I see."

The fancy club was less than a block away. A hundred-fifty strong, they strutted in neatly ordered rows, their ostrich-plume headdresses bobbing, the feathered, mirrored, and bedangled "capes"—more like false wings than capes, for they towered above the marchers and out to the sides—dipping to the odd cadence of the Mummers' strut.

"Who are they?" Fletch asked, indicating a number of darkly dressed, furtive figures slipping quickly through the crowd, roughly parallel to the band.

"Don't look!" he hissed. "You're supposed to pretend you don't see them."

"But who *are* they?"

"Men in Black. They're the spotters. They locate certain people and point them out to the King Clown for a tapping-out or . . . or whatever," he finished lamely. At her questioning glance, he added, "The King Clown is their captain, the one marching in front. King Clown used to be a type of costume, but now there's just the one."

Except for the traditional face paint, King Clown's costume was nothing like a real clown's. His cape was a full twelve feet high, and he glittered with sequins and mirrors and even a bit of diffraction grating, which must have come from somebody's grandmother's trunk. Two guy lines led from the the tips of the cape to his hands, so he could manage the ungainly costume in the light breezes that sometimes blew up. He strutted with great dignity, occasionally bowing slightly to each side in acknowledgment of the cheers that sprang up.

Keith indicated the Men in Black with a sideways nod of his head. "Look. They've marked somebody."

Four Men in Black had slipped up on an unsuspecting watcher, quietly jostling people aside to take up positions immediately behind him.

The Center City troupe Mummer-stepped briskly down Two Street, banjos, glockenspiels, and horns not playing but at ready, and for an instant, looked as if they would pass the man by. Then King Clown raised a gloved hand, and they stopped, wheeling ninety degrees as one man. The Clown strutted around the troupe and into the crowd. They nervously backed away from him.

The Mummer chief strode up to the marked man. The victim flinched away, found himself held firm by the Men in Black. He blanched. King Clown stretched out his arms, took the man by the shoulders.

One arm rose once, twice, again. It fell on the man's shoulders with an audible crack three times. Then King Clown whirled, returning to his troupe. The crowd cheered, and the band broke into "Oh, Dem Golden Slippers," turned, and marched on. The man from the crowd joined a motley band of followers in mufti, strutting happily after the troupe.

"What the hell was *that* all about?" Fletch asked.

"It was a tapping-out. The man was a candidate, and the

Mummers have accepted him. He's one of the lucky ones."

"I wouldn't mind knowing more about all this. Do you think I could get an interview with the captain?"

"Don't do it," Keith said tensely. "Don't have anything at all to do with the Mummers. Just smile and watch the parade."

"Why?"

"Forget I said anything." Keith stared down the street, ignoring her as best he could. The Fancy troupe approached, all glitter and flash, advancing, pausing, and advancing again in their odd half dance, half march. It *was* odd, Keith realized, and strange that it took an out-of-towners' questions to make him aware of such a simple fact.

King Clown's troupe was parallel to them, marching past, when the signal came again. They wheeled to face the crowd. King Clown strutted into the crowd, directly at Keith and Fletch. Sweet Jesus, Keith prayed silently. Let it be somebody else.

People backed away and King Clown stood before Fletch, placed his hands on her shoulders. He waited a beat. Then he leaned down and kissed her gently on both cheeks. She smiled brightly at him and dipped a curtsey. He turned as if to move away.

Then he whirled again, and before Keith could react, the gloved hands were on his shoulders, and he was staring into the man's bloodshot eyes. Keith tried to jerk away, but several pairs of hands held him firm. He could see the weave of the clown's costume, could smell the alcohol on his breath.

Slowly, very slowly, King Clown bent over and kissed his cheeks.

In an instant the restraining hands, Men in Black, King Clown, and all were gone. The band was Mummer-strutting away, playing "Death March of a Marionette."

Fletch's eyes sparkled and she started to say something bright. Keith grabbed her hand, yanked her into a crowd that shrank away from them. Fletch hung back laughingly, and he gave her arm a ferocious tug.

"Come *on!*"
"What's the matter?"
"Shut up and run!"

Away from Two Street the city was virtually empty. By law all citizens had to watch at least the middle third of the parade. This worked to their advantage—there was no one about to report the direction of their flight—but it also made them visible a long way off, if anyone was already on their trail. Rounding a corner, Keith came face to face with a large distraught black man. For an instant he thought he was dead, and then the man had turned and fled, another victim like themselves.

"Why are we running?" Fletch gasped.

"Because they're trying to kill us." He would answer no more of her questions. He needed all his attention to escape.

As a boy he had played Mummer Hunt, both as victim and assassin, with an intensity rivaled only by the real thing. So he fled from the waterfront because he knew that was the first place the hunters would search. He passed by fire escapes and basement windows that looked like they could be forced for much the same reason. North and west he headed, toward the Mummer Hall, which used to be the art museum.

Only when they'd reached their goal did he realize he'd had a goal in mind at all. It was a pre-Meltdown parking garage, its four levels gaping open to the winds. Panting, he arrived at the stairwell. It was dark and too grittily rubbled to take footprints. Once inside they could ascend slowly, try to regain their breaths. As they climbed, Keith explained as best he could.

After the burnings and panic murders of the Meltdown evacuations, Philadelphia's city government collapsed. There was no help to be had from the state, which had just lost its capital, or from the Feds, who were busy with several million refugees. The self-destruction of New York City in a conflagration of riots triggered a worldwide depression almost as a matter of course.

The only organized power remaining in the city was the

Mummers. Clowns and buffoons, they existed only because they *wanted* to. Descent men, they marched and collected money to keep the last hospitals going. When there were no police, they organized volunteers to patrol the neighborhoods. It wasn't long before they controlled the city, and not long after that before they realized that fact.

The Kiss began as a way of flensing mutants and carriers of genetic disease from the population. It was extended to include those who refused vaccination, when the epidemics began. Finally its potential as a political tool was realized, and no reasons were given.

The rooftop was cold and windy. Bent over, Keith scuttled to the tool shed standing in its center and beckoned for Fletch to follow.

"Push on the upper-right corner of the doorway there." He grabbed the opposite corner and tugged as she did so. After a heartbreaking instant's hesitation, the door lurched in its frame and tilted askew. There was a gap wide enough to crawl inside.

Keith led the way and, when Fletch crawled after, slammed the door shut with the heel of his palm. "I found a keg of ten-penny nails here when I was a kid," he said. "Rusty, but I sold them for scrap. So probably nobody else has figured out how to get in."

"Very clever," Fletch said. "Now that we're trapped in here, what do we do next?"

"Look. I think I've done pretty good so far," Keith said angrily. "At least I've bought some time to think." He paced the shed—it wasn't large, maybe eight by ten feet—his footing unsure on the rotting burlap sacks that littered the floor. "Why don't *you* come up with something? *You're* the one who got me into this mess, miss hotshot reporter."

"So you know about that," she said.

"Bowles looked through your pockets. Jesus Christ!—what kind of monster story were you working on to get the Mummers so upset?" It was cold inside the workshed. Dim light seeped through vacant nail holes in the roof. He could see Fletch watching him steadily, a vague grey figure.

"Could we sneak aboard one of the ships going to Boston?" she asked.

"'Could we sneak aboard one of the ships going to Boston?'" he mimicked her bitterly. "No, we could not. There'll be Mummer agents at every—I can't *believe* how you've messed up my life! You know, I was doing okay until you came along."

"Keith," Fletch said quietly.

"At least I didn't have half of Philadelphia trying to gun me down!"

"Keith."

He stopped, looked at her. "Yeah?"

"Stop ranting, and tell me how we're going to get out of here alive."

He angrily thrust his hands in his pockets. There was a slight jangle of metal objects, a few copper coins, a salvageable nail or two—and his key ring.

"Goddamn," he whispered. He drew out the ring, triumphantly separated out the key to his tanker truck. "Hey, I may not be dead after all."

"Let me see." Fletch snapped her fingers and extended her hand. He could tell by her expression that she had already deduced his plan.

Keith shoved the keys back in his pocket. "Forget it. I don't trust you, and I can't think of a single reason to take you along. You've been deadweight so far, and I might be better off without you entirely."

There was a brief silence. "I see." Something rustled in the gloom.

"You want your quid pro quo." With a faint slumping sound, Fletch's kaftan fell to the floor.

"I don't—what do you mean?"

Fletch advanced a step, her eyes steady, her voice preternaturally calm. "You can take what you want, can't you? I can't exactly yell for help."

"Hey, I—"

"It's understandable. You're a man, and you've got me alone. Happens all the time."

She was quite close now. Keith flinched back. "You're twisting what I said."

Her expression was scornful. "But you *are* a man, aren't you? I mean . . . you can still perform?"

Outraged, Keith seized her arms. Cloth bunched up under his head in embarrassment. "Hey, I'm sorry," he said, "I really didn't mean to—"

"Oh, come here." She pulled him back to her.

Their lovemaking was almost tender. Fletch spread out her kaftan to protect them from the icy-cold burlap sacks, and they undressed kneeling atop it. Some of what they did was new to Keith, but he assumed from her lack of criticism, indeed her passionate response, that she could not tell.

When it was over, Fletch tugged and jerked the robe about the two of them like a thick, heavy blanket. It was warm within the robe, and tangled within it, Keith felt oddly secure and sure of himself. He felt a sudden childish urge to shout or yodel or laugh with glee.

"I would've taken you along anyway," he said, not knowing whether it was true or not. "You really didn't have to . . . you know."

Fletch laid a finger on his lips. "It's better this way. Now we can operate as a team."

It was perhaps three in the morning before they made their move. They slipped through the streets cautiously, every sense bristling, avoiding the policed sections. It took an effort to walk slowly, to keep from hunching shoulders and scuttling from shadow to shadow.

Keith was drenched with sweat by the time they made it to the Company's parking lot. Row upon row of trucks stretched into the darkness; all was still. He paced off the way to Slot 97.

Laying a hand on the cold door handle, he grinned and

whispered, "I'm beginning to think this might work." He yanked the door open.

"Stupid," Jimmy Bowles said. "Very stupid, brother man."

Keith jerked back reflexively, froze. Bowles was sitting in the cab, a gun in one hand. It was pointed straight at Keith.

"You've really blown it," Bowles marveled. A corked bottle, half full of some dark fluid, lay in Bowles's lap. Its label was nearly rubbed away from endless handlings and refillings.

Behind Keith, Fletch shifted her weight ever so subtly. The gun flicked in her direction.

"Don't you move, bitch!" The veins in Bowles's forehead stood out angrily. He passed his free hand over his brow, wiping away sweat. Keith realized that the man was deeply, dangerously drunk.

Bowles's eyes glared at Keith for an instant, then dropped. His face underwent a strange alteration of expression, becoming almost maudlin. "Listen, buddy, I didn't know they would bang on you. I just passed the word about your lady friend's papers up the line, the way I was supposed to." He groped absently for the bottle, uncorked it one-handed. "And then a few hours later they called me up to the Hall—in a *car,* man, can you believe that?—to say it all over again to the big cats. And they decided to bang the both of you." He took a long swig from the bottle, holding his head sideways and watching them from the corners of his eyes. "I did my best, man. Told them you didn't know from nothin', but the word was to bang you both."

As he talked, Bowles had let the gun sink slowly to rest on his knees. His eyes were unfocused, half lost in introspection. Keith mentally took a deep breath. It's now or never, he thought. He dove for the gun.

There was time enough to take in an incredible amount of detail. The clumsy way his body moved, not at all smoothly, not at all responsive to his will, so that he more fell than leaped upon Bowles. The way Bowles's hand jerked up involuntarily, the gun's muzzle wobbling in a jagged S through the air. The way his hands connected with Bowles's wrist, pushing past cold steel, gripping aged sinew. Contact made, the hand flew up and to the side, and with a shattering roar, the gun went off.

Keith found himself stomach down on the seat, gun clutched maniacally in both hands. He choked it by the barrel, by the back of the stock. There was a fierce ringing in his ears. His palms tingled.

Jimmy Bowles stared stupidly at a hole in the cab's roof. "Aw, man, you didn't have to do that," he mumbled.

Fletch touched Keith's shoulder, put a hand beneath the gun. He straightened his fingers slowly, letting the gun drop. She snapped it up, held it trained on Bowles.

Bowles ignored it. "Didn't think I could go through with it," he said, almost to himself. Then, "Take the truck, man."

He opened the door, unsteadily climbed out. With a glance at Fletch, Keith straightened, slid behind the wheel, put the key in the ignition.

As they eased out of the lot, Bowles was standing alone in Slot 97, crying drunkenly.

They crashed the barrier at top speed, almost 70 kph, leaving splinters of wood flying behind them. The Mummer agents, caught unprepared, fired after them. Three bullets went through the body of the tanker, making hollow gonging noises. Fortunately the tank was empty, and its last cargo apparently not flammable. Something ricocheted about the underside of the truck, as the guards tried to shoot out the tires. Keith kept going.

Just beyond the barrier some joker had put up a sign reading: RADIOACTIVE CONTAMINATION. DRIVE FAST. He proceeded to do just that.

"I don't like the idea of going through the Drift," he said.

"You can think of a better way to lose them? Take an old combat reporter's advice, son. Move fast and don't look back.

Hey, isn't this where you hit me?"

"No, it's a few miles on." The truck crested a hill, and he pointed off to their left. "See that blue glow just below the horizon?"

"Yeah." It was a light eerie smear in the distant black land. No trees obscured in, and it had curious liquid quality.

"Cherenkov radiation. When the Meltdown happened, there were five trucks loaded with fuel rods they tried to get out. The state police turned them back somewhere around here, so they drove them into the swamps. It makes a good landmark. Your bike's somewhere beyond there."

"Well, keep a sharp eye out for the spot. I want my saddle-bags back."

Keith discovered the hole in the fuel tank when they stopped for the bags. A dribble of alcohol was leaking out, one slow, steady drop at a time. The bullet along the underside of the truck had apparently sent a sliver of something through the tank and, in the process, damaged the fuel gauge. Neither Keith nor Fletch could think of any way to fix it. "We should head east," Keith suggested. "Get as far out of the Drift as we can before it dies."

"Will the Mummers follow us into the Drift?"

"Yes."

"Then New Jersey's not good enough. We go north."

The engine breathed its last at dawn. Following Fletch's directions, he let the truck glide to a halt just off the road in a stand of stunted pines.

Because of the bullet hole in the cab's roof, they were both wearing their masks already. Fletch hopped out, slid her rifle from its sheath in the saddlebags, and snapped, "Let's get moving. You take the bags and I'll lead. Don't step in any patches of snow. We can't afford to leave a trail."

Keith shouldered the saddlebags and followed her down the road the way they had come for perhaps a quarter of a kilometer, and then up a slope on the opposite side from the abandoned truck. In places the ground crunched beneath his feet, and climbing the slope was hard work.

"Hey, we've been running a long time," Keith grumbled.

"We'll rest at the top of the hill. Right now we're exposed."

The sun had risen slightly, and shone weakly through the clouds by the time they could rest. The sky was white and grey, almost colorless. The endless hills beneath were not much better. They huddled behind a tangle of thorny bushes, near to a cluster of spruce trees whose needles had a distinctly brownish tinge. A half hour passed.

"Here they come," Fletch said. "Following our trail." She peered through her binoculars, careful to keep them in shadow.

With a low growl, three four-wheel-drive vehicles swung into view. They sped down the roadway in formation, coming to a halt by the abandoned tanker. Six dark figures climbed out, swarmed over the site. They moved quickly, alertly, keeping each other covered at all times. After ten minutes, they returned to their vehicles and moved on down the road, at a much slower pace.

Fletch stood. "They go that way and we go this way," she said with satisfaction. "Let's go, kid. Miles to go before we sleep, you know."

They were trudging up an endless country road, detouring around the scattered patches of snow. The sun was failing. Keith stepped on a cancerous-looking growth, bent achingly to scoop it up and throw it into the lifeless woods at the side. " . . . snow," Fletch said. Her voice was muffled by the nucleopore, and Keith couldn't make out her words.

"What did you say?" he asked, annoyed.

"I *said* it's like snow!" Then, seeing his difficulty, she fell back a step. "The steam explosions were like a geyser. They sent particulate matter up where the winds could catch it, and it filtered down like snow. Even then, it still got blown about,

so you'll have bare spots and hot spots throughout the Drift.
The concentrations are still too small to see, but you can gauge
them by their effects."

She stopped near an old stone farmhouse nestled within
almost healthy-looking stand of trees, and did a quick scan of
their limited horizons through her binoculars. Save for a collapsed front porch, the house was virtually intact. "Not bad,"
she said. "We'll stay here tonight."

They forced the lock on the kitchen door, and chocked it
shut with an old dresser. The interior was untouched from the
time of the evacuations. Cigars moldered in a humidor atop the
refrigerator. A child's drawing taped to a cupboard crumbled
on being touched.

There was a wood stove in the living room. They broke up
furniture for firewood and heated tins of beef from Fletch's saddlebags. They had to lift their nucleopores for each bite, replac-
ing them immediately after.

When they were done, Fletch scooped up the empty meat
tins and took them outside. She paused on the stoop, cocked
her head. "Listen," she said.

Keith joined her, strained his ears. After a moment he
caught it—a long, almost musical howl. A pause, and there
was another, equally faint howl in reply. "Some kind of mutated dogs," Keith said. "I've seen them. Big shaggy animals, like
wolves."

"Actually, they're a hybrid," Fletch said. "A perfectly natural
cross between a dog and a wolf. They migrated down from
Maine a few years back, and now they're expanding through
the Drift." She paused. "Good luck to them, say I."

Keith stared into the darkness, but trees blocked his vision,
and there was no chance of his seeing the animal. "Hybrid,
mutant, what's the difference?" he asked.

Fletch gawked at him. "They really do keep you poor sods
ignorant, don't they?" she marveled. She threw the tins away
from the house. They fell with a clatter. "The only mutations you
have to worry about coming out of the Drift are the new diseases

that pop up every year." She stood still, listening. "No animals. Usually there'll be rats at least, in the safe spots." She shrugged. "Oh, well, I still say we're okay. Beddy-bye time for me."

She led the way into the house, leaving him to slide the dresser back against the door. When Keith got to the living room, she had dropped her robe and was shedding her shirt. Her breasts were freckled, and they swayed gracefully as she moved. Keith watched them, fascinated, wondered did he really want to make love to this woman again? The passion of the previous night had a strong hold on him, and yet it was tinged with distaste, as if it had been something shameful and unclean.

Fletch caught his glance, looked amused. "Not tonight, boyo. You'll be stiff enough in the morning as it is."

Keith awoke feeling crippled. Fletch had him out on the road before he was awake enough to protest. They passed bleak hours on tedious roads that Fletch puzzled out from a pre-Meltdown Geodesic Survey map.

Once they had to flee the road and hide when a distant growl warned them of an approaching four-wheeler. They watched it go past, two of the Mummer assassins in its seat. Still later they were attacked by a feral cat, a small orange-and-white animal whose ancestors had been domestic pets. It ran at them yowling when they had paused for lunch, and Fletch had to club it to death with the stock of her rifle.

She turned over the small carcass with her boot. "See right there?" she asked. "That big sore on its side? It must've made its lair in a hot spot. It came down with radiation sickness, and the pain made it crazy enough to attack us."

"Fletch," Keith said wearily, "when are we going to be *out* of this hellish place? I don't know how much more of this I can take."

She gathered him into her arms, gave him a hug. "There, there. I've got friends not far from here. There's a small community of Drifters I know of. They're all outcasts and vagabonds,

but reliable in their own way. When we get there we can rest—
maybe tonight, if we're lucky."

Two days passed. A noontime sun was shining when they
reached the mouth of a small shallow valley. A handful of nineteenth-century buildings were clustered below, two or three from
the mid-twentieth anomalously mingled in. "There it is," Fletch
said. She began loading needlelike projectiles into her rifle.

"What's its name?"

"Nameless."

Keith couldn't tell from her answer whether the community
was called Nameless or simply lacked a name. But he was
weary and short-tempered from three days of forced marches
and sexless nights, and he was damned if he was going to ask.
"Not much to look at."

Fletch grunted, flicked the safety on her rifle.

It was a short thing, the rifle, about the length of a sawed-
off shotgun. The stock was carved to fit her forearm, the trigger was far up along its length, and its barrel, though of
normal thickness, had a surprisingly small muzzle. Keith
thought, not for the first time, how handy it would have been
back in Philadelphia.

Fletch removed her mask, stowed it in a kaftan pocket.
"This valley's one of the clean spots I told you about, but you
should keep your mask on anyway. Just in case. When we go
inside, though, take it off. These people are touchy. Say as little as possible. Don't criticize anything. Don't start any fights."

"Some friends," Keith snorted.

Fletch raised the rifle so that its barrel rested against her
shoulder and its muzzle pointed skyward. She led the way down.

The cluster of buildings had once been the industrial core of a
small mill town. Over the years the outlying houses had been
torn down, bit by bit, for building supplies, for firewood, sometimes just for the sake of doing something. Now all that
remained was a miscellany of old factory buildings bordering a

small swift-running river. Sheds and stone additions choked the narrow streets, making the whole a combination windbreak and maze.

There were flickers of movement in the higher windows as they walked past, faces that appeared and were gone, like gold-fish coming to the fore of their bowls and whisking away. "There must be a hundred people in this warren," Keith whispered, awed. "What do they all *do?*"

"Whatever they have to. Now shut up!"

They turned a corner, came face to face with an ancient gas station. Its windows were boarded over, and towers of old tires almost obscured it from view. Keith wondered what possible use anyone could have for them, did not ask. A bell over the door jangled as they went in.

The interior was a packrat's fantasy. Dimly lit by alcohol lamps were clutters and tangles and piles of fishing equipment, furniture, musical instruments, wood stoves—a thousand items, all battered and old, all obviously looted from homes abandoned during he Meltdown. A pale pockmarked face appeared in the shadowy rear. "You after girls?" it asked.

"Hell no," Fletch said. She slid the rifle into its sheath, almost unbalancing Keith with the sudden weight in the saddlebags he still carried. The face advanced, became a tall vacant-eyed man with a slouch belly. She threw him a silver nickel, and he snagged it out of the air. "I want two beers and whatever slop you're serving today."

The man stared at them silently. "Tables to the rear," he said, and was gone.

Fletch went back to sit down. Keith remained standing, poking through the mounds of objects. He came across a mirror, wiped the grime from it. His reflection was grim. Mean lines around the mouth, a scowl creasing his forehead. He blinked, trying to erase the wildness in his eyes. No good. A smile was gobbled up by his mask. He pushed it down. A red triangle of chafe marks remained. He touched them lightly with a fingertip, pushed the uncombed hair back from his forehead. Still he retained the look of a hunted animal.

Keith took a deep breath of air that rushed into his lungs so readily he felt momentarily dizzy. To hell with it, he decided; he was not going to put his mask back on until they left.

"*Susie!*" A gigantic black-bearded man exploded from the rear of the room. He rushed forward, flung his arms around Fletch, lifted her into the air.

Keith had instinctively grabbed for Fletch's rifle, but drew back when he heard her laugh happily. "Bear, you old *pirate!*" She hugged him, thumped his back vigorously.

They sat at the table. Keith drew up a chair and joined them. "But what are you doing *here?*" Fletch asked. "Didn't you have business"—she lowered her voice—"along the coast?"

"Haw! It was a setup. They've got a new administration that's cracking down on smuggling, much good it'll do them. But I've got friends, yes, and they warned me away." He shifted his head toward Keith. "He's okay, right?"

Fletch nodded, performed introductions. Bear was about Fletch's age, perhaps a little older, and he had a bit of a paunch that bulged over the table whenever he leaned forward. "We met when I was covering the Northern Liberation Front," Fletch told Keith. "The guerrillas set up their camps in the Drift because the government troops wouldn't go after them."

The pale man brought their beers and two bowls of watery-looking stew. Bear waited for him to leave, then said quietly, "Listen, Susie. I can see you're planning to rest here a day or so, but I think maybe you and your young friend here should come stay with me in my cabin instead." A stray beam of light glinted on a single gold earring in his matted hair.

Fletch was all serious attentiveness. "Why?"

"I was here two days age, visiting the"—he looked embarrassed—"the girls in back. And some men came in, asking questions about you. So I decided to hang around, in case you might need some help maybe. But they looked like killers to me. Six or eight of them. Southern accents."

"Philadelphia accents?"

"Yeah. I think."

"Damn." Her fingers tapped the table. "Finish your beer, Keith. Bear, have you still got your buggy?"

"Out back. I've got my own fuel still, too. I'm a *rich* man!"

The buggy was an open-pit four-wheel drive, and Bear drove it like a madman. Huddled between Bear and Fletch, Keith concentrated on keeping warm and worried for the first time about frostbite. The others chattered happily over his head, ignoring him and his misery.

"We're here!" Bear roared finally. He drove the buggy along a nearly nonexistent road, across a rough stretch of meadow, and under a stand of gnarled elms. While Bear was covering the vehicle with a tarp, Keith looked about for the cabin. He couldn't see it.

"Back this way." Bear led them up through the trees and gestured with a mittened hand. "How do you like it? Not much, but it's home, hey?"

The cabin was built into the slope of a steep hillside. A long wall with one window and a door and a bit of wood-shingled roof were all that showed.

Bear scooped an armful of wood from a stack beside the door, led them inside. He talked rapidly, as if trying to make a good appearance for a cabin that looked like nothing much. "Built it myself," he said. "Dug it into the hill, so the earth kinda evens out the temperature. I scavenged a lot of Styrofoam, packed it between the walls and the earth. Doesn't need much heating wood. Leave it alone and it stays about thirteen-degrees C constant. Summer and winter."

"Very nice," Keith said politely, not meaning it.

Fletch studied the cabin judiciously, thumping the walls with her fist. She came to an inside door, raised an eyebrow. "Root cellar," Bear explained. Fletch smiled.

"So this is your fabled cabin," she said admiringly. "I never thought I'd actually be here." She examined the shelves crammed with boxes and sacks that covered two walls, while

Bear pulled out prodigious amounts of bedding from several trunks.

He spilled a final armful onto the floor, then stopped and looked ruefully at the mound he'd created, as if seeing it for the first time. "That may be a bit much," he mumbled embarrassedly.

"Do you really think so?" Fletch asked innocently. Their eyes met, and they both laughed in a warm and comfortable way. Their laughter died down, but they remained staring into one another's eyes.

"Keith," Fletch said. "Maybe you should run outside."

"I—"

"That's a good idea," Bear said. He thrust Fletch's binoculars into Keith's hands. "Play with these for awhile." He winked in a conspiratorial fashion, gently pushed Keith toward the door.

Keith stumbled outside. Someone kicked the door shut behind him. He heard the beginning of an intimate chuckle and hastened away.

It was *cold* outside. A wisp of smoke rose from the cabin's flue and disappeared a few feet up into the grey sky. Keith wandered off to one side and came up against a bramble-choked ravine. It was unpassable; he chunked a rock down it, but didn't hear the splash of water.

Choking with rage, Keith slammed a fist against a gnarled tree trunk. Wood crumbled away, leaving a bite-shaped gap in the tree. He felt sick and confused. Could he really be jealous of a man twice his age? Not long ago he hadn't even been sure he wanted to make love with Fletch a second time. They had made love only once, and then under special circumstances, with death nipping at their heels; Fletch had shown no interest since. He had told himself repeatedly that she was too weary or that she had a low sex drive and required the spice of immediate danger to arouse her. But the tryst with Bear disproved both theories.

There was only one answer: Fletch had used him. He held no sexual interest for her; she'd needed a way out of Philadelphia, and she had bought it.

Well, grow up, kid, he told himself. Welcome to the real world. But unbidden memories arose in his mind, of her flesh, of their vigorous coupling, images that were at once compelling and newly repulsive.

Keith stumbled away from the ravine, trying to control his thoughts. He raised the binoculars to his eyes, scanned the horizon in an attempt to distract himself. Beneath the amplified image of dead and winter-barren trees, something moved. A needle. Set inside the binoculars was an unmarked graduated scale, with a small red pointer that sprang up when the glasses were raised to the horizontal.

The needle pointed to a position barely on the scale. Keith shifted the binoculars and the reading held steady. Raise the glasses to the sky, or lower them steady and the position was constant, wherever they were pointed, at rocks or hillside, at darkness or light.

The view through the binoculars misted over and was replaced with an involuntary inner vision of Fletch and Bear pleasuring each other on the cabin floor. Keith blinked angrily, shoved the glasses back into their case, stalked on down the slope a way. His feet were growing numb. He stamped them against the ground, wishing the two would hurry up and get done.

Sometime later, Fletch appeared in the doorway and waved him in. He entered sullenly, made straight for the wood stove, and hunched over it, holding his hands to the warmth and rubbing them together. From the corner of his eye he could not avoid seeing Bear pulling his trousers up. The man's pubic hair was black against his pale skin, and Keith had to admit inwardly that Bear was better endowed than himself. This helped things not one bit.

For the rest of the afternoon and on through the evening, Bear and Fletch talked avidly of politics in the Greenstate Alliance up north and of goings-on within the Drift. Keith listened quietly, having nothing to contribute. He learned a little, but, for the most part, the dialogue relied on knowledge of previous events that he lacked and was absolutely meaningless to him. He fell asleep to their bright, relaxed chatter.

Something roared at the foot of the hill, a great bass noise that peaked and fell and slowly grew less as it became more distant. Keith's eyes flew open. It was late night, and the cabin was flooded with grey shadow. "Fletch?" he said. "Bear?" The cabin was empty.

Keith went to the door, stood shivering in the cold. Downslope there was no shadow where Bear's buggy had been. The distant noise dwindled, faded away. He had been abandoned.

Stunned, he went back inside, built up the fire, lit an alcohol lamp. What did he do now? He was *somewhere* within the Drift, with not the foggiest idea of what roads led out and an unknown number of Mummer assassins scouring the countryside looking for him. His eye was suddenly caught by a square of something white.

It was sheet of paper. Fletch had left her saddlebags behind, open and partially emptied, with a note atop them. The inner seam of one bag had been ripped open and something—it must have been thin and flat and slightly flexible to be hidden there—removed. The rifle was gone too. Keith picked up the note. It began without preamble.

> Heading for coast—Bear thinks he can get me on a ship for Boston. Suggest you keep heading north. Am leaving you most of my supplies & yr partner's gun. Binocs contain ionization meter— don't sleep anywhere that registers over halfway mark. I put a checkmark on map where Nameless is. If you can't figure it out, Bear should be back in a day or two & can help.

Angrily, he crumpled the note and threw it on the floor. "God damn you to hell, Suzette Fletcher," he said aloud. The words seemed foolish and childishly spiteful even as he said them. He took a deep breath and tried to calm himself.

To his surprise, it was not all that difficult. There was a certain grim satisfaction in knowing the worst: that he had been used and then discarded, that Fletch felt no more than a passing affection for him at best, of the sort one might bestow on a stray dog without the least intention of bringing it home. In a way, the knowledge was easier to handle than the sullen suspicion of it had been. He knelt to take inventory of the saddlebags.

He worked briskly, shoving back inside those items he might need and tossing aside those he saw no use for. He lacked a knife and plundered Bear's possessions until he found one—an Arkansas toothpick with a leather sheath—and clipped it to his belt. The ionization counter would come in handy. He set the binoculars carefully beside the bags and began studying the map.

Keith had about decided he could make his way out of the Drift if only he could retrace his way back to Nameless, when he heard another noise. Dousing the lamp, he picked up his pistol and went outside.

There was a deep growling beyond the hills, a changing chord of four bass lines that rose and fell independent of each other, one growl significantly louder than the rest. Crouching in the cold, Keith tried to place its direction. East? West? It echoed and rebounded, rose and fell, so that there was no hope of getting a fix on it. A pale moon floated high in the sky, visible at rare intervals through gaps in the clouds. The noise grew.

Below and to his left a stretch of road was visible through a break in the trees. A shadow slid across it. Keith shifted position, moving behind an outcropping boulder, and waited.

A buggy careened to a halt below, and two figures jumped out. They were immediately running up the slope, one with long graceful strides, and the other lumbering after.

Three grey shadows slipped across the distant roadway. The roar of engines peaked briefly, treble notes coming together in a high angry whine.

Keith drew a bead on the leader of the two coming up the hill, wondered whether he'd actually be able to shoot, to kill a human being in cold blood.

"You'd better have some damn fine weapons up there," the lead figure called over her shoulder. Fletch. Keith lowered his pistol.

"Weapons I got," Bear shouted back. "Miracles I'm fresh out of."

"We'll make our own."

They ran past him, Fletch sparing a single cool glance in passing, and into the cabin. Shoving the gun into his belt, Keith followed.

Bear was wrestling a large chest from one of the shelves. "I'm pretty sure I nailed that fink from back in town," he grunted. "You can bet they wouldn't've been waiting for us without his help. Bastard! If he got away, I'll go back and finish him."

Keith smiled sardonically. "Welcome back, Fletch."

"Later. What've you got?"

Bear rummaged through the box, yanking things out and tossing them across the floor. "Incendiary grenades. Bandoliers. One of those Israeli machine guns from—what was that war again?"

"Before my time."

"It's a museum piece, anyway. But it's in perfect working order, so maybe I'll use it."

"Got into a little trouble, did you?"

"Give me that," Fletch said, reaching for a new weapon Bear had uncovered. "I'm pretty good with those."

Keith's coolness faded as the two armed themselves, steadfastly paying him no attention. He was not at all sure that he was on Bear's and Fletch's side, but he knew that the Mummers would consider him so.

The growl of approaching vehicles died. Bear grabbed his weaponry, bolted for the door.

"I'll take the left," he threw over his shoulder. "Tell the kid how to provide some distraction, and take the right."

"Gotcha." Fletch took her rifle and thrust it into Keith's hands. It felt odd. He realized that he didn't even know how to fire it. She flipped something on the side of the stock. "Okay, now the safety's off. The rifle's ready. I want you to lie down flat in the back of the cabin—they're shooting uphill, so they'll probably fire over you. Shoot at the sky, understand? Don't try to take any of them out when I'm somewhere in front of you— just provide distraction."

"Dammit, I can fight too!" Keith said.

"Like hell. Now, this thing's a compression launcher. The projectiles are small rockets; they ignite about halfway up the barrel, so the thing has a hell of a kick, remember that. The needles hit at supersonic velocities, and the shock wave ruptures every internal organ of the body. Anywhere you hit is lethal. You've got a hundred shots, and don't forget to save the last for yourself. You stick the muzzle in your mouth and aim *up*. Got all that?"

"Yeah, sure," he mumbled.

"Sure you do." She tousled his hair, ran for the door, paused just behind it.

A needle of red light, so brief it almost wasn't there, lanced through the cabin, leaving a small charred hole in the front wall, and another at an angle to it in the back.

"Laser pistols," Fletch snorted. "Kiddie weapons!" She was gone.

Three more needles of light laced the cabin. Keith threw himself to the floor to the rear, as directed. Whatever weird weapon Fletch was handling made high, almost whistling, shrieks. There was a small explosion, followed by the chatter of Bear's machine gun.

Keith suddenly remembered the rifle, lifted it, pointing its muzzle up and through the window. He squeezed the trigger and the window exploded outward, in a fountain of glass and casement splinters. There was a deafening boom as the projectile went supersonic, and the stock slammed into Keith's shoulder, numbing it, half rolling him over. He fired again, sending a shot through the roof. Another incredible roar.

Plaster, earth, bits of wood showered down. There was a

hole the size of a giant's fist in the ceiling.

Four threads of laser light winked in and out of existence, one after the other. Keith's eyes flooded with tears as he realized how right Bear and Fletch had been to leave him behind. He was confused, almost panicked, of no use in a battle that required keeping one's wits.

Somewhere both Fletch and Bear were running, shouting. Their weapons clattered high and low. An incendiary grenade went off, turning night to day for an instant, and there was a hideous garbled scream.

Blindly Keith fired shot after shot, just barely remembering to aim above the horizon. A laser burst struck the hanging alcohol lamp, exploding it, spilling a gout of alcohol over the wood stove.

With a *whoomp,* the alcohol was ignited by the hot iron stove. Flames reached up toward the ceiling, licked against the wall. A dribble of alcohol running across the wooden floor went up, and Keith tried futilely to beat it out with slaps of his jacketed arm. The flames grew and spread.

Time and again laser bursts pierced the walls, but as promised, they were always too high. The cabin was heating up now, and smoke gathering below the ceiling. Some of it slipped out the hole in the roof, but more was generated than left. The cabin was filling with smoke. Keith gasped and choked. Assassins or no, he had to get out.

He crawled to the door, peeked out at floor level. He could see nothing. It was quieter outside now. There was a short burst of weapons fire, then silence. Sweat beaded on his forehead. He drew himself into a crouch, and ran.

The front wall was burning now. As the cool night air hit him, Keith was involuntarily reminded of a time from his childhood, when a bunch of neighborhood kids had torched a house in an abandoned section of Philadelphia. They'd ringed the building, standing with sticks and old baseball bats, waiting for the rats to come out. Then when the rats were forced out, maddened with pain, their fur ablaze, they'd methodically clubbed the animals to death.

Keith ran downslope, flung himself to the ground. He peered into the darkness, circles swimming in front of his eyes as they adjusted. He thought he detected motion *there* and down there.

He snapped his rifle toward a sudden bulking of shadow downslope, and almost fired before he recognized the silhouette as Bear. A sliver of light passed neatly through Bear's head, and he fell. At that same instant, an incendiary grenade went off, briefly illuminating a Mummer assassin. He was on his feet, running and he twisted in surprise at its sudden glare. Awkwardly he fell on his gun hand, the laser pistol skittering into the night.

Keith shot at the man, not taking time to aim. It made a hell of a noise, and probably hit nothing. His nerves crawled, but there was no answering fire.

Something hulked to one side. "Kid . . . "

He whirled and made a snap shot, almost from instinct. The projectile went supersonic with a shattering crash, and the moon broke free of the clouds, briefly flooding the hillside with dim light. He saw Fletch.

He saw her mouth open and neck arch back, as if in the throes of sexual agony. Her blond hair flew forward, back, lashed her face. Her arms thrashed like a rag doll's, impossibly fluid, each broken in several places. She toppled over backward, and he knew even before he fell to his knees beside her body that she was dead.

He reached out gropingly, touched her face with his fingers. They came away warm and sticky with blood. Fletch had another—final—nosebleed. Keith squeezed his eyes shut, let them fall open again. There were no tears. What kind of cold monster have I become? he asked himself. He felt vacant, disbelieving—totally without emotion.

Fletch was dead.

One pocket of her kaftan bulged, the corner of a leather case sticking out of it. For no reason at all he picked up the case, leaving bloody fingerprints across its surface, and opened it.

Her binoculars. For whatever purpose, perhaps unconsciously, she had scooped them up in the cabin. Holding them in his hand, he felt strangely moved by the binoculars. They had been *hers*. She had touched them and used them and left them briefly to his care. Her spirit was in them.

Keith broke down in great racking sobs, his tears totally out of control. He threw back his head and gasped for air, great salty drops of warm fluid running down his cheeks, and along the seal of his nucleopore.

The tears came in a gust, and when he fought them down he was empty again, cold and dry inside. *You* killed her, he told himself harshly. *You* shot her because she ditched you and ran off with Bear. Because you felt rejected and spiteful. But he couldn't gauge the emotional truth of the words. It might have been pure reflex, nerves drawn out to the point of panic and no more. Honesty forced him to admit that he did not know.

Downslope he heard a coughing mechanical noise—the sound of an engine starting up. Keith was on his feet instantly. He ran down through the trees in long rapid strides, heedless of the risk of falling. Branches whipped across his face, leaving raw welts, and he did not notice.

Keith burst though the trees and was beside the buggies just as the engine caught. A short sprint brought him beside the right vehicle, and he was shoving his rifle into the frightened face of a Mummer assassin.

"Cut it off," he said quietly. The Mummer obeyed. Up close Keith could see that the assassin was just a kid—twenty or twenty-two at most, no older than Keith himself. Thin-faced and very, very ordinary. Keith couldn't fix the features in his mind. His subconscious demanded a gargoyle, an ogre, and reality refused to provide. If I closed my eyes, Keith thought, I wouldn't recognize him when they opened again.

"How many of you are left?" Keith asked. He held the rifle's muzzle directly on the kid's face. Scared eyes tried to focus on it.

"None, mister, just me," the kid babbled. "I'm the only one." Keith said nothing. Unnerved, the kid began again. "You killed

all them. I can show you the bodies. You killed the captain . . . "
He broke off when Keith moved the rifle gently, massaging the boy's cheek in a small circular motion.

"Good." His voice was still quiet, preternaturally so. A part of his mind was occupied pushing thought of Fletch's death aside. Like shoveling back the ocean. "Now we come to the good question. Why?"

The kid blinked. Sweat covered his forehead. "Why?" he echoed, bleakly.

"Yes," Keith said sweetly. "Why? Why did you and your friends kill Bear and Suzette Fletcher? Why were you trying to kill me?"

"I don't know," he said feebly.

"That's not good enough Jacko!" Keith's voice rose to a scream, and he jerked back his rifle. He lifted it as if he were about to club the boy in his face, and only controlled the motion at the last instant. "You don't kill people just for the hell of it, you have a reason. You have a goddamned *good* reason! And I . . . want . . . to know." He punctuated the last sentence with short, angry jabs of the rifle. The Mummer, sure he was going to die, began to cry, small quiet tears that squeezed out of the corners of his eyes and slid silently down his cheeks.

"Honest, mister, I don't know. The captain knew. But he didn't tell us. He just said we had to bang the woman. He said to get anyone that was with her, but that the woman was the dangerous one, and we had to bang her."

"Kill her," Keith said. "The word is 'kill.' Let's hear you say it."

"Kill her," the kid choked out. "But that was all we were told, mister that was all I knew."

"You didn't kill her, though," Keith said. The kid looked at him. "I did." The kid said nothing.

Keith still held Fletch's binoculars in his left hand. He dumped them on the Mummer's lap. "Tell that to your owners. Give them her glasses for proof, and tell them I did your dirty work for you." He stood back two paces, said, "Well? What are you waiting for?"

The kid's hands fumbled with the ignition. The motor caught, and he pulled out onto the road like a bat out of Hell. Keith stood watching him, his eyes filling with tears again. He wrapped an arm around a pine tree to keep from falling and once again wept uncontrollably.

By dawn he had dragged both Bear's and Fletch's bodies up to the smoldering remains of the cabin. He laid them side by side, then hesitated. It seemed like a violation of the dead. But he had to have an answer.

Keith opened Fletch's robe and deftly undid the buttons of her shirt. The flesh underneath was an ugly black, massive bruising that had followed her death. Tucked into her belt, protruding over her stomach, was a leather portfolio. He lifted it out, flipped her robe shut.

Standing away from the corpses, his back not quite turned to them, he examined the portfolio's contents. They were handwritten manuscripts, clearly stories Fletch had been working on, cluttered with marginal notes and corrections. They were wrinkled from being carried under Fletch's belt and sewn into the lining of her saddlebags before that, but readable nonetheless.

Keith riffled through thin bundles of paper labeled "Nameless," "Mutations/Disease," "Mutagenic Offspr." and the like. Halfway through, he hit pay dirt: a bundle labeled "Phila/Drift." He returned to the other papers to their sheath, and began reading.

> It's the best-kept secret in Philadelphia. The infant mortality rate is not a matter of public record. People disappear into the hospitals, and the word filters out that they died of "pneumonia" or "flu" or superflu." Not a person in a thousand suspects that Philadelphia lies within the Drift.

Keith stopped reading. Here was his answer, and it didn't make him any happier knowing it. Philadelphia within the

Drift! It was the kiss of death for the city, once the word got out. Philadelphians had a deep, almost superstitious fear of the Drift, and had imbued their home city with mystic faith in its ability to protect them.

A single thicker piece of paper was enclosed in the bundle. Keith thumbed it out idly. It was a copy of the map of the Drift that had been drawn up almost a century ago for the first official reports on the Meltdown. Long curving oblongs had been drawn around the reactor site, the outermost just barely grazing Philadelphia. Fletch had jotted a dozen radiation counts onto the map and redrawn the outermost line. There was no doubt that she had done her homework, no chance of her being mistaken.

Keith tried to imagine the damage this article could do. There were over a million people in Philadelphia—it would be the biggest panic evacuation since the Meltdown. He tried to picture a million people, most of them on foot, streaming out of Philadelphia, clogging the bridges to New Jersey, swooping on the lands beyond like a plague of locusts. The United States was not a rich country the way it had been. It had lost a third of its territory in the turbulent post-Meltdown years. There wouldn't be refugee camps set up for the survivors. There would be, instead, men with guns to mow down the new threat to their economic stability.

It was literally unimaginable. Better to concentrate on matters at hand. Keith checked his rifle, paced thirty yards downhill, and raised it to his shoulder. He aimed at the hillside just above the ruins of the cabin. One after the other he shot the projectiles into the earth, until the clip was emptied, and the hillside—whether from the projectiles themselves or from their thundering reverberations—collapsed over the bodies of his former companions.

He dropped the papers on the ground, started to trudge down past the corpses of the fallen Mummer assassins. He hadn't gone far before a thought occurred to him, and he returned to scoop up the stories again.

He weighed them in his hand. There was power here if he knew how to use them. He didn't kid himself. Politics and the acquisition of power were total unknowns to him. But he could learn.

As he started the buggy, Keith became aware again of the irritation his nucleopore caused. He pulled it off, dropped it on the seat beside him. It hardly mattered now.

He shifted gears, began the long trip home to Philadelphia.

Mummers Day was sunny and blue-skied. Keith stood in the crowd, slapping his arms against his jacket from time to time to keep warm. He was not surprised when the Center City Fancy band stopped in front of him, not at all anxious when King Clown strode straight at him.

The Clown's gloved hands rested on his shoulders, and Keith looked straight into the man's bloodshot eyes. There was a still instant, then whapwhap*whap!* He had been tapped out, and King Clown was striding away. Keith ran to join the ragtag band in mufti strutting happily after the troupe. The crowd cheered.

He was a Mummer now.

Trojan Horse

"IT'S ALL INSIDE MY HEAD," Elin said wonderingly. It was true. A chimney swift flew overhead, and she could feel its passage through her mind. A firefly landed on her knee. It pulsed cold fire, then spread its wings and was gone, and that was a part of her too.

"Please try not to talk too much." The wetware tech tightened a cinch on the table, adjusted a bone inductor. His red-and-green facepaint loomed over her, receded. "This will go much faster if you cooperate."

Elin's head felt light and airy. It was *huge.* It contained all of Magritte, from the uppermost terrace down to the trellis farms that circled the inner lake. Even the blue-and-white Earth that hovered just over one rock wall. They were all within her. They were all, she realized, only a model, the picture her mind assembled from sensory input. The exterior universe—the real universe—lay beyond.

"I feel giddy."

"Contrast high." The tech's voice was neutral, disinterested. "This is a very different mode of perception from what you're used to—you're stoned on the novelty."

A catwalk leading into the nearest farm rattled within Elin's mind as a woman in agricultural blues strode by, gourd-collecting bag swinging from her hip. It was night outside the crater, but biological day within, and the agtechs had activated tiers of arc lights at the cores of the farms. Filtered by greenery, the light was soft and watery.

"I could live like this forever."

"Believe me, you'd get bored." A rose petal fell on her cheek, and the tech brushed it off. He turned to face the two layers standing silently nearby. "Are the legal preliminaries over now?"

The lawyer in orangeface nodded. The one in purple said, "Can't her original personality be restored at all?"

Drawing a briefcase from his pocket, the wetware tech threw up a holographic diagram between himself and the witnesses. The air filled with intricate three-dimensional tracery, red-and-green lines interweaving and intermeshing.

"We've mapped the subject's current personality." He reached out to touch several junctions. "You will note that here, here, and here, we have what are laughingly referred to as impossible emotional syllogisms. Any one of these renders the subject incapable of survival."

A thin waterfall dropped from the dome condensers to a misty pool at the topmost terrace, a bright razor-slash through reality. It meandered to the edge of the next terrace, and fell again.

"A straight yes or no answer will suffice."

The tech frowned. "In theory, yes. In practical terms it's hopeless. Remember, her personality was never recorded. The accident almost completely randomized her emotional structure—technically she's not even human. Given a decade or two of extremely delicate memory probing, we could *maybe* construct a facsimile. But it would only resemble the original; it could never be the primary Elin Donnelly."

Elin could dimly make out the equipment for five more waterfalls, but they were not in operation at the moment. She wondered why.

The attorney made a rude noise. "Well then, go ahead and do it. I wash my hands of this whole mess."

The tech bent over Elin to reposition a bone inductor. "This won't hurt a bit," he promised. "Just pretend that you're at the dentist's, having your teeth replaced."

She ceased to exist.

The new Elin Donnelly gawked at everything she passed by-the desk workers in their open-air offices, a blacksnake sunning itself by the path, the stone stairways cut into the terrace walls. Coming off the topmost of these stairs, into a stand of sapling no higher than she, she stumbled and almost fell. Her companion caught her and roughly set her back on her feet.

"Try to pay attention," the lawyer said, frowning under her loops of purple facepaint. "We have a lot of detail work to go over."

Elin smiled vaguely. They broke out of the saplings into a meadow, and butterflies scattered at their approach. Her gaze went from them to a small cave in the cliffs ahead, then up to the stars, as jumpy and random as their flight.

"—so you'll be stuck on the Moon for a full lunation—almost a month—if you want to collect your settlement. I.G. Feuchtwaren will carry your expenses until then, drawing against their final liability. Got that?"

And then—suddenly, jarringly—Elin could focus again. She took a deep breath. "Yes," she said. "Yes, I—okay."

"Good." The attorney canceled her wetware, yanking the skull plugs and briskly wrapping them around her briefcase. "Then let's have a drink—it's been a long day."

They had arrived at the cave. "Hey, Hans!" the lawyer shouted. "Give us some service here, will you?"

A small man with the roguish face of a comic-opera troll popped into the open, work terminal in hand. "One minute," he said. "I'm on the direct flex time—got to wrap up what I'm working on first."

"Okay." The lawyer dropped to the grass and began toweling her face. Elin watched, fascinated, as a new pattern of fine red-and-black lines, permanently tattooed into the skin, emerged from under the paint.

"Hey!" Elin said. "You're a Jesuit."

"You expected IGF to ship you a lawyer from Earth orbit?" She stuck out a hand. "Donna Landis, S.J. I'm the client-overseer for the Star Maker project, but I'm also available for spiritual guidance. Mass is at nine Sunday mornings."

Elin leaned back against the cliff. Grapevines rustled under her weight. Already she missed the blissed-out feeling of a few minutes before. "Actually, I'm an agnostic."

"You *were.* Things may have changed." Landis folded the towel into one pocket, unfolded a mirror from another. "Speaking of which, how do you like your new look?"

Elin studied her reflection. Blue paint surrounded her eyes, narrowing to a point at the bridge of her nose, swooping down in a long curve to the outside. It was as if she were peering through a large blue moth, or a pair of hawk wings. There was something magical about it, something glamorous. Something very unlike her.

"I feel like a raccoon," she said. "This idiot mask."

"Best get used to it. You'll be wearing it a lot."

"But what's the point?" Elin demanded. She was surprised by her own irritation. "So I've got a new personality; it's still *me* in here. I don't feel any weird compulsion to run amok with a knife or walk out an airlock without a suit. Nothing to warn the citizenry about, certainly."

"Listen," Landis said. "Right now you're like a puppy tripping over its own paws because they're too big for it. You're a stranger to yourself—you're going to feel angry when you don't expect to, get sentimental over surprising things. You can't control your emotions until you learn what they are. And until then, the rest of us deserve—"

"What'll you have?" Hans was back, his forehead smudged black where he had incompletely wiped off his facepaint.

"A little warning. Oh, I don't know, Hans. Whatever you have on tap."

"That'll be Chanty. And you?" he asked Elin.

"What's good?"

He laughed. "There's no such thing as a good lunar wine. The air's too moist. And even if it weren't, it takes a good century to develop an adequate vineyard. But the Chanty is your basic drinkable glug."

"I'll take that, then."

"Good. And I'll bring a mug for your friend, too."

"My friend?" She turned and saw a giant striding through the trees, towering over them, pushing them apart with two enormous hands. For a dizzy instant, she goggled in disbelief, and then the man shrank to human stature as she remembered the size of the saplings.

He grinned, joined them. "Hi. Remember me?"

He was a tall man, built like a spacejack, lean and angular. An untidy mass of black curls framed a face that was not quite handsome, but carried an intense freight of will.

"I'm afraid . . . "

"Tory Shostokovich. I reprogrammed you."

She studied his face carefully. Those *eyes*. They were fierce almost to the point of mania, but there was sadness there, too, and—she might be making this up—a hint of pleading, like a little boy who wants something so desperately he dare not ask for it. She could lose herself in analyzing the nuances of those eyes. "Yes," she said at last, "I see it now—the resemblance."

"I'm pleased." He nodded to the Jesuit. "Father Landis."

She eyed him skeptically. "You don't seem your usual morose self, Shostokovich. Is anything wrong?"

"No, it's just a special kind of morning." He smiled at some private joke, returned his attention to Elin. "I thought I'd drop by and get acquainted with my former patient." He glanced down at the ground, fleetingly shy, and then his eyes were bright and audacious again.

How charming, Elin thought. She hoped he wasn't *too* shy. And then had to glance away herself, the thought was so unlike her. "So you're a wetware surgeon," she said inanely.

Hans reappeared to distribute mugs of wine, then retreated to the cave's mouth. He sat down, workboard in lap, and patched in the skull-plugs. His face went stiff as the wetware took hold.

"Actually," Tony said, "I very rarely work as a wetsurgeon. An accident like yours is rare, you know—maybe once, twice a year. Mostly I work in wetware development. Currently I'm on the Star Maker project."

"I've heard that name before. Just what is it, anyway?"

Tory didn't answer immediately. He stared down into the lake, a cool breeze from above ruffling his curls. Elin caught her breath. *I hardly know this man,* she thought wildly. He pointed to the island in the center of the lake, a thin stony finger that was originally the crater's thrust cone.

"God lives on that island," he said.

Elin laughed. "Think how different human history would be if He'd had a sense of direction!" And then wanted to bite her tongue as she realized that he was not joking.

"Typical," Landis said, glowering at Tory. "Only an atheist would call her that."

"What do you *call* her, then?"

"A victim of technology." She swigged down a mouthful of wine. "*Jeez,* that's vile stuff."

"Uh, guys?" Elin said. "I'm not getting much of an answer."

Tory rubbed the back of his neck ruefully. "*Mea culpa.* Well, let me give you a little background. Most people think of wetware as being software for people. But that's too simplistic, because with machines, you start out blank—with a clean slate—and with people, there's some ten million years of mental programming already crammed into their heads.

"So to date we've been working *with* the natural wetware. We counterfeit surface traits—patience, alertness, creativity—and package them like so many boxes of bonemeal. But the human mind is vast and unmapped, and it's time to move into the interior, to do some basic research.

"And that's the Star Maker project. It's an exploration of the basic substructural programming of the mind. We've redefined the overstructure programs into an integrated system we believe will be capable of essence-programming, and in one-to-one congruence with the inherent substructure of the universe."

"What jargonistic rot!" Landis gestured at Elin's stoneware mug. "Drink up. The Star Maker is a piece of experimental theology that IGF dreamed up. As Tory said, it's basic research into the nature of the mind. The Vatican Synod is providing funding so we can keep an eye on it."

"Nipping heresy in the bud," Tory said sourly.

"That's a good part of it. IGF is trying to create a set of wetware that will reshape a human mind into the popular notion of God. Bad theology, but there it is. They want to computer-model the infinite. Anyway, the specs were drawn up, and it was tried out on—what was the name of the test subject?"

"Doesn't matter," Tory said quickly.

"Coral something-or-other."

Only half-listening by now, Elin unobtrusively studied Tory. He sat, legs wide, staring into the mug of Chanty. There were hard lines on his face, etched by who-knew-what experiences? *I don't believe in love at first sight,* Elin thought. Then again, who knew *what* she might believe in anymore? It was a chilling thought, and she retreated from it.

"So did this Coral become God?"

"Patience. Anyway, the volunteer was plugged in, wiped, reprogrammed, and interviewed. Nothing useful."

Tory raised a finger in objection. "In one hour we learned more about the structure and composition of the universe than in all of the history of science to date."

"It was deranged gibberish." She tapped Elin's knee. "We interviewed her, and then canceled the wetware. And what do you think happened?

"I've never been big on rhetorical questions." She didn't take her eyes off Tory.

"She didn't come down. She was stuck there."

"Stuck?"

Tory plucked a blade of grass, let it fall. "What happened was that we had rewired her to absolute consciousness. She was not only aware of all her mental functions, she was in control of them—right down to the involuntary reflexes. Which also put her in charge of her own metaprogrammer."

"*Metaprogrammer* is just a buzzword for a bundle of functions by which the brain is able to make changes in itself," Landis threw in.

"Yeah. What we didn't take into account, though, was that she'd *like* being God. When we began deprogramming her, she simply overrode our instructions and reprogrammed herself back up."

"The poor woman," Elin said, in part because she knew it was expected of her. And yet—what a glorious experience, to be God! Something within her thrilled to it. It would almost be worth the price.

"Which leaves us with a woman who thinks she's God," Landis said. "I'm just glad we were able to hush it up. If word got out to some of those religious illiterates back on Earth—"

"Listen," Tory said. "I didn't really come here to talk shop. I wanted to invite my former patient on the grand tour of the Steam Grommet Works."

Elin looked at him at him blankly. "Steam . . . "

He swept an arm to take in all of Magritte, the green pillars and grey cliffs alike, and there was something proprietary in his gesture.

Landis eyed him suspiciously. "You two might need a chaperone," she said. "I think I'll tag along to keep you out of trouble."

Elin smiled sweetly. "Fuck off," she said.

A full growth of ivy covered Tory's geodesic trellis hut. He led the way in, stooping to touch a keyout by the doorway. "Something classical?"

"Please." And as he gently began removing her jumpsuit, the holotape sprang into being, surrounding them with rich reds and cobalt blues that coalesced into stained glass patterns in the air. Elin pulled back a bit and clapped her hands. "It's Chartres," she cried, delighted. "The cathedral at Chartres!"

"Mmmm." Tory teased her down onto the grass floor.

The north rose window swelled to fill the hut and slowly revolved overhead. It was all angels and doves, kings and prophets, with gold lilies surrounding the central rosette. Deep and powerful, infused with gloomy light, it lap-dissolved into the lancet of Sainte Anne.

One by one, the hundred and seventy-six windows of Chartres appeared in turn, wheeling about them, slow and stately at first, then more quickly. The holotape panned down the north transept to the choir, to the apse, and then up into the ambulatory. Swiftly then, it cut to the wounded Christ and the Beasts of Revelation set within the dark spaces of the west rose. The outer circle—the instruments of the Passion—closed about them.

Elin gasped.

The tape proceeded down the nave, window by window, still brightening, pausing at the Vendôme chapel and moving on. Until finally the oldest window, the Notre Dame de la Belle Verrière, fairly blazed in a frenzy of raw glory. A breeze rattled the ivy, and two leaves fell through the hologram to tap against their skin and slide to the ground.

The Belle Verrière held for a moment longer then faded again, the light darkening, and the colors ran and were washed away by a noiseless gust of rain.

Elin let herself melt into the grass, drained and lazy, not caring if she never moved again. Beside her Tory chuckled, playfully tickled her ribs. "Do you love me? Hey? Tell me you love me."

"Stop!" She grabbed his arms and bit him in the side—a small nipping bite, more threat than harm—ran a tongue across his left nipple. "Hey, listen, I hit the sack with you a half hour after we met. What do you want?"

"Want?" He broke her hold, rolled over on top of her, pinioning her wrists above her head. "I want you to know"—and suddenly he was absolutely serious, his eyes unblinking and glittery-hard—"that I love you. Without doubt or qualification.

I love you more than words could ever express."

"Tory," she said. "Things like that take time." The wind had died down. Not a blade of grass stirred.

"No, they don't." It was embarrassing looking into those eyes; she refused to look away. "I feel it. I know it. I love every way, shape, and part of you. I love you beyond time and barrier and possibility. We were meant to be lovers, fated for it, and there is *nothing*, absolutely nothing, that could ever keep us apart." His voice was low and steady. Elin couldn't tell whether she was thrilled or scared out of her wits.

"Tory, I don't know—"

"Then wait," he said. "It'll come."

But it was a long night. And a restless hour after Tory had slipped easily into sleep, Elin put on her jumpsuit and went outside.

She walked into a gentle darkness, relieved by Earthshine and the soft glow of walking lights on the catwalks above. There was a rustling in the grass, and a badger passed within ten feet of her, intent on its nightly foraging. She wandered.

There was a lot that had to be sorted out. This evening, to begin with, this sudden sexual adventure. It was like nothing she had ever done before, and it forced her to admit to herself that she had been changed—that nothing was ever going to be the same for her again.

She found a secluded spot away from the cluster of huts Tory lived among, and hunkered down against a boulder. She thought back to her accident. And because it was a matter of stored memory, the images were crisp and undamaged.

Elin had been the end of her shift on Wheel Laboratory 19 in Henry Ford Orbital Industrial Park when it happened. She was doing development work in semiconductors.

"Theta is coming up to temperature," her workboard said.

"Check." Elin put the epsilon lab to bed and switched the controls over. Holding theta up flush against the hub cylinder, she gingerly mixed two molten alloys, one dense, the other light.

Wheel Lab 19 was shaped like a rimless bicycle wheel. Two dozen spindly arms spread out evenly from thick central hub. At various distances along the spokes were twenty-three sliding lab units and a single fixed workspace. The wheel rotated fast enough to give the workspace constant Earth-normal gravity.

When the mix began to cool, Elin dropped the lab a half-kilometer to the end of its arm. Mercury shifted between ballast tanks to keep the rotation constant, and the lab went from fractional Greenwich gravity to a full nine gees.

A dozen different readouts had to be checked. Elin felt a momentary petulant boredom, and then the workboard readjusted her wetware, jacking up her attentiveness so that she ran through the ritual in detached professional fascination.

As the new alloy cooled, its components tried to separate out, creating an even stratification gradient across the sample. Elin waited, unblinking, until all the readouts balanced, then swiftly jabbed a button and quick-froze the wafer. Using waldoes, she lifted the sample from its mold and placed it in a testing device.

"Measurements recorded. Delta is prepped."

"Check." Elin ran the lab back to the hub. The workboard adjusted her wetware again, damping down patience and widening scope of attention. Deftly, she chose the same component alloys, varying the mix slightly, and set them to heat. By then the workboard was demanding her attention on chi.

It was all standard industrial wetware so far, no different from that used by thousands of research workers daily. But then the workboard gave the ten-second warning that the interfacing program was about to be shut off. Her fingers danced across the board, damping down reactions, putting the labs to bed. The wetware went quiescent.

With a shiver, Elin was herself again. She grabbed a towel and wiped off her facepaint. Then she leaned back and transluced the wall—might as well put her feet up until her replacement showed. Stretching, she felt the gold wetware wires dangling from the back of her skull, lazily put off yanking them.

Was I really that indolent? Elin wondered.

Earth bloomed underfoot, crept over her shoulder and disappeared. New Detroit and New Chicago rose from the floor, their mirrors flashing as the twinned residential cylinders slid slowly upward. Bright industrial satellites gleamed to every side: zero-gee factories and fullerspheres, wheels, porcupines, barbells, and cargo grids.

Earth rose again, larger than a dinner plate. Its clouds were a dazzling white on the dayside. Cities gleamed softly in the night.

A load of cargo drifted by. It was a jumble of containers lashed together by nonmagnetic tape and shot into an orbit calculated to avoid the laser cables and power transmission beams that interlaced the Park. A bit of motion caught Elin's eye, and she swiveled to follow it.

A man was riding the cargo, feet braced against a green carton, hauling on a rope slipped through the lashings. He saw her and waved. She could imagine his grin through the mirrored helmet.

That's rather dashing, Elin thought.

Elin snorted, started to look away, and almost missed seeing it happen.

Somehow, in leaning back that fraction more, the cargo-hopper had put too much strain on the lashings. A faulty rivet popped, and the cargo began to slide. Brightly colored cartons drifted apart, and the man went tumbling end-over-end away.

One end of the lashing was still connected to an anchor carton, and the free end writhed like a wounded snake. A bright bit of metal—the failed rivet—broke free and flew toward the juncture of the wheel lab's hub and spokes.

Reliving the incident, Elin's first reaction was to somehow help the man, to suit up and go out with a lifeline before Traffic Control scooped him up.

The old Elin Donnelly snickered. Traffic Control was going to come down on the jerk with both feet, and serve him right too. He was going to have to pay salvage fines not only for the scattered cargo but for himself as well. Which is what you got when you go looking for a free ride.

She was still smiling sardonically when the rivet struck the lab, crashing into a nest of wiring that *should not* have been exposed.

Two wires short-circuited, sending a massive power transient surging up through the workboard. Circuits fused and melted. The board went haywire.

And a microjolt of electricity leaped up two gold wires, hopelessly scrambling the wetware through Elin's skull.

For a moment, everything was blank. Then—

"Whooh." Elin shook her head, reached back, and unplugged the leads. She laughed weakly to herself.

Without bothering to opaque the walls, Elin unjugged a vacuum suit and began to climb the workspace arm to the hub. Ballast tanks whispered to her each time her hands touched a rung. Rings of lights paced her up the arm. She floated into the hub, and the touch of weightlessness was as cold as death.

Automatically, Elin set the mass driver for New Detroit. Through the hub aperture, she could see the twin residential cylinders, oblong lozenges, either of which she could hide with one thumb. Something within her shrieked and gibbered with the desire to pluck them from the sky, dash them to the ground.

"Something is very wrong with my mind," Elin said aloud. She giggled merrily as magnetic forces tugged at the metal bands of her suit, accelerated her to speed, and flung her out into the void.

An hour later the medics recovered her body from New Detroit's magnetic receiving net. It was curled in on itself, arms wrapped about knees, in a fetal position. When they peeled her out of the suit, Elin was alternating between hysterical gusts of laughter and dark gleeful screams.

Morning came, and after a sleepy, romantic breakfast, Tory plugged into his briefcase and went to work. Alone again, Elin wandered off to do some more thinking.

There was no getting around the fact that she was not the metallurgist from Wheel Lab 19, not anymore. That woman was alien to her now. They shared memories, experiences—but how differently they saw things! She no longer understood that woman, could not sympathize with her emotions, indeed found her distasteful.

Elin strolled downslope because that was easiest. She stopped at an administrative cluster and rented a briefcase. Then, at a second-terrace café that was crowded with off-shift biotechs, she rented a table and sat down to try to trace the original owner of her personality.

As Elin had suspected, she found that her new persona was indeed copied from that of a real human being; creating a personality from whole cloth was still beyond the abilities of even the best wetware techs. She was able to determine that it had come from IGF's inventory, and that duplication of personality was illegal—which presumable meant that the original owner was dead.

But she could not locate the original owner. Selection had been made by computer, and the computer wouldn't tell. When she tried to find out, it referred her to the Privacy Act of 2037.

"I think I've exhausted all of the resources of self-discovery available to me," she told the waiter when he came to collect his tip. "And I've still got half the morning left to kill."

He glanced at her powder-blue facepaint, and smiled politely.

"It's selective black."

"Hah?" Elin turned away from the lake, found that an agtech carrying a long-handled net had come up behind her.

"The algae—it absorbs light into the infrared. Makes the lake a great thermal sink." The woman dipped her net into the water, seined up a netful of dark green scum, and dumped it into a nearby trough. Water drained away through the porous bottom.

"Oh," Elin stared at the island. There were a few patches of weeds where drifting soil had settled. "It's funny. I never used to be very touristy. More the contemplative type, sort of home-bodyish. Now I've got to be *doing* something, you know?"

The agtech dumped another load of algae into the trough. "I couldn't say." She tapped her forehead. "It's the wetware. If you want to talk shop, that's fine. Otherwise, I can't."

"I see." Elin dabbed a toe in the warm water. "Well—why not? Let's talk shop."

Someone was moving at the far edge of the island. Elin craned her neck to see. The agtech went on methodically dipping her net into the lake as God walked into view.

"The lake tempers the climate, see. By day it works by evaporative cooling. Absorbs the heat, loses it to evaporation, radiates it out the dome roof via the condensers."

Coral was cute as a button.

A bowl of fruit and vegetables had been left near the waterline. She walked to the bowl, considered it. Her orange jumpsuit nicely complemented her *café-au-lait* skin. She was so small and delicate that by contrast Elin felt ungainly, an awkward if amiable giant.

"We also use passive heat pumps to move the excess heat down to a liquid storage cavern below the lake."

Coral stopped, picked up a tomato. Her features were finely chiseled. Her almond eyes should have had snap and fire in them, to judge by the face, but they were remote and unfocused. Even white teeth nipped at the food.

"At night we pump the heat back up, let the lake radiate it out to keep the crater warm."

On closer examination—Elin had to squint to see so fine—the face was as smooth and lineless as that of an idiot. There was nothing there; no emotion, no purpose, no detectable intellect.

"That's why the number of waterfalls in operation varies."

Now Coral sat down on the rocks. Her feet were dirty, but the toenails pink and perfect. She did not move. Elin wanted to shy a rock at her to see if she would react.

What now? Elin wondered. She had seen the sights, all that

Magritte had to offer, and they were all tiresome, disappointing. Even—no, make that *especially*—God. And she still had
almost a month to kill.

"Keeping the crater tempered is a regular balancing act," the
agtech said.

"Oh, shut up." Elin took out her briefcase, and called Father
Landis. "I'm bored," she said, when the hologram had stabilized.

Landis hardly glanced up from her work. "So get a job," she
snapped.

Magritte had begun as a mining colony. But the first swatches
of lunar soil had hardly been scooped from Mare Imbrium's
surface when the economic winds shifted, and it became more
profitable to mine areas rich in specific minerals than to
process the undifferentiated mélange soil. The miners had left,
and the crater was sold at a loss to a consortium of operations
that were legally debarred from locating Earthside.

From the fifteenth terrace Elin stared down at the patchwork
clusters of open-air laboratories and offices, some separated by
long stretches of undeveloped field, others crammed together in
the hope of synergistic effect. Germ warfare corporations mingled with nuclear-waste engineering firms. The Mid-Asian Population Control Project had half a terrace to itself, and it swarmed
with guards. There were a few off-Swiss banking operations.

"You realize," Tory said, "that I'm not going to be at all happy
about this development." He stood, face impassive in red and
green, watching a rigger bolt together a cot and wire in the sur-
gical equipment.

"You hired me yourself," Elin reminded him.

"Yes, but I'm wired into professional mode at the moment."
The rigger packed up his tools, walked off. "Looks like we're
almost ready."

"Good." Elin flung herself down on the cot, and lay back,
hands folded across her chest. "Hey, I feel like I should be
holding a lily!"

"I'm going to hook you into the project intercom so you don't get too bored between episodes." The air about her flickered, and a clutch of images overlaid her vision. Ghosts walked through the air, stared at her from deep within the ground. "Now we'll shut off the external senses." The world went away, but the illusory people remained, each within a separate hexagonal field of vision. It was like seeing through the eyes of a fly.

There was a sudden overwhelming sense of Tory's presence, and sourceless voice said, "This will take a minute. Amuse yourself by calling up a few friends." Then he was gone.

Elin floated, free of body, free of sensation, almost godlike in her detachment. She idly riffled through the images, bypassing Landis, and stopped at a chubby little man drawing a black line across his forehead. *Hello, Hans,* she thought.

He looked up and winked. "How's it hanging, kid?"

Not so bad. What are you up to?

"My job. I'm the black-box monitor this shift." He added an orange starburst to the band, surveyed the job critically in a pocket mirror. "I sit here with my finger on the button"—one hand disappeared below his terminal—"and if I get the word, I push. That sets off explosives in the condenser units and blows the dome. *Pfffft.* Out goes the air."

She considered it: A sudden volcano of oxygen spouting up and across the lunar plains. Human bodies thrown up from the surface, scattering, bursting under explosive decompression.

That's grotesque, Hans.

"Oh, it's safe. The button doesn't connect unless I'm wetwired into my job."

Even so.

"Just a precaution; a lot of the research that goes on here wouldn't be allowed without this kind of security. Relax—I haven't lost a dome yet."

The intercom cut out, and again Elin felt Tory's presence, a sensation akin to someone unseen staring over her shoulder. "We're trying a series of Trojan Horse programs this time—

inserting you into the desired mental states instead of making you the states. We've encapsulated your surface identity and routed the experimental programs through a secondary level. So with *this* series, rather than identifying with the programs, you'll perceive them all indirectly."

Tory, you have got to be the most jargon-ridden human being in existence. How about repeating that in English?

"I'll show you."

Suddenly Elin was englobed in a sphere of branching crimson lines, dark and dull, that throbbed slowly. Lacy and organic, it looked the way she imagined the veins in her forehead to be like when she had a headache.

"That was anger," Tory said. "You're mind shunted it off into visual imagery because it didn't identify the anger with itself."

That's what you're going to do then—program me into the God-state so that I can see it but not experience it?

"Ultimately. Though I doubt you'll be able to come up with pictures. More likely, you'll feel that you're in the presence of God." He withdrew for a moment, leaving her more than alone, almost nonexistent. Then he was back. "We start slowly, though. The first session runs you up to the basic metaprogramming level, integrates all your mental processes, and puts you in low-level control of them. The nontechnical term for this is 'making the Christ.' Don't fool around with anything you see or sense." His voice faded, she was alone, and then everything changed.

She was in the presence of someone wonderful.

Elin felt that someone near at hand, and struggled to open the eyes she no longer possessed; she had to see. Her existence opened, and people began appearing before her.

"Careful," Tory said. "You've switched on the intercom again."

I want to see!

"There's nobody to see. That's just your own mind. But if you want, you can keep the intercom on."

Oh. It was disappointing. She was surrounded by love, by a crazily happy sense that the universe was holy, by wisdom deeper than the world. By all rights, it *had* come from a source greater than herself.

Reason was not strong enough to override emotion. She riffled through the intercom, bringing up image after image and discarding them all, searching. When she had run through the project staff, she began hungrily scanning the crater's public monitors.

Agtechs in the trellis farms were harvesting strawberries and sweet peas. Elin could taste them on her tongue. Somebody was seining up algae from the inner lake, and she felt the weight of the net in callused hands. Not far from where she lay, a couple was making love in a grove of saplings and she . . .

Tory, I don't think I can take this. It's too intense.

"You're the one who wanted to be a test pilot."

Dammit, Tory—!

Donna Landis materialized on the intercom. "She's right, Shostokovich. You haven't buffered her enough."

"It didn't seem wise to risk dissociative effects by cranking her ego up too high—"

"Who's paying for all this, hah?"

Tory grumbled something inaudible, and dissolved the world.

Elin floated in blackness, soothing and relaxing. She felt good. She had needed this little vacation from the tensions and pressures of her new personality. Taking the position had been the right thing to do, even if it did momentarily displease Tory.

Tory . . . She smiled mentally. He was exasperating at times, but still she was coming to rely on having him around. She was beginning to think she was in love with him.

A lesser love, perhaps. Certainly not the love that is the Christ.

Well, maybe so. Still, on a *human* level, Tory filled needs in her she hadn't known existed. It was too much effort to argue with herself, though. Her thoughts drifted away into a wordless, luxurious reveling in the bodiless state, free from distractions, carefree and disconnected.

Nothing is disconnected. All the universe is a vast net of inter-meshing programs. Elin was amused at herself. That had sounded like something Tory would say. She'd have to watch it; she might love the man, but she certainly didn't want to end up talking like him.

You worry needlessly. The voice of God is subtle, but it is not your own.

Elin started. She searched through her mind for an open intercom channel, didn't find one. *Hello,* she thought. *Who said that?*

The answer came to her not in words, but in a sourceless assertion of identity. It was cool, emotionless, something she could not describe even to herself, but by the same token absolute and undeniable.

It was God.

Then Tory was back and the voice, the presence, was gone. *Tory?* she thought, *I think I just had a religious experience.*

"That's very common under sensory deprivation—the mind clears out a few old programs. Nothing to worry about. Now relax for a jiff while I plug you back in—how does that feel?"

The Presence was back again, but not nearly so strongly as before; she could resist the urge to chase after it. *That's fine, Tory, but listen, I really think—*

"Let's leave analysis to those who have been programmed for it, shall we?"

The lovers strolled aimlessly through a meadow, the grass brushing up higher than their waists. Biological night was coming; the agtechs flicked the daylight off and on twice in warning.

"It was real, Tory. She talked with me; I'm not making it up."

Tory ran a hand through his dark curly hair, looking abstracted. "Well. Assuming that my professional opinion was wrong—and I'll be the first to admit that the program is a bit egocentric—I still don't think we have to stoop to mysticism for an explanation."

To the far side of Magritte, a waterfall was abruptly shut off. The stream of water scattered, seeming to dissolve in the air. "I thought you said she was God."

"I only said that to bait Landis. I don't mean that she's literally God, just god*like*. Mentally, she's a million years more highly developed than we. God is just a convenient metaphor."

"Um. So what's your explanation?"

"There's at least one terminal on the island—the things are everywhere. She probably programmed it to cut into the intercom without the channels seeming to be open."

"Could she do that?"

"Why not? She has that million-year edge on us—and she used to be a wetware tech; all wetware techs are closet computer hacks." He did not look at her, had not looked at her for some time.

"Hey." She reached out to take his hand. "What's wrong with you tonight?"

"Me?" He did not meet her eyes. "Don't mind me, I'm just sulking because you took the job. I'll get over it."

"What's wrong with the job?"

"Nothing. It's just dangerous as sin, is all. Look, I know I can't talk you out of it, and I know I have no business trying. I'm just being moody."

She guided his arm around her waist, pressed up against him. "Well, don't be. It's nothing you can control—I have to have work to do. My boredom threshold is very low."

"I know that." He finally turned to face her, smiled sadly. "I do love you, you know."

"Well . . . maybe I love you, too."

His smile banished all sadness from his face, like a sudden wind that breaks apart the clouds. "Say it again." His hands reached out to touch her shoulders, her neck, her face. "One more time, with feeling."

"Will not!" Laughing, she tried to break away from him, but he would not let go, and they fell in a tangle to the ground. "Beast!" They rolled over and over in the grass. "Brute!" She hammered at his chest, tore open his jumpsuit, tried to bite his neck.

Tory looked embarrassed, tried to pull away. "Hey, not out here! Somebody could be watching."

The agtechs switched off the arc lamps, plunging Magritte into darkness.

Tory reached up to touch Elin's face. They made love.

Physically it was no different from things she had done countless times before with lovers and friends and the occasional stranger. But she had committed herself in a way the old Elin had never dared to, let Tory in past her defenses, laid herself open to pain and hurt, trusting him. He was a part of her now. And everything was transformed, made new and wonderful.

Until they were right at the brink of orgasm, the both of them, and half delirious she could let herself go, murmuring, "I love you, love you, God, I love you, love . . . " And just as she climaxed, Tory stiffened and arced his head back, and in a voice that was wrenched from the depths of passion, whispered, "Coral . . . "

Elin strode furiously among the huts a terrace down from where she had left Tory asleep in the grass. They had lain together silently after making love, and he had no way of knowing that she was holding him so tightly, burying her head behind his, not out of love or passion, but from outraged anger and fear of what she might do if she had to look at his face.

Some few huts, sheltered from each other by scatterings of maple saplings, were dark. The rest glowed softly from the holotapes within—diffuse, scattered rainbow patterns unreadable outside their fields of focus. Elin halted before one hut, stood indecisively. Finally, because she needed somebody to talk to, she rapped on the lintel.

Father Landis stuck her head out the doorway, blinked sleepily. "Oh, it's you, Donnelly. What do you want?"

To her absolute horror, Elin broke into tears.

Landis ducked back inside, reemerged zipping up her jump-suit. She cuddled Elin in her arms, made soothing noises, listened to her story.

"Coral," Landis said. "Ahhh. Suddenly everything falls into place."

"Well, I wish you'd tell me, then!" She tried to blink away the angry tears. Her face felt red and raw and ugly; the wetware paint was all smeared.

"Patience, child." Landis sat down cross-legged beside the hut, patted the ground beside her. "Sit here and pretend that I'm your mommy, and I'll tell you a story."

"Hey, I didn't come here—"

"Who are you to criticize the latest techniques in spiritual nurturing, hey?" Landis chided gently. "Sit."

Elin did so. Landis put an arm about her shoulder.

"Once upon a time, there was a little girl named Coral—I forget her last name. Doesn't matter. Anyway, she was bright and emotional and ambitious and frivolous and just like you in every way." She rocked Elin gently as she spoke.

"Coral was a happy little girl, and she laughed and played and one day she fell in love. Just like *that!*" She snapped her fingers. "I imagine you know how she felt."

"This is kind of embarrassing."

"Hush. Well, she was very lucky, for as much as she loved him, he loved her a hundred times back, and for as much as he loved her, she loved him a thousand times back. And so it went. I think they overdid it a bit, but that's just my personal opinion.

"Now Coral lived in Magritte and worked as a wetware tech. She was an ambitious one, too—they're the worst kind. She came up with a scheme to reprogram people so they could live *outside* the programs that run them in their everyday lives.

Mind you, people are more than sum of their programming, but what did she know about free will? She hadn't any religious training, after all. So she and her boyfriend wrote up a proposal, and applied for funding, and together they ran the new program through her skull. And when it was all done, she thought she was God. Only she wasn't Coral anymore—not so's you'd recognize her."

She paused to give Elin a hug. "Be strong, kid, here comes the rough part. Well, her boyfriend was brokenhearted. He didn't want to eat, and he didn't want to play with his friends. He was a real shit to work with. But then he got an idea.

"You see, anyone who works with experimental wetware has her personality permanently recorded in case there's an accident and it needs to be restored. And if that person dies or becomes God, the personality rights revert to IGF. They're sneaky like that.

"Well. Tory—did I mention his name was Tory?—thought to himself: What if somebody were to come here for a new personality? Happens about twice a year. Bound to get worse in the future. And Magritte is the only place this kind of work can be done. The personality bank is random-accessed by computer, so there'd be a chance of his getting Coral back, just as good as new. Only not a very good chance, because there's *lots* of garbage stuffed into the personality bank.

"And then he had a *bad* thought. But you mustn't blame him for it. He was working from a faulty set of moral precepts. Suppose, he thought, he rigged the computer so that instead of choosing randomly, it would give Coral's personality to the very first little girl who came along? And that was what he did." Landis lapsed into silence.

Elin wiped back a sniffle. "How does the story end?"

"I'm still waiting on that one."

"Well, did Tory really rig the selection—you're not just making that up?"

"Christ, *I* don't know. Maybe it was just a lucky throw of the dice. But the evidence sure is suspicious. You could try snooping around in his personal storage; he might still have the program squirreled away there."

"Oh." She sat silently for a moment, then pulled herself together and stood. Landis followed.

"Feeling any better, kid?"

"I don't know. More in control maybe."

"Listen. Remember what I said about you being a puppy tripping over its paws? Well, you've just stubbed your toes and they hurt. But you'll get over it. People do."

"Yeah. Thanks."

"Today we make a Buddha," Tory said. Elin fixed him with a cold stare, said nothing, even though he was in green and red, immune. Later, she knew, when he came off his programming, he would remember. "This is a higher-level program, integrating all your mental functions and putting them under your conscious control. So it's especially important that you keep your hands to yourself, okay?"

"Rot in hell, you cancer," she muttered beneath her breath.

"I beg your pardon?"

Elin did not respond, and after a puzzled silence Tory continued: "I'm leaving your sensorium operative, so when I switch you over, I want you to pay attention to your surround. Okay?"

The second Trojan Horse program came on. Everything changed.

It wasn't a physical change, not one that could be seen with the eyes. It was more as if the names for everything had gone away. A knee-tall oak grew nearby, very much like the one she had crushed accidentally in New Detroit when she had lost her virginity many years ago. And it meant nothing to her. It was only wood growing out of ground. A mole poked its head out of its burrow, nose crinkling, pink eyes weak. It was just a small biological machine. "Whooh," she said involuntarily. "This is cold."

"Bother you?"

Elin studied him, and there was nothing there. Only a human being, as much an object as the oak, and no more. She felt nothing toward or against him. "No," she said.

"We're getting a good recording." The words meant nothing: they were clumsy, devoid of content.

In the grass around her, Elin saw a grey flickering, as if it were all subtly on fire. Logically she knew the flickering was the firing of nerves in the rods and comes of her eyes, but emotionally it was something else: it was Time. A grey fire that destroyed the world constantly, eating it away and remaking it again and again.

And it didn't matter.

A great calmness wrapped itself around Elin, an intelligent detachment, cold and impersonal. She found herself identifying with it, realizing that existence was simply *not important.* It was all things, objects.

Tory was fussing over his machines, and it seemed to her that he had made himself into one of his own devices. Push a button and get a predictable response. And was this any way for a human being to live?

Then again, how important *was* a human being? She could not see Tory's back, and was no longer willing to assume it even existed. She could look up and see the near side of the Earth. The far side might well not exist, and if it didn't, well *that* didn't matter either.

She stripped away the world, ignored the externalities. *I never realized how dependent I am on sensory input,* she thought. And if you ignored it—

—there was the Void. It had no shape or color or position, but it was what underlay the bright interplay of colors that was constantly being destroyed by the grey fires of time. She contemplated the raw stuff of existence.

"Please don't monkey around with your programming," Tory said.

The body was unimportant too; it was only the focal point for her senses. Ignore them, and you could ignore *it*. Elin could feel herself fading in the presence of the Void. It had no material existence, but how much less had what she'd always taken for granted: the world and all its glitters.

It was like being a program in a machine and realizing it for the first time.

Landis's voice flooded her existence. "Donnelly, for God's sake, keep your fingers off the experiment!" The thing was, the underlying nothingness was *real*—if "real" had any meaning. If meaning had meaning. But beyond real and beyond meaning, there is something that is. And she had found it.

"Donnelly, you're treading on dangerous ground. You've—" Landis's voice was a distraction, and she shut it off. Elin felt the desire to achieve unity with what *was;* one simply had to stop the desire for it, she realized, and it was done.

But before she could realize the union, horror collapsed upon her. Orange flames shot up; they seared and burned and crisped, and there were snakes among them, great slimy things that reached out with disgusting mouth and needle-sharp fangs.

She recoiled in panic, and they were upon her. The flames were drawn up into her lungs, and hot maggots wallowed through her brain tissues. She fled through a mind that writhed under the onslaught, turning things on and off.

Until abruptly she was back in her body, and there was nothing pursuing her. She shivered, and her body responded. It felt wonderful.

"Well, that worked at least," Tory said.

"What—" her voice croaked. She cleared her throat and tried again. "What happened?"

"Just what we hoped would. Your primary identity was threatened with dissolution, and it moved to protect itself."

Elin realized that her eyes were still closed; she opened them now and convulsively closed her hand around the edge of the cot. It was solid and real to the touch. So good.

"I'll be down in a minute," Tory said. "Just now, though, I think you need to rest." He touched a bone inductor, and Elin fell into blackness.

Floating again, every metaphorical nerve on edge, Elin found herself hypersensitive to outside influences, preternaturally aware, even suggestible. Still, she suspected more than sensed Coral's presence. *Go away,* she thought. *This is my mind now.* She was not surprised when she was answered.

I am here and I am always. You have set foot in my country, and are dimly aware of my presence. Later, when you have climbed into the mountains, you will truly know me; and then you will be as I.

Everyone tells me what I'm going to do, Elin though angrily. *Don't I get any say in this?*

The thought was almost amused: *You are only a program caught in a universal web of programming. You will do as your program dictates. To be free of the programs is to be God.*

Despite her anger, despite her hurt, despite the cold trickle of fear she tried to keep to the background, Elin was curious. *What's it like?* She couldn't help asking.

It is golden freedom. The universe is a bubble infinitely large, and we who are God are the film on its outside. We interact and we program. We make the stars shine and the willows grow. We program what you want for lunch. The programming flows through us, and we alter it and maintain the universe.

Elin pounced on this last statement. *Haven't done a very good job of it, have you?*

We do not tamper. When you are one with us, you will understand.

This was, Elin realized, the kind of question-and-answer session Coral must have gone through repeatedly as part of the Star Maker project. She searched for a question that no one else would have asked, one that would be hers alone. And after some thought she found it.

Do you still—personally—love Tory Shostokovich?

There was a slight pause, then—*The kind of love you mean is characteristic of lower-order programming. Not of program-free intelligence.*

A moment later Tory canceled all programming, and she floated to the surface, leaving God behind. But even before then she was acutely aware that she had not received a straight answer.

When Tory finally found her, Elin was patched into the outside monitors, staring across Mare Imbrium. It was a straight visual program; she could feel the wetwire leads dangling down her neck, the warm humid air of Magritte against her skin.

"Elin, we've got to talk."

The thing about Outside was its airless clarity. Rocks and shadows were so preternaturally *sharp.* From a sensor on the crater's seaward slope, she stared off into Mare Imbrium; it was monotonously dull, but in a comforting sort of way. A little like when she had made a Buddha. There was no meaning out there, nothing to impose itself between her and the surface. "Nothing to talk *about,*" she said.

"Dammit, yes there is! I'm not about to lose you again because of a misunderstanding, a—a matter of semantics."

Elin hopscotched down the slope to the surface, where the abandoned surface mine abutted on the mass driver. "How very melodramatic."

The mass driver was a thin monorail stretching kilometers into Mare Imbrium, its gentle slope all but imperceptible. Repair robots prowled its length, stopping occasionally for a spot-weld; blue sparks sputtered soundlessly over the surface.

"I don't know how you found out about Coral, and I guess it doesn't matter. I always figured you'd find out sooner or later. That's not important. What matters is that I love you—"

"Oh, hush up!" Below the hulking repair robots scurried

dozens of smaller devices, quick and tiny, almost cute. They were privately owned, directed by hobbyists within the crater. Elin redirected a camera to follow one little fellow zipping about in the old strip mine, dragging a cloth sack in one claw, holding a pick in another, waving the third free. A rockhound.

"—and that you love me. You can't pretend you don't."

Elin felt her nails dig into her palms. "Sure I can," she said. The robot was chipping away at a rock outcrop. Dust powdered up, fell quickly. It scanned the sample it had chipped, turning it over and over before the camera lens, then let it drop. It scooted on.

"You're identifying with the woman who used to be Elin Donnelly. There's nothing wrong with that; speaking as a wet-ware tech, it's a healthy sign. But it's something you've got to grow out of."

At the edge of the slope, another robot had set up a holograph generator. It fussed over the machine, set a final switch, then lapsed into quiescence. There was a moment's hesitation, and then a field of blue pillars appeared on the floor of Imbrium.

"Listen, Shostokovich, tinkering around with my emotions doesn't change who I am. I'm not your dead lady-friend, and I'm not about to take her place. So why don't you just go away and stop jerking me around, huh?"

The pillars grew to perhaps a third the height of Magritte before resolution began to fail, and they drifted toward insubstantiality. The unseen operator adjusted their height downward.

"You're not the old Elin Donnelly either, and I think you know it. Bodies are transient, memories are nothing. Your spontaneity and grace, your quiet strength, your impatience—the thousand little quirks of you I've known and loved for years—are what make you yourself. The name doesn't matter, nor the past. You are who you are, and I love you for it."

A host of butterflies appeared, fluttering out of the rock. They danced erratically, yellow and red and orange, each moving randomly, but as a whole drifting through vacuum toward the field of pillars.

"Yeah, well, what I am does not love you, buster."

Several hobbyist robots had abandoned their tasks to follow the flight. Two rockhounds crawled up to the edge of the mine so their owners could see better.

Tory was silent for a bit, his voice almost sad when he finally spoke. "You do, though. You can't hide that from me. I know you as your lover and as your wetware surgeon. You've let me become a part of you, and no matter how angry you might temporarily be, you'll come back to me."

Elin's body trembled with rage; she could feel it. "Yeah, well if that's true then why tell *me*? Hah? Why not just go back to your hut and wait for me to come crawling?"

Emerald green snakes boiled out of the surface, writhed just outside the pillars. Now and again one would snap futilely at the butterflies hesitating, just out of reach, before the pillars.

"Because I want a favor from you. I want you to quit your job."

"Say what?"

There was an odd hesitancy to Tory's voice, as if he were already defeated and knew it. "I don't want you to become God. It was a mistake the last time, and I'm afraid it won't be any better with the new programs. If you go up and become God and can't get down this time, you'll do it the next. I'll spend my life here waiting for you, re-creating you, losing you. Can't you see it—year after year, replaying the same tired old tape?"

Now Tory's voice fell to a whisper. "And I don't think I could take it even once more."

With a surge the butterflies were among the pillars, and the snakes leapt and slithered after them. The instant they were all encompassed, the cold blue pillars flashed violent red, bursting into great gouts of flame, incinerating them all.

"If you know me as well as you say, then I guess you know my answer," Elin said coldly.

The rockhounds waved their claws in applause. The fiery pillars faded away. Switching sensors, Elin could see the robot packing up the hologram generator for the day.

Tory's footsteps sounded, moving away, fading, defeat echoing after.

Only when she was sure he was gone did Elin realize that her sensor had been scanning the same empty bit of Magritte's slope for at least five minutes.

It was time for the final Trojan Horse. "Today we make a God," Tory said. "This is a total conscious integration of the mid in an optimal efficiency pattern. Close your eyes and count to three."

One. The hell of it, Elin realized, was that Tory was right. She still loved him. He was the one man for her, and she wanted him, was empty without him.

Two. Worse, she didn't know how long she could go on without coming back to him—and, good God, would that be humiliating!

She was either cursed or blessed; cursed perhaps for the agonies and humiliations she would willingly undergo for the sake of this one obsessive and manipulative human being. Or maybe blessed in that at least there was *someone* who could move her so, deserving or not. Many went through their lives without.

Three. She opened her eyes.

Nothing was different. Magritte was as ordinary, as mundane, as ever, and she felt no special reaction to it one way or another. Certainly she did not feel the presence of God.

"I don't think this is working," she tried to say. The words did not come. From the corner of her eye, she saw Tory wiping clean his facepaint, shucking off his jumpsuit. But when she tried to sit up to see, she found she was paralyzed.

What is this maniac doing?

Tory's face loomed over her, his eyes glassy, almost fearful. He smiled reassuringly. His hair was a tangled mess; her fingers itched with the impulse to run a comb through it. "Forgive me, love." He kissed her forehead lightly, her lips ever so gently. Then he was out of her field of vision, stretching out on the grass beside the cot.

Elin stared up at the dome roof, thinking: *No.* She heard him strap the bone inductors to his body, one by one, and then a sharp click as he switched on a recorder. The programming began to flow into him.

A long wait—perhaps twenty seconds viewed objectively—as the wetware was loaded. Another click as the recorder shut off. A moment of silence, and then—

Tory gasped. One arm flew up into her field of vision, swooped down out of it, and he began choking. Elin struggled against her paralysis, could not move. Something broke noisily, a piece of equipment by the sound of it, and the choking and gasping continued as he began to thrash about wildly.

Tory, Tory, what's happening to you? He was having a seizure, that much was clear. But inside—within the confines of his skull—what horrors ran rampant? An arm smashed against her cot, rocking it, jolting her mildly.

Whatever was happening, it was bad. And Elin could do nothing about it.

"It's just a *grand mal* seizure," Landis said. "Nothing we can't cope with, nothing we weren't prepared for." She touched Elin's shoulder reassuringly, called back at the crowd huddled about Tory, "Hey! One of you loopheads—somebody there know any programming? Get the lady out of this."

A tech scurried up, made a few simple adjustments with her machinery. The others—still gathering, Landis had been only the third on the scene—were trying to hold Tory still, to fit a bone inductor against his neck. There was a sudden gabble of comment, and Tory flopped wildly. Then a collective sigh as his muscles eased, and his convulsions ceased.

"There," the tech said, and Elin scrabbled off the couch.

She pushed through the people (and a small voice in the back of her head marveled: A crowd! How strange) and knelt before Tory, cradling his head in her arms.

He shivered, eyes wide and unblinking. "Tory, what's the matter?"

He turned those terrible eyes on her. *"Nichevo."*

"What?"

"Nothing," Landis said. "Or maybe 'it doesn't matter,' is a better translation."

A wetware tech had taken control, shoving the crowd back. He reported to Landis, his mouth moving calmly under the interplay of green and red. "Looks like a flaw in the programming philosophy. We were guessing that bringing the ego along would make God such an unpleasant experience that the subject would let us deprogram without interfering—now we know better."

Elin stroked Tory's forehead. His muscles clenched, then loosened, as a medtech reprogrammed the body response. "Why isn't anyone *doing* anything?" she demanded.

"Take a look," Landis said, and patched her into the intercom. In her mind's eye, Elin could see dozens of wetware techs submitting program after program. A branching wetware diagram filled one channel, and as she watched, minor changes would occur as programs took hold, then be unmade as Tory's mind rejected them. "We've got an imagery tap of his *Weltanschauung* coming up," some nameless tech reported, and then something horrible appeared on a blank channel.

Elin could only take an instant's exposure before her mind reflexively shut the channel down, but that instant was more than enough. She stood in a room infinitely large and cluttered in all dimensions with great noisome machines. They were tended by malevolent demons who shrieked and cackled and were machines themselves, and they generated pain and madness.

The disgust and revulsion she felt was absolute. It could not be put into words—no more than could the actual experience of what she had seen. And yet—she knew this much about wet-ware techniques—it was only a rough approximation, a cartoon of what was going through Tory's head.

Elin's body trembled with shock, and by slow degrees she realized that she had retreated to the surface world. Tory's head was still cradled in her arms. A wetware tech standing nearby looked stunned, her face grey.

Elin gathered herself together, said as gently as she could, "Tory, what *is* that you're seeing?"

Tory turned his stark, haunted eyes on her, and it took an effort of will not to flinch. Then he spoke, his words shock-ingly calm.

"It is—what is. It's reality. The universe is a damned cold machine, and all of us only programs within it. We perform the actions we have no choice but to perform, and then we fade into nothingness. It's a cruel and noisy place."

"I don't understand—didn't you always say that we were just programs? Wasn't that what you always believed?"

"Yes, but now I experience it."

Elin noticed that her hand was slowly stroking his hair; she did not try to stop it. "Then come down, Tory. Let them depro-gram you."

He did not look away. "*Nichevo,*" he said.

The tech, recovered from her shock, reached toward a piece of equipment. Landis batted her hand away. "Hold it right there, techie! Just what do you think you're doing?"

The woman looked impatient. "He left instructions that if the experiment turned out badly, I was to pull the terminator switch."

"That's what I thought. They'll be no mercy killings while *I'm* on the job, Mac."

"I don't understand." The tech backed away, puzzled. "Sure-ly you don't want him to suffer."

Landis was gathering herself for a withering reply when the intercom cut them all off. A flash of red shot through the sensorium, along with the smell of bitter almond, a prickle of static electricity, the taste of *kimchi*. An urgent voice cried, "Emergency! We've got an emergency!" A black-and-white face materialized in Elin's mind. "Emergency!"

Landis flipped into the circuit. "What's the problem? Show us."

"You're not going to believe this." The face disappeared, was replaced by a wide-angle shot of the lake.

The greenish-black water was calm and stagnant. The thrust-cone island, with its scattered grass and weeds, slumbered.

And God walked upon the water.

They gawked, all of them, unable to accept what they saw. Coral walked across the lake, her pace determined but not hurried, her face serene. The pink soles of her bare feet only just touched the surface.

I didn't believe her, Elin thought wildly. She saw Father Landis begin to cross herself, her mouth hanging open, eyes wide in disbelief. Halfway through her gesture, the Jesuitical wetware took hold. Her mouth snapped shut, and her face became cold and controlled. She pulled herself up straight.

"Hans," the priest said. "push the button."

"No!" Elin shrieked, but it was too late. Still hooked into the intercom, she saw the funny little man briskly, efficiently obey.

For an instant, nothing happened. Then bright glints of light appeared at all of the condenser units, harsh and actinic. Steam and smoke gushed from the machinery, and a fraction of a second later, there was an ear-slapping gout of sound.

Bits of the sky were blown away.

Elin turned twisted, fell. She scrambled across the ground, and threw her arms around Tory. He did not respond. "I *can't* lose you now," she cried.

Tory smiled sadly, said, "It doesn't matter. You live, you die, you are aware or ignorant—the universe doesn't change. None of it makes any difference." He said something more, but she could not catch it, though she strained to hear.

The air was thinner. The holes in the dome roof—small at

first—expanded as more of the dome flaked away, subjected to stresses it was designed not to take. An uncanny whistling filled the air, grew to a screech, then a scream, and then there was an all-encompassing *whoomph* and the dome shattered.

Elin was thrown up into the air, torn away from Tory, painfully flung high and away. All the crater was in motion, the rock tearing out of the floor, the trees splintering upward, the lake exploding into steam.

The screaming died, and for an instant the air was gone. Elin's ears rang, and her skin stung everywhere. A universal pressure built within her, the desire of her blood to mate with the vacuum, and Elin realized that she was about to die.

A quiet voice said: *This must not be.*

Time stopped.

Suspended between Moon and death, Elin experienced a strange interplay of sensations. The shards and fragments of an instant past crystallized and shifted. The world became . . . not misty, actually, but appositional. Both grew tentative, probabilities rather than actual things.

Come be God with me now, Coral said, but not to Elin.

Tory's presence flooded the soupy uncertainty, a vast and powerful thing, but wrong somehow, twisted. But even as Elin felt this, there was a change within him, a sloughing off of identity, and he seemed to straighten, to heal.

All around, the world began to grow more numinous, more real. Elin felt tugged in five directions at once. Tory's presence swelled briefly, then dwindled, became a spark, less than a spark, nothing.

Yes.

With a roaring of waters and a shattering of rocks, with an audible thump, the world returned.

Elin unsteadily climbed down the last flight of stone stairs from the terraces to the lakefront. She passed by two guards at the

foot of the stairs, their facepaint as hastily applied as their programming, several more on the way to the nearest trellis farm.
They were everywhere since the incident.

She found the ladder up into the farm and began climbing.
It was biological night, and the agtechs were long gone.

Hand over hand she climbed, as far and high as she could,
until she was afraid she would miss a rung and tumble off.
Then she swung herself onto a ledge, wedging herself between
strawberry and yam planters. She looked down on the island,
and though she was dizzyingly high, she was only a third of
the way up.

"Now what the hell am I doing here?" she mumbled to herself.
She swung her legs back and forth, answered her own question: "Being piss-ass drunk." She cackled. *There* was something she didn't have to share with Coral. She was capable of
getting absolutely blitzed, and walking away from the bar
before it hit her. It was something metabolic.

Below, Tory and Coral sat quietly on their monkey island.
They did not touch, did not make love or hold hands or even
glance one at the other—they just sat. Being Gods.

Elin squinted down at the two. "Like to upchuck all over
you," she mumbled. Then she squeezed her eyes and fists
tight, drawing tears and pain. *Dammit, Tory!*

Blinking hard, she looked away from the island, down into
the jet-black waters of the lake. The brighter stars were reflected there. A slight breeze rippled the water, making them twin-
kle and blink, as if lodged in a Terran sky. They floated lightly
on the surface, swarmed and coalesced, and formed Tory's face
in the lake. He smiled warmly, invitingly. Elin stared hungrily
at his lips as he whispered, "Come. Join me."

A hand closed around her arm, and she looked up into the
stern face of a security guard. "You're drunk, Ms.," he said,
"and you're endangering property."

She looked where he pointed, at a young yam plant she had
squashed in the process of sitting, and began to laugh. Smooth-

ly, professionally, the guard rolled up her sleeve, clamped a plastic bracelet around her wrist. "Time to go," he said.

By the time the guard had walked Elin up four terraces, she was nearly sober. A steady trickle of her blood wound through the bracelet, was returned to her body cleansed of alcohol. A sacrilegious waste of wine, in her opinion.

In another twenty steps, the bracelet fell off her wrist. The guard snapped it neatly from the air, disappeared. Despair closed in on her again. *Tory, my love!* And since there was no hope of sleep, she kept on trudging up the terraces, back toward Han's rathskeller, for another bellyful of wine.

There was a small crowd seated about the rock that served Hans as a table, lit by a circle of hologram-generated fairy lights. Father Landis was there, and drinking heavily. "Tomorrow I file my report," she announced. "The Synod is pulling out of this, withdrawing funding."

Hans sighed, took a long swig of his own wine, winced at its taste. "I guess that's it for the Star Maker project, huh?"

Landis crossed her fingers. "Pray God." Elin, standing just outside the circle, stood silently, listening.

"I don't ever want to hear that name again," a tech grumbled.

"You mustn't confuse God with what you've just seen," Landis admonished.

"Hey," Hans said. "She moved time backward or something. I saw it. This place exploded—doesn't that prove something?"

Landis grinned, reached out to ruffle his hair. "Sometimes I worry about you, Hans. You have an awfully *small* concept of God." Several of the drinkers laughed.

He blushed, said, "No, really."

"Well, I'll try to keep this—" she leaned forward, rapped her mug against the rock, "fill this up again, hey?—keep it simple. We had analysts crawl up and down Coral's description of the universe, and did you know there was no place in it *anywhere* for such things as mercy, hope, faith? No, we got an amalgam of substrates, supra-programs, and self-metaediting physics. Now what makes God superior is not just intellect—we've all known some damn clever bastards. And it's not power, or I could buy and atomic device on the black market and start my own religion.

"No, by *definition* God is my moral superior. Now I am myself but indifferent honest—but to Coral moral considerations don't even exist. Get it?"

Only Elin noticed the hunted, hopeless light in Landis's eyes, or realized that she was spinning words effortlessly, without conscious control. That deep within, the woman was caught in a private crisis of faith.

"Yeah, I guess." Hans scratched his head. "I'd still like to know just what happened between her and Tory there at the end."

"I can answer that," a wetware tech said. The others turned to face her, and she smirked, the center of attention. "What the hell, they plant the censor blocks in us all tomorrow—this is probably my only chance to talk about it.

"We reviewed all the tapes, and found that the original problem stemmed from a basic design flaw. Shostokovich should never have brought his ego along. The God-state is very ego-threatening; he couldn't accept it. His mind twisted it, denied it, make it into a thing of horror. Because to accept it would mean giving up his identity." She paused for emphasis.

"Now we don't understand the why or how of what happened. But *what* was done is very clearly recorded. Coral came along and stripped away his identity."

"Hogwash!" Landis was on her feet, belligerent and unsteady. "After all that happened, you can't say they don't have any identity! Look at the mess that Coral made to join Tory to her—that wasn't the work of an unfeeling identity-free creature."

"Our measurements showed no trace of identity at all," the

tech said in a miffed tone.

"Measurements! Well, isn't that just scientific as all get-out?" The priest's face was flushed with drunken anger. "Have any of you clowns given any thought to just what we've created here? This gestalt being is still young—a newborn infant. Someday it's going to grow up. What happens to us all when it decides to leave the island, hey? I—" She stopped, her voice trailing away. The drinkers were silent, had drawn away from her.

"'Scuse me," she muttered. "Too much wine." And sat.

"Well." Hans cleared his throat, quirked a smile. "Anybody for refills?"

The crowd came back to life, a little too boisterous, too noisily, determinedly cheerful. Watching from the fringes, outside the circle of light, Elin had a sudden dark fantasy, a waking nightmare.

A desk tech glanced her way. He had Tory's eyes. When he looked away, Tory smiled out of another's face. The drinkers shifted restlessly, chattering and laughing, like dancers pantomiming a party in some light opera, and the eyes danced with them. They flitted from person to person, materializing now here, now there, surfacing whenever an individual chanced to look her way. A quiet voice said, "We were fated to be lovers."

Go away, go away, go away, Elin thought furiously, and the hallucination ceased.

After a moment spent composing herself, Elin quietly slipped around to where Landis sat. "I'm leaving in the morning," she said. The new persona had taken; they would not remove her facepaint until just before the lift up, but that was mere formality. She was cleared to leave.

Landis looked up, and for an instant the woman's doubt and suffering were writ plain on her face. Then the mask was back, and she smiled. "Just stay away from experimental religion, hey kid?" They hugged briefly. "And remember what I told you about stubbing your toes."

Elin nodded wordlessly. She realized now that she had returned to the rathskeller looking for the priest's advice and comfort. She had wanted to say, "Look. For a moment there I thought I could get Tory back, the same way he got Coral back. But when I tried to raid the computer, I found out they've jacked their security *way* up. So it's only now hitting me that Tory is actually gone, and I want you to talk me out of doing something stupid." But Landis was in bad shape, and one more emotional burden might break her. And Elin would not be the one to do that to her.

She went back home to Tory's hut.

There was one final temptation to be faced. Sitting in the center of the hut, Tory's terminal in her lap, Elin let the soothing green light of its alphanumerics wash over her. She thought of Tory. Of his saying, "We were meant to be lovers," of his lean body under hers in the pale blue Earthlight. She thought of what life would be like without him.

The terminal was the only artifact Tory had left behind that held any sense of his spirit. It had been his plaything, his diary, and his toolbox, and its memory still held the series of Trojan Horse programs he had been working with when he had—been transformed.

One of those programs would make her a God.

She stared up through the ivy at the domed sky. Only a few stars were visible between the black silhouetted leaves, and these winked off and on with the small movements breathing imparted to her body. She thought back to Coral's statement that Elin would soon join her, merge into the unselfed autistic state that only Tory's meddling had spared her.

"God always keeps her promises," Tory said quietly.

Elin started, looked down, and saw that the grass to the far side of the hut was moving, flowing. Swiftly it formed the familiar, half-amused, half-embittered features of her lover, continued to flow until all of his head and part of his torso rose up from the floor.

She was not half so startled as she would have liked to be. Of *course* the earlier manifestations of Tory had been real, not phantoms thrown up by her grief. They were simply not her style.

Still, Elin rose to her feet apprehensively. "What do you want from me?"

The loam-and-grass figure beckoned. "Come. It is time you join us."

"I am not a program," Elin whispered convulsively. She backed away from the thing. "I can make my own decisions!"

She turned and plunged outside, into the fresh, cleansing night air. It braced her, cleared her head, returned to her some measure of control.

A tangle of honeysuckle vines on the next terrace wall up moved softly. Slowly, gently, they became another manifestation, of Coral this time, with blossoms for the pupils of her eyes. But she spoke with Tory's voice.

"You would not enjoy Godhood," he said, "but the being you become will."

"Give me time to think!" she cried. She wheeled and strode rapidly away. Out of the residential cluster, through a scattering of boulders, and into a dark meadow.

There was a quiet kind of peace here, and Elin wrapped it about her. She needed that peace for she had to decide between her humanity and Tory. It should have been an easy choice, but—the pain of being without!

Elin stared up at the Earth; it was a world full of pain. If she could reach out and shake all the human misery loose, it would flood all of Creation, extinguishing the stars and poisoning the space between.

There was, if not comfort, then a kind of cold perspective in that, in realizing that she was not alone, that she was merely another member of the commonality of pain. It was the heritage of her race. And yet—somehow—people kept on going.

If they could do it, so could she.

Some slight noise made her look back at the boulder field.

Tory's face was appearing on each of the stones, each face slightly different, so that he gazed upon her with a dozen expressions of love. This strange multiple manifestation brought home to Elin how alien he had become, and she shivered involuntarily. "Your desire is greater than your fear," he said, the words bouncing back and fourth between his faces. "No matter what you think now, by morning you will be part of us."

Elin did not reply immediately. There was something in her hand—Tory's terminal. It was small, and weighed hardly at all. She had brought it along without thinking.

A small bleak cry came from overhead, then several others. Nighthawks were feeding on insects near the dome roof. They were too far, too fast, and too dark to be visible from here.

"The price is too high," she said at last. "Can you understand that? I won't give up my humanity for you."

She hefted the terminal in her hand, then threw it as far and as hard as she could. She did not hear it fall.

"Good-bye, Tory," she said. "I still love you, but—good-bye." She turned and walked away.

Behind her, the rocks smiled knowingly.

Snow Angels

YOU COULDN'T SEE IT, but the sun was low over the mountains, hidden by the same featureless cloud layer that kept the temperature hovering just above zero. Grey shadows were gathering in the depths of the wood, and gloom filled the hollows.

The man stopped and stared into the dark firs and skeletal oaks, frowning with indecision. A stand of white birches loomed like ghosts. He'd been struggling up the old logging trail for hours now, hoping for a hunting lodge he could break into. But he wasn't going to find one—not before sunset. And it was no joke to be out after dark in this weather.

He started forward again, pushing his stride. The snow was waist-deep, and it was slow going without snowshoes. He half floundered up the trail, arms held high.

Not long after, he broke through into a stretch of trail swept almost clear by the wind. To one side the snow drifted up against a granite outcrop, cresting higher than his head. He bit off a mitten and undid his waist cinch. Slowly, achingly, he shrugged off the pack. His legs hurt and his body was sweaty and itchy under its layers of clothing. He unholstered his hatchet.

It took only a few minutes to chop out a snow cave. He tunneled down into the drift, kicking the loose fill out with his pacs, and dug a hollow big enough to squat in by the sheltering rock.

It took somewhat longer to cut the armfuls of pine boughs he needed to insulate him from the cold floor. The last light was fading when he backed in for the final time, dragging his rucksack after him.

It was dark. He spread out his sleeping bag and knelt atop it, unpacking by feel. Then he blocked the tunnel with his rucksack and set up the stove. He'd made it himself from a coffee can, cutting off the top and punching airholes at top and bottom with a church key. Three dimples halfway down held a small grill. He put a handful of birch bark curlings in the bottom of the can. Then he unwrapped his precious supply of charcoal briquets and placed five atop the grill. Seating the stove firmly where the pack would help reflect the heat back at him, he carefully struck a match and poked it through a bottom vent hole.

The bark went up with a roar. White light danced on walls and ceiling. While the charcoal was catching, the hiker leaned back and took off his pacs, thrusting them deep into his bag. Then he removed the three pairs of wool socks, one thick, two thin, that he wore beneath them. His feet were sweaty. He scratched them long and hard, holding them up to the stove.

He stripped quickly, carefully placing each item of clothing in his sleeping bag, where his body heat would keep it supple. Cold like this could freeze cloth stiff as a board. Naked, he waited a second before slipping into his bag, so the cold air could brace his skin. He lay on his stomach, shivering at first and then warmer, and stared at the stove.

The small space was already getting cozy. The briquets gave off a dull, red light. If he held out his hands, the hiker could see their outlines floating before him. He idly dropped a curl of birch bark atop the coals, just to see it flare. He wondered could the light be seen through the snow, a faint starlike glimmer? Would a passerby see fairy lights at play in the drift, or just walk on unseeing?

The snow over the stove was slightly slick, partially melting from the heat and refreezing into ice. If he kept the fire going long enough it would glaze over the entire cave.

For a moment he thought he heard something—a helicopter thrumming through the sky?—and cocked an ear, listening . . . and afraid. A whine rose in his throat. But it was only imagination. Slowly, he relaxed.

The coals were ready now; he scooped a smaller can full of snow and placed it directly atop them. As the snow melted he was careful to stir it occasionally. If you didn't, you could burn out the can, raising a stink that would drive you out into the cold. Several times he added more snow, and when the water was boiling, he stirred in a packet of dehydrated stew mix.

Sometime later, he pulled the sleeping bag over his face and fell asleep. He dreamed of giant cave bears swimming through the stars, and of baby mastodons frozen in the ice.

In the morning, the hiker emerged from his cave, pushing his pack before him, and discovered that the clouds had cleared during the night. A far sun was beginning its climb through a sky of purest pale blue. It was cold, too, a lot colder than it had been the night before. The kind of cold that stings your face and scours it raw.

A faint breeze stirred the air, passing effortlessly through his many layers of clothing. "Damn." He stamped his feet, and spat onto the snow. The spittle froze the instant it hit, with a sharp *crack*. That meant it was at least thirty below.

The man ducked back into the cave. Kneeling within the body-warm pocket of air, he carefully undid his clothes and took a leak. The smell of urine mingled with pine. Pungent, but it was better than exposing himself outside.

Carefully, then, he wrapped his scarf about his face, leaving only the eyes exposed, laced up his parka hood, and put his mittens back on. Then he re-emerged into the day.

The air bit at his eyes, and he blinked in pain. He shouldered his pack, adjusted its straps, and waded back to the trail. Yesterday's trace was almost undisturbed. If he chose, he could make it down the mountain to where he'd abandoned the Land Rover in half the time it had taken him to get this far.

He headed upslope.

There was an inch-thick crust on the snow, not quite enough to support his weight. He had to break his way through. As he struggled forward, he thought of something he had been told once, that personality exists only in interactions between people. That when a man is alone, he has no traits, no characteristics. He is no different from anyone else.

Do I have no personality? the man wondered. He laughed. Here I go, up the mountain, a spirit of purest ethereality. The sky was heartbreakingly clear. The day was going to be a bright one.

Around noon he stopped to rest, lying with his eyes closed and his feet up on the rucksack. He began cooling off immediately. The problem was that he had to keep moving to maintain his body heat. It was getting tougher to breathe, too, because the scarf before his nose and mouth had stiffened with frost, the moisture frozen out of his breath.

He forced himself to squint into the sky. It was bright and hurt his eyes. When he looked down, the snow was dazzling and he couldn't keep his eyes open at all. Iridescent red shapes swam in his vision.

He was in trouble.

He wasn't prepared for real cold. He needed arctic gear, snowshoes, goggles to protect himself from snow blindness. There hadn't been the time to gather it together; he'd taken what he had, counting on temperatures staying above zero this late in the winter, going to maybe ten below at worst. Even his pacs, with their wool liners and thick rubber soles, were only guaranteed to twenty below.

He pulled a hand free of its mitten and crammed the last of his pemmican bar into his mouth so he could chew as he walked. Then he tugged at his scarf, readjusting it so that one eye was covered completely, and the other nearly so. Through the slit between folds he could see a slice of snow at his feet.

He moved his head up and down, and though pain lanced through his skull, it gave him a rough picture of what was before him. He put his mitten back on and shoved the mittened hand under an armpit to warm it. Time to move on.

Already his toes were getting cold.

As he walked uptrail, he worried what to do. He'd gone too far to turn back now. No way he was going to get down the mountain before dark. He had to find shelter somewhere ahead. Or die, he supposed. He wondered what the gang back at the Data Center in Burlington would think of that? It was hard to imagine people's lives going on after your own death. It didn't seem right. The world ought to come to an end. Out of respect.

He laughed again.

He'd gone maybe a half a mile up the road when he halted. He smelled smoke. Hastily he moved up his scarf for a better sniff. Cold, *cold* air. But there was the faintest tang of woodsmoke on it. The wind was not coming from up the trail, though. He'd have to strike out into the woods to find its source.

By the time he had his face rewrapped his lips were numb and cracked. He felt a warm trickle of blood from one tiny cut.

The way was steep at first. He struggled downslope a step at a time, thrashing through a drift where only the tiniest fingers of brush poked free of the snow, but that was all snarl and tangle underneath. At the bottom of the slope was a small, long-frozen stream. Trying to clamber up the far bank, he took a tumble and went sprawling. One legging pulled free, and he took in a little snow before he could get it tucked back in and the pac laced up again. The snow was cold at first, but then it melted and pooled in the toe, warm and sloshy.

Upslope was tough going. In places he had to pull himself up by grabbing onto scrub trees. He moved with the same slow, awkward motions that the astronauts made as they struggled across the surface of the moon. It was easier for them, though; they hadn't had it so treacherous underfoot.

At the top of the ridge, he looked over his shoulder at his straggling trail and moved to the side to compensate for drift.

Then he picked out a landmark ahead to aim for—a black, wasted tree. If you didn't watch out, traveling in the woods, you'd go in a large, slow circle. Something about favoring one leg over the other. He started downhill again.

The hours passed with bleak monotony as he traveled up one slope and down another. The warm water in the one pac cooled. He lost feeling in his toes, and then his feet. His parka was too bulky for him to keep both hands pressed under his arms, so he took turns warming them, waiting until one was screaming with pain before releasing the other. Neither ever really got warm.

The wind shifted, and it was a long time since he had smelled smoke. He concentrated on traveling in a straight line. The shadows lengthened. The sun was not high above the mountains.

He was beyond weary; his entire body felt dead. He couldn't imagine how he kept going. Just a little further, he kept telling himself, night comes fast in the mountains.

When it was night, he would give up.

There came a time when he was struggling up a slope and sliding down, struggling up and sliding down, and he realized that he did not have the strength to make it all the way up. Not with that rucksack on his back. So he left the pack behind. It made him a little sad, because losing it cut his chances of survival at least in half.

The shadows were dark now, and he could not see the sun. His eyes felt a little better, though his head still ached crushingly, resoundingly. Is it night yet, he asked himself, can I quit now? Just a little further. He topped the rise.

There was a cabin.

He stood looking at the cabin, not sure what to do. Smoke lifted thin and blue into dark evening sky. Orange light spilled from a small window. You couldn't see inside, because a lace curtain covered the window. It was a little room-and-a-half hunting cabin, better made than most, probably hammered together over the course of five or six alcoholic weekends.

He stumbled forward, the end of his scarf swinging free

where it had started to unwind from his face. He tried to run, and couldn't. His feet hit the short wooden porch clumsily. He pawed up the latch, and lurched within.

"Come in." A woman smiled up at him from an overstuffed chair in front of the fireplace. "I've been waiting for you."

He stood there. The woman rose, geisha-graceful in loose chinos and plaid flannel shirt. Hardwood logs blazed at her feet. There was a woodstove going too, behind her, with a kettle steaming on the stovetop. It seemed too much. He couldn't think what to say. Numbly, he shut the door and tried to unwrap his scarf. His mittens kept getting in the way.

"Let me help." She had crew-cut red hair and green eyes as pure and merciless as laser light. Glint of silver at her neck. Her fingers danced over him, undoing the tie strings of his parka. "Poor baby, you went and got yourself all cold."

I'm okay, the man thought. You don't have to. Then his legs buckled and he hit the floor hard. He was lying on his back. Bang. He imagined little white stars.

The woman laughed. Like glass bells afloat in midsummer evening air. She scooped him up in her arms, whirled him around, and set him gently down on the bed. That is one strong woman, he thought. She unlaced his pacs, taking a knife to one where the compacted snow had frozen the thongs, and tugged them off. Looking down the length of his body, the hiker saw that his feet were both corpse-white, turning to grey. He tried to move one, and the pain was like needles of ice lancing his flesh. The woman was singing softly to herself, something calm and sweet.

Somehow his eyes were closed. He listened to the woman bustle about the room. She took a metal bowl from a cupboard, and poured water from the kettle into it. Then she added more water from something that gurgled just like a plastic gallon jug. Nice homey sounds. When the temperature was right, she put the bowl on the bed. "Easy-breezy," she said, easing his feet in. "This'll help." She rolled up her sleeves and began chafing his feet, rubbing them hard between her hands. It hurt, but the pain was distant, almost lost in the universal warmth and ache of his every muscle. His head still throbbed darkly, and he felt queasy. It was too much trouble to tell her that current theory was that rubbing was bad for frostbite.

He opened his eyes and immediately closed them again. Seeing the snowlands he had crossed glowing a radioactive blue, rising and falling to the rhythm of the woman's hands. Every now and then she bent to kiss his feet, chafing all the while.

He fell asleep.

He awoke under a pile of quilts and comforters. It was morning and he was alone. His head felt awful. He wanted simply to burrow deep into bed and darkness forever. "You'll never get to Heaven that way," he grumbled, and throwing back the blankets, swung his feet off the bed.

It was agony to stand. The floorboards were like ice. But there was a fire in the stove and the enameled kettle bubbling away atop it, so the air was almost warm.

Wrapping himself in a blanket, he hobbled about the cabin. It was cluttered in the way that a ship's cabin is cluttered, with crowded tidiness and logical economy. A console wind-up gramopohone stood by the bed, its belly crammed with old 78s. A gun rack was bolted over the bathroom door. But the rack was empty, there was no ammunition in its drawer, and a portable cassette player rested atop the gramophone. A hurricane lamp had been rehung on its ceiling hook, the chain looped to give more headroom. The woman didn't belong here any more than he did.

The bathroom was crammed with kerosene cans, crates of toilet paper and cardboard boxes of dusty paperbacks—nothing he could use. Old sports and hunting magazines lay atop the stacks, covers slightly greasy with age. Poking about, he found one that had been angrily folded in three and shoved behind a crate. He teased it out, stuck it under his arm, wrapped himself in the blanket again.

He prowled the room, laying hands on everything. He found the woman's clothes in an empty liquor cabinet. Atop the mantelpiece was a chunk of Lebanese hashish bigger than his fist, the maker's mark stamped in its side. A brass and ebony pipe leaned against an unmarked bottle with a hundred or so small white pills. Jesus, he thought. Then, in a nightstand drawer he found a leather case that unzipped to reveal row upon row of fine tools—picks, scalpels, wire cutters, needle-nose pliers— that glittered like gems. There were three syringes and a small vial of clear liquid. A set of optically flat palm mirrors, a jeweler's loupe, pencil flashlight, loops of silver cable no thicker than string. This is it, the man thought. Here was the heart of last night's weirdness. But it told him nothing, and he put it back. He turned on the cassette player.

Alien music filled the room.

He stopped, transfixed. Long, trilling ululations swelled and receded, came to sudden stops, chuckled and began again. He'd heard these songs before, the songs the humpback whales sing. But not atop a mountain. It made him aware of what great masses of air there were about him, how far they extended, and how alone he was.

Then he heard the woman outside, stamping her feet on the porch, and hastily retreated to the bed. She came in with a gust of cold air, dangling his rucksack from one hand. She dumped it in the middle of the floor, and snapped off the cassette. Silence, sudden and absolute. Then she went to the stove and pulled off her mittens so she could start warming her hands. She hadn't once looked his way.

"Uh, I suppose I owe you thanks," the man said awkwardly. He was suddenly aware how inadequate words were. "For saving my life, I guess. So, um, thank you." He waited, and when she didn't respond, said, "My name is—"

She whirled, her parka hood still up, and her pupils were cold black holes afloat in green fire. "Mister, I don't give a royal fuck what your name is. All I want to know is when you're leaving, okay?"

He flinched back, startled, but said nothing. He just stared at her hands, at the fine silver cables that looped over pale

skin, tiny flexible tendrils dipping into Teflon sockets implanted in the flesh above each joint. The cable was restrained at the
wrist by a black rubber bracelet before sliding under her
sleeve. He glanced up. A thicker cable emerged from her jersey,
looped through a neck strap, and plugged into a false vertebra
at the base of her skull. "You've got biochip augments," the
man said stupidly.

"Have I?" Her mouth was bitter. "I hadn't noticed." She
shucked her parka, the motions as graceful as a marionette bal-
lerina's. Each small movement was smooth and discrete from
the next. The man watched, fascinated by how complex a set of
gestures went into removing a coat. "Well?" she said.

He looked at her.

"When are you leaving?"

Her contempt took his breath away. But he bit down on his
anger before it could find expression, and kept his voice casual, impersonal. "What's the weather like? Still cold?" No reply.
"I guess I could make it down the foot of the mountain and
hitch a ride out if I started early enough in the morning. I'll
have to wait for it to warm up some, though. I doubt I could
weather over."

Hard, stony face. She glided to the mantelpiece, shook a pill
from the unmarked bottle and threw it down her throat without water. "You *are* real, aren't you?"

"Well, yeah, sure. I mean, I guess so."

"I'd hoped otherwise." With sudden decisiveness she threw
on her parka, pulled a ski mask over her face. Bright, mod-
ernized African tribal pattern. No mouth. She turned to him,
eyes burning from that archetypal terrorist face, and said, "I'm
going skiing. When I get back, I expect to find you gone."

"My feet—"

She stamped outside, slamming the door after her. He could
hear her putting on her skis, and then she was gone.

"Wow." Shaking his head, he got out of bed, began dresss-
ing. "Lady, you are the strangest—" His feet ached. No way he

was going down the mountain today. He yanked the magazine from where he'd shoved it under the mattress.

It was a three-year-old copy of *Sports Illustrated*. A marginally younger version of the woman smiled from the cover, above the headline *Great White Hope?* Inside was an article titled *Fire on the Slopes*. Two-page trick shot the photographer had taken in near dusk, a low sun setting her hair ablaze so that she etched a bright time-exposed line of fire down the shadowy slope, twisting and shifting to create a long, cryptic rune to which she alone had the key.

Magic.

He remembered her now. Jessie James, the desperado of the slopes. A local girl in a place where that counted, born and raised in Montpelier, heart of the Green Mountains, at age nineteen the girl wonder everyone agreed was going to bring Olympic gold home to Vermont. But more than that, an exciting skier, so the article said, an athlete who redefined the possible, a creature of the edges.

"A creature of the edges," he said aloud. He liked that. According to the magazine she practiced her art right on the cutting edge of disaster, courting the kind of perfection found only a reflex-twitch from death or disfigurement. *At peak form,* the article read, *she is harrowing even to watch.*

The man didn't know the first thing about skiing. But these shots of Jessie James in action, they were beautiful. The human body at its best. One in particular, face keen with concentration, hunched low on her skis, making a difficult turn, roostertail of snow rising in a complexly beautiful four-dimensional curve behind her. What could it possibly feel like to be able to do that?

He found a broom, began vigorously sweeping the floor. Trying to remember just what had happened to the famous Jessie James anyway. It wasn't all that long ago that something had stopped her career dead in its tracks. An accident of some kind. Something about an ultralight. A downdraft had slammed her into high-tension lines, burned out her peripheral nervous system, and she'd fallen, crisped and broken, to the ground.

Hell of a way to end your dreams.

At noon he opened a pouch of soup. He ate, then donned his parka and stepped out on the porch. Air bit his face, forcing tears to his eyes. The snow before the cabin was crisscrossed by ski tracks. Down the trail a break in the trees afforded a narrow glimpse of distant mountains and far-below valleys. Directly under him a thin vein of road followed a small frozen river. Something trembled in the still air like a violin string about to snap. The weather was going to change soon. He could feel it.

He went inside to warm up some powdered milk. Thinking about a yogi he'd read of who'd agreed to stop his heart while wired to an EKG machine. They'd found that he didn't slow it down at all, but actually sped it up until it was vibrating so fast and erratically it couldn't beat, and began to fibrillate. His life had been accelerating like that, faster and faster, in increasingly violent jolts, moving toward a sudden stop. He felt himself being pushed to the edges. If he could, he'd leave now. But he didn't dare. People died in weather like this. After a minute he burned a peephole in the window rime with the heel of his hand, and peered out. A puff of wind blew a few crystals of snow past, pick-up from the drifts. The woods were still. As soon as he turned away, he had to stifle the urge to look again.

The fifth time he looked out the window he saw Jessie struggling up the trail. She was leaning on a bundle of skis and poles, as if they were a staff, using them to drag herself forward. One leg was loose and trembling. She fell, and he hurried out to help. He wrestled her into the cabin, let her fall across the bed. She lay there, her leg twitching spasmodically, while he shut the door.

"Damn, damn, damn," she muttered softly. He peeled the mask from her face. She was sobbing with exhaustion and humiliation. "Please." Her eyes were soft and imploring, pupils enormous and black. "My repair kit. It's—it's in the drawer."

"Let me," he said. He laid out the kit, caught her spasming leg between his knees. There were velcroed slits up the sides of her leggings, and he ripped the one open. "I do electronics work all the time, it's my job. Back down the mountain." The knee-ring held the mother cable and three daughter cables. It looked to be the calf muscle that was malfunctioning. He slid a pick into the Teflon cuff and twisted, unlocking the sleeve. Then he yanked the cable, and her leg went dead. "We'll have this fixed in a jiffy." He fitted the jeweler's loupe to his eye, examined the cuff with the pencil flash. It was clean. "Took a spill, didn't you? Probably bruised the cable just above the lead. That's easy enough to take care of."

"I didn't take enough mellow. Should've doubled the dosage. Stupid of me."

"Well, nobody can think of everything." The cable network was fitted in short, modular lengths to make just this sort of repair feasible. He got out a coil of new cabling, eyeballed length, and cut. "You know, I remember when I was in high school, my guidance counselor said to me, 'Your problem is that you're bright, but you're a plodder. You can make a good living at anything you care to put your mind to, but you'll never be the best at anything.' At the time, it felt like being sentenced to death." Jessie's attention was total now, her gaze as focused as a scorpion's. He grinned. "But you know what? For something like this you're better off in my hands than with the best electronics tech who ever lived. And you know why?" She shook her head. "Because I'm not good enough to take any shortcuts. I have to do everything a step at a time, carefully. Story of my life. Jack of all trades, master of none. There." He plugged in the new cable, rocked back on his heels. "How's that?"

Slowly she raised her foot a fraction, lowered it. The leg worked perfectly. She sat up, looked at him expressionlessly. "I envy you, Jack."

"Jack—? Oh, right. Jack of all trades, I get it." He chuckled, shook his head. Lightly touched her knee. "So tell me, Jessie. Just what happened to you out there?"

She didn't ask how he knew her name. "Like I said, not enough mellow." She began removing her outside things. "There's a nice stretch of climax forest not far down from here, no brush at all, just big trees and empty space. That's where I like to break away from the trail. You know how it is when it's really cold—nothing moving anywhere, no wind, perfect silence. And with no trail it takes all your concentration to keep going, so your ego dwindles down to almost nothing. You're just a pair of eyes floating along, moving, gliding, not thinking a thing. The hit I took in the cabin was just kicking in, and it was like the air was filled with liquid God and my body had dissolved into it. So I'd got up a little speed, and I found a short slope I liked, picked out a five-tree slalom, and went down it. But right around the last tree, there was a low limb I hadn't noticed. It just leaped up in front of me. I could have ducked, but it came to me that it was time and I could just pass *through*. Only before I could center myself, everything welled up, and I was lying on the ground, skis and poles scattered about, and this leg flopping over and over.

"That was awful. I hadn't broken anything, but I was a mile from the cabin with a bruised cable and an implant that kept cycling on and off. It was a nightmare getting back."

He listened attentively, hands clasped below his chin, index fingers forming a steeple that peaked at his lips. When she stopped, he said, "But you weren't really expecting to go through that branch, were you? Not actually."

"Oh yes." Her smile was sunshine and confidence. "That's the whole idea."

"Ah. And the pills—?" He nodded toward the bottle on the mantel.

"MDA. It's an amphetamine-related psychedelic. Very big with the suburban-bohemian crowd—they call it mellow. It's sort of like LSD, only without the hallucinations. You know what they used to call LSD, don't you? Acid." She giggled. "That's a good one. A little acid to etch some new circuits in my brain."

"You took drugs and went skiing?" He thought that one over for a minute. Then he turned away, slid the pot of milk from the stove's warming shelf, and began fixing her a mug of cocoa. "Well, it's your business."

Jessie took the cocoa in her hands, set it down untasted. "No," she said. "I want you to understand. It's important to me." She looked over her shoulder. "Where's that hash pipe?"

After a small ceremony of whittling crumbs from the brick of hashish, toasting them in the pipe, and drawing in a lungful of smoke, Jessie raised an eyebrow and smiled with little-girl mischievousness. He shrugged, accepted, inhaled. Everything grew very still.

He exhaled.

As they smoked, Jessie spoke of her accident. Of knowing she was going to die, and then knowing she was paralyzed for life, and then knowing that there was a new series of operations that could return her freedom of movement but that she'd never be able to afford them. And when a Swiss foundation for sports medicine—one she had never even heard of— paid for her implants, she knew then that anything was possible.

At first she was helpless as a baby. "It's like learning to move all over again. You have to consciously think commands, like 'green triangle three' to make a single muscle twitch, and it's so hard to do sometimes you cry with frustration. Your body is one big phantom pain, overlaid with the visual feedback alphanumerics, and it's months before the simplest little motion comes naturally." But she'd given herself to the therapy with the same concentration she'd put into her sport, and by the end of the first year she was walking again. By the end of the second year she was skiing. It wasn't until her third year that her coach—gently, regretfully—explained to her that not everything was possible after all. That no matter how hard or virtuously she practiced, she was never going to reach the Olympics.

He looked around for the pipe, saw it lying on its side by his feet. But when he reached for it his arm wouldn't move, and he couldn't bend forward. Just as well, he thought. As well. Just. He felt as big as God and as distant.

"You have to understand that I was eleven when I started serious training for the Olympics. Even before that—I can't remember not knowing I was going to win the gold. It was my entire life, and when they took it away from me, I was devastated."

"What did you do?"

"I cried a lot. Broke furniture, hurt my friends." Her chuckle was warm and throaty. "At last I decided to do something a little more positive. I thought, if I couldn't excel in the body, then I'd have to excel in the spirit. I was doing a lot of yoga then, for muscle control, and there's this discipline of meditation by which you transcend the body entirely, if you keep at it long enough. I mean, you're actually transported into a higher spiritual realm. So I thought, aim high. Nothing is impossible."

But decades of meditation were not for Jessie, not if there was a shortcut. She learned that researchers had found that large doses of psychedelics could actually reprogram the brain— change personality, rewire modes of thought—if the subject was imprinted by a strong stimulus when the drug's effects were greatest. These experiments were usually conducted in isolation tanks to eliminate outside impressions, but Jessie didn't like the helplessness of that technique. She figured a mountaintop in midwinter would be isolate enough.

"One of my doctors had an unlimited supply of mellow. He had these parties . . . They were a little weird to get used to at first. But if you were a regular, he was willing to share." She stopped. "I know what you're thinking, but it wasn't like that."

"I didn't—"

"Nothing is like that when you're on mellow. You're filled with love for everyone, genuine love. It was perfect for me, because I was steeped in darkness. I needed to purge that. You've seen what I'm like straight—I used to be like that all the time. And I brought along whale tapes to play while I was peaking. Because whales are a superior intelligence, aren't they? More spiritual than us."

The man shook his head. He really didn't know.

Once she'd found this cabin, it had taken five trips to back-pack supplies in. That was two weeks ago. Since then she'd been on a rigorous schedule of vitamins, exercise, and meditation. Once a day she popped the MDA and went out. "It's like skiing through the inside of your own skull," she said. "The body is gone, and only the discipline of will provides motion. The world flows by, and you're that close to breaking through it entirely." As the drug peaked, she'd return to meditate to the tapes. Slowly reprogramming herself into a new consciousness.

When Jessie had finally finished, the afternoon was gone, darkened into evening. The only light in the cabin came from the embered logs in the fireplace. The man shook his head admiringly. "That's brilliant," he said. "I'd never have thought of that myself." Jessie reached out to take his hands in hers. ""Your skin is like ice!" he cried.

"Touch my face. The feedback capability in the augments is just numbers. I can't feel anything below my neck."

Hesitantly, he touched her cheek, the soft skin under one ear. She shivered and rubbed his hand with her face, like a cat. "That's nice," she murmured. Then, "Both hands, please?" And when he did, she started to unbutton his shirt.

"Wait, no," the man said.

"I can make love as well as any woman," she said. "Better. I have perfect conscious control over every muscle in my body." She unbuckled his belt, tugged it from its loops.

"But you can't feel anything."

"Caress my face. I'd like that." She toppled him down on the bed, and knelt over him. "Don't be shy, babe. I almost tran-scended the material world today. That makes me a holy woman, doesn't it? When was the last time you got to fuck a saint?"

Her body was cool and pale, like marble, and the cables of her harness gleamed in the firelight.

He entered her carefully. Slowly Jesssie clamped tight about him, warm and moist. She rose up slightly like a flame riding high on its wick, settled back down like a wave subsiding. He slid a hand up one side of her neck, and his forefinger explored her lips, the tip of her tongue, the wet interior of her mouth. In a kind of wondering stillness, he realized that he believed in her. This very strange woman. It was either belief or a wild kind of love. She bent over him, a jungle cat to the feeding, and the cables dug into his flesh.

She was ferocious. Crouched atop him as if negotiating a difficult slope, her concentration was total, pure, and holy. Long before they were done, he could no longer tell which body was his and which hers, where he ended and she began. If only, he thought crazily, he could become her and flee with her, the both of them, out of this world altogether. Into someplace better.

He melted into her.

Afterward, they lay in each other's arms, under that big mound of quilts, talking quietly about this and that. Things of no matter. "I thought you were a god when you first showed up," Jessie said. "Just for a minute there."

He laughed at the idea. "Why would you think that?"

"When you're meditating, you progress through higher and higher mental levels. And just as you're making real progress, you break through into the realm of the gods, and they approach you with gifts and power, and say, 'Give up your quest. Stay here with us. We'll make you a god.' So I was kind of expecting them.

"I'd reached that state of perfect clarity where you're riding the top of the rush and everything's going faster and faster, in a kind of controlled explosion, an endless expansion of reality, right? When there was this sudden *hush*, this sense of . . . immanence in the air. Like something important was about to happen. And just at that precise instant, in you walked. Anybody would've made my mistake."

He hesitated, then said, "Suppose it's not true? What if there aren't any other levels of reality? No gods. No . . . other world to move into."

"Then I haven't lost anything by trying, have I?"

"No, I suppose not." He felt her dig her face into the side of his neck, the tip of her nose small and cool. "It must be hard on you. Knowing that you used to be the best."

"I still am," she said sleepily. "Even better than before the accident. Everybody says so. But the bastards won't let me compete."

Something within him grew very still. "How's that?"

"There was a big scandal, year before last, a couple of members of the U.S. fencing team had the nerves to their wrists severed, and augments implanted. See, a nerve fires slow compared to electrical current through silver wire, so they were upping their reflex time by a few hundred nanoseconds. That was right after the stink about the Bulgarian peptide treatments and the big Finnish operant conditioning scandal. So they came down hard, rewrote the rules book, red-lined me out of the Olympics forever." Her voice was flat with the monotone of a tale repeated so many times all residual trace of bitterness had been worn away. "But I'm putting all that behind me now."

"But you can ski as well as before?" he insisted.

"They told me I should get a gig in Austria or one of the new resorts in Kenya, teaching rich—'scuse me—rich tourists." She yawned again. Her voice was low, murmurous. "Bastards wanted me to coach."

In the morning the sky was a uniform grey and the temperature had risen above zero again. He carried his rucksack on the porch, glanced toward the woods, and cocked his arm. He threw as hard as he could. The bottle made a silent hole in the snow by the trunk of an old pine. He hoisted the pack.

He'd meant to slip away before Jessie awoke. Just be off and gone without having to confront her. But now he looked down the mountain and saw a grey dragon creep into the valley below. It flowed smoothly across the frozen river, rippled over a fence and came to a halt on the roadway. One of the army's new personnel carriers.

He knew the carrier's operational specs by heart. Those carbon whisker reinforced "legs" were capable of 45 mph on the straightaway, and lesser but dependable speeds on slopes of up to sixty degrees. Any terrain a man could cross, it could follow. It could swarm right up the mountain after him.

"So why don't you?" he said bitterly. "Come and get me."

The dragon stirred, twisted, and sped down the highway. It would be back, though, he knew it. A few snowflakes blew past. The man looked up, over the rooftop, and was startled how dark it was getting to the north, how fast the clouds were coming on. It was going to be a real bitch in a few minutes.

By the time he stepped back inside the cabin the first slanting flurries were coming down.

He slammed the door. Jessie sat up in bed, eyes shadowy and cryptic. In the morning light her skin was ashen under its metal harness, with small, puckered black nipples. "I don't suppose you have a gun?" he said. "A hunting rifle, a pistol? One of those ladylike little electronic jobs you see on TV?"

"Cram it up your ass," Jessie said drowsily. She gathered her clothes and the palm mirrors from her kit, then disappeared into the bathroom. The wind boomed and shook the cabin. With a pounce and crunch of airy fangs and claws, the storm was upon them.

He spent the morning packing and repacking his gear, while Jessie ran through an endless series of exercises in the middle of the floor. Always he kept one ear on the blizzard, its shrieks and moans and sudden silences. It had come on too fast, too eager—he guessed it would blow itself out by noon.

Jessie grunted and rose to a kneeling position. Their eyes met, and she snapped, "What are *you* looking at?"

The unrelenting silence between them had eaten away at him through all these long hours, gnawed at his patience until there was none left in him at all. He blurted, "You know, I believed in you!"

She blinked.

"I thought . . . I met you here, I heard your story, and I thought, Here's someone special." He stood, walked to the far side of the cabin and back again. There was no room. He peered out the window. Still snowing. He let the curtain drop. "You know, there was a nineteenth-century sculptor somewhere, in Bennington I think it was. Maybe Brattleboro. One Christmas Eve, while everyone else was at services, he created his masterpiece—a life-sized angel in snow, right out in front of the church. All the local people, they came out from midnight mass, and there it was. This . . . beautiful angel. Waiting for them in the moonlight."

Green eyes, reptilian calm. "So?"

"So okay, I've never done anything remarkable in my life. I accept that. But I've never even seen something special. Those townspeople, they couldn't have made the snow angel themselves, but at least they saw it. They bore witness. And you, I thought you were special, a snow angel, someone like nobody's ever seen before. But you're just one more quitter. You say you're the best, but you're giving it up because you can't get a lousy gold medal. What does a medal have to do with anything?"

She lifted the pipe from the floor and with feathery touch brushed a few unburnt crumbs of hash from the end table into the bowl. "Okay, I give up. I wasn't going to ask, but just who the fuck are you, Jack? What are you doing in my life?" She fired up the pipe and handed it to him.

He took a puff. Suddenly he was dizzy and had to sit down. The fabric on the easy chair's arms was frayed and white. When he tried to draw on the pipe again, there was nothing in the bowl but ashes. "I'm not doing anything," he said unhappily. "I'm just a guy. The government's after me."

Jessie said nothing.

"We were doing contract work for the Canadians. Harmless enough stuff, really, but then the government stepped in and classified everything. They wanted us to falsify the results. To cover up that we'd come up with something valuable. I guess I did something stupid." He brushed a hand through his hair. "I couldn't cheat them like that. We accepted their money."

Without warning, Jessie roared with laughter. It was spooky how her features twisted and reddened, her head bobbed and shook, and yet her body sat immobile, hands on knees, feet on floor, like a dynastic Egyptian statue. At last she calmed. "Ah God," she said. "Ah God. What a sad creature you are, Jack."

"Well, maybe I am!" he said angrily. "Maybe I'm on the run. But at least I'm *running*. I'm not sitting in the middle of nowhere, burning my brains out, waiting for gods to walk in the door. Committing suicide—that's what you're doing."

"How you talk." She sounded genuinely amused. Then, cold again, "When are you leaving?"

A burst of wind howled like a celestial freight train chasing its tail across the mountaintop. The personnel carrier would be stalled down below; it couldn't travel in this. Still, it was brightening up outside. The wind was carrying less snow. "Soon."

Jessie nodded and stood with stately grace. The hashish flashed him an iceberg avalanching upward to rejoin its mother glacier. She snapped on the cassette player and went to the mantelpiece. Delicate cetacean music mingled with the wind in a swirl of dissonances and chance harmonies. "Jack," she said. "What happened to my pills?"

"I threw them away."

Her back was to him. "Why would you do a thing like that?"

For the same reason a man would take a can of poison from a child, or a loaded gun from a drunk. For the same reason that same man might suddenly find himself homeless, without career or friends, alone and hunted. Because he'd been brought up that way. Because he had no choice.

"Those things are making you crazy," he said. "Trying to ski through a branch. Next time it'll be a tree. Or a cliff. You're not the Buddha, Jessie, and you're not any kind of saint. You're just plain deluding youself."

In one swift, frictionless motion, she turned and seized his hand between hers. Her face glittered with tightly restrained violence, and for the first time he was a little afraid of her. "How does my skin feel?"

"Cold."

"Wait." She fell silent. After a second her flesh felt less chill. He thought it an illusion at first, their shared hands reaching for isothermy. But then her hands were definitely warmer than his own. Much warmer. They were actually hot, as if she were flushed and running a fever. They grew hotter yet, until finally he yanked his hand away in pain. "How did I do that?" Jessie demanded. "How could I do that if I'm deluded?"

"Biofeedback—" he began falteringly.

"Biofeedback, my ass!" she folded her hands open, as if making the sign for book. "Look at my palms!"

He could feel the heat radiating from her. As he watched, the angry red skin blossomed with clusters of white blisters. They swelled and ballooned, and the skin edging them darkened, blackened, and crisped. He could smell her flesh burning.

Small hairs rose on the back of his neck. Abruptly the room seemed all color and shimmering surface, unreal, impermanent, the floor ready to give way underfoot, the walls about to melt into starless void. He staggered back a step and cried, "You can't do that!"

"I'm a god, baby. I can do what I want." She thrust her hands almost into his face. "Look at them. Touch them. Is this a trick? Am I faking?" When he shook his head, she stuck her hands under her arms, as if to warm them. "The body is only illusion, Jack. It does what the mind tells it to do. But that's only the beginning. The body is easiest to control because you grow up thinking of it as yours. But everything is illusion. Existence is illusion, being is illusion, the world is illusion—it'll do whatever you tell it to. You only have to learn confidence."

She held out her hands again and the charring was gone, the skin whole. He opened his mouth, could say nothing. The last blisters dwindled to nothing and were gone, like soap bubbles winking out of existence. "Bring me my pills, Jack."

He stumbled outside, hastily zipping his parka. He'd forgotten his mittens. The snow was falling lightly now, the storm over. The hole by the old pine had been swept away, of course, but he remembered where it had been. Falling to his knees, he swept about under the snow with both hands. The bottle stung his fingers as he carried it in.

"Thank you, Jack." Jessie popped two pills in her mouth, hesitated, and then shook out two more. She raised an eyebrow, a look of almost malicious caprice on her face. "Tell you what, Jack, I'll take you along with me. That's what you'd like, isn't it?" She proffered the pills.

He was stunned. The pills stared up at him from her palm, and the afterimage of her smile burned beneath them like neon. In that instant he wanted it so badly, this form of escape she offered, that he almost bent his lips to her hand. He was never going to make it over the border. Not without some kind of miracle. Beam me up, he thought. Get me the hell out of this shitful world.

She could do it, too. It would be easy for her. Just reach out a hand from the other side and drag him after her, leaving nothing behind but a cooling woodstove and a cabin surrounded by virgin snow. Jessie swam in his sight, all but sparkling with impermanence, anchored to existence by the most fragile ties of habit and nostalgia. But it wasn't his way. Everything he'd gotten in this life had been by his own efforts, even the trouble he was in. He wasn't about to start cheating now.

"You don't understand." He took a deep breath, shouldered his rucksack, turned away. "You don't understand a thing."

The way down a mountain is always easier than the way up. Still, night comes quickly in the winter, and it wouldn't do to reach the state highway at sunset. Best keep an eye out for a spot to dig a cave so he could sleep over. When the clouds rose, they'd be able to lift a copter over the mountain. He'd have to keep under the trees then.

Canada wasn't more than fifteen miles distant, twenty at the outside, but he doubted he'd ever reach it. Now he was glad he hadn't found a gun. Those things weren't protection. The most he could do with one was take some poor grunt with him.

The trail turned, and he suddenly came face to face with a stretch of sheer cliff. The slow seepage of water from bedrock had covered the rock with organ pipes of ice, hundreds of them, cascading one over the other, some thicker than both his legs together, others as slim as his little finger. Pale colors lurked in the depths, yellows and blues and pinks in rippling curtains, as if the aurora borealis had been frozen and slammed down to earth. He bared his head to the cold, shoving back his hood and snatching off his cap, struck by the presence of something holy.

For a long minute he stood there, not even thinking.

But there were still soldiers down the mountain. They'd likely found the Land Rover by now. If so, they'd be coming up after him.

He couldn't stay.

Reluctantly he trudged on, repeatedly staring back over his shoulder, until the old logging road turned into a stand of dark firs, and the ice was gone.

A few light, fluffy flakes of snow were falling now. Slow, puffy things that nobody could possibly take seriously. He tried to catch one on his tongue. Then he stepped up his pace, swinging his arms. After a while he began to sing. "Oh, the bear went over the mountain . . ." For some reason he felt wonderful.

He thought of snow angels then. The kind you make as a child, lying down in the snow, kicking arms and legs to form the wings and skirts. He hadn't made a snow angel since he was a boy. The man laughed. He promised himself that before the day was over, he would find an open space and make one.

Perhaps several.

The Man Who Met Picasso

IN ANOTHER TIME, another place, the shop could have been a magician's lair. A gargoyle crouched, stone wings spread, above the shabby brownstone's doorway. Submerged within dark windows were cracked Tiffany lampshades and statuettes of Grecian gods and maidens, lacking here an arm, there a head, that on the originals had survived into modern times. Weathered gilt lettering on the panes read: FRANZ WEIL—RESTORATIONS.

Half a block away a gas station stood at the corner of an expressway feeder. Beyond it, air shimmered over the pavement. It mingled with exhaust fumes, was blasted apart by loud cars bright with hot chrome. Somewhere, a burglar alarm warbled monotonously, endlessly.

But inside, the shop was quiet, the traffic muted. Shadowed shelving reared over a nondescript desk and a few square yards of carpet. The vases and platters, cracked goblets and broken figurines, might have been the slow limestone growths of a cave. An air conditioner in some distant part of the house took the edge off the heat, kept the windows closed.

The old man positioned himself by the desk, reached a gnarled hand to the side, closed it about a circle of glass. He shuffled to the window, where a solitary sunbeam pierced the gloom. It caught his white hair and suffused it with holy light.

The glass plate flashed purple fire as he held it up, turning it over and over again in his hands. "The fragments had to be baked together, or else with the first little touch of tension they would snap again." His voice was gentle and contemplative. "It's no great trick if you have the clamps to hold the pieces together perfectly. But they don't sell such things; there's not the market. You have to build them yourself, you see?"

The customer nodded his head respectfully.

Weil put the glass down and started to turn, then stopped to pick up a Hummel figurine. It was a fat boy with rouged cheeks; he was playing an accordion. "Look at this," he said with mild disgust. "People collect these things, you know. Tell me—would *you* waste your time repairing a thing like this?"

The man smiled slightly, and shook his head.

"That's good. Time is precious, it's the one limitation you can't ignore. When I was young, I spent a *month* building a single set of clamps—imagine that! Well, at least I had the skill. I was a sculptor then; yes, I was." He straightened slightly, to stare off into some nonexistent distance, and his voice grew reminiscent. "How I wasted my youth! When I think of all I had—and I spent my life on trash like this."

Still the customer said nothing, but it was an encouraging sort of silence, and after a quick glance through his shaggy eyebrows, Weil gestured the man to a chair.

"It was so very long ago," he mused.

It was an early autumn evening. Paris was wet and miserable, and I was on my way to hear Georges Thill at the Opéra. This was a ridiculous expense for an art student—there were days when all I had to eat was one lousy apple—but my friend Marissa had received the tickets from her parents, and invited me along. I remember that I had been working in granite that day, and my hands were slightly red, and tingled pleasantly.

We were just chums, Marissa and I, not lovers, and she was

not a good-looking woman. No, I lie—she was extremely beautiful. But it was all internal; to the eye, she was quite ugly.

We were walking along a drab and weary street—quickly, for our coats were light—and the buildings were all huddled together and soaked with *tristesse*. I was making some laughing comment when Marissa grabbed my arm and pointed across the street.

"Le Boeuf!" she hissed. We'd nicknamed Picasso the Bull because at that time he was painting all those pictures of minotaurs. I looked, and there he was. Seated at a café table by the curb, hunched over a drink, with that little black beret of his slouched across his head.

I shrugged. "So?"

"This is your chance," she whispered urgently. "Go up and ask him about the navel our teacher was telling us about."

"You want me—a student, a nobody—to go up to *Le Boeuf* and ask about a painting?" I snorted. "He wouldn't give me the time of day."

"You must go up and ask," she insisted fiercely.

"No, no, I couldn't."

"Well, if you won't, then I *will*." And looking into those blazing green eyes, I knew that she meant it. My heart sank.

"No, don't do that—he would only be rude to you." He had a reputation for that kind of behavior. "Better that I go."

"Then go!"

I waited a beat by the curb, then darted between the cars to the other side. Taking a deep breath, I approached Picasso's table and stood across from him, not daring to speak before he noticed me.

Slowly he raised his head, lifted those baleful eyes to mine. They glared with a malevolent light, and his mouth moved like that of a camel.

"Crétin!" he spat.

I bowed politely. *"Oui, Maître."* If the Master told me I was a cretin, who was I to disagree?

"Maître?" he asked. "You are one of us, then—an artist?"

"*Un élève,*" I said. "Only a student."

"Sit!" He pointed imperiously at the wire chair opposite him, and I obeyed. He glanced at my rough callused hands. "A sculptor, eh?"

I admitted this was so, and he looked pleased. "You will have a drink with me."

"Thank you, *Maître,* but I—"

"*Garçon!*" He snapped his fingers and a waiter materialized. He pointed at his glass. "Another for my companion."

The waiter brought anisette, a drink I had always loathed. I took a sip, trying not to grimace.

For a moment he studied me silently. A leaf fell to the table, and he glanced at it, deemed it unworthy, and swept it away. "You have a girlfriend across the street?" he asked suddenly.

Marissa was indeed standing where I'd left her, clutching her light cloth coat about her, and peering anxiously at us. But Picasso was facing away from her; he must have seen my glances. "She is not exactly my girlfriend," I began.

"Bring her over!"

Back across the street I ran, to where Marissa stood shivering. I took her hand, and led her back. She stood humbly before the great man, and he looked her up and down with those basilisk eyes. "You know," he said, "you are a remarkably ugly woman."

"*Oui, Maître.*"

"Sit down!"

Picasso snapped his fingers for the waiter, pointed to his glass again, the man darted away. "And yet—there is something about that chin. Come by my studio next week, and I will paint you."

"*Merci, Maître.*"

"Bah!" he snorted in disgust. Marissa's anisette arrived, and she drank it with apparent pleasure. Picasso turned to me again.

"So. Obviously you have a question, or you would not have dared approach me—out with it!"

I stared into the milky liquid in my glass. "You did a painting," I said hesitantly, "some ten years ago, of a woman—a nude. It was called *La Belle*—"

"Bah! Do you have any idea of how many women I have painted in my life? Hundreds! Thousands! And out of all these years you expect me to remember *one* painting?"

"She had an orange navel," I said. The principal of our school had lectured us for a full day on that one painting.

"Ahhh," Picasso said. "I know the one you speak of—what about it?"

"Our teacher, the dean of our school, he said that the navel should not have been orange—that it should have been green."

Picasso's attention was absolute. A truck smashed through a nearby puddle, throwing up a rooster tail of water that almost sprayed the table, and he did not notice. "And what did he say about my painting it orange?"

"He said that you were a fool."

"Der Scheisskopf!" The Master's face turned red, and he began swearing in German, an endless stream of truly foul words. I wriggled in my chair in embarrassment.

He noticed my reaction, and stopped in midcurse. "So," he said. *"Sie können Deutsch."*

"Ein klein Plattdeutsch," I admitted. I was by no means fluent, but I knew enough German to follow his outburst.

"Well then, you go back to your teacher, and tell him he plays with himself."

"What!" I cried in astonishment. Marissa's hand flew up to her mouth, tried unsuccessfully to stifle a giggle.

"Tell this pig that he plays with himself—tell him that *Picasso* says so."

I shook my head politely but firmly. "You want me to tell the dean of my school this? No, I am afraid not."

"Ahhh," he said. "You are one of *those.*" I had managed to choke down my anisette, and he noticed that the glasses were empty, gestured for refills. I winced inwardly. Picasso glared at me. "And what do *you* think, eh?"

"I do not know why you painted it thus," I said. "But I know that Picasso had a reason."

"Oh? And how do you know that?" There was something dangerous, something very animal, about the way he hunched forward over the table, and I found myself tongue-tied, unable to reply.

Marissa, silent until now, said, "The painting has become almost an obsession with Franz; we have discussed it often. And he told me that you must have had a reason because, he said, Picasso is a wizard!"

Picasso rocked back in his chair, bellowing with laughter. "A wizard! That's good! So you think I am a wizard, eh, my little sculptor?"

"Oui, Maître," I said humbly.

"Then, my young sorcerer's apprentice, I must *be* your wizard, eh?" His eyes filled with dark demonic mirth. "But understand first of all that I do not speak about my work. The paintings themselves must do the talking, or else it is only words."

He was silent for a moment, but it was a compelling silence. He was in control of it.

"But," he said at last, "if you really wish to learn, then I will tell you what to do. Are you familiar with the works of El Greco?"

"Yes, certainly, in reproductions."

"Reproductions—bah! Reproductions are nothing. You cannot know a work until you have seen it. But I'll tell you what— you must go to the Prado."

"Me? Go to Madrid?" I was astonished all over again.

"Yes. To the Prado. On the second floor you will find an El Greco called *Rooftops of Toledo.* You go there and stand before it. Look at it. There is a vast spread of roofs, all the city laid out under either a sunrise or a sunset. Just off the center is one orange roof, the only orange one among all the others. Hold your thumb so that it covers that roof and no more. You must study the painting, see it as a whole. Then *pull* your thumb away, and you will have your answer."

"And for this I have only to go to the Prado?" It was so ludicrous a suggestion that I had to struggle not to laugh aloud.

"Yes, that is your quest—your wizard is sending you there."

I shrugged. "I know you can tell by my accent that I am an American. But you must understand that my family is poor, and I am here on a scholarship. Where would I come up with that kind of money?"

He stared at me for a moment. Then he took out a leather wallet, ran a thumb through its contents. Calmly he counted out five hundred francs and gave them to me! "Take this," he said, "and go. Take her"—he jerked his head at Marissa—"your girlfriend, with you. Both of you do as I have directed." The night was beginning to fall, the street going dark. We had missed the opening of *Faust*.

"Now I am not giving this to you. If you go to Madrid and spend your time foolishly, *you owe me this back*. But—if you do as I have instructed, and return with the answer, then you owe me nothing. The money is yours. And I will tell you why I painted the woman's navel orange."

I sat there, his money in my hand, not knowing what to say or do. I opened my mouth and shut it again.

Picasso grew suddenly angry. "Go away!" he snapped. "You are disturbing me—get out of here!"

So we went.

It was an interesting trip. Marissa costumed herself as a *haute-bourgeoise*, and with a constant stream of demands and complaints made life miserable for the staff. It got so that the porter would hunch his shoulders and try to bull his way past our compartment. To no avail. Marissa darted out, fox stole swinging, and seized the man's arm with her long red nails. "My pillows!" she shrilled. "They are *flat!*"

The man threw up his hands in dismay. His little mustache drew in on itself. "Madame—"

"And the sandwiches in the luncheon car—the lettuce is quite definitely wilted!"

The porter could not edge away, for Marissa still clung to his arm. She leaned quite close to the poor man, and with an air of final triumph, added, "And my lover—this morose young artist here—he is *lousy* in bed!" Then she released him.

The porter fled down the corridor. As soon as he was out of sight, Marissa collapsed across her seat in laughter.

I sat cracking my knuckles, thinking of Picasso, of all the money I owed.

The Prado was all smooth marble floors and cold echoes. We arrived early—I had not even allowed us time to freshen up— and the galleries were practically deserted. Now and then we'd hear twinned sets of heels click-click by, or a scattered fragment of light conversation. It did not take us long to find the *Rooftops of Toledo.*

Humbly, like supplicants, we stood before the work. It was a grandiose sweep of roofs caught in the rich low-lying Spanish sun. I could have eaten an apple in the time we stood there, core, seeds, and all. Then slowly, hesitantly, I raised my thumb at arm's length until it just covered the orange roof near the center of the painting.

Agonized minutes crept by. My thumb wavered slightly, but I held it stationary until my entire arm ached with fatigue poisons. Cold sweat beaded up on my forehead. And finally I *pulled* my thumb away triumphantly.

And I saw—nothing.

I almost collapsed. The painting floated before me, flat, daubed with colors, the speck of orange enigmatic and mocking. Sweaty and pale, I turned to Marissa to ask: Had *she* seen it?

She shrugged—no. Whatever this great secret was, she had not seen it either, nor did she especially care.

That was Marissa. She had shrewd intelligence, verve and self-confidence, and a cool discerning eye. But she was only a *dilettante,* a dabbler. She had enrolled in the school because it was fashionable, the thing to do. There is no discredit to her in this, only—she was not an artist. She didn't care.

But I had to care, because to fail this test would be to admit that I also was no artist. So again I tried, only this time differently.

You cannot actually *see* a painting unless it fills you. I had been thinking of Picasso, feeling the weight of his money and the fear of his disapproval. All of this I forced myself to forget. I stood and simply let the painting grow, until it was all I saw and all I thought of. Instead of seeking answers, I waited.

Marissa wandered away to look at other works, but I did not notice. Only dimly, distantly, was I aware of the slow passage of time, of the still air, the quiet. Moving like a somnambulist I raised my thumb, held it steadily before me. I studied the painting, without demands or expectations.

Then I snapped my thumb away. And I saw.

I could have sobbed in relief. The museum gallery seemed to swim about me. I turned to Marissa, saw that she was not there, that she was several paintings away, and hurried to her side.

"Do you want to try again?" I asked.

"No," she said. She looked at me oddly. "You have the most idiotic grin on your face."

I realized suddenly that my cheeks hurt. But what did I care? I grabbed Marissa, swung her around, kissed her right there in the middle of Prado!

Events kept me from reporting back to Picasso immediately on my return. But one bright October morning found me on the rue des Grands-Augustins, where his studio was. The seventeenth-century mansion houses along the street had been subdivided into offices and businesses, a little worn but not quite shabby. Balzac had lumbered ponderously down this very way, a walrus touched by divine fire, and I followed in his footsteps. The day was unseasonably warm, so bright and fine that I almost forgot my troubles.

At number 7, I plunged within and hurried up a gloomy spiral stairway. I took the steps two and three at a time, past a process server's office, up to a simple door on which was tacked a handwritten note. *"C'est ici,"* it said—here it is. I knocked.

For a moment, nothing. Then the door flew open, and Picasso stood before me, wearing a striped sailor's shirt and white duck pants. He carried a mop under one arm, and in the hand of that same arm held a galvanized steel bucket of whitewash.

"Herr Weil," he said threateningly. I was flattered that he had remembered my name. "Come in!"

Flooded with cool northern light, the studio was a vast and colorful pigsty. Frayed chairs were half-buried under piles of tin cans, pegboards, burlap, and steel rods. Canvas flats leaned against walls brightened by here a Matisse, there a Rousseau. And everywhere, of course, were his own canvases—but they were placed facing the walls, not to be seen.

"You have interrupted me in the middle of my work," Picasso said, steering me around a pile of newspapers and paintpots, out of which poked an old rusting bicycle. "Stand *there*—and do not make a sound until I am done."

He planted me beside a broken-seated cane chair on which rested several canvases, a Modigliani peeking out from the rear. I almost caught my ankle in a snarl of wire when I realized that I was standing on one of the Master's sketches, and frantically hopped away. I steadied myself with one hand on a paint-flecked ladder, and watched him work.

One wall of the studio was all plate glass, with clear autumn light streaming through. Beyond, I could see the tail end of a line of brick rowhouses, with tiny walled-in yards, and a cemetery. The sky was as flatly blue as that of any Miró, and the graveyard, with its orchardlike lines of small white tombstones, was all grass gone brown.

Picasso was painting goats on the window. He dipped the mop into the bucket of whitewash, then smoothly, surely, painted directly onto the glass, as if the mop were a gigantic brush. I stood entranced.

Those goats—! The man had an uncanny, a perfect knowledge of animal anatomy. The goats gamboled joyfully on the glass, and though they were drawn with broad strokes, almost as cartoons, every detail was perfect. In a single continuous sweep he drew a head, continuing the line to include the bump on the back, the upswelling behind the cranium.

The mop danced across the glass, creating ritual, making these creatures of the spring into something sacred, something that could not be expressed in words alone.

Finally, he was done. He stepped back to study the work, and without looking at me, said, "What do you think?"

I kissed my fingertips. *"C'est magnifique!* You are truly a great artist."

"No," he snarled. "I want your honest opinion."

There was some small movement in the cemetery beyond the glass, but I could not look past those luminous sprightly goats. "No opinion was ever more honest," I said. "You are magnificent, a great artist—a wizard!"

Grasping a large sponge, he advanced menacingly on the window. "It is not good enough for *Picasso,*" he said, and wiped it all clean.

I could have cried to see first one goat, then another, disappear in ugly white smears. The Master worked vigorously, attacking the glass, until it was all clean. I could look beyond now, and see the tiny figures on the dying grass, gathered about a small hole in the ground, a funeral.

Picasso threw the sponge away and turned to me. "You have been to the Prado, otherwise you would not dare show your stupid face before me. And now you think you have seen what I instructed you to see, eh? Well—I am waiting."

I faced him squarely. He could not bully me; I knew what I had seen. "I have done as you told me, and I have two observations."

"Eh! I send you to see one thing, and you come back with two," he sneered.

"The first thing I saw was that it was not a sunrise, but a sunset."

"That is so," he said impatiently. "And the other?"

"The second thing I saw was that the orange roof spreads the color of the setting sun about the rooftops, so that the eye sees its warmth on them all, even though there is not a touch of orange paint on any of the others."

"Exactly!" he cried. *"That* was what I sent you to see. El Greco had set himself a problem: he wanted to show the rich glow of sunset on the roofs, but without daubing pigment on each and every roof. He wanted to do it in the most economical fashion possible. It is a *trompe l'oeil,* a trick of the eye. The orange roof spreads its glow, but only in the eye of the viewer—not on the canvas itself. It supports the others without touching them.

"And *that* is why I painted the woman's navel orange. That painting had given me a lot of trouble, the stomach and limbs were too angular, too flat, and I wanted them to be rounded— soft. But I did not want to ring in the third dimension—that is *your* province, my young sculptor, not the painter's.

"Painting is merely design. It is flat. To bring in the third dimension is to cheat. But still I wanted that illusion of round-ness.

"It was a problem that I thought about for weeks—at the easel, in the cafés, on the crapper. Until finally I remembered El Greco, and painted her navel not green, but orange.

"The orange, you see, spreads its glow across her belly and breasts, her arms and legs—and the eye is tricked into seeing them as rounded and soft. *Yes,* I broke the rules—but knowing-ly. For that is the artist's chore—to first master the rules, and then overcome them. The rules exist, but they can all be cir-cumvented."

He fixed those cold eyes on me. "And there is the gist of it. The actual painting is nothing, it is dead. It is only the work-ing out of problems that the artist sets for himself that matters. The learning." Behind him, the coffin was being lowered into the cold earth.

"You—you will be an artist. You have the eye for it. But you must learn to never stop learning. Discipline, sure you need discipline, you must work constantly, every minute of every day. But that is something you pick up along the way. Even you already have that kind of discipline, eh?"

I reddened, and muttered. *"Oui, Maître."* It was true.

"You have called me a great artist—I do not believe there is such a thing. You have called me a wizard. Well," he smiled oddly, "perhaps I am. But first and foremost I am a Student, now and for the rest of my life."

I fell back a pace from the intensity of his harangue. The Master came after me, grabbed my collar, and said: "Now. Recite back to me what you have learned, my apprentice sorcerer."

"First, about the roof," I said. "It supports without touching."

Picasso released his grip. "Hah! Good—your artist's eye sees right to the core of it. Yes, it is very much like the artist in that sense, aloof yet supporting all, lending color and meaning to the world. Go on."

"Next, that the rules exist to be learned, and then overcome." Outside, the prayers were done, and dirt being shoveled into the grave.

He almost smiled. "One more."

"That one never ceases to learn."

"That an *artist* never ceases to learn," he corrected. "All very good. But you came back with only two observations, and I have given you three answers. How shall we correct this imbalance, eh?"

"I—"

"I have it! You will go now—today! You will make a bust of your girlfriend, the ugly one, and you will return with it to me within the week. If it is good, I will see that it is sold. If not—" He made a gesture with his hands, as if balling up discarding a scrap paper.

The joy I had been feeling all died at once. Rather than face the Master, I stared out at the funeral, which was slowly beginning to break up. "I am sorry, *Maître,* but I cannot."

Picasso was outraged. "You say no to me?" He grabbed the mop from the floor, hurled it away to crash noisily against a stack of corrugated iron sheeting.

"I am sorrier than words can say, *Maître.* But I have just

received a telegram from home, and—" I fished the piece of paper from my pocket, and he snatched it out of my hand.

His face sour, Picasso read the telegram aloud. "COME HOME. YOUR FATHER IS DYING." He threw it on the floor in disgust.

"All the preparations have been made," I said. "I leave in the morning."

"Shall I tell you what will happen?" he asked. He took me by the shoulders, turned me face to face the funeral party. "First of all, you will go home and your father will die. Never doubt it—fathers die."

He pointed at the small black figures. "That woman—there— the one apart from the others. She is your mother. She will take you aside, as soon as the funeral is over."

The woman was joined by another small speck—from this distance it could as well have been me as anyone else.

"She will say to you: There's me, and the five children. And there's you. While he was alive, your father took care of us. Now it's your turn."

Perhaps the two were talking; it was impossible to tell. I saw the woman place an arm around the other's shoulder.

"And you will say: You mean—my career? It's over?" His voice became mocking, whiney, and he shook me ferociously as he predicted the words.

"And do you know what she will say then, this mother of yours? She will say: It's a tough world." He flung me away from him. His eyes were savage. "Haven't you heard a single god-damned word of what I've told you?"

Turning my back on the funeral, I gave him a small bow, and headed for the door. "I'm sorry, *Maître.*"

"Then go!" he screamed. "Pass by your chance to be a sor-cerer—what do I care? But you have wasted my time, and in the final reckoning, that sin will weigh heaviest against you!"

He slammed the door behind me.

The old man sighed. "Ah, well," he said. "The Master was a prophet. The conversation went almost word for word as he said it would. And then came the war, and then I married and raised a family. I tell myself that when I retire, I will return to sculpting. But I won't. I'll never retire."

The man said nothing.

"Picasso said that I would be an artist! I could laugh, if it weren't so sad. For the greatest artist of our times to be wrong on a matter of art—!"

Midway through this story, weariness had forced Weil to sit down. Now he grasped the arms of his chair, still staring down at the desktop. "I could have been an artist—once. No more. An artist needs to have an enormous ego in order to create, and I don't have it now. It was all kicked out of me."

Slowly, painfully, he stood. Holding the plate up into the light, he watched it flash and sparkle. "There is a lesson in this for you. I tried to support everyone with my work—my mother, my family, my country, and then my other family. Now all the people I loved are dead, and I realize that this was wrong. I should have been like that little orange roof. Supporting from a distance."

He glanced up. "Eh? What do you think?"

But the customer was no longer there. His chair contained nothing but shadows, and save it for the old man the shop was empty. Weil shook his head in chagrined puzzlement. If his maunderings had driven a customer away, well, he could understand that. But the man had left without his plate.

Then too, he should have *heard* the man leave. No matter how deeply sunk in his reveries he had been, he should at least have heard the bell over the door.

"I truly am growing old," he thought sadly.

Mocking laughter burst out of nowhere and filled the room. Dark and sardonic, it roared and reverberated.

Weil spun about fearfully, and saw nothing. Only a solid wall separating the shop from the rest of the house. The laughter must have come from beyond, he decided, and took a step backward.

And Picasso walked jauntily through the wall.

"So, my sorcerer's apprentice—not so young now, eh? I tell you there were times I thought you would *never* get the lesson."

The old man leaned heavily against his desk. "*Maître!*" he gasped. "But you—you are dead."

The Master laughed scornfully. "Death—bah! Death is just another goddamned limitation. The artist's job is to go beyond these limits." His manner was so quick and alert that by his very presence he made the shop a dreary and confining place.

Weil gingerly stretched out a hand, not daring to touch. His heart was pounding wildly. "You—*look* like him. But perhaps I am going mad."

Picasso's voice was almost gentle as he took Weil's hand. "My poor little apprentice! The first lesson, though, is always the roughest. Come, we have unfinished business in Paris."

But the old man hung back. "Can it be?" he murmured to himself. Then, "No, I am too old."

"Old!" Picasso sneered. Weil shivered as if touched by a crisp autumn breeze. "Age is just another limitation—move *around* it." He looked stern. "In time, you must learn to do this yourself. I am not your daddy, to look after you every instant of every day. But this once, I am at your disposal. I can return to you your youth, your will, the years you have wasted. Only tell me what you want."

"I—" He stopped and swallowed. "I want to be an artist! I want to form stone and clay and bronze into shapes that have never been seen before, that no one but I could create!"

"All this you shall have," Picasso promised. He seized Weil's shoulders, turned him toward the wall. "Come, it is time for your next lesson."

And as the wizard shoved him through the wall, through the cold decades and vast distances and weary regrets that were, after all, only limitations, he snarled, "But from now on, let's get it right the *first* time!"

Foresight

HE DIED.

They killed John Fox in the unlit parking lot behind an abandoned Safeway on the outskirts of the Altoona Reclamation Area. There were four of them, tall and slender in Italian suits. Two knelt on his arms, and another held his legs while the fourth injected a cardioparalytic into his heart.

He whited out for an instant as his head hit the tarmac, and when he came to, the pavement was gritty under his cheek, and he could see a flattened section of rusted tail pipe, the Styrofoam sleeve from a Coke bottle, and a galaxy of broken glass. A cigarette coal tumbled inches from his face, a tiny midnight sun. It was the cheery reddish-orange of Halloween pumpkins and midwinter bonfires. The wind puffed it away. Crickets chirped in the tangle of deadwood, chickweed, and thistle at the verge of the lot.

There was a momentary thrill of horror as he looked down the narrowing tunnel of his life at the instant of approaching death. So near, and beyond it . . . blackness, mystery. It might be that all men die alike, but it was still awful to die in ignorance. "Why are you doing this?" he cried.

The three with the stiff robotlike expressions of predeterminists went about their business as if he were about to say nothing—but the fourth smiled sadly, even fondly. He paused, the needle case halfway out of his inner jacket pocket. "Who can say? The past is unknowable, and the future is fixed—only in the present moment can we act with grace. You are about to die well. Let that comfort you." He made a short, formal bow.

They were Chinese, all of them, corporate assassins from Neue Telefunken's Taiwanese division. They stepped from their stretch Cadillac smoothly, calmly. They knew he was about to die as well as he did. Their faces were white triangles, and they had shadows in place of their eyes. One rolled down his window to flick away his cigarette. The coal was knocked free.

Fox leaned against his car, trying to compose himself. All that was important now, as his assassin would soon say, was to die well. The Camaro was a ruin—a hole had been punched through the engine block by an illegal, but quite effective, Israeli combat laser.

The long midnight-black limo whispered to a halt just ten yards behind him.

An hour before, Fox sat naked on a chair beside an unmade motel bed, alone. His trousers, belt still in the loops, lay at his feet, but he made no move to pick them up. He smoked a Marlboro slowly, thinking about his death. The killers must be on their way already. They probably had some kind of tracer on his car, because he wasn't going to notice anyone following him when he left. Then again—they were *going* to find him. They might not need a mechanism; maybe Fate would simply bring them to him when the time came.

The woman left. She picked up her handbag.

Lying on the bed, Fox watched her dress. Her suit was expensive; grey wool, cut for success, with a little corporate jacket and a single string of pearls so luminous they glowed on her neck. She wore an imported German *fikt-nicht* skirt, and authoritative mid-height heels. But under that were a black lace bra, silk panties so sheer her pubic triangle showed through, and a frilly garter belt to hold up those smoke-grey boardroom stockings. It was both luscious and impersonal watching this stranger dress, like viewing an erotic movie. He wondered who she was. A pickup? She wasn't a hooker—not with those clothes, that expensive three-color gold wedding band. (There was no ring on his hand, so probably he wasn't her husband.) Those were intimate underthings. Maybe they had meant a lot to each other. No one could tell.

The woman pulled her lingerie on quickly, discomforted by his presence but too proud to ask him not to look. She wouldn't meet his eyes. Fox found her embarrassment and tension arousing. She was obviously wondering who he was, how deeply involved they were. Possibly she was thinking forward to her husband finding out. Her breasts were large and lovely. He'd left bite marks on one; the marks were red and angry, and when she put on the bra, it didn't cover them all.

They made love. There were occasional awkwardnesses, for they no longer knew each other's bodies or tastes. But his coming death, the knowledge that this was his last time with a woman, made Fox hot and desperate. The woman too—though he had no idea why. Maybe it would be a long time after this before her next good session in bed. When she took her clothes off, she paused briefly to give him the chance to look away politely. He didn't.

"We might as well get on with this," she said, touching the top button of her pewter silk blouse. She was blushing. "Since we're going to do it anyway."

"No," he had just said. "Whatever we do, let's not do it because we have to. For this one present moment, we're free to do whatever we wish. If we don't act that way, we might just as well be zombies."

He thought forward to his assassin, and wished he knew the man's name.

"Go with God then, Fox," Gingrich said. There were tears in his eyes.

A moment before he had asked, "You won't tell me how you're going to die?" and Fox had replied, "What would be the point?" It was time he left for his last meeting with Carolyn.

Gingrich's apartment had multicolored Aztec-cut carpeting, uncluttered walls, and a bachelor's fussy tidiness. Solemn music soothed the ear, and holographic abstracts played against the gently curving beige ceiling. It was new construction, a rarity in these days. There were few enough luxuries to go around, with nine-tenths of the world in virtual chaos and anarchy.

"I can't imagine how I ever got this job," Gingrich said. He ran a hand over his round hairless head. "I'm too soft. It hurts me to see one of my boys walk out to die."

Unmoved, Fox had said nothing. A moment before Gingrich sighed and said, "You've got a good record, Fox—I'll read your files after you leave. A *very* good record, I—well, never mind. This is the last time we'll talk, and I still have to give you your recruitment pitch."

"Go ahead," Fox had said.

"John, there was a time—not too long ago, we think—when consciousness was . . . different. Memory extended not just a few seconds into the past, but all the way back to birth. And, if you can believe the records from that period, they could not remember any of their future. Not an instant." He shook his head. "Almost unimaginable. You know, it'll be said that life is like climbing a very long stairway, able to see from your feet to that closed door at the top, while the steps you've left behind crumble to nothing. I think life then must have been like climbing that same stairway backwards, able to see all the past, but none of what was about to happen to you." He'd paused for effect. "Then came the Event." Before this, he went on to describe the chaos that had followed the change of consciousness—if that was what the Event had been—and the rise of the Reclamation Authority, as would be reconstructed by scholars forty years hence. Then he had explained what the Authority had expected of Fox, what it had given him in return. Fox listened mechanically, his thoughts on Carolyn Mies. She was a hot number, whoever she was, and he liked her style. The speech was for the benefit of his earlier, younger self, and he presumed he'd have thought it over long before. If not—well, it was too late now.

Standing in the hallway, overseen by a dozen mechanicals, Fox made a face. He disliked his superior's false camaraderie, that forced jowly heartiness. A battered Sony bodycounter strapped to the wall by the door clocked softly. A Chase-Geigy genesniffer hummed to itself. Cameras telemetered his image in infrared, visual, and ultraviolet to Central Accountability. He wouldn't let Gingrich see how he felt, though. It must be rough on the poor bastard, sending old friends out to die, and then knowing that he had as good as killed total strangers.

The night before, he and Carolyn met in a hotel built a century before the chaos. The building was old and shadowy, drenched in mystery and forgotten time. It was a good hour's drive from Pittsburgh, deep in dreamlogic Pennsylvania, and the desk clerk was a thin, pinched man with wire rims and the dusty-glass eyes of a predeterminist. He moved like an automaton—stiffly, impersonally—never quite focusing on Fox.

Fox paid with a large bill. Carolyn was already waiting in the car.

It was all so mechanical. What would happen if he yanked the bill back from the clerk? Probably the man's hand would close about empty air, transport nothing to the register, dole out the change, slam the money drawer shut. I won't pay, he thought in sudden rebellion. I'll resist. But of course he would forget his resolve an instant after he made it.

The room was Victorian in proportion, small with high walls. The ceiling was molded plaster—fruit clusters, vine, cornucopias, all gone soft and vague from uncounted coats of paint. The wallpaper had been rubbed all but transparent by generations of feather-light touches, the pattern gone and indistinct shapes threatening to emerge from beneath. The thick wood door fit clumsily in its frame, and its brass knob was pitted with corrosion.

Carolyn's beeper lay neatly atop her folded clothing. They

stood by the window, lights out, watching.

Directly across the street was a dark Rite-Aid. The Reclamation Authority had restored electricity as a prelude to opening a local office, and the red neon DRUGS sign sputtered and hissed. To one side of the Ride-Aid was a burned-out Florsheim's, and to the other, a 7-Eleven. Cold white light flared from the 7-Eleven, and occasionally people wandered in and out.

"No responsibility, no guilt, no conscience," Carolyn concluded.

"I suppose that, in our different ways, this is what each of us is fighting," Fox said.

A bonfire had been built in the middle of the street, and the locals were drawn to its light. A line of middle-class respectables had set up folding chairs at the flickering edge of light. A heavy woman with the jaw of a snapping turtle knitted.

Beside the fire a woman was pulling the train. She looked young because she was skinny and beautiful because she was naked and her hair was long and blond, but a closer look revealed her as old and plain. The men standing in line for her looked considerably less interested than did the spectators.

Beside the turtle woman an old man in John Deere cap, plaid shirt, and grey chinos belted above the waist stood, unzipped, and casually urinated. Nobody turned to look. The watchers gasped, and then a woman ran out of the darkness, seized one of the men in line, and with a sudden wrench tumbled him into the fire. He leaped up, frantically beating down the flames in his hair. Fox saw that the hair was previously charred.

A nondescript man walked up to the fire, shook his head, walked away. He returned, shook his head, walked away again. And again. Once started, he was incapable of stopping, caught in a behavior loop by his own sense of futility.

"Grotesque," Carolyn said. She nudged Fox, pointing off to the side. The desk clerk stood in the shadows, watching. There was a gleam of life in those taxidermy eyes, a sour lascivious smile on those thin lips.

As they moved to the window, Fox wondered at his meeting

Carolyn two nights in a row. Could her husband be away? Or had he—horrible possibility, but by now Fox barely knew the woman—agreed to this, as part of some mousetrap operation, some elaborate plot to snare him?

As if reading his mind, Carolyn had said, "Helmut is a zombie. It doesn't matter if he finds out—he won't do anything because he's not *going* to do anything. He just does whatever he knows he's going to do."

A dark flash of doubt had hit Fox. "That's all we do too—really. It's not as if we can change anything that's going to happen. So what's the difference between us and him?"

She'd laughed then, and said, "Intent."

The sheets were a sticky crumpled mass hanging off the foot of the bed. Sometime during their hours of sex, the mattress had been all but kicked bare. Between bouts, their talk was as urgent and passionate as their lovemaking. By the time they first got intimate they were already half in love.

Taking off his shirt, Fox had said, "I know that you're going to turn me over to your assassins tomorrow."

"Oh, yes?" She did not meet his eyes.

"I wrote myself a letter a year ago. When we first met. With a note to read it tomorrow morning." He talked rapidly, anxious to get it said while he still felt for her. "It says to tell you that it's all right, that I understand. That if I'd had a choice, I'd still have done everything we did."

"Only a year?" she'd said wistfully.

Checking in, with Carolyn waiting impatiently by the ancient Otis elevator—the black ironwork doors open, the interior walnut-paneled and erotically snug—he had a brief conversation with the desk clerk. "The Reclamation will be coming through here soon," he said. "I imagine you're excited about the changes that are coming."

"No, I'm not," the man had snapped. His eyes still focused somewhere beyond Fox. A hand touched the register. "You've been here off and on some dozen times, all with the same woman. Did you know that?"

"No."

"Well, I do. I write it down. I write down what happens on the street every night too. When they bring in their machines, their location meters, their policemen, and their *orders,* that'll all end. The only pleasure those fuckers leave me will be reading the goddamned book."

On the way in, Fox realized that the man was angry because he was losing his position. Soon, he would be obeying orders. Then he would no longer be the detached observer and recorder, the omnipotent voyeur. He would no longer be God.

The Porsche eased out of the parking garage. Carcounters tagged it and automatically flashed holographic directional arrows onto his windshield. Fox followed their directions exactly. He assumed there was some good reason for their orders.

He was at a training seminar in the old Koppers Building. Behind the conference table, the mirror glass towers and soaring crenellations of the PPG Place dominated the horizon. Most of the trainees were old, factory managers and economic analysts, about to ease into retirement and the senility of fatalism. But there was also a twenty-five-year-old, a victim of an impending industrial accident.

The table fed him a program. The only interesting item was number eight, Technology Creep Through Temporal Backfeed. He was sorry to have forgotten that. He also got a machine printout of his activities in the past week. Fox saw that he'd left the surveillance-net areas five times. There was a computer-generated reprimand at the bottom of the page. It probably would've been stronger, he surmised, had he stayed in town. One thing he disliked about the new order was its latent puritanism; lust was too dreamlogic for the system to condone.

Gingrich closed with a little speech: "What was the collapse itself like—the time when the flow of memory abruptly and totally changed in nature and direction? Scholars will be able to tell us surprisingly little. The Event is like a black hole in history, surrounded by impenetrable mystery. It cannot even be dated. Records from that period are confusing and contradictory. Most likely the Event was a natural occurrence—we know so little about time or consciousness, it seems highly dubious the disaster was man-made."

While Gingrich preceded in a historical vein, Fox doodled on his notepad: long spiraling stairways that led nowhere and ended in whiteness. He tried to imagine experience and memory both running forward. He didn't think it would change much. Water would still run downhill. Modern times probably differed very little from ancient. Conversations were held backward, but that was only a social convention, a polite means of those speaking retaining some understanding of what they were saying as the conversation unraveled beneath them.

"Our struggle is not entirely against the blind forces of ignorance and confusion, though," Gingrich concluded. "Speaking in complete confidence, many of the multinational corporations would like nothing better than to grab control of big chunks of real estate and create corporate states—the way they will in Italy and Japan. In addition to the work of reconstruction, we are engaged in an extended covert war for control of North America."

"Who's going to win?" someone has asked.

"We are." Gingrich squared up his notes even with the edge of the table. He wasn't going to glance at them once, so far. "Ultimately. Before I retire. But it'll be nip and tuck there for a time to come. We're lucky to have leverage over one of the major multinationals. Soon they'll be as good as in our pockets."

Oddly enough, Gingrich was looking directly at Fox when he said this. And smiling.

In the preceding months, Fox grew closer to Carolyn. They met more and more frequently, and he learned more than he wanted to know about Helmut Mies. Until finally, their first time in the dreamlogic hotel with the mad desk clerk, he had put the question to her directly, and Carolyn told him, "I married Helmut to get control of Telefunken-Amerika. I held eight percent of the stock and a seat on the board, and it was the only way to go any higher."

Just before that she began to cry. "No, I married him because I was going to. I hate the fat son of a bitch. It's like fucking a robot. What do *I* care about Telefunken-Amerika? Hell, it's only a regional, an outcolony of the real thing. Do you know what's going to happen to me?"

"No, I don't," he'd said quietly.

"I'm going to grow extremely old and bitter, and I'll have nominal control over Telefunken-Amerika, and I won't give a shit. It's your people who will be making the decisions anyway. When you're gone, all I have to look forward to is going predeterministic and then senile."

One of Gingrich's clever young men came and took the stacks of floppies away, hands cupped protectively about each load. The office was as fastidiously neat as Gingrich's apartment would be, with clear work surfaces and not so much as a spent staple on the cream shag rug. The heavy cranberry drapes were kept shut.

Gingrich unloaded the ostrich-hide briefcase slowly, examining the label of each floppy disk and piling them into short stacks. "This is beautiful," he chortled. "John, I don't believe you have any idea what you've got here."

In the coming year, Fox would learn to respect his boss, and even to like the man—though he suspected they had never actually been friends. "Samuel," he had said, "I don't want to ask her for these. Can you understand that? I love the woman, and if I could change *one* act of my life, it would be to not ask her to do this tomorrow." He slammed his fist into his leg, hard, with the knuckles down, and savored the pain.

Awkwardly, Gingrich put a hand on Fox's shoulder. It rested there like an inanimate object—a banana, or a box of cornmeal. Before a long silence, he said, "She's already given them to you. I think we can assume that—how else could you have gotten them? If you don't ask for them, then all the guilt rests on her alone, and none on you. If you love her, you'll be as eloquent and persuasive as you know how tomorrow."

Fox gave him the briefcase.

The hotel was right in the middle of town, with location meters in every hall, and genesniffer/bodycounter units over the doors. They weren't ashamed of their love, and they didn't care who knew about it.

It was late afternoon when Carolyn left, called away to an emergency session of Telefunken-Amerika's security people. She nodded to the briefcase on the way out and said, "Now we're even. I'm going to have you killed, and you've made me betray my husband, my career, everything I've worked for all my life." She was smiling as she said it.

"It must be a relief to have done with it," he'd said. "To forget. Now you'll never know who it was that sold you out."

"I don't want to forget a thing. But I suppose it's not my choice, is it?"

A slash of honey-colored sunlight knifed through the air from the gap between the drapes. It caressed Carolyn's naked cheeks as she struggled into her blouse, danced to her thighs, then leaped from her body as she reached for her panties.

The beeper went off, and she slapped it silent.

A moment before they were sprawled lazily across the bed, legs tangled, skin slippery. "Do you keep a diary?" Carolyn asked.

"No," he'd said. "What would be the use?"

"I'm going to burn mine just before I betray you. So I won't remember that you ever existed. Do you understand that? If I can't have you, I don't want the least trace of you to survive."

"You're a romantic."

He'd gasped with pleasure on entering her. Having known all his life that it was going to be like this didn't spoil the present instant one bit.

Beneath her business suit Carolyn wore the same lacy underthings she would wear on their last night together . . . a bleak joke that made them both laugh.

"I'd do anything for you," she said. "You know that. I wish you wanted to do something filthy to me, I wish you wanted to hit me. I'd let you do that." In the elevator, her long red nails left love tracks down his back. She ran her hands up under his shirt, and a small white button went flying. He stroked her back, as if he could melt the silk of her blouse with the heat of his palms. They were only seconds away from lovemaking, and the memory of it aroused them both to feverish heat. Fox guessed that this would be their first time together. They stepped into the elevator. The door opened.

A few minutes earlier, they met for the first time.

Ginungagap

ABIGAIL CHECKED OUT of Mother of Mercy and rode the translator web to Toledo Cylinder in Juno Industrial Park. Stars bloomed, dwindled, disappeared five times. It was a long trek, halfway around the sun.

Toledo was one of the older commercial cylinders, now given over almost entirely to bureaucrats, paper pushers, and freelance professionals. It was not Abigail's favorite place to visit, but she needed work and 3M had already bought out of her contract.

The job broker had dyed his chest hairs blond and his leg hairs red. They clashed wildly with his green cache-sexe and turquoise jewelry. His fingers played on a keyout, bringing up an endless flow of career trivia. "Cute trick you played," he said.

Abigail flexed her new arm negligently. It was a good job, but pinker than the rest of her. And weak of course, but exercise would correct that. "Thanks," she said. She laid the arm underneath one breast and compared the colors. It matched the nipple perfectly. Definitely too pink. "Work outlook any good?"

"Naw," the broker said. A hummingbird flew past his ear, a nearly undetectable parting of the air. "I see here that you applied for the Proxima colony."

"They were full up," Abigail said. "No openings for a gravity bum, hey?"

"I didn't say that," the broker grumbled. "I'll find—hello! What's this?" Abigail craned her neck, couldn't get a clear look at the screen. "There's a tag on your employment record."

"What's that mean?"

"Let me read." A honeysuckle flower fell on Abigail's hair, and she brushed it off impatiently. The broker had an open-air office, framed by hedges and roofed over with a trellis. Sometimes Abigail found the older Belt cylinders a little too lavish for her taste.

"Mmp." The broker looked up. "Bell-Sandia wants to hire you. Indefinite term one-shot contract." He swung the keyout around so she could see. "*Very* nice terms, but that's normal for a high-risk contract."

"High risk? From B-S, the Friendly Communications People? What kind of risk?"

The broker scrolled up new material. "There." He tapped the screen with a finger. "The language is involved, but what it boils down to is they're looking for a test passenger for a device they've got that uses black holes for interstellar travel."

"Couldn't work," Abigail said. "The tidal forces—"

"Spare me. Presumable they've found a way around that problem. The question is, are you interested or not?"

Abigail stared up through the trellis at a stream meandering across the curved land overhead. Children were wading in it. She counted to a hundred very slowly, trying to look as if she needed to think it over.

Abigail strapped herself into the transition harness and nodded to the technician outside the chamber. The tech touched her console, and a light stasis field immobilized Abigail and the air about her while the chamber wall irised open. In a fluid bit of technological sleight-of-hand, the translator rechanneled her inertia and gifted her with a velocity almost, but not quite, that of the speed of light.

Stars bloomed about her, and the sun dwindled. She breathed in deeply and—

—was in the receiver device. Relativity had cheated her of all but a fraction of the transit time. She shrugged out of harness and frog-kicked her way to the lip station's tugdock.

The tug pilot grinned at her as she entered, then turned his attention to his controls. He was young and wore streaks of brown makeup across his chest and thighs—only slightly darker than his skin. His mesh vest was almost in bad taste. But he wore it well, and looked roguish rather than overdressed. Abigail found herself wishing she had more than a cache-sexe and nail polish on—some jewelry or makeup, perhaps. She felt drab in comparison.

The starfield wraparound held two inserts routed in by synchronous cameras. Alphanumerics flickered beneath them. One showed her immediate destination, the Bell-Sandia base *Arthur C. Clarke.* It consisted of five wheels, each set inside the other and rotating at slightly differing speeds. The base was done up in red-and-orange supergraphics. Considering its distance from the Belt factories, it was respectably sized.

Abigail latched herself into the passenger seat as the engines cut in. The second insert—

Ginungagap, the only known black hole in the sun's gravity field, was discovered in 2023, a small voice murmured. *Its presence explained the long-puzzling variations in the orbits of the outer planets. The* Arthur C. Clarke *was*

"Is this necessary?" Abigail asked.

"Absolutely," the pilot said. "We abandoned the tourist program a year or so ago, but somehow the rules never caught up. They're very strict about the regs here." He winked at Abigail's dismayed expression. "Hold tight a minute while—" His voice faded as he tinkered with the controls.

established forty years later and communications with the Proxima colony began shortly thereafter. Ginungagap

The voice cut off. She grinned thanks. "Abigail Vanderhoek."

"Cheyney," the pilot said. "You're the gravity bum, right?"

"Yeah."

"I used to be a vacuum bum myself. But I got tired of it, and grabbed the first semipermanent contract that came along."

"I kind of went the other way."

"Probably what I should have done," Cheyney said amiably. "Still, it's a rough road. I picked up three scars along the way." He pointed them out: a thick slash across his abdomen, a red splotch beside one nipple, and a white crescent half obscured by his scalp. "I could've had them cleaned up, but the way I figure, life is just a process of picking up scars and experience. So I kept 'em."

If she had thought he was trying to impress her, Abigail would have slapped him down. But it was clearly just part of an ongoing self-dramatization, possibly justified, probably not. Abigail suspected that, tour trips to Earth excepted, the *Clarke* was as far down a gravity well as Cheyney had ever been. Still, he did have an irresponsible boyish appeal. "Take me past the net?" she asked.

Cheyney looped the tug around the communications net trailing the *Clarke*. Kilometers of steel lace passed beneath them. He pointed out a small dish antenna on the edge and a cluster of antennae on the back. "The loner on the edge transmits into Ginungagap," he said. "The others relay information to and from Mother."

"Mother?"

"That's the traditional name for the *Arthur C. Clarke*." He swung the tug about with a careless sweep of one arm, and launched into a long and scurrilous story about the origin of the nickname. Abigail laughed, and Cheyney pointed a finger. "There's Ginungagap."

Abigail peered intently. "Where? I don't see a thing." She glanced at the second wraparound insert, which displayed a magnified view of the black hole. It wasn't at all impressive; a red smear against black nothingness. In the starfield it was all but invisible.

"Disappointing, hey? But still dangerous. Even this far out, there's a lot of ionization from the accretion disk."

"Is that why there's a lip station?"

"Yeah. Particle concentration varies, but if the translator were right at the *Clarke*, we'd probably lose about a third of the passengers."

Cheyney dropped Abigail off at Mother's crewlock and looped the tug off and away. Abigail wondered where to go, what to do now.

"You're the gravity bum we're dumping down Ginungagap." The short, solid man was upon her before she saw him. His eyes were intense. His cache-sexe was a conservative orange. "I like the stunt with the arm. "I'm Paul Girard. Head of external security. In charge of your training. You play verbal Ping-Pong?"

"Why do you ask?" she countered automatically.

"Don't you know?"

"Should I?"

"Do you mean now or later?"

"Will the answer be different later?"

A smile creased Paul's solid face. "You'll do." He took her arm, led her along a sloping corridor. "There isn't much prep time. The dry run is scheduled in two weeks. Things will move pretty quickly after that. You want to start your training now?"

"Do I have a choice?" Abigail asked, amused.

Paul came to a dead stop. "Listen," he said. "Rule number one. Don't play games with *me*. You understand? Because I always win. Not sometimes, not usually—always."

Abigail yanked her arm free. "You maneuvered me into that," she said angrily.

"Consider it part of your training." He stared directly into her eyes. "No matter how many gravity wells you've climbed down, you're still the product of a near-space culture—protected, trusting, willing to take things on face value. This is a dangerous attitude, and I want you to realize it. I want you to learn to look behind the mask of events. I want you to grow up. And you will."

Don't be so sure. A small smile quirked Paul's face as if he could read her thoughts. Aloud, Abigail said, "That sounds a little excessive for a trip to Promixa."

"Lesson number two," Paul said. "Don't make easy assumptions. You're not going to Proxima." He led her outward—down the ramp to the next wheel, pausing briefly at the juncture to acclimatize to the slower rate of revolution. "You're going to visit spiders." He gestured. "The crewroom is this way."

The crewroom was vast and cavernous, twilight gloomy. Keyouts were set up along winding paths that wandered aimlessly through the workspace. Puddles of light fell on each board and operator. Dark-loving foliage was set between the keyouts.

"This is the heart of the beast," Paul said. "The green keyouts handle all Proxima communications—pretty routine by now. But the blue . . . " His eyes glinting oddly, he pointed. Over the keyouts hung silvery screens with harsh grainy images floating on their surfaces, black-and-white blobs that Abigail could not resolve into recognizable forms.

"Those," Paul said, "are the spiders. We're talking to them in real time. Response delay is almost all due to machine translation."

In a sudden shift of perception, the blobs became arachnid forms. That mass of black flickering across the screen was a spiderleg and *that* was its thorax. Abigail felt an immediate primal aversion, and then was swept by an all-encompassing wonder.

"Aliens?" she breathed.

"Aliens."

They actually looked no more like spiders than humans looked like apes. The eight legs had an extra joint each, and the mandible configuration was all wrong. But to an untrained eye they would do.

"But this is—how long have you—why in God's name are you keeping this a secret?" An indefinable joy arose in Abigail. This opened a universe of possibilities, as if after a lifetime of being confined in a box someone had removed the lid.

"Industrial security," Paul said. "The gadget that'll send you through Ginungagap to *their* black hole is a spider invention. We're trading optical data for it, but the law won't protect our rights until we've demonstrated its use. We don't want the other corporations cutting in." He nodded toward the nearest black-and-white screen. "As you can see, they're weak on optics."

"I'd love to talk . . . " Abigail's voice trailed off as she realized how little-girl hopeful she sounded.

"I'll arrange an introduction."

There was a rustling to Abigail's side. She turned and saw a large black tomcat with white boots and belly emerge from the bushes. "This is the esteemed head of Alien Communications," Paul said sourly.

Abigail started to laugh, choked it back in embarrassment as she realized that he was not speaking of the cat. "Julio Dominguez, section chief for translation," Paul said. "Abigail Vanderhoek, gravity specialist."

The wizened old man smiled professorially. "I assume our resident gadfly has explained how the communications net works, has he not?"

"Well—" Abigail began.

Dominguez clucked his tongue. He wore a yellow cache-sexe and matching bow tie; just a little too garish for a man his age. "Quite simple, actually. Escape velocity from a black hole is greater than the speed of light. Therefore, within Ginungagap the speed of light is no longer the limit to the speed of communications."

He paused just long enough for Abigail to look baffled. "Which is just a stuffy way of saying that when we aim a stream of electrons into the boundary of the stationary limit, they emerge elsewhere—out of another black hole. And if we aim them *just so*"—his voice rose whimsically—"they'll emerge from the black hole of our choosing. The physics is simple. The finesse is in aiming the electrons."

The cat stalked up to Abigail, pushed its forehead against her leg, and mewed insistently. She bent over and picked it up.

"But nothing can emerge from a black hole," she objected.

Dominguez chuckled. "Ah, but anything can fall in, hey? A positron can fall in. But a positron falling into Ginungagap in positive time is only an electron falling out in negative time. Which means that a positron falling into a black hole in negative time is actually an electron falling out in positive time—exactly the effect we want. Think of Ginungagap as being the physical manifestation of an equivalence sign in mathematics."

"Oh," Abigail said, feeling very firmly put in her place. Three white moths flittered along the path. The cat watched, fascinated, while she stroked its head.

"At any rate, the electrons do emerge, and once the data is in, the theory has to follow along meekly."

"Tell me about the spiders," Abigail said, before he could continue. The moths were darting up, sideward, down, a chance ballet in three dimensions.

"The *aliens*," Dominguez said, frowning at Paul, "are still a mystery to us. We exchange facts, descriptions, recipes for tools, but the important questions do not lend themselves to our clumsy mathematical codes. Do they know of love, do they appreciate beauty? Do they believe in God, hey?"

"Do they want to eat us?" Paul threw in.

"Don't be ridiculous," Dominguez snapped. "Of course they don't."

The moths parted when they came to Abigail. Two went to either side; one flew over her shoulder. The cat batted at it with one paw. "The cat's name is Garble," Paul said. "The kids in Bio cloned him up."

Dominguez opened his mouth, closed it again.

Abigail scratched Garble under the chin. He arched his neck and purred all but noiselessly. "With your permission," Paul said. He stepped over to a keyout and waved its operator aside.

"Technically you're supposed to speak a convenience language, but if you keep it simple and nonidiomatic, there shouldn't be any difficulty." He touched the keyout. "Ritual greetings, spider." There was a blank pause. Then the spider moved, a hairy leg flickering across the screen.

"Hello, human."

"Introductions: Abigail Vanderhoek. She is our representative. She will ride the spinner." Another pause. More leg waving.

"Hello, Abigail Vanderhoek. Transition of vacuum garble resting garble commercial benefits garble still point in space."

"Tricky translation," Paul said. He signed to Abigail to take over.

Abigail hesitated, then said, "Will you come to visit us? The way we will visit you?"

"No, you see—" Dominguez began, but Paul waved him to silence.

"No, Abigail Vanderhoek. We are sulfur-based life."

"I do not understand."

"You can garble black hole through garble spinner because you are carbon-based life. Carbon forms chains easily, but sulfur combines in lattices or rosettes. Our garble simple form garble. Sometimes sulfur forms short chains."

"We'll explain later," Paul said. "Go on, you're doing fine."

Abigail hesitated again. What do you say to a spider, anyway? Finally, she asked, "Do you want to eat us?"

"Oh, Christ, get her off that thing," Dominguez said, reaching for the keyout.

Paul blocked his arm. "No," he said. "I want to hear this."

Several of the spiderlegs wove intricate patterns. "The question is false. Sulfur-based life derives no benefit from eating carbon-based life."

"You see," Dominguez said.

"But if it were possible," Abigail persisted. "If you *could* eat us and derive benefit. Would you?"

"Yes, Abigail Vanderhoek. With great pleasure."

Dominguez pushed her aside. "We're terribly sorry," he said to the alien. "This is a horrible, horrible misunderstanding. You!" he shouted to the operator. "Get back on and clear this mess up."

Paul was grinning wickedly. "Come," he said to Abigail. "We've accomplished enough here for one day."

As they started to walk away, Garble twisted in Abigail's arms and leapt free. He hit the floor on all fours and disappeared into the greenery. "Would they really eat us?" Abigail asked. Then amended it to, "Does that mean they're hostile?"

Paul shrugged. "Maybe they thought we'd be insulted if they *didn't* offer to eat us." He led her to her quarters. "Tomorrow we start training for real. In the meantime, you might make up a list of all the ways the spiders could hurt us if we set up transportation and they are hostile. Then another list of all the reasons we shouldn't trust them." He paused. "I've done it myself. You'll find that the lists get rather extensive."

Abigail's quarters weren't flashy, but they fit her well. A full starfield was routed to the walls, floor, and ceiling, only partially obscured by a trellis inner-frame that supported foxgrape vines. Somebody had done research into her tastes.

"Hi." The cheery greeting startled her. She whirled, saw that her hammock was occupied.

Cheyney sat up, swung his legs over the edge of the hammock, causing it to rock lightly. "Come on in." He touched an invisible control, and the starfield blueshifted down to a deep erotic purple.

"Just what do you think you're doing here?" Abigail asked.

"I had a few hours free." Cheyney said, "so I thought I'd drop by and seduce you."

"Well, Cheyney, I appreciate your honesty," Abigail said. "So I won't say no."

"Thank you."

"I'll say maybe some other time. Now get lost. I'm tired."

"Okay." Cheyney hopped down, walked jauntily to the door. He paused. "You said 'later,' right?"

"I said *maybe* later."

"Later. Gotcha." He winked and was gone.

Abigail threw herself into the hammock, redshifted the starfield until the universe was a sparse smattering of dying embers. Annoying creature! There was no hope for anything more than the most superficial of relationships with him. She closed her eyes, smiled. Fortunately, she wasn't currently in the market for a serious relationship.

She slept.

She was falling . . .

Abigail had landed the ship an easy walk from 3M's robot laboratory. The lab's geodesic dome echoed white clouds to the north, where Nix Olympus peeked over the horizon. Otherwise all—land, sky, rocks—was standard-issue Martian orange. She had clambered to the ground and shrugged on the supply backpack.

Resupplying 3M-RL stations was a gut contract; easy but dull. So perhaps she was less cautious than usual going down the steep rock-strewn hillside, or perhaps the rock would have turned under her no matter how carefully she placed her feet. Her ankle twisted and she lurched sideways, but the backpack had shifted her center of gravity too much for her to be able to recover.

Arms windmilling, she fell.

The rockslide carried her downhill in a panicky flurry of dust and motion, tearing her flesh and splintering her bones. But before she could feel pain, her suit shot her full of a nerve synesthetic, translating sensation into colors: reds, russets, and browns, with staccato yellow spikes when a rock smashed into her ribs. So that she fell in a whirling rainbow of glorious light.

She came to rest in a burst of orange. The rocks were settling about her. A spume of dust drifted away, out toward the distant red horizon. A large jagged slab of stone slid by, gently shearing off her backpack. Tools, supplies, airpacks, flew up and softly rained down.

A spanner as long as her arm slammed down inches from Abigail's helmet. She flinched and suddenly events became real. She kicked her legs, and sand and dust fountained up. Drawing her feet under her body—the one ankle bright gold— she started to stand.

And was jerked to the ground by a sudden tug on one arm. Even as she turned her head, she became aware of a deep, profound purple sensation in her left hand. It was pinioned by a rock not quite large enough to stake a claim to. There was no color in the fingers.

"Cute," she muttered. She tugged at the arm, pushed at the rock. Nothing budged.

Abigail nudged the radio switch with her chin. "Grounder to Lip Station," she said. She hesitated, feeling foolish, then said, "Mayday. Repeat, Mayday. Could you guys send a rescue party down for me?"

There was no reply. With a sick green feeling in the pit of her stomach, Abigail reached a gloved hand around the back of her helmet. She touched something jagged, a sensation of mottled rust, the broken remains of her radio.

"I think I'm in trouble." She said it aloud and listened to the sound of it. Flat, unemotional—probably true. But nothing to get panicky about.

She took quick stock of what she had to work with. One intact suit and helmet. One spanner. A worldful of rocks, many close at hand. Enough air for—she checked the helmet read-out—almost an hour. Assuming the lip station ran its checks on schedule and was fast on the uptake, she had almost half the air she needed.

Most of the backpack's contents were scattered too far away to reach. One rectangular gaspack, however, had landed nearby. She reached for it but could not touch it; squinted but could not read the label on its nozzle. It was almost certainly liquid gas—either nitrogen or oxygen—for the robot lab. But there was a slim chance it was the spare airpack. If it was, she might live to be rescued.

Abigail studied the landscape carefully, but there was nothing more. "Okay, then, it's an airpack." She reached as far as her tethered arm would allow. The gaspack remained a tantalizing centimeter out of reach.

For an instant she was stymied. Then, feeling like an idiot, she grabbed the spanner. She hooked it over the gaspack. Felt the gaspack move grudgingly. Slowly nudged it toward herself.

By the time Abigail could drop the spanner and draw in the gaspack, her good arm was blue with fatigue. Sweat running down her face, she juggled the gaspack to read its nozzle markings.

It was liquid oxygen—useless. She could hook it to her suit and feed in the contents, but the first breath would freeze her lungs. She released the gaspack and lay back, staring vacantly at the sky.

Up there was civilization; tens of thousands of human stations strung together by webs of communication and transportation. Messages flowed endlessly on laser cables. Translators borrowed and lent momentum, moving streams of travelers and cargo at almost (but not quite) the speed of light. A starship was being readied to carry a third load of colonists to Proxima. Up there, free from gravity's relentless clutch, people lived in luxury and ease. Here, however . . . "

"I'm going to die." She said it softly and was filled with wondering awe. Because it was true. She was going to die.

Death was a black wall. It lay before her, extending to infinity in all directions, smooth and featureless and mysterious. She could almost reach out an arm and touch it. Soon she would come up against it and, if anything lay beyond, pass through. Soon, very soon, she would *know*.

She touched the seal to her helmet. It felt grey—smooth and inviting. Her fingers moved absently, tracing the seal about her neck. With sudden horror, Abigail realized that she was thinking about undoing it, releasing her air, throwing away the little time she had left . . .

She shuddered. With sudden resolve, she reached out and

unsealed the shoulder seam of her captive arm.

The seal clamped down, automatically cutting off air loss. The flesh of her damaged arm was exposed to the raw Martian atmosphere. Abigail took up the gaspack and cradled it in the pit of her good arm. Awkwardly, she opened the nozzle with the spanner.

She sprayed the exposed arm with liquid oxygen for over a minute before she was certain it had frozen solid. Then she dropped the gaspack, picked up the spanner, and swung.

Her arm shattered into a thousand fragments.

She stood up.

Abigail awoke, tense and sweaty. She blueshifted the walls up to normal light, and sat up. After a few minutes of clearing her head, she set the walls to cycle from red to blue in a rhythm matching her normal pulse. Eventually the womb-cycle lulled her back to sleep.

"Not even close," Paul said. He ran the tape backward, froze it on a still shot of the spider twisting two legs about each other. "That's the morpheme for 'extreme disgust,' remember. It's easy to pick out, and the language kids say any statement with this gesture should be reversed in meaning. Irony, see? So when the spider says that the strong should protect the weak, it means—"

"How long have we been doing this?"

"Practically forever," Paul said cheerfully. "You want to call it a day?"

"Only if it won't hurt my standing."

"Hah! Very good." He switched off the keyout. "Nicely thought out. You're absolutely right; it would have. However, as a reward for realizing this, you can take off early *without* it being noted on your record."

"Thank you," Abigail said sourly.

Like most large installations, the *Clarke* had a dozen or so smaller structures tagging along after it in minimum maintenance orbits. When Abigail discovered that these included a small wheel gymnasium, she had taken to putting in an hour's exercise after each training shift. Today, she put in two.

The first hour she spent shadow-boxing and practicing savate in heavy-gee to work up a sweat. The second hour she spent in the axis room, performing free-fall gymnastics. After the first workout, it made her fell light and nimble and good about her body.

She returned from the wheel gym sweaty and cheerful to find Cheyney in her hammock again. "Cheyney," she said. "this is not the first time I've had to kick you out of there. Or even the third, for that matter."

Cheyney held his palms up in mock protest. "Hey, no," he said. "Nothing like that today. I just came by to watch the raft debate with you."

Abigail felt pleasantly weary, decidedly uncerebral. "Paul said something about it, but . . . "

"Turn it on, then. You don't want to miss it." Cheyney touched her wall, and a cluster of images sprang to life at the far end of the room.

"Just what is a raft debate, anyway?" Abigail asked, giving in gracefully. She hoisted herself onto the hammock, sat beside him. They rocked gently for a moment.

"There's this raft, see? It's adrift and powerless, and there's only enough oxygen on board to keep one person alive until rescue. Only there are three on board—two humans and a spider."

"Do spiders breathe oxygen?"

"It doesn't matter. This is a hypothetical situation." Two-thirds of the image area were taken up by Dominguez and Paul, quietly waiting for the debate to begin. The remainder showed a flat spider image.

"Okay, what then?"

"They argue over who gets to survive. Dominguez argues that he should, since he's human and human culture is superior to spider culture. The spider argues for itself and its culture." He put an arm around her waist. "You smell nice."

"Thank you." She ignored the arm. "What does Paul argue?"

"He's the devil's advocate. He argues that no one deserves to live and they should dump the oxygen."

"Paul would enjoy that role," Abigail said. Then, "What's the point to this debate?"

"It's entertainment. There isn't *supposed* to be a point."

Abigail doubted it was that simple. The debate could reveal a good deal about the spiders and how they thought, once the language types were done with it. Conversely, the spiders would doubtless be studying the human responses. *This could be interesting,* she thought. Cheyney was stroking her side now, lightly but with great authority. She postponed reaction, not sure whether she liked it or not.

Louise Chang, a vaguely high placed administrator, blossomed in the center of the image cluster. "Welcome," she said, and explained the rules of the debate. "The winner will be decided by acclaim," she said. "with half the vote being human and half alien. Please remember not to base your vote on racial chauvinism, but on the strengths of the arguments and how well they are presented." Cheyney's hand brushed casually across her nipples; they stiffened. The hand lingered. "The debate will begin with the gentleman representing the aliens presenting his thesis."

The image flickered as the spider waved several legs. "Thank you, Ms. Chairman. I argue that I should survive. My culture is superior because of our technological advancement. Three examples. Humans have used translation travel only briefly, yet we have used it for sixteens of garble. Our black-hole technology is superior. And our garble has garble for the duration of our society."

"Thank you. The gentlemen representing humanity?"

"Thank you, Ms. Chairman." Dominguez adjusted an armlet. Cheyney leaned back and let Abigail rest against him. Her head fit comfortably against his shoulder. "My argument is that technology is neither the sole nor most important measure of a culture. By these standards dolphins would be considered brute animals. The aesthetic considerations—the arts, theology, and the tradition of philosophy—are of greater import. As I shall endeavor to prove."

"He's chosen the wrong tactic," Cheyney whispered in Abigail's ear. "That must have come across as pure garble to the spiders."

"Thank you. Mr. Girard?"

Paul's image expanded. He theatrically swigged from a small flask and hoisted it high in the air. "Alcohol! There's the greatest achievement of the human race!" Abigail snorted. Cheyney laughed out loud. "But I hold that neither Mr. Dominguez nor the distinguished spider deserves to live, because of the disregard both cultures have for sentient life." Abigail looked at Cheyney, who shrugged. "As I shall endeavor to prove." His image dwindled.

Chang said, "The arguments will show now proceed, beginning with the distinguished alien."

The spider and then Dominguez ran through their arguments, and to Abigail they seemed markedly lackluster. She didn't give them her full attention, because Cheyney's hands were moving most interestingly across unexpected parts of her body. He might not be too bright, but he was certainly good at some things. She nuzzled her face into his neck, gave him a small peck, returned her attention to the debate.

Paul blossomed again. He juggled something in his palm, held his hand open to reveal three ball bearings. "When I was a kid I used to short out the school module and sneak up to the axis room to play marbles." Abigail smiled, remembering similar stunts she had played. "For the sake of those of us who are spiders, I'll explain that marbles is a game played in free-fall for the purpose of developing coordination and spatial perception. You make a six-armed star of marbles in the center . . . "

One of the bearings fell from his hand, bounced noisily, and disappeared as it rolled out of camera range. "Well, obviously it can't be played here. But the point is that when you shoot the marble just right, it hits the end of one arm and its kinetic energy is transferred from marble to marble along that arm. So that the shooter stops and the marble at the far end of the arm flies away." Cheyney was stroking her absently now, engrossed in the argument.

"Now, we plan to send a courier into Ginungagap and out the spiders' black hole. At least, that's what we say we're going to do.

"But what exits from a black hole is not necessarily the same as what went into its partner hole. We throw an electron into Ginungagap, and another one pops out elsewhere. It's identical. It's a direct casual relationship. But it's like the marbles—they're identical to each other and have the same kinetic force. It's simply not the same electron."

Cheyney's hand was still, motionless. Abigail prodded him gently, touching his inner thigh. "Anyone who's interested can see the equations. Now, when we send messages, this doesn't matter. The message is important, not the medium. However, when we send a human being in . . . what emerges from the other hole will be cell for cell, gene for gene, atom for atom identical. *But it will not be the same person.*" He paused a beat, smiled.

"I submit, then, that this is murder. And further, that by conspiring to commit murder, both the spider and the human races display absolute disregard for intelligent life. In short, no one on the raft deserves to live. And I rest my case."

"Mr. Girard!" Dominguez objected, even before his image was restored to full-size. "The simplest mathematical proof is an identity: that A equals A. Are you trying to deny this?"

Paul held up the two ball bearings he had left. "These marbles are identical too. But they are not the same marble."

"We know the phenomenon you speak of," the spider said. "It is as if garble the black hole bulges out simultaneously. There is no violation of continuity. The two entities are the same. There is no death."

Abigail pulled Cheyney down, so that they were both lying on their sides, still able to watch the images. "So long as you happen to be the second marble and not the first," Paul said. Abigail tentatively licked Cheyney's ear.

"He's right," Cheyney murmured.

"No, he's not," Abigail retorted. She bit his earlobe.

"You mean that?"

"Of course I mean that. He's confusing semantics with reality." She engrossed herself in a study of the back of his neck.

"Okay."

Abigail suddenly sensed that she was missing something. "Why do you ask?" She struggled into a sitting position. Cheyney followed.

"No particular reason." Cheyney's hands began touching her again. But Abigail was sure something had been slipped past her.

They caressed each other lightly, while the debate dragged to an end. Not paying much attention, Abigail voted for Dominguez and Cheyney voted for Paul. As a result of a nearly undivided spider vote, the spider won. "I told you Dominguez was taking the wrong approach," Cheyney said. He hopped off the hammock. "Look, I've got to see somebody about something. I'll be right back."

"You're not leaving now?" Abigail protested, dumbfounded. The door irised shut.

Angry and hurt, she leapt down, determined to follow him. She couldn't remember ever feeling so insulted.

Cheyney didn't try to be evasive; it apparently did not occur to him that she might follow. Abigail stalked him down a corridor, up an inramp, and to a door that irised open for him. She recognized that door.

Thoughtfully, she squatted on her heels behind an untrimmed boxwood and waited. A minute later, Garble wandered by, saw her, and demanded attention. "Scat!" she hissed. He butted his head against her knee. "Then be quiet, at least." She scooped him up. His expression was smug.

The door irised open and Cheyney exited, whistling. Abigail waited until he was gone, stood, went to the door and entered. Fish darted between long fronds under a transparent floor. It was an austere room, almost featureless. Abigail looked, but did not see a hammock.

"So Cheyney's working for you now," she said coldly. Paul looked up from a corner keyout.

"As a matter of fact, I've just signed him to permanent contract in the crewroom. He's bright enough. A bit green. Ought to do well."

"Then you admit that you put him up to grilling me about your puerile argument in the debate?" Garble struggled in her arms. She juggled him into a more comfortable position. "And that you staged the argument for my benefit in the first place?"

"Ah," Paul said. "I knew the training was going somewhere. You've become very wary in an extremely short time."

"Don't evade the question."

"I needed your honest reaction," Paul said. "Not the answer you would have given me, knowing your chances of crossing Ginungagap rode on it."

Garble made an angry noise. "You tell him, Garble!" she said. "That goes double for me." She stepped out the door. "You lost the debate," she snapped.

Long after the door had irised shut, she could feel Paul's amused smile burning into her back.

Two days after she returned to kick Cheyney out of her hammock for the final time, Abigail was called to the crewroom. "Dry run," Paul said. "Attendance is mandatory," and cut off.

The crewroom was crowded with technicians, triple the number of keyouts. Small knots of them clustered before the screens, watching. Paul waved her to him.

"There," he motioned to one screen. "That's Clotho—the platform we built for the transmission device. It's a hundred kilometers off. I wanted more, but Dominguez overruled me. The device that'll unravel you and dump you down Ginungagap is that doo-hickey in the center." He tapped a keyout, and the platform zoomed up to fill the screen. It was covered by a clear transparent bubble. Inside, a spacesuited figure was placing something into a machine that looked like nothing so much as a giant armor-clad clamshell. Abigail looked, blinked, looked again.

"That's Garble," she said indignantly.

"Complain to Dominguez. I wanted a baboon."

The clamshell device closed. The spacesuited tech left in his tug, and alphanumerics flickered, indicating the device was in operation. As they watched, the spider-designed machinery immobilized Garble, transformed his molecules into one long continuous polymer chain, and spun it out an invisible opening at near-light speed. The water in his body was separated out, piped away, and preserved. The electrolyte balances were recorded and simultaneously transmitted in a parallel stream of electrons. It would reach the spider receiver along with the lead end of the cat-polymer, to be used in the reconstruction.

Thirty seconds passed. Now Garble was only partially in Clotho. The polymer chain, invisible and incredibly long, was passing into Ginungagap. On the far side of the spiders were beginning to knit it up.

If all was going well.

Ninety-two seconds after they flashed on, the alphanumerics stopped twinkling on the screen. Garble was gone from Clotho. The clamshell opened, and the remote cameras showed it to be empty. A cheer arose.

Somebody boosted Dominguez atop a keyout. Intercom cameras swiveled to follow. He wavered fractionally, said "My friends," and launched into a speech. Abigail didn't even listen.

Paul's hand fell on her shoulder. It was the first time he had touched her since their initial meeting. "He's only a scientist," he said. "He had no idea how close you are to the cat."

"Look, I *asked* to go. I knew the risks. But Garble's just an animal; he wasn't given the choice."

Paul groped for words. "In a way, this is what your training has been about; the reason you're going across instead of someone like Dominguez. He projects his own reactions onto other people. If—"

Then, seeing that she wasn't listening, he said, "Anyway, you'll have a cat to play with in a few hours. They're only keeping him long enough to test out the life-support systems."

There was a festive air to the second gathering. The spiders reported that Garble had translated flawlessly. A brief visual display showed him stalking about Clotho's sister platform, irritable but apparently unharmed.

"There," somebody said. The screen indicated that the receiver net had taken in the running end of the cat's polymer chain. They waited a minute and a half, and the operation was over.

It was like a conjuring trick: the clamshell closed on emptiness. Water was piped in. Then it opened and Garble floated over its center, quietly licking one paw.

Abigail smiled at the homeliness of it. "Welcome back, Garble," she said quietly. "I'll get the guys in Bio to brew up some cream for you."

Paul's eyes flicked in her direction. They lingered for no time at all; long enough to file away another datum for future use, and then his attention was elsewhere. She waited until his back was turned and stuck out her tongue ant him.

The tug docked with Clotho, and a technician floated in. She removed her helmet self-consciously, aware of her audience. One hand extended, she bobbed toward the cat, calling softly.

"Get that jerk on the line," Paul snapped. "I want her helmet back on. That's sloppy. That's real—"

And in that instant Garble sprang.

Garble was a black-and-white streak that flashed past the astonished tech, through the airlock, and into the open tug. The cat pounced on the pilot panel. Its forelegs hit the controls. The hatch slammed shut, and the tug's motors burst into life.

Crewroom techs grabbed wildly at their keyouts. The tech

on Clotho frantically tried to fit her helmet back on. And the tug took off, blasting away half the protective dome and all the platform's air.

The screens showed a dozen different scenes, lenses shifting from close to distant and back. "Cheyney," Paul said quietly. Dominguez was frozen looking bewildered. "Take it out."

"It's coming right at us!" somebody shouted.

Cheyney's fingers flicked: rap-tap-rap.

A bright nuclear flower blossomed.

There was silence, dead and complete, in the crewroom. *I'm missing something,* Abigail thought. *We just blew up five percent of our tug fleet to kill a cat.*

"*Pull* that transmitter!" Paul strode through the crewroom, scattering orders. "Nothing goes out! You, you, and you"—he yanked techs away from their keyouts—"*off* those things. I want the whole goddamned net shut *down.*"

"Paul . . . " an operator said.

"Keep on receiving." He didn't bother to look. "Whatever they want to send. Dump it all in storage and don't merge any of it with our data until we've gone over it."

Alone and useless in the center of the room, Dominguez stuttered, "What—what happened?"

"You blind idiot!" Paul turned on him viciously. "Your precious aliens have just made their first hostile move. The cat that came back was nothing like the one we sent. They made changes. They retransmitted it with instructions wetwired into its brain."

"But why would they want to steal a tug?"

"*We don't know!*" Paul roared. "Get that through your head. "We don't know their motives, and we don't know how they think. But we would have known a lot more about their intentions than we wanted if I hadn't rigged that tug with an abort device."

"You didn't—" Dominguez began. He thought better of the statement.

"—have the authority to rig that device," Paul finished for

him. "That's right. I didn't." His voice was heavy with sarcasm.

Dominguez seemed to shrivel. He stared bleakly, blankly, about him, then turned and left, slightly hunched over. Thoroughly discredited in front of people who worked for him.

That was cold, Abigail thought. She marveled at Paul's cruelty. Not for an instant did she believe that the anger in his voice was real, that he was capable of losing control.

Which meant that in the midst of confusion and stress, Paul had found time to make a swift play for more power. To Abigail's newly suspicious eye, it looked like a successful one, too.

For five days, Paul held the net shut by sheer willpower and force of personality. Information came in but did not go out. Bell-Sandia administration was not behind him—too much time and money had been sunk into Clotho to abandon the project. But Paul had the support of the tech crew, and he knew how to use it.

"Nothing as big as Bell-Sandia runs on popularity," Paul explained. "But I've got enough sympathy from above, and enough hesitation and official cowardice, to keep this place shut down long enough to get a message across."

The incoming information flow fluctuated wildly, shifting from subject to subject. Data sequences were dropped halfway through and incomplete. Nonsense came in. The spiders were shifting through strategies in search of the key that would reopen the net.

"When they start repeating themselves," Paul said, "We can assume they understand the threat."

"But we *wouldn't* shut the net down permanently," Abigail pointed out.

Paul shrugged. "So it's a bluff."

They were sharing an aftershift drink in a fifth-level bar. Small red lizards scuttled about the rock wall behind the bartender. "And if your bluff doesn't work?" Abigail asked. "If it's all for nothing—what then?"

Paul's shoulders sagged, a minute shifting of tensions. "Then we trust in the good will of the spiders," he said. "We let them call the shots. And they will treat us benevolently or not, depending. In either case," his voice became dark, "I'll have played a lot of games and manipulated a lot of people for no reason at all." He took her hand. "If that happens, I'd like to apologize." His grip was tight; his knuckles pale.

That night Abigail dreamt she was falling.

Light rainbowed all about her, in a violent splintering of bone and tearing of flesh. She flung out an arm, and it bounced on something warm and yielding.

"Abigail."

She twisted and tumbled, and something smashed into her ribs. Bright spikes of yellow darted up.

"Abigail!" Someone was shaking her, speaking loudly into her face. The rocks and sky went grey, were overlaid by unresolved images. Her eyelids struggled apart, fell together, opened.

"Oh," she said.

Paul rocked back on his heels. Fish darted about in the water beneath him. "There now," he said. Blue-green lights shifted gently underwater, moving in long, slow arcs. "Dream over?"

Abigail shivered, clutched his arm, let go of it almost immediately. She nodded.

"Good. Tell me about it."

"I—" Abigail began. "Are you asking me as a human being or in your official capacity?"

"I don't make that distinction."

She stretched out a leg and scratched her big toe, to gain time to think. She really didn't have any appropriate thoughts. "Okay," she said, and told him the entire dream.

Paul listened intently, rubbed a thumb across his chin thoughtfully when she was done. "We hired you on the basis of that incident, you know," he said. "Coolness under stress. Weak body image. There were a lot of gravity bums to choose from. But I figured you were just a hair tougher, a little bit grittier."

"What are you trying to tell me? That I'm replaceable?"

Paul shrugged. "Everybody's replaceable. I just wanted to be sure you knew that you could back out if you want. It wouldn't wreck our project."

"I don't want to back out." Abigail chose her words carefully, spoke them slowly, to avoid giving vent to the anger she felt building up inside. "Look, I've been on the gravity circuit for ten years. I've been everywhere in the system there is to go. Did you know that there are less than two thousand people alive who've set foot on Mercury *and* Pluto? We've got a little club; we get together once a year." Seaweed shifted about her; reflections of the floor lights formed nebulous swimming shapes on the walls. "I've spent my entire life going around and around and around the sun, and never really getting anywhere. I want to travel, and there's nowhere left for me to go. So you offer me a way out and then ask if I want to back down. Like hell I do!"

"Why don't you believe that going through Ginungagap is death?" Paul asked quietly. She looked into his eyes, saw cool calculations going on behind them. It frightened her, almost. He was measuring her, passing judgment, warping events into long logical chains that did not take human factors into account. He was an alien presence.

"It's—common sense, is all. I'll be the same when I exit as when I go in. There'll be no difference, no an atom's worth, not a scintilla."

"The *substance* will be different. Every atom will be different. Not a single electron in your body will be the same one you have now."

"Well, how does that differ so much from normal life?" Abigail demanded. "All our bodies are in constant flux. Molecules come and go. Bit by bit, we're replaced. Does that make us different people from moment to moment? 'All that is body is as coursing vapors,' right?"

Paul's eyes narrowed. "Marcus Aurelius. Your quotation isn't complete, though; it goes on: 'all that is of the soul is dreams and vapors.'"

"What's that supposed to mean?"

"It means that the quotation doesn't say what you claimed it did. If you care to read it literally, it argues the opposite of what you're saying."

"Still, you can't have it both ways. Either the me that comes out of the spider black hole is the same as the one who went in, or I'm not the same person as I was an instant ago."

"I'd argue differently," Paul said. "But no matter. Let's go back to sleep."

He held out a hand, but Abigail felt no inclination to accept it. "Does this mean I've passed your test?"

Paul closed his eyes, stretched a little. "You're still reasonably afraid of dying, and you don't believe that you will," he said. "Yeah. You pass."

"Thanks a heap," Abigail said. They slept, not touching, for the rest of the night.

Three days later Abigail woke up, and Paul was gone. She touched the wall and spoke his name. A recording appeared. "Dominguez has been called up to Administration," it said. Paul appeared slightly distracted; he had not looked directly into the recorder, and his image avoided Abigail's eyes. "I'm going to reopen the net before he returns. It's best we beat him to the punch." The recording clicked off.

Abigail routed an intercom call through to the crewroom. A small chime notified him of her call, and he waved a hand in combined greeting and direction to remain silent. He was hunched over a keyout. The screen above it came to life.

"Ritual greetings, spider," he said.

"Hello, human. We wish to pursue our previous inquiry: the meaning of the term 'art' which was used by the human Dominguez six-sixteenths of the way through his major presentation."

"This is a difficult question. To understand a definition of art, you must first know the philosophy of aesthetics. This is a comprehensive field of knowledge comparable to the study of perception. In many ways it is related."

"What is the trade value of this field of knowledge?"

Dominguez appeared, looking upset. He opened his mouth, and Paul touched a finger to his own lips, nodding his head toward the screen.

"Significant. Our society considers art and science as being of roughly equal value."

"We will consider what to offer in exchange."

"Good. We also have a question for you. Please wait while we select the phrasing." He cut the translation lines, turned to Dominguez. "Looks like your raft gambit paid off. Though I'm surprised they bit at that particular piece of bait."

Dominguez looked weary. "Did they mention the incident with the cat?"

"No, nor the communications blackout."

The old man sighed. "I always felt close to the aliens," he said. "Now they seem—cold, inhuman." He attempted a chuckle. "That was almost a pun, wasn't it?"

"In a human, we'd call it a professional attitude. Don't let it spoil your accomplishment," Paul said. "This could be as big as optics." He opened the communications line again. "Our question is now phrased." Abigail noted he had not told Dominguez of her presence.

"Please go ahead."

"Why did you alter our test animal?"

Much leg waving. "We improved the ratios garble centers of perception garble wetware garble making the animal twelve-sixteenths as intelligent as a human. We thought you would be pleased."

"We were not. Why did the test animal behave in a hostile manner toward us?"

The spider's legs jerked quickly, and it disappeared from the screen. Like an echo, the machine said, "Please wait."

Abigail watched Dominguez throw Paul a puzzled look. In the background, a man with a leather sack looped over one shoulder was walking slowly along the twisty access path. His hand dipped into the sack, came out, sprinkled fireflies among the greenery. Dipped in, came out again. Even in the midst of crisis, the trivia of day-to-day existence went on.

The spider reappeared, accompanied by two of its own kind. Their legs interlaced and retreated rapidly, a visual pantomime of an excited conversation. Finally, one of their number addressed the screen.

"We have discussed the matter."

"So I see."

"It is our conclusion that the experience of translation through Ginungagap had a negative effect on the test animal. This was not anticipated. It is new knowledge. We know little of the psychology of carbon-based life."

"You're saying the test animal was driven mad?"

"Key word did not translate. We assume understanding. Steps must be taken to prevent a recurrence of this damage. Can you do this?"

Paul said nothing.

"Is this the reason why communications were interrupted?"

No reply.

"There is a cultural gap. Can you clarify?"

"Thank you for your cooperation," Paul said, and switched the screen off. "You can set your people to work," he told Dominguez. "No reason why they should answer the last few questions, though."

"Were they telling the truth?" Dominguez asked wonderingly.

"Probably not. But at least now they'll think twice before trying to jerk us around again." He winked at Abigail, and she switched off the intercom.

They reran the test using a baboon shipped out from the Belt Zoological Gardens. Abigail watched it arrive from the lip station, crated and snarling.

"They're a lot stronger than we are," Paul said. "Very agile. If the spiders want to try any more tricks, we couldn't offer them better bait."

The test went smooth as silk. The baboon was shot through

Ginungagap, held by the spiders for several hours, and returned. Exhaustive testing showed no tampering with the animal.

Abigail asked how accurate the tests were. Paul hooked his hands behind his back. "We're returning the baboon to the Belt. We wouldn't do that if we had any doubts. But—" He raised an eyebrow, asking Abigail to finish the thought.

"But if they're really hostile, they won't underestimate us twice. They'll wait for a human to tamper with."

Paul nodded.

The night before Abigail's send-off they made love. It was a frenzied and desperate act, performed wordlessly and without tenderness. Afterward they lay together, Abigail idly playing with Paul's curls.

"Gail . . . " His head was hidden in her shoulder; she couldn't see his face. His voice was muffled.

"Mmmm?"

"Don't go."

She wanted to cry. Because as soon as he said it, she knew it was another test, the final one. And she also knew that Paul wanted her to fail it. That he honestly believed that traversing Ginungagap would kill her, and that the woman who emerged from the spiders' black hole would not be her.

His eyes were shut; she could tell by the creases in his forehead. He knew what her answer was. There was no way he could avoid knowing.

Abigail sensed that this was as close to a declaration of emotion as Paul was capable of. She felt how he despised himself for using his real emotions as yet another test, and how he could not even pretend to himself that there were circumstances under which he would not so test her. *This must be how it feels to think as he does,* she thought. *To constantly scrabble after every last implication, like eternally picking at a scab.*

"Oh, Paul," she said.

He wrenched about, turning his back to her. "Sometimes I wish"—his hands rose in front of his face like claws; they moved toward his eyes, closed into fists—"that for just ten goddamned minutes I could turn my mind *off.*" His voice was bitter.

Abigail huddled against him, looped a hand over his side and onto his chest. "Hush," she said.

The tug backed away from Clotho, dwindling until it was one of a ring of bright sparks pacing the platform. Mother was a point source lost in the starfield. Abigail shivered, pulled off her armbands, and shoved them into a storage sack. She reached for her cache-sexe, hesitated.

The hell with it, she thought. *It's nothing they haven't seen before.* She shucked it off, stood naked. Gooseflesh rose on the backs of her legs. She swam to the transmittal device, feeling awkward under the distant watching eyes.

Abigail groped into the clamshell. "Go," she said.

The metal closed about her seamlessly, encasing her in darkness. She floated in a lotus position, bobbing slightly.

A light gripping field touched her, stilling her motion. On cue, hypnotic commands took hold in her brain. Her breathing became shallow; her heart slowed. She felt her body ease into stasis. The final command took hold.

Abigail weighed fifty keys. Even though the water in her body would not be transmitted, the polymer chain she was to be transformed into would be two hundred seventy-five kilometers long. It would take fifteen minutes and seventeen seconds to unravel at light speed, negligibly longer at translation speed. She would still be sitting in Clotho when the spiders began knitting her up.

It was possible that Garble had gone mad from a relatively swift transit. Paul doubted it, but he wasn't taking any chances. To protect Abigail's sanity, the meds had wetwired a travel fantasy into her brain. It would blind her to external reality while she traveled.

She was an eagle. Great feathered wings extended out from her shoulders. Clotho was gone, leaving her alone in space. Her skin was red and leathery, her breasts hard and unyielding. Feathers covered her thighs, giving way at the knees to talons.

She moved her wings, bouncing lightly against the thin solar wind swirling down into Ginungagap. The vacuum felt like absolute freedom. She screamed a predator's exultant shrill. Nothing enclosed her; she was free of restrictions forever.

Below her lay Ginungagap, the primal chasm, an invisible challenge marked by a red smudge of glowing gases. It was inchoate madness, a gibbering impersonal force that wanted to draw her in, to crush her in its embrace. Its hunger was fierce and insatiable.

Abigail held her place briefly, effortlessly. Then she folded her wings and dove.

A rain of X rays stung through her, the scattering of Ginungagap's accretion disk. They were molten iron passing through a ghost. Shrieking defiance, she attacked, scattering sparks in her wake.

Ginungagap grew, swelled, until it swallowed up her vision. It was purest black, unseeable, unknowable, a thing of madness. It was Enemy.

A distant objective part of her knew that she was still in Clotho, the polymer chain being unraveled from her body, accelerated by a translator, passing through two black holes, and simultaneously being knit up by the spiders. It didn't matter.

She plunged into Ginungagap as effortlessly as if it were the film of a soap bubble.

In—

—and out.

It was like being reversed in a mirror, or watching an entertainment run backward. She was instantly flying out the way she came. The sky was a mottled mass of violet light.

The stars before her brightened, from violet to blue. She craned her neck, looked back at Ginungagap, saw its disk-shaped nothingness recede, and screamed in frustration because it had escaped her. She spread her wings to slow her flight and—

—was sitting in a dark place. Her hand reached out, touched metal, recognized the inside of a clamshell device.

A hairlike crack of light looped over her, widened. The clamshell opened.

Oceans of color bathed her face. Abigail straightened, and the act of doing so lifted her up gently. She stared through the transparent bubble at a phosphorescent foreverness of light.

My God, she thought. *The stars.*

The stars were thicker, more numerous that she was used to, large and bright and glitter-rich. She was probably some-place significant, a star cluster or the center of the galaxy; she couldn't guess. She felt irrationally happy to simply *be;* she took a deep breath, then laughed.

"Abigail Vanderhoek."

She turned to face the voice, and found that it came from a machine. Spiders crouched beside it, legs moving silently. Out-side, in the hard vacuum, were more spiders.

"We regret any pain this may cause," the machine said.

Then the spiders rushed forward. She had no time to react. Sharp mandibles loomed before her, then dipped to her neck. Impossibly swift, they sliced through her throat, severed her spine. A sudden jerk, and her head was separated from her body.

It happened in an instant. She felt brief pain, and the dis-sociation of actually seeing her decapitated body just begin-ning to react. And then she died.

A spark. A light. *I'm alive*, she thought. Consciousness returned like an ancient cathode tube warming up. Abigail stretched slowly, bobbing gently in the air, collecting her thoughts. She was in the sister-Clotho again, not in pain, her head and neck firmly on her shoulders. There were spiders on the platform, and a few floating outside.

"Abigail Vanderhoek," the machine said. "We are ready to begin negotiations."

Abigail said nothing.

After a moment, the machine said, "Are you damaged? Are your thoughts impaired?" A pause, then, "Was your mind not protected during transit?"

"Is that you waving the legs out there? Outside the platform?"

"Yes. It is important that you talk with the other humans. You must convey our questions. They will not communicate with us."

"I have a few questions of my own," Abigail said. "I won't cooperate until you answer them."

"We will answer any questions provided you neither garble nor garble."

"What do you take me for?" Abigail asked. "Of course I won't."

Long hours later she spoke to Paul and Dominguez. At her request, the spiders had withdrawn, leaving her alone. Dominguez looked drawn and haggard. "I swear we had no idea the spiders would attack you," Dominguez said. "We saw it on the screens. I was certain you'd been killed . . . " His voice trailed off.

"Well, I'm alive, no thanks to you guys. Just what is this crap about an explosive substance in my bones, anyway?"

"An explosive—I swear we know nothing of anything of the kind."

"A close relative to plastique," Paul said. "I had a small editing device attached to Clotho's translator. It altered roughly half the bone marrow in your sternum, pelvis, and femurs in transmission. I'd hoped the spiders wouldn't pick up on it so quickly."

"You actually did," Abigail marveled. "The spiders weren't lying; they decapitated me in self-defense. What the holy hell did you think you were *doing?*"

"Just a precaution," Paul said. "We wetwired you to trigger the stuff on command. That way, we could have taken out the spider installation if they'd tried something funny.

"Um," Dominguez said, "this *is* being recorded. What I'd like to know, Ms. Vanderhoek, is how you escaped being destroyed."

"I didn't," Abigail said. "The spiders killed me. Fortunately, they anticipated the situation, and recorded the transmission.

It was easy for them to re-create me—after they edited out the plastique."

Dominguez gave her an odd look. "You don't—feel anything particular about this?"

"Like what?"

"Well—" He turned to Paul helplessly.

"Like the real Abigail Vanderhoek died and you're simply a very realistic copy," Paul said.

"Look, we've been through this garbage before," Abigail began angrily.

Paul smiled formally at Dominguez. It was hard to adjust to seeing the two in flat black-and-white. "She doesn't believe a word of it."

"If you guys can pull yourselves up out of your navels for a minute," Abigail said, "I've got a line on something the spiders have that you want. They claim they've sent probes through their black hole."

"Probes?" Paul stiffened. Abigail could sense the thoughts coursing through his skull, of defenses and military applications.

"Carbon-hydrogen chain probes. Organic probes. Self-constructing transmitters. They've got a carbon-based secondary technology."

"Nonsense," Dominguez said. "How could they convert back to coherent matter without a receiver?"

Abigail shrugged. "They claim to have found a loophole."

"How does it work?" Paul snapped.

"They wouldn't say. They seemed to think you'd pay well for it."

"That's very true," Paul said slowly. "Oh, yes."

The conference took almost as long as her session with the spiders had. Abigail was bone weary when Dominguez finally said, "That ties up the official minutes. We now stop recording." A line tracked across the screen, was gone. "If you want to speak to anyone off the record, now's your chance. Perhaps there is someone close to you . . . "

"Close? No." Abigail almost laughed. "I'll speak to Paul alone, though."

A spider floated by outside Clotho II. It was a golden crablike being, its body slightly opalescent. It skittered along unseen threads strung between the open platforms of the spider star-city. "I'm listening," Paul said.

"You turned me into a bomb, you freak."

"So?"

"I could have been killed."

"Am I supposed to care?"

"You damn well ought to, considering the liberties you've taken with my fair white body."

"Let's get one thing understood," Paul said. "The woman I slept with, the woman I cared for, is dead. I have no feelings toward or obligations to you whatsoever."

"Paul," Abigail said. "*I'm not dead.* Believe me, I'd know if I were."

"How could I possibly trust what you think or feel? It could all be attitudes the spiders wetwired into you. We know they have the technology."

"How do you know that *your* attitudes aren't wetwired in? For that matter, how do you know anything is real? I mean, these are the most sophomoric philosophic ideas there are. But I'm the same woman I was a few hours ago. My memories, opinions, feelings—they're all the same as they were. There's absolutely no difference between me and the woman you slept with on the *Clarke.*"

"I know." Paul's eyes were cold. "That's the horror of it." He snapped off the screen.

Abigail found herself staring at the lifeless machinery. God, that hurt, she thought. It shouldn't, but it hurt. She went to her quarters.

The spiders had done a respectable job of preparing for her. There were no green plants, but otherwise the room was the same as the one she'd had on the Clarke. They'd even been able to spin the platform, giving her an adequate down-orientation. She sat in her hammock, determined to think pleasanter thoughts. About the offer the spiders had made, for example. The one she hadn't told Paul and Dominguez about.

Banned by their chemistry from using black holes to travel, the spiders needed a representative to see to their interests among the stars. They had offered her the job.

Or perhaps the plural would be more appropriate—they had offered her the jobs. Because there were too many places to go for one woman to handle them all. They needed a dozen, in time perhaps a hundred Abigail Vanderhoeks.

In exchange for licensing rights to her personality, the right to make as many duplicates of her as were needed, they were willing to give her the rights to the self-reconstructing black-hole platforms.

It would make her a rich woman—a hundred rich women— back in human space. And it would open the universe. She hadn't committed herself yet, but there was no way she was going to turn down the offer. The chance to see a thousand stars. No, she would not pass it by.

When she got old, too, they could create another Abigail from their recording, burn her new memories into it, and destroy her old body.

I'm going to see the stars, she thought. *I'm going to live forever.* She couldn't understand why she didn't feel elated, wondered at the sudden rush of melancholy that ran through her like the precursor of tears.

Garble jumped into her lap, offered his belly to be scratched. The spiders had recorded him, too. They had been glad to restore him to his unaltered state when she made the first request. She stroked his stomach and buried her face in his fur.

"Pretty little cat," she told him. "I thought you were dead."

The Edge of the World

THE DAY THAT DONNA and Piggy and Russ went to see the Edge of the World was a hot one. They were sitting on the curb by the gas station that noontime, sharing a Coke and watching the big Starlifters lumber up into the air, one by one, out of Toldenarba AFB. The sky rumbled with their passing. There'd been an incident in the Persian Gulf, and half the American forces in the Twilight Emirates were on alert.

"My old man says when the Big One goes up, the base will be the first to go," Piggy said speculatively. "Treaties won't allow us to defend it. One bomber comes in high and wha-boom—" he made soft nuclear explosion noises—"it's all gone." He was wearing camouflage pants and a khaki teeshirt with an iron-on reading KILL 'EM ALL AND LET GOD SORT 'EM OUT. Donna watched as he took off his glasses to polish them on his shirt. His face went slack and vacant, then livened as he put them back on again, as if he were playing with a mask.

"You should be so lucky," Donna said. "Mrs. Khashoggi is still going to want that paper done on Monday morning, Armageddon or not."

"Yeah, can you believe her?" Piggy said. "That weird accent! And all that memorization! Cut me some slack. I mean, who cares whether Ackronnion was part of the Mezentian Dynasty?"

"You ought to care, dipshit," Russ said. "Local history's the only decent class the school's got." Russ was the smartest boy Donna had ever met, never mind the fact that he was flunking out. He had soulful eyes and a radical haircut, short on the sides with a dyed-blond punklock down the back of his neck. "Man, I opened the Excerpts from Epics text that first night, thinking it was going to be the same old bullshit, and I stayed up 'til dawn. Got to school without a wink of sleep, but I'd managed to read every last word. This is one weird part of the world; its history is full of dragons and magic and all kinds of weird monsters. Do you realize that in the eighteenth century three members of the British legation were eaten by demons? That's in the historical record!"

Russ was an enigma to Donna. The first time they'd met, hanging with the misfits at an American School dance, he'd tried to put a hand down her pants, and she'd slugged him good, almost breaking his nose. She could still hear his surprised laughter as blood ran down his chin. They'd been friends ever since. Only there were limits to friendship, and now she was waiting for him to make his move and hoping he'd get down to it before her father was rotated out.

In Japan she'd known a girl who had taken a razor blade and carved her boyfriend's name in the palm of her hand. How could she do that, Donna had wanted to know? Her friend had shrugged, said, "As long as it gets me noticed." It wasn't until Russ that Donna understood.

"Strange country," Russ said dreamily. "The sky beyond the Edge is supposed to be full of demons and serpents and shit. They say that if you stare into it long enough, you'll go mad."

They all three looked at one another.

"Well, hell," Piggy said. "What are we waiting for?"

The Edge of the World lay beyond the railroad tracks. They bicycled through the American enclave into the old native quarter. The streets were narrow here, the sideyards crammed with broken trucks, rusted out buses, even yachts up in cradles with staved-in sides. Garage doors were black mouths hissing and spitting welding sparks, throbbing to the hammered sound of worked metal. They hid their bikes in a patch of scrub apricot trees where the railroad crossed the industrial canal and hiked across.

Time had altered the character of the city where it bordered the Edge. Gone were the archers in their towers, vigilant against a threat that never came. Gone were the rose quartz palaces with their thousand windows, not a one of which overlooked the Edge. The battlements where blind musicians once piped up the dawn now survived only in Mrs. Khashoggi's texts. Where they had been was now a drear line of weary factory buildings, their lower windows cinderblocked or bricked up and those beyond reach of vandals' stones painted over in patchwork squares of grey and faded blue.

A steam whistle sounded and lines of factory workers shambled back inside, brown men in chinos and white shirts, Syrian and Lebanese laborers imported to do work no native Toldenarban would touch. A shredded net waved forlornly from a basketball hoop set up by the loading dock.

There was a section of hurricane fence down. They scrambled through.

As they cut across the grounds, a loud whine arose from within the factory building. Down the way another plant lifted its voice in a solid wham-wham-wham as rhythmic and unrelenting as a headache. One by one the factories shook themselves from their midday drowse and went back to work. "Why do they locate these things along the Edge?" Donna asked.

"It's so they can dump their chemical waste over the Edge," Russ explained. "These were all erected before the Emir nationalized the culverts that the Russian Protectorate built."

Behind the factory was a chest-high concrete wall, roughedged and pebbly with the slow erosion of cement. Weeds grew in clumps at its foot. Beyond was nothing but sky.

Piggy ran ahead and spat over the Edge. "Hey, remember what Nixon said when he came here? *It is indeed a long way down.* What a guy!"

Donna leaned against the wall. A film of haze tinted the sky grey, intensifying at the focal point to dirty brown, as if a dead spot were burned into the center of her vision. When she looked down, her eyes kept grabbing for ground and finding more sky. There were a few wispy clouds in the distance and nothing more. No serpents coiled in the air. She should have felt disappointed but, really, she hadn't expected better. This was of a piece with all the natural wonders she had ever seen, the waterfalls, geysers, and scenic vistas that inevitably included power lines, railings, and parking lots absent from the postcards. Russ was staring intently ahead, hawklike, frowning. His jaw worked slightly, and she wondered what he saw.

"Hey, look what I found!" Piggy whooped. "It's a stairway!"

They joined him at the top of an institutional-looking concrete and iron stairway. It zigzagged down the cliff toward an infinitely distant and nonexistent Below, dwindling into hazy blue. Quietly, as if he'd impressed himself, Piggy said, "What do you suppose is down there?"

"Only one way to find out, isn't there?" Russ said.

Russ went first, then Piggy, then Donna, the steps ringing dully under their feet. Graffiti covered the rocks, worn spray-paint letters in yellow and black and red scrawled one over the other and faded by time and weather into mutual unreadability, and on the iron railings, words and arrows and triangles had been markered onto or dug into the paint with knife or nail: JURGEN = SCHEISSKOPF. MOTLEY CRUE. DEATH TO SATAN AMERICA IMPERIALIST. Seventeen steps down, the first landing was filthy with broken brown glass, bits of crumbled concrete, cigarette butts, soggy, half-melted cardboard. The stairway folded back on itself and they followed it down.

"You ever had *fugu?*" Piggy asked. Without waiting for an

answer, he said, "It's Japanese poisonous blowfish. It has to be prepared very carefully—they license the chefs—and even so, several people die every year. It's considered a great delicacy."

"Nothing tastes that good," Russ said.

"It's not the flavor," Piggy said enthusiastically. "It's the poison. Properly prepared, see, there's a very small amount left in the sashimi and you get a threshold dose. Your lips and the tips of your fingers turn cold. Numb. That's how you know you're having the real thing. That's how you know you're living right on the edge."

"I'm already living on the edge," Russ said. He looked startled when Piggy laughed.

A fat moon floated in the sky, pale as a disk of ice melting in blue water. It bounced after them as they descended, kicking aside loose soda bottles in Styrofoam sleeves, crushed Marlboro boxes, a scattering of carbonized sparkplugs. On one landing they found a crumpled shopping cart, and Piggy had to muscle it over the railing and watch it fall. "Sure is a lot of crap here," he observed. The landing smelled faintly of urine.

"It'll get better farther down," Russ said. "We're still near the top, where people can come to get drunk after work." He pushed on down. Far to one side they could see the brown flow from the industrial canal where it spilled into space, widening and then slowly dispersing into rainbowed mist, distance glamoring it beauty.

"How far are we planning to go?" Donna asked apprehensively.

"Don't be a weak sister," Piggy sneered. Russ said nothing.

The deeper they went, the shabbier the stairway grew, and the spottier its maintenance. Pipes were missing from the railing. Where patches of paint had fallen away the bolts anchoring the stair to the rock were walnut-sized lumps of rust.

Needle-clawed marsupials chittered warningly from niches in the rock as they passed. Tufts of grass and moth-white gentians grew in the loess-filled cracks.

Hours passed. Donna's feet and calves and the small of her back grew increasingly sore, but she refused to be the one to complain. By degrees she stopped looking over the side and out into the sky, and stared instead at her feet flashing in and out of sight while one hand went slap grab tug on the rail. She felt sweaty and miserable.

Back home she had a half-finished paper on the Three Days Incident of March, 1810, when the French Occupation, by order of Napoleon himself, had fired cannonade after cannonade over the Edge into nothingness. They had hoped to make rainstorms of devastating force that would lash and destroy their enemies, and created instead only a gunpowder haze, history's first great failure in weather control. This descent was equally futile, Donna thought, an endless and wearying exercise in nothing. Just the same as the rest of her life. Every time her father was reposted, she had resolved to change, to be somebody different this time around, whatever the price, even if—no, especially if—it meant playacting something she was not. Last year in Germany when she'd gone out with that local boy with the Alfa Romeo and instead of jerking him off had used her mouth, she had thought: Everything's going to be different now. But no.

Nothing ever changed.

"Heads up!" Russ said. "There's some steps missing here!" He leaped, and the landing gonged hollowly under his sneakers. Then again as Piggy jumped after.

Donna hesitated. There were five steps gone and a drop of twenty feet before the stairway cut back beneath itself. The cliff bulged outward here, and if she slipped she'd probably miss the stairs altogether.

She felt the rock draw away from her to either side, and was suddenly aware that she was connected to the world by the merest speck of matter, barely enough to anchor her feet. The sky wrapped itself about her, extending to infinity, depthless and absolute. She could extend her arms and fall into it forever. What would happen to her then, she wondered. Would she die of thirst and starvation, or would the speed of her fall grow so great that the oxygen would be sucked from her lungs, leaving her to strangle in a sea of air? "Come on, Donna!" Piggy shouted up at her. "Don't be a pussy!"

"Russ—" she said quaveringly.

But Russ wasn't looking her way. He was frowning downward, anxious to be going. "Don't push the lady," he said. "We can go on by ourselves."

Donna choked with anger and hurt and desperation all at once. She took a deep breath and, heart scudding, leaped. Sky and rock wheeled over her head. For an instant she was floating, falling, totally lost and filled with a panicky awareness that she was about to die. Then she crashed onto the landing. It hurt like hell, and at first she feared she'd pulled an ankle. Piggy grabbed her shoulders and rubbed the side of her head with his knuckles. "I knew you could do it, you wimp."

Donna knocked away his arm. "Okay, wiseass. How are you expecting to get us back up?"

The smile disappeared from Piggy's face. His mouth opened, closed. His head jerked fearfully upward. An acrobat could leap across, grab the step and flip up without any trouble at all. "I—I mean, I—"

"Don't worry about it," Russ said impatiently. "We'll think of something." He started down again.

It wasn't natural, Donna realized, his attitude. There was something obsessive about his desire to descend the stairway. It was like the time he'd brought his father's revolver to school along with a story about playing Russian roulette that morning before breakfast. "Three times!" he'd said proudly.

He'd had that same crazy look on him, and she hadn't the slightest notion then or now how she could help him.

Russ walked like an automaton, wordlessly, tirelessly, never hurrying up or slowing down. Donna followed in concerned silence, while Piggy scurried between them, chattering like somebody's pet Pekinese. This struck Donna as so apt as to be almost allegorical: the two of them together yet alone, the distance between filled with noise. She thought of this distance, this silence, as the sun passed behind the cliff and the afternoon heat lost its edge.

The stairs changed to cement-jacketed brick with small buttresses cut into the rock. There was a pile of stems and cherry pits on one landing, and the railing above them was white with bird droppings. Piggy leaned over the rail and said, "Hey, I can see seagulls down there. Flying around."

"Where?" Russ leaned over the railing, then said scornfully, "Those are pigeons. The Ghazoddis used to release them for rifle practice."

As Piggy turned to follow Russ down again, Donna caught a glimpse into his eyes, liquid and trembling with helplessness and despair. She'd seen that fear in him only once before, months ago when she'd stopped by his house on the way to school, just after the Emir's assassination.

The living room windows were draped and the room seemed unnaturally gloomy after being out in the morning sun. Blue television light flickered over shelves of shadowy ceramic figurines: Dresden milkmaids, Chantilly Chinamen, Meissen pugdogs connected by a gold chain held in their champed jaws, naked Delft nymphs dancing.

Piggy's mother sat in a limp dressing gown, hair unbrushed, watching the funeral. She held a cup of oily looking coffee in one hand. Donna was surprised to see her up so early. Everyone said that she had a bad problem with alcohol, that even by service wife standards she was out of control.

"Look at them," Piggy's mother said. On the screen were solemn processions of camels and Cadillacs, sheikhs in jellaba, keffigeh and mirrorshades, European dignitaries with wives in tasteful grey Parisian fashions. "They've got their nerve."

"Where did you put my lunch?" Piggy said loudly from the kitchen.

"Making fun of the Kennedys, like that!" The Emir's youngest son, no more than four years old, salaamed his father's casket as it passed before him. "That kid's bad enough, but you should see the mother, crying as if her heart were broken. It's enough to turn your stomach. If I were Jackie, I'd—"

Donna and Piggy and Russ had gone bowling the night the Emir was shot. This was out in the ruck of cheap joints that surrounded the base, catering almost exclusively to servicemen. When the Muzak piped through overhead speakers was interrupted for the news bulletin, everyone had stood up and cheered. *Up we go* someone had begun singing, and the rest had joined in, *into the wild blue yonder* . . . Donna had felt so sick with fear and disgust she had thrown up in the parking lot. " I don't think they're making fun of anyone," Donna said. "They're just—"

"Don't talk to her!" The refrigerator door slammed shut. A cupboard door slammed open.

Piggy's mother smiled bitterly. "This is exactly what you'd expect from these ragheads. Pretending they're white people, deliberately mocking their betters. Filthy brown animals."

"Mother! Where is my fucking lunch?"

She looked at him then, jaw tightening. "Don't you use that kind of language on me, young man."

"All right!" Piggy shouted. "All right, I'm going to school without lunch! Shows how much you care!"

He turned to Donna and in the instant before he grabbed her wrist and dragged her out of the house, Donna could no longer hear the words, could only see that universe of baffled futility haunting Piggy's eyes. That same look she glimpsed today.

The railings were wooden now, half the posts rotting at their bases, with an occasional plank missing, wrenched off and thrown over the side by previous visitors. Donna's knees buckled and she stumbled, almost lurching into the rock. "I have to stop," she said, hating herself for it. "I cannot go one more step."

Piggy immediately collapsed on the landing. Russ hesitated,

then climbed up to join them. They three sat staring out into nothing, legs over the Edge, arms clutching the rail.

Piggy found a Pepsi can, logo in flowing Arabic, among the rubble. He held it in his left hand and began sticking holes in it with his butterfly knife, again and again, cackling like a demented sex criminal. "Exterminate the brutes!" he said happily. Then, with absolutely no transition he asked, "How are we ever going to get back up?" so dolorously Donna had to bite back her laughter.

"Look, I just want to go on down a little bit more," Russ said.

"Why?" Piggy sounded petulant.

"So I can get down enough to get away from this garbage." He gestured at the cigarette butts, the broken brown glass, sparser than above but still there. "Just a little further, okay guys?" There an edge to his voice, and under that the faintest hint of a plea. Donna felt helpless before those eyes. She wished they were alone, so she could ask him what was wrong.

Donna doubted that Russ himself knew what he expected to find down below. Did he think that if he went down far enough, he'd never have to climb back? She remembered the time in Mr. Herriman's algebra class when a sudden tension in the air had made her glance across the room at Russ, and he was, with great concentration, tearing the pages out of his math text and dropping them one by one on the floor. He'd taken a five-day suspension for that, and Donna had never found out what it was all about. But there was a kind of glorious arrogance to the act; Russ had been born out of time. He really should have been a medieval prince, a Medici or one of the Sabakan pretenders.

"Okay," Donna said, and Piggy of course had to go along.

Seven flights farther down the modern stairs came to an end. The wooden railing of the last short, septambic flight had been torn off entire, and laid across the steps. They had to step carefully between the uprights and the rails. But when they stood at the absolute bottom, they saw that there were stairs beyond the final landing, steps that had been cut into the stone itself. They were curving swaybacked things that millenia of rain and foot traffic had worn so uneven they were almost unpassable.

Piggy groaned. "Man, you can't expect us to go down that thing."

"Nobody's asking you," Russ said.

They descended the old stairway backwards and on all fours. The wind breezed up, hitting them with the force of an unexpected shove first to one side and then the other. There were times when Donna was so frightened she thought she was going to freeze up and never move again. But at last the stone broadened and became a wide, even ledge, with caves leading back into the rock.

The cliff face here was green-white with lichen, and had in ancient times been laboriously smoothed and carved. Between each cave (their mouths alone left in a natural state, unaltered) were heavy-thighed women—goddesses, perhaps, or demons or sacred dancers—their breasts and faces chipped away by the image-hating followers of the Prophet at a time when Mohammed yet lived. Their hands held loops of vines in which were entangled moons, cycling from new through waxing quarter and gibbous to full and then back through gibbous and waning quarter to dark. Piggy was gasping, his face bright with sweat, but he kept up his blustery front. "What the fuck is all this shit, man?"

"It was a monastery," Russ said. He walked along the ledge dazedly, a wondering half smile on his lips. "I read about this." He stopped at a turquoise automobile door someone had flung over the Edge to be caught and tossed by fluke winds, the only piece of trash that had made it down this far. "Give me a hand."

He and Piggy lifted the door, swung it back and forth three times to build up momentum, then lofted it over the lip of the rock. They all three lay down on their stomachs to watch it fall away, turning end over end and seeming finally to flicker as it dwindled smaller and smaller, still falling. At last it shrank below the threshold of visibility and became one of a number of shifting motes in the downbelow, part of the slow, mazy movement of dead blood cells in the eyes' vitreous humors. Donna turned over on her back, drew her head back from the rim, stared upward. The cliff seemed to be slowly tumbling forward, all the world inexorably, dizzyingly leaning down to crush her.

"Let's go explore the caves," Piggy suggested.

They were empty. The interiors of the caves extended no more than thirty feet into the rock, but they had all been elaborately worked, arched ceilings carved with thousands of faux tesserae, walls adorned with bas-relief pillars. Between the pillars the walls were taken up with long shelves carved into the stone. No artifacts remained, not so much as a potsherd or a splinter of bone. Piggy shone his pocket flash into every shadowy niche. "Somebody's been here before us and taken everything," he said.

"The Historic Registry people, probably." Russ ran a hand over one shelf. It was the perfect depth and height for a line of three-pound coffee cans. "This is where they stowed the skulls. When a monk grew so spiritually developed he no longer needed the crutch of physical existence, his fellows would render the flesh from his bones and enshrine his skull. They poured wax in the sockets, then pushed in opals while it was still warm. They slept beneath the faintly gleaming eyes of their superiors."

When they emerged it was twilight, the first stars appearing from behind a sky fading from blue to purple. Donna looked down on the moon. It was as big as a plate, full and bright. The rilles, dry seas, and mountain chains were preternaturally distinct. Somewhere in the middle was Tranquility Base, where Neil Armstrong had planted the American flag.

"Jeez, it's late," Donna said. "If we don't start home soon, my mom is going to have a cow."

"We still haven't figured a way to get back up," Piggy reminded her. Then, "We'll probably have to stay here. Learn to eat owls and grow crops sideways on the cliff face. Start our own civilization. Our only serious problem is the imbalance of sexes, but even that's not insurmountable." He put an arm around Donna's shoulders, grabbed at her breast. "You'd pull the train for us, wouldn't you, Donna?"

Angrily she pushed him away and said, "You keep a clean mouth! I'm so tired of your juvenile talk and behavior."

"Hey, calm down, it's cool." That panicky look was back in his eyes, the forced knowledge that he was not in control, could never be in control, that there was no such thing as control. He smiled weakly, placatingly.

"No, it is not. It is most emphatically not 'cool.'" Suddenly she was white and shaking with fury. Piggy was a spoiler. His simple presence ruined any chance she might have had to talk with Russ, find out just what was bugging him, get him to finally, really notice her. "I am sick of having to deal with your immaturity, your filthy language, and your crude behavior."

Piggy turned pink and began stuttering.

Russ reached a hand into his pocket, pulled out a chunk of foil-wrapped hash, and a native tin pipe with a carved coral bowl. The kind of thing the local beggar kids sold for twenty-nine cents. "Anybody want to get stoned?" he asked suavely.

"You bastard!" Piggy laughed. "You told me you were out!"

Russ shrugged. "I lied." He lit the pipe carefully, drew in, passed it to Donna. She took it from his fingers, felt how cold they were to her touch, looked up over the pipe and saw his face, thin and ascetic, eyelids closed, pale and Christlike through the blue smoke. She loved him intensely in that instant and wished she could sacrifice herself for his happiness. The pipe's stem was overwarm, almost hot, between her lips. She drew in deep.

The smoke was raspy in her throat, then tight and swirling in her lungs. It shot up into her head, filled it with buzzing harmonics: the air, the sky, the rock behind her back all buzzing, ballooning her skull outward in a visionary rush that forced wide open first her eyes and then her mouth. She choked and spasmodically coughed. More smoke than she could imagine possibly holding in her lungs gushed out into the universe.

"Hey, watch that pipe!" Piggy snatched it from her distant fingers. They tingled with pinpricks of pain like tiny stars in the darkness of her flesh. "You were spilling the hash!" The evening light was abuzz with energy, the sky swarming up into her eyes. Staring out into the darkening air, the moon rising below her and the stars as close and friendly as those in a children's book illustration, she felt at peace, detached from worldly cares. "Tell us about the monastery, Russ," she said, in the same voice she might have used a decade before to ask her father for a story.

"Yeah, tell us about the monastery, Unca Russ," Piggy said, but with jeering undertones. Piggy was always sucking up to Russ, but there was tension there too, and his sarcastic little challenges were far from rare. It was classic beta male jealousy, straight out of Primate Psychology 101.

"It's very old," Russ said. "Before the Sufis, before Mohammed, even before the Zoroastrians crossed the gulf, the native mystics would renounce the world and go to live in cliffs on the Edge of the World. They cut the steps down, and once down, they never went back up again."

"How did they eat then?" Piggy asked skeptically.

"They wished their food into existence. No, really! It was all in their creation myth: In the beginning all was Chaos and Desire. The world was brought out of Chaos—by which they meant unformed matter—by Desire, or Will. It gets a little inconsistent after that, because it wasn't really a religion, but more like a system of magic. They believed that the world wasn't complete yet, that for some complicated reason it could never be complete. So there's still traces of the old Chaos lingering just beyond the Edge, and it can be tapped by those who desire it strongly enough, if they have distanced themselves from the things of the world. These mystics used to come down here to meditate against the moon and work miracles.

"This wasn't sophisticated stuff like the Tantric monks in Tibet or anything, remember. It was like a primitive form of animism, a way to force the universe to give you what you wanted. So the holy men would come down here and they'd wish for . . . like riches, you know? Filigreed silver goblets with rubies, mounds of moonstones, elfinbone daggers sharper than Damascene steel. Only once they got them they weren't supposed to want them. They'd just throw them over the Edge. There were these monasteries all along the cliffs. The farther from the world they were, the more spiritually advanced."

"So what happened to the monks?"

"There was a king—Althazar? I forget his name. He was this real greedhead, started sending his tax collectors down to gather up everything the monks brought into existence. Must've figured, hey, the monks weren't using them. Which as it turned out was like a real major blasphemy, and the monks got pissed. The boss mystics, all the real spiritual heavies, got together for this big confab. Nobody knows how. There's one of the classics claims they could run sideways on the cliff just like it was the ground, but I don't know. Doesn't matter. So one night they all of them, every monk in the world, meditated at the same time. They chanted together, they said, It is not enough that Althazar should die, for he has blasphemed. He must suffer a doom such as has been visited on no man before. He must be unmade, uncreated, reduced to less than has ever been. And they prayed that there be no such king as Althazar, that his life and history be unmade, so that there never had been such king as Althazar.

"And he was no more.

"But so great was their yearning for oblivion that when Althazar ceased to be, his history and family as well, they were left feeling embittered and did not know why. And not knowing why, their hatred turned upon themselves, and their wish for destruction, and they too all of a single night, ceased to be." He fell silent.

At last Piggy said, "You believe that crap?" Then, when there was no answer, "It's none of it true, man! Got that? There's no magic, and there never was." Donna could see that he was really angry, threatened on some primal level by the possibility that someone he respected could even begin to believe in magic. His face got pink, the way it always did when he lost control.

"No, it's all bullshit," Russ said bitterly. "Like everything else."

They passed the pipe around again. Then Donna leaned back, stared straight out, and said, "If I could wish for anything, you know what I'd wish for?"

"Bigger tits?"

She was so weary now, so pleasantly washed out, that it was easy to ignore Piggy. "I'd wish I knew what the situation was."

"What situation?" Piggy asked. Donna was feeling languorous, not at all eager to explain herself, and she waved away the question. But he persisted. "What situation?"

"Any situation. I mean, all the time, I find myself talking with people and I don't know what's really going on. What games they're playing. Why they're acting the way they are. I wish I knew what the situation was."

The moon floated before her, big and fat and round as a griffin's egg, shining with power. She could feel that power washing through her, the background radiation of decayed chaos spread across the sky at a uniform three degrees Kelvin. Even now, spent and respent, a coin fingered and thinned to the worn edge of nonexistence, there was power out there, enough to flatten planets.

Staring out at that great fat boojum snark of a moon, she felt the flow of potential worlds, and within the cold silver disk of that jester's skull, rank with magic, sensed the invisible presence of Russ's primitive monks, men whose minds were nowhere near comprehensible to her, yet vibrated with power, existing as matrices of patterned stress, no more actual than Donald Duck, but no less powerful either. She was caught in a waking fantasy, in which the sky was full of power and all of it accessible to her. Monks sat empty-handed over their wishing bowls, separated from her by the least fictions of time and reality. For an eternal instant all possibilities fanned out to either side, equally valid, no one more real than any other. Then the world turned under her, and her brain shifted back to realtime.

"Me," Piggy said, "I just wish I knew how to get back up the stairs."

They were silent for a moment. Then it occurred to Donna that here was the perfect opportunity to find out what was bugging Russ. If she asked cautiously enough, if the question hit him just right, if she were just plain lucky, he might tell her everything. She cleared her throat. "Russ? What do you wish?"

In the bleakest voice imaginable, Russ said, "I wish I'd never been born."

She turned to ask him why, and he wasn't there.

"Hey," Donna said. "Where'd Russ go?"

Piggy looked at her oddly. "Who's Russ?"

It was a long trip back up. They carried the length of wooden railing between them, and every now and then Piggy said, "Hey, wasn't this a great idea of mine? This'll make a swell ladder."

"Yeah, great," Donna would say, because he got mad when she didn't respond. He got mad too, whenever she started to cry, but there wasn't anything she could do about that. She couldn't even explain why she was crying, because in all the world—of all his friends, acquaintances, teachers, even his parents—she was the only one who remembered that Russ had ever existed.

The horrible thing was that she had no specific memories of him, only a vague feeling of what his presence had been like, and a lingering sense of longing and frustration.

She no longer even remembered his face.

"Do you want to go first or last?" Piggy had asked her.

When she'd replied, "Last. If I go first, you'll stare at my ass all the way up," he'd actually blushed. Without Russ to show off in front of, Piggy was a completely different person, quiet and not at all abusive. He even kept his language clean. But that didn't help, for just being in his presence was enough to force understanding on her: That his bravado was fueled by his insecurities and aspirations, that he masturbated nightly and with self-loathing, that he despised his parents and longed in vain for the least sign of love from them. That the way he treated her was the sum and total of all of this and more.

She knew exactly what the situation was.

Dear God, she prayed, let it be that I won't have this kind of understanding when I reach the top. Or else make it so that situations won't be so painful up there, that knowledge won't hurt like this, that horrible secrets won't lie under the most innocent word.

They carried their wooden burden upward, back toward the world.